Praise for Bertrice Small,

"THE REIGNING QUEEN OF THE HISTORICAL GENRE"*

and Her Novels

"Bertrice Small creates cover-to-cover passion, a keen sense of history, and suspense." —*Publishers Weekly*

"Ms. Small delights and thrills." —*Rendezvous*

"An insatiable delight for the senses. [Small's] amazing historical detail . . . will captivate the reader . . . potent sensuality." —*Romance Junkies

"[Her novels] tell an intriguing story, they are rich in detail, and they are all so very hard to put down." —The Best Reviews

"Sweeps the ages with skill and finesse." —*Affaire de Coeur*

"[A] captivating blend of sensuality and rich historical drama." —Rosemary Rogers

"Small is why I read historical romance. It doesn't get any better than this!" —*Romantic Times* (top pick)

"Small's boldly sensual love story is certain to please her many devoted readers." —*Booklist*

"[A] delight to all readers of historical fiction." —Fresh Fiction

"[A] style that garnered her legions of fans. . . . When she's at the top of her form, nobody does it quite like Bertrice Small." —The Romance Reader

"Small never ceases to bring us an amazing story of love and happiness." —Night Owl Romance

BOOKS BY
BERTRICE SMALL

**THE SILK MERCHANT'S
DAUGHTERS**
Bianca

THE BORDER CHRONICLES
A Dangerous Love
The Border Lord's Bride
The Captive Heart
The Border Lord and the Lady
The Border Vixen
Bond of Passion

**THE FRIARSGATE
INHERITANCE**
Rosamund
Until You
Philippa
The Last Heiress

**CONTEMPORARY
EROTICA**
Private Pleasures
Forbidden Pleasures
Sudden Pleasures
Dangerous Pleasures
Passionate Pleasures
Guilty Pleasures

THE O'MALLEY SAGA
Skye O'Malley
All the Sweet Tomorrows
A Love for All Time
This Heart of Mine
Lost Love Found
Wild Jasmine

SKYE'S LEGACY SERIES
Darling Jasmine

Bedazzled
Besieged
Intrigued
Just Beyond Tomorrow
Vixens

THE WORLD OF HETAR
Lara
A Distant Tomorrow
The Twilight Lord
Crown of Destiny
The Sorceress of Belmair
The Shadow Queen
Crown of Destiny

**MORE BY
BERTRICE SMALL**
The Kadin
Love Wild and Fair
Adora
Unconquered
Beloved
Enchantress Mine
Blaze Wyndham
The Spitfire
A Moment in Time
To Love Again
Love, Remember Me
The Love Slave
Hellion
Betrayed
Deceived
The Innocent
A Memory of Love
The Duchess

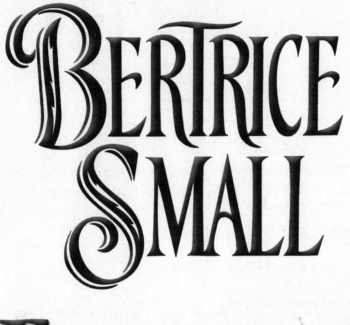

BERTRICE SMALL

FRANCESCA

The Silk Merchant's Daughters

 NEW AMERICAN LIBRARY

New American Library
Published by the Penguin Group
Penguin Group (USA) Inc., 375 Hudson Street,
New York, New York 10014, USA

USA I Canada I UK I Ireland I Australia I New Zealand I India I South Africa I China

Penguin Books Ltd., Registered Offices: 80 Strand, London WC2R 0RL, England
For more information about the Penguin Group visit penguin.com.

First published by New American Library,
a division of Penguin Group (USA) Inc.

First Printing, April 2013
10 9 8 7 6 5 4 3 2 1

REGISTERED TRADEMARK—MARCA REGISTRADA

LIBRARY OF CONGRESS CATALOGING-IN-PUBLICATION DATA:

Small, Bertrice.
  Francesca/Bertrice Small.
    p. cm.—(The silk merchant's daughters)
  ISBN 978-0-451-41373-4
  1. Florence (Italy)—History—1421–1737—Fiction. I. Title.
  PS3569.M28F73 2013
  813'.54—dc23   2012043575

Set in Sabon
Designed by Spring Hoteling

Printed in the United States of America

PUBLISHER'S NOTE
This is a work of fiction. Names, characters, places, and incidents either are the product
of the author's imagination or are used fictitiously, and any resemblance to actual per-
sons, living or dead, business establishments, events, or locales is entirely coincidental.
  The publisher does not have any control over and does not assume any responsibility
for author or third-party Web sites or their content.

To the man who first believed in me,
who always believed in me, and
who always encouraged me,
my late husband, George, my hero, my love.
March 6, 1923–July 5, 2012
Till we meet again, Toodle.
R.I.P.

FRANCESCA

Prologue

"You will choose a wife and wed within the next year," Titus Cesare, Duke of Terreno Boscoso, told his son and heir. He was a tall, distinguished man with a head full of wavy snow-white hair and had warm brown eyes that now looked directly at his only child.

"I am too young to marry," his offspring replied casually, sprawling in a tapestried chair by the fire in his father's library. He was taller than his sire by at least two inches and had rich dark auburn hair and his deceased mother's green eyes. Those eyes were a slightly deeper shade than an emerald, more the color of a pool in the forest—dark yet filled with golden light.

"Need I remind you, brash youth, that we have both just celebrated our natal day?"

It was considered a rarity that both father and son had been born on the same day in May. The Duchess Antonia had always considered it her greatest achievement to have delivered her husband's only child on the day he celebrated forty years upon this earth. She had been twenty years old, and his second wife.

Duke Titus adored her not just for the precious gift she had given him, but for her loving and sweet nature. His first wife, Elisabetta, had been plucked from the convent where she had been educated and seriously contemplating taking the veil. She had tried very hard to be a good wife to him, but she was frail of body and died at eighteen years of age, having been married to him for but four years. Duke Titus had not remarried until he was thirty-eight to his beloved Antonia, who in less than two years' time delivered him his son, Rafaello.

Antonia had been a wonderful and nurturing mother to their son. He was fifteen when she had died, and remembered her well. She had fostered a strong bond between father and son. When she had died suddenly of a winter flux they had had each other to lean upon and mourn her loss. Now as the duke contemplated his son he thought of how Antonia might have handled this situation.

"You are twenty-nine," he finally said. "I am sixty-nine. I want to see you happy with a bride before I die. I want to see my grandchildren. I am considered very old."

"You are an old fraud," his son replied, laughing.

"How can I go to my grave unable to tell your sweet mother that you are happy?" the duke said.

"Are you ill, Papa?" the younger man asked anxiously.

"No, but remember your mama was in the best of health before that flux struck her and she was so suddenly carried off," the duke reminded his son. The duke saw that his words had caught his son unawares.

"You have already made a plan to accomplish your purpose," Rafaello said quietly. Then he smiled at his father. "Tell me. When does my bride arrive? And who is she, Papa?"

"Actually I have sent for three young women to come so you may have a small choice in your selection of a wife," the duke said, surprising his son. "I know damned well if I waited for you to go courting, God only knows if you would ever find a maiden to suit you. On my seventieth natal day I will retire and turn my dukedom over to you and your bride, Rafaello. You are more than capable of governing Terreno Boscoso. You've been sitting by my side in all matters of governance since you were ten. I think you can learn no more from me. It is time for you to make the decisions."

Rafaello Cesare was astounded. "Three women? You sent for three women, Papa? What will happen to the losers, then, and how will their angry families feel about my rejecting two? And who are these three peerless virgins you think suitable to marry your precious son?" Then he laughed, for the situation, he thought, was ridiculous.

"I have investigated carefully and chosen as carefully," Duke Titus answered his son. "The maidens are Aceline Marie du Barry, the daughter of the Comte du Barry. The family line is ancient, and the comte wealthy. The second girl is Louisa Maria di Genoa, a bastard daughter of the Duke of Genoa. She is particularly loved by her father, and he has offered quite an enormous dower portion for her. The third virgin is Francesca Allegra Liliana Maria Pietro d'Angelo, the daughter of a very important Florentine silk merchant who stands quite high in Lorenzo di Medici's favor. The dower her father offers is even larger than the one Genoa proffers me for his daughter."

"Large dowers usually mean ugly faces or some physical deformity," Rafaello noted dryly.

"No, I have sent my own agent to observe these three candidates for your hand. He did not make himself known to the families, but obtained a place in each household for a brief time so he might view these girls within their own familial setting. He claims he was almost struck blind by the beauty he saw. The faces are flawless, and he saw no physical deformity on any of the trio."

"So when do these paragons of virtue—for I assume they are virtuous virgins—arrive, Papa?" Rafaello chuckled.

The duke grinned at his son. "Next month," he replied. "I expect that by next June you will have chosen one for your bride and will marry. If you are quick perhaps you will have already planted your seed in her belly, and I may look forward to a grandson or granddaughter."

"You are in a great hurry, Papa," Rafaello responded.

"I hardly consider requesting my twenty-nine-year-old heir to settle down and produce an heir an onerous task. You have a summer before you and three beautiful girls to court. I am sure that Valiant and the rest of those young rascals you run with will be delighted to help you out, Rafaello," the duke told him. "Ahh, were I young once again and my Antonia with me." His handsome face briefly grew sorrowful.

Seeing the look, his son answered him, "I thank you for all you have done in this matter. I will dutifully inspect my three virgins, and hopefully I can find one suitable with whom I can live. I promise to do my duty as I know Mama would want."

Duke Titus smiled and lifted the wineglass on the table by his arm. "To my Antonia," he said.

"To Mama," Rafaello Cesare replied, lifting his own glass. "To Mama!"

Chapter 1

"He is too fat, *Madre*. I will not wed with an over-dressed pig," Francesca Pietro d'Angelo said irritably to her anxious mother.

"He is an Orsini!" her mother exclaimed. "They are one of the richest and most distinguished families in Rome. They descend from emperors."

"He is still too porcine, and if he were emperor I still would not have him," Francesca declared. "Besides, he is from a lesser branch of his family. I doubt there is any money there. He has come to Florence to obtain a rich wife and restore his fortunes."

Lorenzo di Medici, who had been listening to this exchange between mother and daughter, chuckled. "She is absolutely correct, *signora*," he said, and he turned to Francesca. "You would be wasted on such a *buffone*."

"Do not encourage her, *signore*, I beg of you," Orianna

Pietro d'Angelo pleaded. "Have you any idea how many fine young men she has turned away? I thought when she returned home from my father's house in Venice, so properly contrite over her bad behavior, I might add, that she might prove reasonable. But no! There has been something wrong with every young man who has sought her hand. One walks like a duck! Another has the face of one of the apes your daughters keep, or legs like a stork, or breath like the banks of the river Arno at low tide, or looks like a gaping fish just caught. She asked Paulo Torrelli where he hid his tail, because she declared he resembled a rat!"

Lorenzo di Medici restrained the great guffaw that bubbled up in his throat. The truth was, young Torrelli did look a bit like a rodent, even as his father did. Gaining a mastery of himself he said, "I asked you to my reception tonight, *signora*, with a specific purpose in mind. I have already spoken with your good husband about it. I see how the local gentlemen avoid your company. Francesca's shrewish reputation is beginning to spread, and we cannot have the loveliest maiden in Florence since the fair Bianca scorned. Her behavior could indeed reflect on your two younger daughters."

Orianna Pietro d'Angelo grew pale. Her eldest daughter was no longer spoken of in their house, for her audacity in running off with an Ottoman prince.

Lorenzo di Medici saw her distress and immediately apologized for his thoughtlessness. Then he said, "Go home, *signora*, and see if my solution to your problem suits you. Your husband was quite pleased by it."

"Thank you, *signore*," Orianna said, curtsying to him. "We are grateful for your concern." Then she turned away and moved off in the direction of where her husband stood waiting for her and for Francesca.

Francesca did not immediately follow. Raising her beautiful green eyes to Lorenzo di Medici, she smiled at him flirtatiously. "What have you done, *signore*? Would you send me to some convent away from Florence?" She put a hand on his silk sleeve.

He chuckled. "Do not attempt to wield your wiles on me, Francesca," he told her. "If you weren't a virgin I would have probably made you my mistress by now. But, like your parents, I want you happy, and you must marry if you are to be content. Now go and join your *madre, inamorata*."

Francesca pouted prettily, but then seeing he couldn't be moved, left him. Crossing the crowded reception chamber, she rejoined her parents. Together the trio departed the Medici palazzo in the family litter to return home. While they traveled through the busy late-afternoon streets, Francesca asked her parents, "What is it that *Signore* di Medici would have me do?"

"We will speak on it when we get home," Giovanni Pietro d'Angelo told his daughter firmly, "and not before."

"It is my life you are deciding," Francesca replied sharply. "Am I to have no say in it at all?"

"*Madre di Dios!*" Orianna exclaimed. "Be quiet! Your father has said it will be discussed when we reach home and not before. Just once, you impossible child, do as you are told. I raised you to be dutiful, but you seem to have left all your manners behind since your return from your grandfather's palazzo in Venice. He has spoiled you and allowed you to run wild. We are fortunate you caused no greater scandal than you did running after Enzo Ziani so shamelessly and giving rise to rumors that your virtue was not quite all it should be. You offered up my family, the Veniers, to ridicule, and we have been leaders in Venice for centuries, even having a *doge* among our antecedents."

"I know, *Madre*. I know," Francesca responded wearily. "My grandfather was forever drumming the history of your house into my head."

Orianna glared across the litter at her daughter, and Francesca finally grew quiet.

A faint smile played across Giovanni Pietro d'Angelo's mouth. His wife and their daughters were well matched. While their lamented eldest, Bianca, had been stubborn and very determined to follow her heart even if it meant losing her family, Francesca was even more like their fiery mother. Once Bianca attained her goal she would settle back to exhibiting a sweet and amiable nature. Francesca, however, fought her battles with great passion, refusing to yield in the slightest. It would take a very strong man to control her. He smiled again to himself. Lorenzo di Medici had come up with an excellent solution to the problem of his difficult daughter. Now he must convince her of it, and it would not be easy at all. Because he was a quiet man, many thought his women ruled him. This could not have been further from the truth. Though Giovanni Pietro d'Angelo spoke softly he was a hard but fair man when it came to having his own way. No one who had ever done business with the respected leader of the Arti di Por Santa Maria, the silk merchants' guild, would have said otherwise.

At last the litter reached their palazzo on the Piazza Santa Anna. Its occupants exited the vehicle and entered through the great ironbound double oak doors. Leading the way, the silk merchant brought his wife and daughter to his library. A small fire was burning in the fireplace, taking the chill off the early-spring afternoon. A servant brought refreshments, and when he had departed the chamber Giovanni began to speak.

"There is a large duchy located well northwest of the Duchy

of Milano. It is called Terreno Boscoso. It is an ancient holding ruled by a distinguished family of wealth and good reputation."

Francesca yawned, bored. Seeing it, Orianna frowned and, reaching out, pinched her daughter to attention. Francesca jumped with a little squeak, glaring back at Orianna.

Though he had seen the action between mother and daughter, Giovanni gave no hint of it, and continued smoothly. "Duke Titus has one child, a son, born to him late in life. He wishes to retire from his duties shortly, but first he must see his son wed. To this end he has asked for three maidens to be brought to Terreno Boscoso so his son may get to know them and choose a bride from among the three. Since, like many heads of state, he does business with the di Medici bank, he wrote to Lorenzo himself and asked if Florence might offer up a candidate for his son's hand. Lorenzo believes Francesca is the perfect choice. He is certain that Francesca will be chosen." Giovanni looked at his daughter.

"You would be a *duchessa*, my daughter," he said quietly, "but you would be treated like a queen."

"A *duchessa*!" Orianna responded breathlessly, her eyes wide with pride and excitement. "What an honor for you, Francesca, for our family, for Florence."

"No!" Francesca said.

"*No?*" her mother gasped, disbelieving. "*No?* You dare say no to such a magnificent offer? You are heartless, you ungrateful girl. Heartless!"

"I will not be shipped off to some unknown place and put in a contest for the hand of a strange man," Francesca said. "The man who wants to marry me must court me properly, *Madre*. I am appalled you would even consider such a thing."

Orianna Pietro d'Angelo's beautiful face turned a very unattractive shade somewhere between crimson and purple. "Refuse, and you will be shipped off to a cloistered convent as far away from Florence as I can find," she replied angrily. "They will shave your head of your glorious hair. You will be nourished on stale bread and water, and beaten twice daily until you learn obedience again. And there you will remain, imprisoned for the remainder of your days, you wicked child! And do not look to your father for help. You know that in all matters having to do with the household and our children it is my word that rules supreme, Francesca, not his."

Having allowed his wife to vent her anger, the master of the house now spoke up once again. "Francesca, *cara*, you must wed. You have just celebrated your fifteenth natal day." He smiled warmly at her. "I remember the day you were born quite well. It was a perfect day in early April. The sky was cloudless and blue. The sun bright and warm upon the back. The flowers in the garden had begun to bloom early that year. I had found a large bud on one of the roses several days earlier, which I cut and was forcing into bloom right here in my library. It opened that day, and I brought it to your mother after she had safely delivered you. Father Bonamico said it was a sign from God."

Orianna's face grew soft as her husband renewed her own memory of that day.

"I realize," Giovanni continued, "that Enzo Ziani proved a great disappointment to you, *cara mia*, but I believe in my heart of hearts that you know now he was the wrong man for you. An unimportant Venetian prince among many unimportant Venetian princes. We can do far better for our daughter. This is a golden opportunity for you. Go to Terreno Boscoso. Show this ducal family the caliber of Florentine maidens. You are certain to win the heart of the duke's son. The old man has promised as soon as his son is wed, he will abdicate in his son's immediate favor. You will be a *duchessa*, Francesca!"

"A horse fair is what you are sending me into," she replied, but her tone was less strident and more thoughtful.

"What do you mean, we are sending you into a horse fair?" Orianna demanded.

"Are not three fresh young mares being brought to Terreno Boscoso to see which one pleases the duke's stallion?" Francesca responded.

Giovanni Pietro d'Angelo burst out laughing, and he laughed so hard tears fell from his eyes.

His wife, however, exhibited shock. "Francesca! What an indelicate thought. I hope you will not voice such sentiments aloud in Terreno Boscoso."

A mutinous look crossed Francesca's beautiful face. "I did not say I was going anywhere," she murmured.

The silk merchant shot his wife a hard look, silently warning her that she should say nothing more. Orianna pressed her lips together as her husband spoke again. "Of course you will go, *cara*. It doesn't mean you have to stay. But you will spend an adventurous summer away from your family. You will not have to go to our villa in the Tuscan hills to be bored or aggravated daily by your siblings.

"You will have a splendid new wardrobe, so that not only will your natural beauty outshine the other two girls, but your clothing will as well. I shall send you with an impressive train of men-at-arms in livery to escort you, a priest, two maids to serve you, and two nuns from your mother's favorite convent to chaperone you. You will have two horses of your own, which we will choose together, and a casket full of jewels.

"This is a great honor Lorenzo di Medici has offered you,

Francesca. You will represent our city of Florence. Even you must admit that you must wed, and at fifteen you are just on the cusp of becoming too old to be desirable." He chuckled at the flash of anger that crossed her face. But then, unable to help herself, Francesca smiled ruefully. "Remember, if this young man proves unsuitable I will bring you home again, but God only knows where we will find a husband for you then. You have frightened away every suitable man from Florence and a hundred leagues around, my daughter."

"Can I have a stallion, *Padre*?" Francesca asked sweetly.

"Perhaps two geldings," he counteroffered. "A stallion might prove too intimidating and difficult to handle."

She nodded her agreement.

"Would not a lovely white mare be suitable?" Orianna ventured, hoping as she spoke that her suggestion would not prove cause for argument.

"It is a lovely thought, *Madre*, but I am not docile and neither should my horse be," Francesca answered in a nonconfrontational tone.

"Do you have a preference among the priests?" her father asked her.

"Bonamico is too old for such a journey," his daughter answered. "Father Silvio is the youngest among them. He could make the journey easily and he is most amusing." She turned to her mother. "Will you obtain the two nuns from the convent of Santa Maria del Fiore, *Madre*? I'm certain the Reverend Mother knows which of her sisters would be suitable." Francesca gave her mother a small smile. "Hopefully they will not be too dull," she concluded.

"Then you will go?" Orianna asked nervously.

"Of course I will go, *Madre*. A summer away in a new place will hopefully be entertaining, and I can return in the autumn."

"*If* I find the young man unsuitable, *cara*," her father reminded her.

"Of course he is unsuitable if his father has to send away in order to find a wife for him," Francesca said, laughing. "He will be a tall gawk of a boy with pimples who will stutter. It will be amusing, and my new clothing and jewelry are a good incentive for me to go. You are thoughtful, *Padre*, to allow me this respite away from Florence and family. Perhaps I shall never marry," Francesca told her parents.

Madre di Dios, Orianna thought to herself. This child of mine has a very hard heart. How on earth did it happen? She must marry or enter a convent. There is no other life for a respectable maiden of good family.

"If I do not, then perhaps I shall become a courtesan," Francesca added.

Orianna grew pale and swayed in her chair.

"Do not distress your *madre*," Giovanni Pietro d'Angelo said sternly to his daughter. "And know that I do not find such thoughts becoming of you. You have agreed you will go to Terreno Boscoso. I accept your word in this matter. Tomorrow I shall go to Lorenzo di Medici and tell him. He will be pleased at the honor you bring to us all."

Francesca said nothing more. Her interests lay in all the wonderful things her father had promised her if she would spend her summer in this duchy. She insisted that her horses be chosen first. She wanted to become accustomed to their gait and to their personalities before she embarked on the long journey she would take to Terreno Boscoso. She wanted to have saddles and bridles made that suited them.

Informing the merchant who sold the finest horseflesh of his needs, Giovanni Pietro d'Angelo made arrangements for a private showing of the animals for his daughter. It was extremely unusual for the wife or daughters of a wealthy or highborn gentleman to appear in public. They went several days later to an indoor marketplace, where the beasts would be displayed. Arriving in a curtained litter they entered the showroom and were greeted by the very effusive merchant who bustled forward to welcome them.

"I am honored you have chosen my establishment," the horse seller said.

"Lorenzo himself recommended your merchandise," the silk merchant replied.

"Yes, yes, I supply many of the mounts he stables, Maestro Pietro d'Angelo," came the answer. "Now, I have picked several horses for your most honorable daughter to choose among." He turned and called, "Bring a seat for the young *signorina*," and a boy ran forth with a small chair for Francesca.

She sat down, her glance modestly lowered, for she knew what was expected of her in public. She would behave as she had been taught.

The horse seller snapped his fingers, and at once a parade of young blackamoors came forth, each leading a beautiful animal. "Each of these creatures is well mannered, *signorina*," he told her, "and well trained as well." He snapped his fingers again and one by one the grooms led their animals forward, walking them about so she might gain a better view of them. "Each comes with its own groom as part of the price. They are slaves, so other than feeding them and keeping them clothed, there is no additional expense."

"We will want two horses," Giovanni Pietro d'Angelo said. "Is it necessary to take two grooms?"

"It is better, *maestro*, for each horse has been raised with its keeper, who is aware of its every foible and character," the horse seller explained.

"I see, I see," was the silk merchant's response. Then he turned to his daughter. "Do you see anything you like?" he asked her.

"The white with the black mane and tail is most striking," she remarked.

"You have a sharp eye, *signorina*."

"And the bay with the dark brown mane and tail," Francesca said.

"Another excellent choice," the horse seller enthused.

Ignoring him, Francesca got up and walked over to where the white gelding stood quietly. She stroked his nose gently, allowing him to sniff her. She whispered to him, "Will you be mine, my beauty?"

The horse nickered softly and stamped his hoof gently.

"He says he would be pleased to be yours," the small black groom murmured to her softly. "He says he will serve you well, *signorina*."

Francesca smiled. "You speak with him?" she asked.

"Yes, *signorina*," came the shy reply.

"I will take this one, *Padre*," Francesca said to her father. Then she walked to where the bay stood, greeting him as she had the white. "And you, my handsome one. Are you ready to join your fate to mine too?"

The bay looked her directly in the eye and then he nodded slowly up and down, never breaking eye contact with her.

Francesca clapped her hands delightedly. "Did you see that, *Padre*? This clever beast answered my question. I must have him as well!" She turned back to the groom holding the bay. "What is your name?"

"I am called Ib, *signorina*."

She looked to the groom holding the white.

"I am Adon, *signorina*," he answered her.

"I must have both horses and their grooms, *Padre*. My animals must be happy and they cannot be without their familiar companions."

Giovanni Pietro d'Angelo smiled and agreed. It had been quite a while since he had seen Francesca enthusiastic and happy over anything. She must remain this way if they were to get her successfully on the road to Terreno Boscoso. Her show of greediness actually delighted him, and he could well afford the cost, he thought as he negotiated the price with the horse seller, took out his purse, and paid. "I will ask you to send them to my own stables on the morrow," he said.

"It shall be done, *Maestro*, as you instruct."

As they returned to the palazzo Giovanni grumbled to his daughter, "Those two black extravagances you have wheedled me into taking will have to have suitable wardrobes. I can guarantee they will be sent to us in rags. You are becoming a great expense to me."

"But I am so happy, *Padre*," she said with a mischievous grin.

"You are happy with new clothing and all the accoutrements that go with a young girl who might wed in several months," he said.

"Or who will return to you, *Padre*. This boy may find me not to his taste at all. He may decide one of the other two maidens is far more suitable to take for a wife," Francesca told him. And I shall see that he does, she thought to herself. I have no intention of remaining in some rural duchy away from my family, even if they do irritate me.

He looked sharply at her, but Francesca's green eyes were delicately lowered. He could only imagine what she was thinking. God help them all if she was returned to them. He must pray more diligently. Like most men he remembered to pray only when he found himself in a situation that he was unable to handle by himself. But he did attend Mass more than most men. Hopefully that would count in his favor with God.

Francesca wanted to help pick the fabrics that would be used in her new wardrobe. Disappointed but taking direction from her husband's behavior, Orianna said she would go to the convent of Santa Maria del Fiore and request two nuns who would serve as Francesca's chaperones while she was in Terreno Boscoso. "I am certain two of the nuns can be spared."

"Do not let the Reverend Mother palm off two old ladies on you," Francesca said. "I will have no patience with them, for they will complain the entire journey about their aches and pains. It is too long an expedition for such elders to make."

Orianna had to admit that her daughter was correct, although she had hoped to send Francesca with two stern older women who would keep her daughter's behavior as it should be. She wasn't surprised to have her cousin, the Reverend Mother Baptista, agree with Francesca's assessment.

"It's too long a time for any of my elders to be away from their home. Do you even know how long it will be before you return my sisters to me, Orianna?"

Orianna shook her head. "Francesca leaves at the end of May. It will be a good month or more before she reaches Terreno Boscoso. She will remain at least for several months, until Duke Titus's heir picks his bride from among the three maidens who have been sent for. Lorenzo believes the duke's son cannot fail to fall in love with my daughter, but we cannot be certain."

"Yes," Reverend Mother Baptista said, "especially given

Francesca's reputation for discrimination when dealing with her suitors. I heard she said the Torrelli boy resembled a rat. Is it so?"

"Yes," Orianna said, openly mortified. "You are well informed, cousin."

Reverend Mother Baptista laughed a short sharp laugh. "I think I should rather like the girl," she remarked. "Too bad she doesn't have a calling, but let us get to your problem. I have thought about your request ever since you wrote to me, Orianna. I believe I have two young nuns who would be very suitable traveling companions and chaperones for your daughter. One has already taken her final vows. The other has not. I did not believe she was quite ready. This foray into the world may help her decide if she would really join her life to ours forever." Reaching out, she rang a small bell on the table next to her chair. "Fetch Sister Maria Annunziata and Sister Maria Benigna," she told the answering postulant, who nodded silently and scurried off.

"Annunziata is the elder and quite sensible. Benigna is gentler, and perhaps a bit shy. Together they will keep Francesca's behavior as it should be and see that she says her daily devotions. You're sending one of your priests?"

"Silvio, the younger of the three. The other two are too old to make such a trip."

"Do you expect to get her back?" the nun asked candidly.

"It would be a miracle if he chose her and she agreed. If that should happen, Francesca will return your nuns and our priest along with our men-at-arms. If she is not chosen, then the return journey will be made in mid-autumn," Orianna said.

The door to Reverend Mother Baptista's privy chamber opened, and two nuns entered, bowing to their mistress.

"You sent for us, *Madre*?" the taller of the two said, coming to stand before her.

"Yes, Annunziata. I need you, my daughters, to accompany my cousin's daughter a long distance to a duchy called Terreno Boscoso, which is to the north and west of Milano. The party you travel with will be a safe one. A priest will also accompany the young *signorina*, along with servants. The duke of Terreno Boscoso has sent for three maidens, from which his heir will choose a wife. You must remain with the *signorina* until that choice is made. It will take several months. If my cousin's daughter is chosen to be the bride, I will want you to remain with her until the marriage is celebrated. If she is not, then you will all return home this autumn. You are both young enough to make such an arduous journey and return. This will give you, Benigna, the opportunity to decide if you would really live your life here with us at Santa Maria del Fiore, or go elsewhere out into the world."

"I would rather remain here, *Madre*," the younger nun said quickly. "I would take my life vows now."

"God has directed that you face this great temptation a final time, Benigna," the Reverend Mother said. "I know you can overcome your fears, and make the right decision by the time you return."

"We will supply these good women with additional clothing and horses to ride. Mules would be too slow, and the trip will be long," Orianna said. "It is agreed upon, then, cousin?" She pressed a plump purse into the nun's hand.

"It is agreed," Reverend Mother Baptista said serenely. "When would you have me send these two to you, Orianna?"

"Let them remain with you until it is time. We will pass this convent on our way out of the city. They can join Francesca's caravan then. Until then let them be comfortable within their own surroundings," the silk merchant's wife answered.

"You are kind," came the reply.

Orianna returned home satisfied. Finding Francesca in the garden she said, "Have you had a busy day selecting your fabrics? May I see your choices?"

"Oh, *Madre*," exclaimed Lucianna, her third daughter. "Her choices are simply splendid. I hope when I marry I may have the privilege of choosing the materials from which my trousseau will be made."

Orianna smiled and caressed Lucianna's red-gold hair.

"She will be easy," Francesca said, amused. "She likes everything. Yes, of course, *Madre*, come and see my choices."

They went to the household storerooms, where the fabric chosen had been laid aside. Orianna was very impressed by Francesca's good taste, and she had not stinted herself, the mother noted of her daughter. There were silks and silk brocades of every hue. There were velvets, both cloth of gold and cloth of silver. There were lace and furs and several small dishes of beads for trimming, along with a great number of spools of thread in many colors.

"We will send for the shoemaker and the glove makers," Orianna said.

"And the saddle maker to make the saddles and bridles for my horses," Francesca replied. "I'll want a third bridle trimmed with silver bells too."

"Oh, I wish I could go with you!" Lucianna said. "I wonder if he is handsome. Are his eyes blue or brown or green? Is his mouth made for kissing?"

"*Lucianna!*" Orianna was shocked, but Francesca giggled. "Who has ever suggested to you that men's mouths were made or not made for kissing?"

"Oh, *Madre*, do not fear. I only overheard the serving women talking," Lucianna reassured her mother.

Orianna was far from reassured, however. God only knew what else those sluts in the kitchens had said. Well, as soon as Francesca was off for Terreno Boscoso, the family would depart for their villa in Tuscany, where her children were less likely to hear such sophisticated chatter. Lucianna would spend her days running barefoot with her village friends in the fields as she did each summer, Giulia fast behind her. At twelve and ten these two youngest daughters of hers were closer than the eldest two had been.

It was just a matter of getting Francesca on her way. Just a few more weeks, Orianna thought, and she sighed with relief. And with luck, Francesca would find her happiness with this young duke and be married into Terreno Boscoso. She certainly already had all the mannerisms of a *duchessa*.

Chapter 2

The day for her departure came at last. Her beautiful new wardrobe, along with her jewelry, was carefully packed into six wooden trunks lined in cedar. The trunks were made of sturdy oak and bound with iron. There were two separate trunks for Francesca's bedding. One held fine linen sheets and a feather bed. The other a down comforter covered in silk, and several plump pillows. There was a trunk that held the garments she would wear as she traveled to Terreno Boscoso. There was a small trunk containing items of embellishment, such as gloves, adornments for her hair, her silk stockings, and shoes, several pairs of which had been made for her.

There was a trunk containing the possessions of her maid, Terza, who had been given a fine new wardrobe, indicating that Francesca's family was one of importance and means and valued her. Terza was a pleasant plain-faced woman in her twenties. She had light brown hair and brown eyes. She had been raised within the Pietro d'Angelo household, the daughter of the cook. She had been trained by Orianna's own personal maid, Fabia, who recommended her to her mistress.

Terza was well-spoken, mannerly, and devout without being annoying. She had been assigned Francesca's care upon her return from Venice and was content to follow her. Francesca actually enjoyed her company, for Terza was far more adventurous than her quiet demeanor indicated to others, as her mistress discovered one day when she caught her gambling with several menservants from whom she gleefully took her winnings.

When one of the men proved a bad loser and accused her of cheating, Terza whipped out a small dagger that had been hidden in the pocket of her skirts. Then she asked him if he had anything more than his stupidity and poor judgment to back up his accusation. If he did not, she would accept his apology. If he did not apologize, she threatened to geld him with her knife. The serving man began to bluster, and Terza moved closer to him, humming a naughty street song. Another servant gave his companion a warning push. The apology was reluctantly forthcoming. Terza gathered up her winnings and sauntered off, whistling. Francesca was very impressed, and told her serving woman so. From that moment they became friends.

There were to be fifty Pietro d'Angelo men-at-arms escorting Francesca, and Lorenzo di Medici had hired twenty-five more who wore his badge of household service.

It was a huge honor, but old Duke Titus would have no doubts as to the importance Francesca Pietro d'Angelo held to Florence. There were the two grooms who would take care of Francesca's two horses, as well as the animals ridden by the two nuns, the priest, and the sturdy chestnut mare that served as Terza's mount. They would also see to the two greyhounds gifted to Francesca by Lorenzo di Medici. She named the dark gray one Tuono, which meant "thunder," and the paler gray Nebbia, meaning "fog." A Pietro d'Angelo cook who would accompany them and prepare their meals had his own wagon with all his equipment and supplies. He also carried a small bathing tub for Francesca.

Giovanni Pietro d'Angelo looked at the great train assembled before his house. While not a parsimonious man, he nonetheless added up in his head the great expense that this venture was costing him. Pray God that Francesca liked the Duke of Terreno Boscoso's son. Pray God the duke's son be taken by Francesca's beauty and choose her as his bride. If not, they would all be the laughingstock of Florence, and he named a fool.

Yet a man could not send his daughter off as the possible bride to such a distinguished family in a niggardly fashion. Lorenzo di Medici's kindness had proved to have a very high price. And if Francesca failed to gain the prize, the di Medici family would not be pleased at all.

Orianna had bid her daughter a tearful farewell. "I still think we should have had the wedding gown made," she fretted.

"The seamstress has my measurements. Make the gown if it pleases you, and if I decide to allow this duke's heir to have the honor of wedding me, I will send for it," Francesca said in placating tones. "If not, we will save it for another bridegroom."

"Madre di Dios!" Orianna half sobbed with her anxiety. "How can you speak so casually about this? It could well be your last chance at a good marriage."

Oddly Francesca felt a small surge of guilt at her mother's

distress. She put a hand upon her parent's arm, comforting her. "*Madre*, do not fear. I am aware of what is involved. I promise to do nothing too awful to discourage this young man."

"You will do nothing to discourage him," Orianna said, rallying.

Francesca laughed. "I will try," she promised.

Her siblings surrounded her. "If you win the prince's hand, we shall never see you again," her sisters noted sanguinely.

"Why not?" Francesca asked.

"It's so far away. You'll disappear from our lives, as the eldest of us did," Lucianna remarked.

Orianna said nothing to this veiled reference to her eldest daughter, Bianca.

Giulia began to sob. "I'll miss you," she said.

"In another few years it will be your turn to wed," Francesca told her.

"*Madre* says Luci and I will go far away too. None of us will ever be together again." And Giulia cried harder.

"That is usually the way of it for girls of good family," Orianna pointed out.

"I must go," Francesca said. Her sisters' words had unsettled her. What if she didn't come back from Terreno Boscoso? She quickly kissed her mother and her two younger sisters and, turning, departed the palazzo.

Outside Giovanni and his sons awaited her. Her brothers bid her a fond farewell, reminding her of her duty to both her family and to Florence. Then they returned inside the palazzo, leaving Francesca with her father. He took her by her shoulders and looked into her face. "You know what is expected of you, Francesca. This is no longer a game. I want you to be happy, but should you return to us it will be difficult to find a husband for a girl who has been refused by a duke's son. Remember that you've turned down every respectable offer in Florence."

For a moment Francesca was frightened by the seriousness of his tone and by his blunt words. Was it actually possible a husband could not be found for her when she came home? No! She was Francesca Pietro d'Angelo. She was wealthy and beautiful. There was always a man available for such a girl. Still, she considered her father's speech to her as his duty. "I will hope to find this duke's son pleasing," she said.

"You had best hope he finds you pleasing," Giovanni said sharply. Then he kissed her cheek and helped her mount the beautiful white gelding. "God bless you, my daughter. May our own Santa Anna travel with you."

Settled securely in her saddle, Francesca pulled her beautiful golden-brown leather gloves onto her hands. "Thank you, *Padre*," she replied, smiling down at him.

Giovanni Pietro d'Angelo raised his hand to signal the captain of his household's men-at-arms to proceed. He stood watching as his second daughter and her personal attendants, surrounded by well-armed men-at-arms, slowly rode across the piazza through the small park that led out into the public streets. The baggage train had already gone on ahead of them. Old Father Bonamico stood on the steps of the church and blessed them as they passed by Santa Anna. When they were gone the silk merchant climbed into his waiting litter and went to his warehouses, for there was a new shipment of silk arriving today. It had come directly from Cathay.

Francesca looked beautiful in her rich brown riding outfit. She knew it, and held herself proudly as they rode through the streets and out the gates onto the road leading to Milano. The normally rude streets, so bustling and busy, opened for her, allowing them easy access. She heard whispers and saw fingers pointing now and again in her direction.

At the gate the sentry examined their travel papers. She heard the man say to the captain of her guard, "Don't blame 'em for sending her away to find a husband. No man in Florence will have such a shrew." Her cheeks grew hot but she didn't deign to give the soldier a glance as they passed him. She was, after all, Francesca Pietro d'Angelo, and the opinion of a low soldier didn't count.

Because it was late spring coming into summer they rode each day from dawn until dusk. The baggage train was gone each morning before they finished their simple meal of bread, cheese, hard-cooked eggs, and fruit. As the light began to wane at day's end they would reach the halt designated for the night. Within an hour the baggage carts would arrive, the cook fires would be lit, and Francesca's silk pavilion would be raised on its sturdy wooden platform for the women. A smaller tent would be set up for the priest. Camp beds, tables, and chairs would be unloaded and placed within the pavilion. Father Silvio would take his evening meal with the women. The cook would bring in a hot delicious meal. The goblets would be filled with wine.

Most days of the late spring as it moved into early summer were warm and pleasant, but some days they were forced to ride in the rain. Giovanni Pietro d'Angelo did not want his daughter stopping at any public inns. Most were flea-ridden, and not all of the travelers they housed were apt to be respectable or honest. The silk merchant wanted his daughter's journey to be as pleasant as it could be given the distance they would travel. He wanted Francesca happy when she reached Terreno Boscoso.

The Duke of Milano had at the personal request of Lorenzo di Medici given Francesca's party leave to travel through his domain. He sent a scout to observe her train's passing and was impressed by what he was told afterwards. He already knew the reason for her travels. Perhaps if old Duke Titus's son did not choose her, he should consider this girl for one of his own relations.

They had departed at the end of the month of May. They passed through several small holdings after leaving the Duchy of Milano but faced no border guards. The landscape around them began to change from farmland into rolling hills and forestland. Then suddenly there were larger and much larger hills in the distance. Francesca realized these were mountains, although she had never seen any before; she had asked the priest and he had and told her so. She asked why some of the larger mountains were white on top, and the priest explained it was snow. Francesca had seen snow once or twice in her lifetime, although most Florentine winters were just wet and chilly.

As June slid into July the captain of her men-at-arms told her they were now on the road that would take them directly to Duke Titus's great *castello*. Shortly they came to territorial markings indicating they were in Duke Titus's duchy. A few leagues farther on they were met by an official crossing. Its keeper said that they were expected, and he had been watching for the train from Florence for several days now.

"You traveled slowly, or did you meet with some misfortune along your route?" the border keeper asked.

"It's our large baggage train. It's about an hour behind us," the captain of the men-at-arms said in reply.

"But your lady hasn't been chosen from among the three yet," the border keeper noted slyly.

"Do you think that Florence would send an applicant unprepared and arriving like a pauper?" the captain returned proudly. "Half the men-at-arms with me come from the house of the di Medici. Our candidate is both well respected and of a good and honorable family. She was chosen by Lorenzo the Magnificent himself."

"I am suitably awed," the border keeper said, grinning. He opened the crossing gate for them and waved them through. "I'll send your baggage train on as soon as it arrives."

"My thanks," the captain responded politely. "How far are we from the duke's *castello*?"

"The rest of today and a half day tomorrow should bring you safely to it," the border keeper said.

They traveled onward until almost sunset. The baggage train arrived, and the encampment was set up for the evening. When the dinner had been brought and the blessing said Father Silvio told them what the captain had learned from the border keeper.

"You must surely be glad to finally reach your destination, *madonna*. I will be glad when we do, I am not loath to admit. He tore a piece from the loaf of bread and mopped up the rich gravy from the rabbit stew that had been served. "And you will finally meet the duke's young heir. He cannot fail to be taken by you. It is hoped you will not frighten him away." He smiled mischievously at her as the two nuns, usually silent, and Terza laughed at his words. The priest was well aware he was baiting Francesca.

"I will withhold my judgment on this young lordling until I have spent some time with him," she answered sweetly, adding, "*Then* I will frighten him away, good priest."

"I am relieved you will at least give him an opportunity to know you, *signorina*," Father Silvio responded drolly. "I must have at least a month's respite before you force our return to Florence and your eternal spinsterhood."

"Perhaps I shall join a convent after all," Francesca said pertly. "What think you, Annunziata? Benigna?" she queried her two chaperones.

"I think that you should be a great trial for any convent, and particularly its novice mistress," Annunziata, the more outspoken of the two nuns, said candidly. Benigna nodded but there was a small smile upon her lips.

"I believe as soon as Terza clears our dishes away it will be time for prayers, and then you must seek your beds, my daughters," Father Silvio said.

When all had been accomplished and before she prepared herself for bed Francesca called for Terza, and together the two sought out the captain of the men-at-arms. "Send scouts ahead in the morning as soon as it is light enough to see," she told him. "I want to know exactly how many hours it will take to reach the duke's *castello*.

"When we are an hour away I would stop, bathe, and don fresh garments. I will not meet this duke or his son smelling of horse and the road. You need not raise my pavilion. The priest's small tent will do and give me the shelter I need. I will change horses when we again proceed. I want the bay for my entrance into the *castello*."

"I'll see the priest's small tent is carried by our men-at-arms on the morrow. Your tub, however, is another matter. We will have to put it on wheels and drag it behind us."

"You will know best," Francesca said. Then she and Terza left the captain to return to the pavilion and settle themselves for the night. She slept surprisingly well, but was immediately awake when Terza touched her shoulder even before the dawn. Outside Francesca could hear the birds already stirring, their cheerful chirps quite audible through the walls of the silk tent.

She joined the two nuns and the priest for their early-morning devotionals and breakfast, even as the pavilion was being torn down around them.

They were on the forest road again as the sunrise began to creep over the unseen horizon, sending bright golden rays through the tall trees. Finally when the sun had reached its midday position they stopped where the forest opened out into a large meadow. As the priest's small undistinguished tent was being raised to shield her from prying eyes, she bathed, and Francesca was pleased to see a fire had been started and two kettles of water were being heated. It occurred to her that she had not considered water when she was so busy giving instructions the previous evening.

"Where do you think they got the water?" she said to Terza.

"There's a nice big brook on the edge of this meadow," Terza replied. "I heard the captain this morning instructing his scouts to be certain to find a halt where water could easily be obtained."

"He's clever," Francesca remarked. "I must tell my father of his resourcefulness when we return to Florence in a few months' time."

When the tub was full Francesca and Terza entered the tent, where the serving woman stripped the clothing from her mistress, pinned up her single thick plait, and helped her into the tub. The girl sank down into the water with a sigh of delight.

"I'll repack these smelly things and fetch what you are to wear," Terza said. "Enjoy your bath, and I'll be back to scrub you down properly." Then she exited the tent quickly.

Francesca closed her eyes. In a few hours this day would be concluded. She would sleep in a comfortable bed and enjoy herself for the next few weeks until she could properly satisfy the duke that she was not a good choice to be his son's wife. Then they would return to Florence. She felt a tiny modicum of guilt knowing that both her family and the di Medicis hoped for a match between her and Terreno Boscoso. Each had other motives than her happiness. She could only marry a man she loved beyond all reason. She had realized months ago that her fascination with Enzo Ziani's charms was childish.

Her grandfather, her parents, the priests, had all been correct. At thirteen she had been too immature to wed. Many girls, however, were not, but she certainly was, as her reckless behavior in taking her sister's place on the wedding gondola had proven. And then she had caused further scandal by refusing to accept Enzo's decision to marry an older girl of sixteen who came from a large family of sons. She made a grimace.

The girl had been ugly too, which made it more hurtful that Francesca Pietro d'Angelo with her beauty could be overlooked. But she had been, and now she was about to join two other girls in attempting to win the favor of this duke's son. Well, they would try. She didn't think she would. If he could like her for her, that would be fine. But she would not debase herself in order to gain anyone's favor.

Terza returned with the rich brown silk riding outfit, which Francesca had not worn since the day she departed Florence. It was a beautiful garment embellished with fine cream-colored lace, its bodice decorated with bits of sparkling topaz. The maidservant laid it carefully aside, and then, taking up the scrub brush, began to quickly wash her mistress. When she was done Francesca stepped from the tub to be rubbed briskly dry. Then came her clothing, beginning with silk undergarments, stockings, and finally the lavish brown skirts and fitted bodice.

Terza unpinned the braid Francesca favored when riding.

She brushed out her mistress's long thick tresses. They were a rich gold in color with a hint of flame. The hair, while not curly, had a natural tendency to wave, which Terza now encouraged by brushing it around her fingers and her hand. She wanted Francesca to show to her best advantage as she rode up to the duke's gates, especially as she had not yet gotten a look at her lady's competition. Once she knew what the other two girls looked like she would be certain that Francesca outshined them. The silk merchant had promised her that if Francesca wed with the duke's son, he would give her a small purse of gold in reward and she would always have a place in his house, even in old age. Of course, even Terza knew that if her mistress did indeed marry the duke's son, they were unlikely, either of them, to ever see Florence again. Still the gold would be paid, and gold was good no matter where you lived. "You're done," she told Francesca. "The horses are awaiting us."

Outside, Francesca reluctantly positioned herself in her side-saddle. She far preferred her leather pants, which allowed her to ride astride, but as Terza artfully arranged the silk skirts around her and over the bay's flanks, she knew how beautiful she looked. The serving woman handed her a riding crop and mounted her own animal, and they were ready to depart on this final leg of their long journey.

They had barely gone a short distance along the forest road when a troupe of riders galloped from the trees, surrounding them. The men-at-arms, caught unawares, began reaching for their swords, but the leader of this group called out, "We are the king's huntsmen, and have come to escort you to Castello Forestavista. Welcome to Terreno Boscoso! My name is Valiant. The duke awaits you." Then with a wave of his hand he signaled the large party onward.

"Oh, my," Terza said. "He's a handsome fellow, isn't he? Do you think he is the duke's son?"

"I doubt it," Francesca said. "My host and his son will greet me dressed in their very best so I may be impressed."

The duke's huntsmen rode among their ranks while Valiant settled himself next to the captain of the men-at-arms. One man, with a bushy beard and nasty scar that ran from the corner of his left eye to the corner of his mouth, nodded in her direction as he rode near her.

Francesca tossed her head, ignoring him. "Does he think I am some strumpet from the streets of Florence that he can look at me like that?" she whispered to Terza.

"He does look dangerous," Terza admitted.

They came to a wide drawbridge that opened into the castle's yard. Crossing it, they entered. There were servants to help them down off their horses. A higher-level servant came forward. "*Signorina* Pietro d'Angelo, welcome," he greeted her. "I am Piero, Duke Titus's majordomo. If you will please follow me I will take you to the duke. He awaits you in his library. Is this your maid?"

"Yes, it is," Francesca replied. "Her name is Terza."

Piero turned to Terza as he drew a young footman forward. "This is Matteo, Terza. He will take you to your apartments. Your luggage will be brought up to you as soon as it arrives. Shall I kennel your dogs, *madonna*?"

"Nay, Piero. I prefer them with me," Francesca told him. "Go with Terza, Nebbia, Tuono," she said to the two greyhounds. Then, turning, she followed Piero into the castle and to the chamber where the duke awaited her.

The majordomo ushered her into a beautiful room lined with bookcases whose shelves were filled with ancient volumes and scrolls. "My lord, *Signorina* Pietro d'Angelo," he announced, then left her.

The tall, distinguished white-haired man stepped forward, and, taking Francesca's two hands in his, lifted them up to kiss. "Lorenzo di Medici wrote that you were quite beautiful. I am pleased to see that for once that Florentine rogue did not lie. Welcome to Terreno Boscoso, my child. You have traveled a long distance to reach us."

"I thank you for your kindness, my lord," Francesca answered him, curtsying deeply. "I am pleased to have finally arrived."

"I am told you have a bit of a temper and speak your mind, Francesca. I may call you Francesca, mayn't I?" Then, without awaiting her answer, he continued. "I hope that is so. Of the other two who have been sent, one is sweet but quite dull. The other is overproud. I doubt either of them will hold my son's interest." He laughed aloud. "Come, sit by the fire, and we will talk now. It may be July but the late afternoons can get a bit chilly."

He took her quite by surprise and yet she knew she already liked this old man. "Who are the others?" she asked him. "Neither Lorenzo nor my father claimed to know."

She settled herself in a tapestried chair while Duke Titus sat opposite her.

"Ah yes, your rivals," he chuckled. "There is the little French girl, Aceline Marie du Barry, daughter of the Comte du Barry. She is dark and petite and has a sharp tongue, I have already noticed. The other is a sweet child, Louisa Maria di Genoa, the bastard daughter of the Duke of Genoa. How old were you on your last natal day, Francesca?"

"Fifteen," she answered him. "My natal day is in April, my lord."

"The other two have just turned fourteen, both in June," Duke Titus told her.

"When will I meet them?" Francesca asked him.

"Tonight in the hall. A small feast has been prepared to celebrate your arrival," he informed her. "You will want to bathe and change, my child, so I shall release you to do so. I watched you ride into the courtyard. You sit your horse well, and the garment you wear suits you well. I could not help but notice how prettily your skirts were displayed."

"I prefer to ride astride, and wear leather britches when I do," Francesca told Duke Titus. "Skirts are such a bother ahorse."

"Excellent! You shall be able to keep up with us in the hunt," he approved as he stood up and escorted her to the door. Opening it he said, "I shall look forward to this evening. You will meet my son, Rafaello, then."

Piero stepped from the shadows in the hallway. "If you will follow me, *madonna*," he said, leading her away.

Francesca could not have found her way back to the library by the time they reached a broad corridor at whose end was a double oak door. The man-at-arms at the door flung it open for her.

"I will leave you here," Piero said. "You will find Terza awaiting you."

She stepped into the antechamber of her apartment. Terza hurried forward.

The room was filled with her luggage. The dogs were in the dayroom, sprawled before a cheerful fireplace. "I've met the duke. He's clever and he's courtly. If his son is like him I might actually find myself interested. I will meet him and the other two maidens tonight at a small banquet to celebrate my arrival. I'll need a spectacular gown to wear if I am to put my rivals out of sorts and stun the duke's son."

"I've already found a gown and set two housemaids to getting the wrinkles out of it," Terza answered. "I'll want to wash your hair, and you must bathe again. I've called for hot water and a tub. Your travel tub will not do."

The footman who had escorted Terza to these guest apartments now returned. "There are things I would show you and your mistress." Leading them to the large bedchamber, he pointed to a door. Opening it, he ushered them inside. "This is your bathing room," he said. He opened a small door in the stone wall to reveal a platform.

There were several buckets of steaming water on the platform. As he removed each in its turn, dumping them into the tall round oaken tub that sat in the room's center, he explained, "This is how the hot water is brought up." He sent the platform back down to from wherever it had come, and a moment later was pulling it up again with six more large buckets. "When you have filled the tub leave the platform at this level with its empty buckets, until you need them again. Your garderobe is through this other door," he explained without opening it. "Are there any questions you need ask of me?"

Terza thanked him, and he left them again. "How cleverly thought out this is," she remarked.

"Go and explore while I get your tub ready," Terza said, and began emptying the new buckets on the platform before sending them back down into the kitchens again.

She walked back out to the antechamber, noting the two little maids who were busy with a heated flat iron to remove any wrinkles from her turquoise gown. Francesca smiled at them. "Thank you for your labors on my behalf." Shyly the duo bobbed their heads up and down. The antechamber had several straight-back chairs lined up against and around the stone walls. It had a large stone fireplace with a late-afternoon fire in it.

The dayroom was comfortably furnished. Its walls were paneled in a warm lightish wood. Windows gave view to the forest surrounding the castle and the high mountains beyond. The stone fireplace was flanked by two carved, seated lions. The furniture was a golden oak, old but well cared for. Tapestries hung on the paneled walls, and carpets adorned the stone floors.

Returning to the bedchamber, she admired the bucolic and romantic scenes painted upon the walls. Even the ceilings showed plump naked and seminaked gods, goddesses, and cupids enjoying a picnic within a summer meadow. Like the furniture in the dayroom, that within this room was golden oak. Her bed was hung with pale green velvet, and Terza had already made it up with Francesca's scented sheets, pillows, and silk and down comforter. I am really looking forward to a good sleep tonight, Francesca thought.

Terza bustled out of the bathing room. "Let's get you into your tub. Then you will have time for a short nap before I must dress you," she said. She quickly undressed her mistress and led her quickly into the hot tub.

Francesca sank down into the water. She closed her eyes and a small smile touched her features. The little travel tub this morning had not been scented with exotic rose oil, nor held the heat as well as this wonderful tub did. Terza climbed the steps to the tub, and, kneeling, began to wash Francesca's beautiful hair as her mistress rubbed a finely milled soap containing the rose fragrance over her body. She loved the sensation of luxury on her body and suddenly wondered if a man's hands upon her would rouse those same feelings.

When she had finished bathing and her hair had been toweled and brushed dry, then rubbed with silk cloth to bring up its shine, Francesca donned a delicate silk chemise and lay down to rest. When she finally awoke she rose so Terza might dress her.

The gown chosen was elegant but reasonably simple. Softly pleated, its turquoise, light velvet skirts were neither fitted nor full, but hung gracefully over two silk petticoats and a sleeveless cloth of silver underdress. The bodice was tightly fitted with an open center panel that revealed the underdress. The neckline was square, not so low as to reveal her breasts, but low enough to show a bit of ripe cleavage. The turned-back cuffs on her sleeves were trimmed with exquisite cream-colored lace. She wore plain silk stockings and heelless leather slippers, but neither could be seen beneath her long skirts.

About her neck Francesca wore a red-gold chain from which hung a heart-shaped pink diamond that flashed and sparkled. Her long reddish-golden hair had been brushed into loose waves, and against all tradition she wore nothing in her hair or on her head.

Terza stepped back and smiled gleefully. "He cannot fail to be taken by you, and your rivals will have a bitter taste in their mouths this night."

"But it's so simple," Francesca said.

"Precisely!" Terza crowed. "And your attitude must match your garments. Do not endeavor to deliberately attract his attention. Allow him to come to you, and then be nothing more than polite. Do not fawn over him like the others will do. Speak with his father instead. It will drive this boy wild with jealousy." Then the maidservant escorted her mistress from her apartments to the Great Hall of the castle. "Remember my words," she hissed softly, leaving her at the entrance.

Francesca entered the hall, her carriage tall and straight as she directed her feet towards the high board where she knew she would be seated tonight.

Duke Titus leaned over to his son and whispered into his ear. "Is she not glorious, Rafaello? What grace, what elegance and style, what hair! And a mother who has produced seven living children."

"It is all as you point out, *Padre*, but I want more in a woman, as you well know," the younger man responded. "I rode disguised with the huntsmen and Valiant this morning to welcome the Florentines. I found the girl arrogant. She did not smile or exclaim with delight at her forester escort. I would have thought her pleased and honored that your men came out to greet her."

"She is a Florentine, Rafaello. She has been brought up to have elegant manners. I imagine had either of the other two been greeted in such an enthusiastic manner they would have been taken aback as well," Duke Titus told his son. "Give her a chance."

Farther down the high board Francesca's two rivals attempted to study her as she came into the hall. She mounted the dais and was seated between Duke Titus and his heir.

Aceline du Barry narrowed her dark blue eyes. "She has a proud air about her for a silk merchant's daughter," the French girl observed.

"Her gown is lovely," Louisa di Genoa said.

"She appears overproud," Aceline replied.

"Don't you recall how nervous you were the first night you arrived when the banquet was for you?"

"The du Barrys are never afraid or nervous," Aceline answered her.

"Well, I certainly was," Louisa admitted.

"Of course you were," Aceline agreed. "You are, after all, only a duke's *bastarda*."

"I am rarely reminded of the low status I hold," Louisa said quietly. "My family is far too polite to do so, and my father would have whipped anyone who dared to voice it. You are thoughtful to recollect it for me." She smiled a sweet smile that did not extend to her amber eyes.

"We should not be enemies," Aceline murmured. "If we band together against the Florentine it makes our chances with Rafaello all the better."

Louisa laughed low. "You can have the duke's heir," she said. "He scares me quite to death. He is so big and powerful. I want a gentler man for my husband."

"How can you not want Rafaello? He is handsome and very rich," the French girl responded. "Since girls have no choice in a husband I should just as soon have one like Rafaello than a poor, weak man."

"I think his friend, Valiant, even more handsome, and he is so kind," Louisa said.

"And poor. He is a third son, for goodness's sake." Aceline was shocked that any sensible girl would want a poor man, no matter his appearance.

"Keep your rivalry for *Signorina* Francesca, Aceline," Louisa told the French girl.

The servers began arriving with a variety of dishes that were passed among the guests. There was local trout, sliced and served on a bed of bright green watercress, stewed eels in wine sauce, and creamed salted cod. There was a roasted wild boar and venison, along with roasted capons and ducks. There was pasta with butter and freshly grated cheese, and green salad. Several loaves of newly baked breads were scattered on each table, along with butter. And when the main meal had been cleared away, bowls of fresh fruit were offered, including individual little bowls of mixed berries that were for the high board alone. As the duke had promised it was a very simple meal.

The entertainment was quiet, just a few musicians playing softly in a small gallery above the hall itself. Francesca had been introduced to Rafaello upon being seated. She greeted him politely and even gave him a small smile. But following Terza's advice it was the duke she engaged in conversation for much of the meal. Rafaello did not know whether to be amused or offended, but how could he take offense because she spoke with his father?

The diners descended from the dais, and now it was the duke who drew Francesca forward to introduce her to the two other girls. "This, my child, is Aceline Marie du Barry," Duke Titus said. He reached for the French girl's hand and brought her so that she stood before Francesca. "She is the daughter of the Comte du Barry, who makes his home in the Franche-Comté."

Francesca curtsied politely to the French girl, noting that she was very pretty with her shiny deep brown hair and rosy complexion. "I am pleased to meet you, mademoiselle," the silk merchant's daughter said in perfect French.

"You may speak to me in your own language," Aceline replied, surprised that Francesca spoke French and had been polite enough to use it. She curtsied back. What a bitch, she thought irritably as she stepped back so Duke Titus might bring the other girl forth for introductions.

"And this, my dear Francesca, is Louisa Maria di Genoa, of the Duke of Genoa's family," the old man said.

"I'm so glad to meet you at last," Louisa said, curtsying. "I want to hear all about Florence. I've never been outside of Genoa until now."

"I spent a bit over a year in Venice at my grandfather, Prince Venier's, palazzo," Francesca replied, curtsying back. "Florence is a bit dull for me, but Venice is all color!"

She had decided she already liked Louisa, with her lovely amber eyes and her black hair.

There was genuine warmth about the girl. Francesca was quite certain that they would be friends by the time they parted. Aceline du Barry was another matter altogether.

Duke Titus smiled. "I am pleased to see that you are all so amenable to one another," he told them. "We will have a fine summer together and hopefully a very happy ending for one of you. But the two my son declines will not go unrewarded for their efforts, I promise you."

Chapter 3

Francesca slept well her first night in Terreno Boscoso. The bed was more than comfortable. Terza had left the leaded, paned windows open just a crack before finding her rest in her own small chamber. She was extremely pleased to have it. The dawn came and Terza finally rose, washed, and dressed herself. Then she went to rouse her mistress, but seeing Francesca still sleeping soundly, she simply opened the windows wide to allow in the fresh summer air and left her. It had been a long journey from Florence, and while her mistress had held up well, a little extra sleep wouldn't harm her.

Francesca agreed when she finally awoke in midmorning. She broke her fast with a dish of warm grain mixed with fresh fruit, bread, butter, and jam. Her cup was filled with a mixture of water and light wine. When she had satisfied her appetite she rose and was dressed. Then she descended to the hall to find Aceline and Louisa there.

"Ohh," the French girl cooed, "you have missed our morning ride with Rafaello. He is like a magnificent centaur ahorse. Now you probably won't see him until tonight. What a great pity."

"If Duke Titus's son wishes to further our acquaintance, I'm sure he will make time for me," Francesca said. "And if he is too busy, then so be it." She smiled.

Aceline was somewhat taken aback. "Do you not want to marry Rafaello?"

"Only if he wants to marry me, and I wish the same," Francesca said casually.

Aceline was briefly speechless, but Louisa laughed. "Frankly," she said, "he frightens me. He is so proud and fierce. But my father believes this is a wonderful opportunity for me. He will be very disappointed when I am sent home, I fear."

"Of course it is a wonderful opportunity for you," Aceline said sharply. "For a bastard daughter to make a respectable marriage of such magnificence is unheard of, and you might even have a chance with him if you tried."

"I do try, but I prefer his friend Valiant's company," Louisa responded.

"Who is he?" Francesca said.

"He's always by Rafaello's side," Louisa explained. "Tall with light brown hair and those northern blue eyes," she sighed. He speaks so gently to me and is kind. That is the kind of man I would have. Not one who growls and scowls all the time."

"You are a simpleton," Aceline told her. "If Rafaello chooses me, he will not look so dark all the time, for I shall keep him happy and smiling."

"Because you are such a charming maiden, I have not a doubt," Francesca said wickedly. "Who wants to show me the gardens? You have both been here over a week, and I am newly arrived and do not know my way."

"I have more important things to do than waste my time in a garden," Aceline said sourly. "I am already sewing a silk shirt for Rafaello." She turned, and hurried off.

"I love gardens," Louisa spoke up. "Walk with me. Duke Titus has a beautiful garden, Francesca, and the day is fair."

Together the two young women found their way outside. The area was filled with both flowers and a small display of fruit trees. Gravel paths led the way through the planted area. Francesca was particularly intrigued to find that half of the fruit trees were growing heavy with peaches, and the other with half-formed apples that would be ready to pick in the early autumn.

"It must be beautiful in the springtime," she remarked to Louisa.

"My father's palazzo has peach trees in its gardens. Their blossoms are lovely and sometimes even faintly fragrant," Louisa replied.

"Aceline made a great to-do about your circumstances," Francesca said. "I think she is very rude and unkind."

"She only seeks to make herself seem more important and therefore more worthy of Rafaello Cesare than either you or I are," Louisa said shrewdly. "When you arrived last night with your great baggage train, your servants, horses, and dogs, she was very taken aback, for she considers you of little importance, being a merchant's daughter. Yet the numerous men-at-arms accompanying your train were quite impressive. She isn't certain now what to make of you."

Francesca smiled wickedly. "I am sorry to have confused her."

Louisa laughed. "No, you aren't," she replied. "My mother's sire is a ship's captain. He is very direct in his dealings, which is confusing to many who look for plots in the simplest matters. I know all the gossip that has emanated from Florence and Venice about you, for mariners hear everything. When my father told me you were one of the girls chosen to compete for Rafaello's hand I was delighted, for I longed to meet you."

Francesca was very surprised. "Why?" she asked.

"You are brave and daring," Louisa said admiringly. "If I am chosen to be the bride I will be obedient, but the truth is I don't want to be the bride. But if you are chosen you will rebel, and perhaps I will gain some of your courage. I am far too meek and mild, as you have probably already seen."

"I am neither brave nor daring," Francesca said. "I am just stubborn and say no. Your perfect obedience is what a man looks for in a wife. Even I know that."

"I hope not," came the reply. "Of course I would wed, but to a less-fierce man."

"Well, we both know that Aceline wants the dark and brooding Rafaello," Francesca said. "She has made no secret of it, has she?" And she laughed.

"She would make his life a misery," Louisa answered. "All she wants is to be a *duchessa* and squander his wealth on herself."

Francesca tucked her arm into Louisa's. "Let us go pick a peach and eat it," she suggested. "It is a shame to allow them to go to waste."

They walked a short distance amid the trees, and then each picked a peach, which they began eating. The juice from the ripe fruits drizzled down their chins as they sat beneath the trees, and they giggled like children. Then suddenly looming up before them was Rafaello Cesare and his friend, Valiant.

"What is this?" Valiant said in a mock-serious tone. "Have we caught us a pair of pretty poachers in your father's orchards?" he teased them.

"Alas, we are discovered!" Francesca cried. "What will you do with us, *signores*?" She feigned fright.

Louisa giggled.

Rafaello Cesare looked down at Francesca. "Stop eating," he said. "I would walk with you so we may learn more about each other."

"But the peach is delicious, *signore*," Francesca protested.

Before he might complain, his companion, Valiant, bent and, capturing Louisa's little hand, pulled her to her feet. "This lady has finished her fruit," he said. "I shall take her for a walk. You remain here, Rafaello. It would be a great shame to waste that peach." Then he turned to the startled Louisa. "Your fingers are very sticky," he told her as he led her off.

Rafaello sat in the grass beneath the tree. "You are very stubborn," he said to Francesca as he settled himself.

"Yes," she agreed, "I am." *Madre di Dios*, he was hardly the child she had believed him to be. Exhausted from her journey, she had barely looked at him last night. He was a man, not a boy. And he was handsome in a very rugged and masculine way.

"Did no one ever tell you that you cannot always have your own way?"

"They did," she admitted. His eyes were a deep foresty green.

"But you paid them no mind," he said.

"Sometimes I do if the reasoning is sound," Francesca told him.

He laughed at that and his face was transformed from stern and fierce into something else entirely. His eyes crinkled with his amusement. "You are a woman of logic, then," he said to her.

"I am not an obedient little simpleton who will agree with your every thought," she told him.

"No, you are not," he replied, intrigued. "The other two, however, are.

"Louisa is sweet and kind," Rafaello said. "I see that. I'm certain she would make me an admirable wife if she weren't scared to death of me. She is pretty. Obedient. And she seems to possess all the proper virtues a good wife should have," Rafaello noted. "So does Aceline, though I find her tongue far too sharp—although I suspect she would be a tigress in the marital bed. You, however, are a puzzle."

"Not really," Francesca responded. "I simply do not like being called forth from Florence to partake in this horse fair where the three nubile mares are paraded before the young stallion so he may choose which one he will mount to breed with."

He laughed at her analogy, but said, "Is that not a bit harsh?"

"How old are you?" Francesca asked him.

She is maddening, Rafaello thought. "Twenty-nine. How old are you?"

"Fifteen," she replied. "I am told I am almost too old now to make a young man a wife, but you are not so young. Why have you not married before?" She had finished her peach and tossed away the pit. Then she began to lick and suck on her fingers to remove the stickiness from them.

His breath caught in his throat. Her actions were incredibly sensuous and he actually felt a tightening in his groin. Was she even aware of what she was doing and the effect it was having on him? No, he didn't believe she was. She was, he could see, spoiled and outspoken, but she was not a flirt. He swallowed and made an attempt at another topic with her. "Tell me about your life in Florence. Terreno Boscoso is a very different place if you have lived in a large city most of your life."

"We live in our father's palazzo. I have two older brothers and a younger one. I have three sisters, an older one and two little ones. Our days are regulated by the church and our lessons. In the summers we go to our villa in the Tuscan hills. There is nothing unusual about my life. It is the same as any girl's."

"So you have never left Florence before, and yet were brave enough to make this journey," he said.

"Oh no, *signore*, this is not my first voyage from Florence. I lived in Venice with my grandfather for a year," Francesca admitted.

"Here you are! Here you are!" Aceline du Barry came to where they were seated and joined them. "When I saw your companion, Valiant, walking with Louisa, I thought you might be here in the gardens." Then she paused and clapped her hand over her mouth. "You did know Louisa was with Valiant. Didn't you?" she finally said.

The bitch! Francesca thought. She would put Louisa in a bad light to further her own cause. Well, she could play this game better than the French girl. Florentines were noted for their deviousness. "Louisa is with Valiant?" she exclaimed, her eyes wide. "Oh, dear! Oh, dear! Did you know that, Rafaello?"

"Well, given her background, the child of a courtesan, what can one expect of her behavior?" Aceline said quickly before he might reply.

Rafaello almost laughed at Francesca's response to Aceline du Barry. Well, the wench deserved to be taken down a peg or two, especially as Valiant and Louisa were now approaching them. He stood and, reaching out, pulled Francesca up from the grass. Then he hailed his best friend and the charming Louisa.

Aceline now realized the precariousness of her situation. *"You knew!"* she hissed at Francesca.

"We knew," Francesca replied, implying there was something deeper between her and Rafaello Cesare.

The French girl's face flushed with her anger. "You are nothing more than a vile Florentine tradesman's daughter," she snarled.

"And you a lying and conniving wench who believes she can win a bridegroom by vilifying another's reputation. I have been here but a day, yet I can tell you that Louisa di Genoa is a sweet, kind girl. How dare you attempt to tarnish her good name? Do you think Rafaello is a fool? Are you not even aware of how you make yourself look?" Francesca demanded. She kept her voice low, so as to not involve the others. Now she turned away from Aceline du Barry and, putting her hand through Rafaello's arm, said, "Will you walk us back to the *castello*? The sun is becoming quite hot."

"Now I have learned something else about you," Rafaello said as they strolled.

"That I have a temper?" Francesca said, realizing he had heard her outburst.

"Yes, but I learned another thing as well. You are loyal to friends. It is a trait I find admirable in a man or a woman," Rafaello responded.

"Louisa is a sweet person. The circumstances of her birth are not her fault. I will tell you that they certainly neither offend nor distress my sensibilities," Francesca said.

He smiled again. She wondered if it hurt his face to smile, since his handsome visage usually wore a look of such seriousness. They returned to the Great Hall. It was already the noon hour, and the servants were preparing to set out the main meal of the day.

"I plan to ride again this afternoon," Rafaello said to her. "Come with me."

"Nay," Francesca told him. "I am yet weary from my travels and will nap after we have eaten."

He looked genuinely disappointed. "Then tomorrow morning," he said.

"Perhaps if I do not decide to stay abed as I did this morning, although I was not aware that you rode in the mornings," Francesca answered him.

"Piero was told to inform you," he responded. "I will speak to him. It is unlike him to forget an order," Rafaello said.

"Do not scold him, *signore*," she replied. "I would not have come this morning under any circumstances, and I know now."

She had a good heart. Something else learned in this brief time. "I will leave you to rejoin your two companions," Rafaello said as they stopped where Louisa and Aceline were now waiting. She curtsied and turned away. Rafaello walked over to where his friend, Valiant, stood with a cup of wine in his hand. Valiant looked happy and at the same time he looked unhappy. "What is wrong?" Rafaello said.

"I know they were sent for so you might pick among them for a wife. Will you pick her?" the young man wanted to know.

Rafaello knew exactly to whom his best friend referred. He had never seen him that way over any female. "No, I will not pick Louisa, although I really should. She is beautiful, sweet-natured, soft-spoken, and obedient. Only two things prevent me from ending this summer fiasco my father has arranged. The first is that she is frightened of me, and I really could not wed a wife who appears to believe I will gobble her up. The second is that my best friend fell in love with her at first sight, and I believe she returns his sentiments. Do not declare yourself yet, though, my friend. I must make my own choice first in order to please my father. When I do I will ask him to approach the Duke of Genoa about arranging a match between you and your lady love. You are of noble birth and have lands of your own, Valiant. If I wed, then so must you. I shall not venture into this new world without my best friend by my side as you have always been."

Both relief and joy lit Valiant Cordassci's handsome face. "Thank you," he said. Then he added, "But which of the other two? You hardly know the Florentine. She arrived only yesterday."

"And yet in that short time we were alone beneath the peach trees I learned much. There is more I would know, and the French girl, despite her difficult nature, has noble blood while the Florentine is just a wealthy merchant's daughter. Which would be better suited to be my *duchessa* is what I must decide," Rafaello said.

"Let your heart decide, my friend. You will be happier that way," Valiant wisely counseled Rafaello.

With the arrival of the final aspirant for the hand of his son, Duke Titus signaled a summer of festivities so Rafaello might become better acquainted with his potential bride. He had no idea that his son had already yielded the sweet Louisa to Valiant. It would seem that the French girl had the edge, for she was always in his company, while the beautiful Florentine, Francesca Pietro d'Angelo, seemed to always be by the duke's side.

"Do you not like Rafaello?" he asked her one afternoon as they picnicked in the orchards of his gardens. His warm brown eyes searched her face. He already knew that this was the girl he would choose for his son.

"I do like him," Francesca said. "But he must like me for who and what I am. Not what he believes he could make me."

"And yet you seem to be always in my company. Not that I mind it," Duke Titus said with a smile. "It has been quite a while since I had so beautiful a young companion by my side. Not since my beloved Antonia died. She was many years my junior, you know, and gave me my only child."

"You miss her," Francesca replied putting a comforting hand on his. "I am sorry to have made you sad, *signore*."

"No, child, you did not. I can never, it seems, think of Antonia without growing tearful, despite the many years she has been gone," the old duke admitted.

They had been watching a small jousting tournament, and now in an effort to distract him from his sad thoughts Francesca said, "Oh, look! Rafaello and Valiant are going to go up against each other."

"Valiant will win," Duke Titus said with a chuckle. "My own son is little interested in jousting. He says there is no practical use for it. Now and again he will overcome Valiant but 'tis only by chance."

Francesca felt Louisa grab her hand and squeeze it hard as the two horsemen sat at either end of the jousting course, awaiting a signal from the tourney's master at arms.

"Tell me what happens," she whispered. "I can't look."

Francesca repressed a chuckle, knowing Louisa's fear was for Valiant, not Rafaello.

"Ohh," squealed Aceline. "Are they not magnificent? But of course my Rafaello will win. He is so brave and so very gallant."

A horn sounded and the two riders began their gallop down the field, lances lowered. The sound of the horses' hooves was almost like distant thunder. The tip of Valiant's lance hit the direct center of Rafaello's shield. He struggled to stay ahorse, but lost his seat and went down with an audible thump. The crowd burst into laughter, for this was an old story to them and they knew no harm had been done the duke's heir by his best friend. The fallen warrior gave them a good-natured wave of his armored gauntlet, and it was then they cheered him and Valiant.

Aceline gasped, shocked, and pushed her way from the duke's box to run down onto the jousting field, shrieking at the top of her lungs. "Rafaello! Rafaello!" She turned angrily on Valiant, who had dismounted, and was checking on his friend. "Monster! If you have killed him I will kill you! How dare you win? He is your lord's son, and when we are wed you will be forbidden from the court, I swear it."

Valiant ignored her and knelt by Rafaello's side. "Are you all right?" he asked.

Rafaello laughed. "If you do not take into consideration my bruised bottom and my equally bruised ego, I'm fine. Help me up." He had already removed his helmet.

Valiant and a squire pulled Rafaello to his feet.

Aceline pushed Valiant away and clung to Rafaello. "You are sooo brave," she cooed at him. "I am so very proud of you. He took you off guard, else you should never have fallen victim to this coward," she declared vehemently.

Rafaello shook her off angrily. "Valiant and I have been jousting ever since we were small boys," he told her. "He is the better warrior and everyone knows it. How dare you call him a coward, you little shrew?" He pushed her away when she attempted to reattach herself to him again. "And how dare you make a spectacle of yourself here on a field of honor? You shame your family by your behavior."

Aceline burst into fulsome tears, but cleverly disguised her outrage at him by saying loudly for many to hear, "Thank God you are safe, *amore mia*!"

"I am *not* your *amore*," Rafaello snapped irritably. She was fair to the eye. She was of noble blood, but she was spoiled beyond redemption and had a sharp tongue. She was obviously determined to have him, no matter the cost. He was surprised she hadn't thrown off her clothing and had her way with him on the jousting field before all the spectators watching. "Valiant," he said to his friend, "you must crown your queen of love and beauty, having triumphed over me this day."

Together the two men turned away from Aceline and walked to Duke Titus's box. The French girl, now in serious danger of being publicly embarrassed, scrambled after them, attempting to make a trio. Reaching their destination, she reentered the box.

Duke Titus gave her a sharp look of disapproval before turning to the two young men standing below him.

"It is time to crown the queen of love and beauty," he said, taking a wreath of gilded laurel leaves and placing it carefully upon Valiant's couched lance.

Valiant moved his stallion sideways but a foot or two and then offered the wreath to Louisa di Genoa. "*Signorina*," he said quietly, his blue eyes meeting her adoring ones.

With a blush and a murmur of thanks, Louisa accepted and slowly placed the wreath upon her dark head. A cheer went up from the onlookers.

"It suits you perfectly," Francesca said with a smile, kissing her friend's cheek.

"I've never been the queen of love and beauty before," Louisa said shyly. "Valiant should not draw attention to me. He should have offered the crown to you."

"Or me!" Aceline said angrily. "In birth I outrank you both."

"After that scene you caused upon the field you are fortunate the duke allowed you back in the box," Francesca said sharply.

"I was only showing my love and concern for Rafaello," Aceline defended herself.

"You are ridiculous," Francesca told the girl.

"He won't choose you," Aceline murmured. "You are barely polite to him. Ohh, I know all about how you scorned and turned down every suitor who came your way," she continued. "My father sought out information on both of the others chosen to be my rivals. He laughed when he saw who you both were. A *bastarda* and a tradesman's brat. He said he did not see why Duke Titus had not simply asked for my hand for his son, since it was obvious Rafaello would have no other choice."

"I know he won't choose me," Francesca said. "And, believe me, I shall be happy to return home to Florence, though my family will be disappointed. But I should not try on the ducal jewelry quite yet, Aceline. I suspect it will not fit your skinny throat."

"You had best beware of me, for I also know about Venice," Aceline threatened.

Francesca laughed. "I suspect most of the known world does," she replied. "It was quite an adventure, as I recall it."

"Stop it!" Louisa said. "You both shame us all by this quarreling. Are you so perfect, Aceline, that you dare threaten Francesca by repeating lurid gossip? I understand that your father has been shopping you around for two years now and has had no takers."

Aceline turned a bright scarlet, but she clamped her lips tightly together.

Francesca fought back her giggle over that fascinating bit of information. Louisa was correct, and this imbroglio between herself and the French girl must cease. Besides, Aceline was clever. She would turn their squabble so that she would appear the victim and put Francesca in a poor light. It wasn't that she cared, but old Duke Titus was being so very kind to her. She did not want to disappoint him.

The summer moved slowly, and Francesca found she was actually enjoying herself. She had a friend in Louisa di Genoa, and she had never had a friend before. Bianca, her eldest sister, had gone away more than two years ago, and her two little sisters had just been too young. They had each other. The three girls rode out together daily into the beautiful forests surrounding the *castello*. They hunted with Rafaello, Valiant, and a few other gentlemen of the duke's court. They picnicked in the flower-filled meadows. In the evenings they danced informally, played cards, and sang. Oddly Aceline had a very sweet voice, but it did not, unfortunately, make up for her shrewish behavior.

Although Rafaello spent time alone with Louisa to take any suspicion off Valiant's attraction to her, and a little time with Aceline, it was Francesca who frustrated him. She managed to find more ways to avoid him. She would slip away into the forest with the two nuns who were her chaperones to pick berries. In the company of her serving woman, Terza, she would ride into the nearby village to make small purchases. She closeted herself with her women, and Father Silvio for hours on end. Sometimes Louisa was invited.

"What do you do?" he inquired of Louisa.

"Do? We do many things," Louisa said to him. "If you are

curious, why not ask Francesca? I'm sure she would tell you. After all, what mischief can she get into surrounded by two holy women and a priest?"

"I would ask if I could corner her," Rafaello said. "Why does she avoid me?"

"Does she?" Louisa said innocently, eyes wide.

"Be careful, you devious wench," Rafaello warned her. "I could always tell my father I have chosen you for my bride." He gave her his best glower.

Louisa laughed. "I am no longer afraid of you," she said. "Valiant says you are a fraud. He says you are a very kind man, and I have seen incidents of it these past weeks."

"Have you indeed?" Rafaello answered her. Then he said, "She intrigues me, Louisa. I want to get to know her better, but she will not allow it. Why? Surely she is not still bedazzled by that Venetian popinjay who refused her."

"Gracious, no! She laughs about her time in Venice and tells us the funniest stories. It is her pride, Rafaello. She is offended to have been summoned to Terreno Boscoso for the purpose of being considered as your bride."

"But women have no choice in the matter of their husbands," he replied, surprised, although she had once told him much the same although in more colorful language.

"Francesca's older sister was wed at her parents' hand to a monster. I do not know all of the story behind it, but I do know when he died, Bianca—that is her name—ran off with the man with whom she was deeply in love. She is happy now. Francesca wants to choose her own husband," Louisa told him.

"But how can she fall in love with me if she will not at least take time to know me?" he asked. "You are a sensible girl. Speak to her, but do not say I asked it of you."

Poor man, Louisa thought to herself. I believe he might be falling in love with the mystery that is Francesca. "I will help you," she said.

In the morning Louisa sent word that she was feeling poorly and would not ride. Aceline du Barry found herself riding with Valiant by her side. "Get out of my way," she hissed at him. "I will ride by Rafaello's side, as I do every morning."

"He has ordered me to keep you by my side," Valiant lied boldly. "You allow him no time to get to know Francesca better."

"He knows all he needs know about her," Aceline responded. "She is the daughter of a low tradesman. Whatever you do, he will pick me in the end because I am of noble blood as he is."

"Her father is head of the silk merchants' guild in Florence, an important position in the second most important guild in that city. His wealth is great. Her mother is the daughter of one of the noblest houses in Venice, the Veniers. She is hardly low."

Aceline was actually surprised. She had not realized that Francesca's family was so important or that she had noble blood in her veins. Her parents both had noble blood, but their wealth was sparse. It was important that she make this marriage to Rafaello Cesare. It would add to the prestige of the du Barry family, and they could find a suitable heiress for her brother to wed. She said nothing more to Valiant and rode by his side without complaint. Making a scene would not aid her cause.

She already had a plan to entrap Rafaello, should he appear to be becoming interested in choosing anyone but her. Her maidservant, Oriel, had suggested it. It was a foolproof strategy that would leave him no other choice than to wed her. Aceline smiled.

Ahead of her Rafaello and Francesca were bickering over something.

"Why do you want to know?" Aceline heard Francesca say.

"Why do you want to keep it secret?" Rafaello demanded.

"What mischief can I get into with a priest and two nuns by my side?" Francesca said. "You are ridiculous."

"I hear riotous laughter when you are closed up in your apartments. Asking what you do that causes you to laugh so is no intrusion," he responded.

"Oh, very well," Francesca replied, sounding irritated. "We gamble. Annunziata just took her final vows, and Benigna soon will. They are not so far from the world yet that they have forgotten how to have fun, but as you surely know gambling is not allowed in the convent. We play cards and throw the dice for ridiculous wagers, like the Holy Father's undergarments or the King of Naples' throne. Sometimes *Padre* Silvio joins us, but his wagers are so innocent we laugh at him. Mostly he attempts to keep us honest in our play. There! Now you know my dark secret."

He was very surprised by what she had told him. He had not thought of her as a girl with a particularly active sense of humor. Her choice of activities was, however, very amusing. "I hope the good priest gives you all a proper penance for your unholy behavior," he told her. "Are you good with the bones?"

"I never lose," Francesca said. "My brothers taught me well."

"It is but a game of chance," he told her.

"For some who do not know how to throw dice properly, perhaps, but not for me. I know how to control those little ivory squares."

"Then we shall dice together tonight, you and I. What shall we play for?" he asked her wickedly.

"Kisses," she answered him. "Since I shall win, you will get none, so I do not endanger my virtue by offering them."

Rafaello laughed heartily. "By evening's end you will have been kissed most thoroughly," he promised her. Then he set his stallion into a gallop, and Francesca, taken unawares by his actions, quickly galloped after him.

She was surprised to find her heart pounding at his words. She had never been kissed but for one time in Venice when Enzo Ziani had angered her and she had flung herself at him and kissed him. He had not really kissed her back. She wondered what it would be like to be kissed by Rafaello Cesare. Well, she had to begin with someone who was at least interested in kissing her back.

The day was warm, and a fine sheen of moisture formed on her face and neck. The air caused by the motion of her horse dried it, but when they came to a halt in a lovely forest clearing it bloomed again. He lifted her from her animal and, taking her hand, began to walk with her. At first he spoke not a word. Then he said, "I am taking you to one of my favorite places. No one will find us for a while. Valiant will know where we have gone, but he will keep Aceline away."

"Don't you like her?" Francesca asked.

"She has noble blood, but there is something that tells me it is the prospect of being my *duchessa* that pleases her more than being a wife to me. I expect if I were ugly and crippled she would still pay me court. Do I like her? I think not, and certainly not enough to wed her."

"Then it is Louisa you will choose. She is a fine choice, Rafaello. Gentle, loving, obedient. Everything a good wife should be. I have grown quite fond of her these past summer months. Aceline will be disappointed, I expect."

"Will you be disappointed, Francesca?" he queried her.

"I did not expect you to choose me, Rafaello. I know what I am. Stubborn. Outspoken and quite determined to have my own way. I shall probably, as my mother predicts, end up as the family spinster." But even as she said the words, Francesca realized that she found them distasteful. And yet did she really want to wed at all?

"You are far too beautiful to remain a spinster," he told her.

"Is that all men look for in a woman?" she replied. "Someone beautiful? And after you have taken your pleasure is there nothing more a woman can offer to you? And if the chamber is dark, what matter if she is beautiful or ugly as long as the parts fit properly? And if a man demands beauty in his wife, should not a woman be permitted to request the same?"

He was astounded by her once more, and he laughed aloud again. "You have been told, I am certain, that you are a most outrageous maiden," he said. "I have never before heard a female voice such thoughts aloud, if indeed she even had such thoughts," he admitted.

"Oh, all women have such thoughts at one time or another in their lives," Francesca told him. "I really believe that most do not voice them aloud, but there is another of my thoughts. I seem to speak whatever I am thinking, Rafaello."

"I find it charming," he surprised her by saying.

"Then you are unique among men," she answered. "In most households I should be beaten for speaking my mind, and I should be admonished severely by the priest."

"You will make an interesting wife," he told her. "Ahh, here we are."

They came out of the woodland trail and there before them was a beautiful small pond fed by a stony brook. The ground around the pool was moss covered. In the center of the water a heart-shaped rock. There were two large willow trees, one on the far side of the pond and the other at its end.

"It's called Heart's Wish Pond," Rafaello said. "It's believed that a faerie with the ability to grant your dearest wishes lives in the pond. She has been seen sitting on the rock, combing her long silver hair in the light of a full moon. If you whisper your desire to her, seen or unseen, she may sometime grant you your wish if she considers it worthy."

"Have you whispered a wish to her, Rafaello?"

"Many times," he admitted.

"And were they granted?" Francesca wanted to know.

"Sometimes," he said with a small smile. "Today I shall ask the faerie to help me choose the right wife, and that my bride may come to love me."

"I have no wish to make," Francesca told him. "Make yours!"

He did silently.

Behind them there came the sound of voices as they moved through the forest.

"Quickly!" Francesca said. "Let us go back before Aceline can see this pond. I do not want her to view it."

He agreed and, taking her hand again, they turned back and walked away from the magical little area. Around a bend they met Valiant coming along, Aceline behind him, complaining that he walked too fast and that the briars were pulling at her hair and gown.

"There is nothing ahead but more woods, and I can see that your companion has had enough of nature this day."

"I certainly have!" Aceline said sharply, looking at Francesca to see if she was showing any signs of having been kissed.

Francesca smiled a wicked little smile back, convincing Aceline that she had been the little slut the French girl thought. Rafaello had not kissed her at any time during their stay. Now

Aceline wondered if he had possibly kissed Louisa and Valiant's interest in the girl had been a ruse to keep people guessing. She ground her teeth. She needed to win this contest. If she was sent home, her father intended to marry her off to a neighboring nobleman. The man was twenty years older than she was, had bad breath, and wanted an heir desperately. He had offered to take her with half the dowry her father was willing to pay the Duke of Terreno Boscoso for his son. The man had already attempted to take liberties with her, Aceline recalled with a shudder.

"Wear your most beautiful gowns tonight," Rafaello said when they had returned to the *castello*. "I would make it a special occasion," he told them. And when he was alone again with Valiant he said, "Tonight I will choose."

"Which one?" his friend asked.

"You must wait and be surprised with all the rest," Rafaello said, "but I will keep my promise to you, Valiant. You shall have your Louisa."

Chapter 4

*T*erza looked at Oriel, Aceline's maidservant, and said, "You have monopolized the women servants long enough. Elda and I need help with the preparations for tonight's announcement. Our mistresses are part of this too."

"But it is my beautiful mistress who this duke's son will choose," Oriel said smugly. "Be careful, girl, with that undergown!" she called out sharply to a little maid. Do you wish to iron it again?"

"Put the undergown there across the chair," Terza instructed the nervous girl. "Then go help Elda with *Signorina* Louisa."

When Oriel began to protest, Terza silenced the older French-woman with a hard look and a sharp word. "Enough! I do not care which of them is chosen, but the other two will have the opportunity to look their best."

"Your mistress has the finest clothes," Oriel whined. "And

the little Genoese may be born on the wrong side of the blanket, but her mother is loved and respected by her duke. They will have other chances for marriage. This may be my mistress's only opportunity."

"I have heard it said among the other servants that you bragged a wealthy nobleman awaits your mistress's return, and her father has promised him the girl if the duke's son does not choose her."

Oriel flushed at this reminder of her indiscretion. "But the Comte du Lyonnais is not a duke with his own kingdom," she said.

"How unfortunate for your mistress," Terza said sarcastically.

Her confident attitude made Oriel afraid. "What do you know?" she demanded of Terza. "You must tell me what you know!"

"No more than you," Terza replied, a little smile playing at the corners of her mouth. "I know nothing. We shall all learn the young lord's decision together. Perhaps he finds none of the candidates worthy or compatible to his hand." Terza then walked away, leaving the older woman in a quandary.

Francesca was just exiting her bath when Terza reached her apartments. She had been helped by two little maidservants and the two young nuns. There was much laughter coming from the bedchamber when she entered it. "You have time to take a brief nap before you must dress," she said to her mistress, who was being thoroughly toweled dry by the maidservants.

"Is it true he will make his decision tonight?" Sister Annunziata asked Terza.

"That is the rumor going about," Terza answered her. "It's time. They have had two and a half months to become acquainted. Autumn is almost upon us, and if we are to return home to Florence, we will have to depart soon."

"We are returning home to Florence," Francesca broke in.

"But what if the duke's son chooses you?" the trusting Sister Benigna wondered.

"He won't," Francesca said. "Louisa is in love with Valiant, and Rafaello knows it. He will pick the French girl. Her pedigree matches his, and she is beautiful. She'll quickly do her duty, give him several heirs, grow a bit thicker in the waist, and in five years settle down to spend his money quite happily. He'll find a mistress to keep him happy and satisfied. A perfect ending, eh?"

All the women laughed at her analysis of the situation. There was nothing outrageous about it. It was how many marriages were begun and eventually settled.

"But what will happen to you?" Sister Benigna asked.

"Well," Francesca said, "I shall not join you at Santa Maria della Fiore."

There was more laughter when Sister Annunziata said, "To be honest, I believe the good Reverend Mother Baptista will find that a mighty relief."

"But what will you do?" Sister Benigna persisted.

"I shall become the daughter who remains at home to care for her parents in their old age. Perhaps I shall learn something of the silk trade. I shall do as I please and as long as I cause no scandal I shall be allowed to do it," Francesca said.

"But what of love?" one of the little maids, a girl who looked no older than twelve, asked softly. "Don't you want to be loved, *signorina*?"

"I don't know if what is called love actually exists. And what exactly is love?" Francesca inquired of her companions. "I surely do not know."

"Too much serious thought," Terza said. "Your chances with the duke's son are as good as the other two. I think I will wait until he announces his choice tonight before I begin packing for our return journey."

"We are going home," Francesca said stubbornly. "My father promised me if this man did not suit I could come home."

"Get into bed. Tonight, whatever happens, will be an exciting night," Terza replied. "I will choose a gown for you, and when you awaken all will be in readiness." She slipped a clean silk chemise over Francesca, and firmly led her to the bed, helped her into it, and drew the goose-down coverlet over her. "Now rest," she said. Ushering the other women out of the room, she thanked the little maids for their aid and sent them off. Then she sat down by the dayroom fireplace with the two nuns. For a few moments they sat in silence. The sunset filled the blue sky of the September evening.

It was Sister Annunziata who finally spoke up. "You think he will choose her. Don't you, Terza?"

Terza nodded. "*Signore* Valiant is openly in love with the little Louisa, and she with him. Rafaello knows it, and would not steal the maiden his best friend loves away from him. He is wise enough to know she would not be a good choice for him. She is gentle and soft-spoken. He's already bored with her."

"But what of the French girl?" Sister Benigna asked. "Her bloodline is an excellent one, there is no denying."

"But her avid quest to be his *duchessa* first and her sharp tongue put him off. There is no sweetness in her at all. She has virtually ignored the duke these past weeks. If she were wise, she would know it is he who will actually make the decision, but she is not a wise woman. She is greedy and selfish. She does not hide it, and I doubt she would be surprised to be told she is," Terza concluded.

"So it must of necessity be Francesca," Annunziata replied.

"Or none of the trio," Terza answered, "but from what I have observed I believe that he will choose my mistress."

"What of her father's promise?" Benigna asked softly.

"I was hidden behind a tapestry during that conversation that day," Terza said. "I wanted to know exactly where *Signore* Pietro d'Angelo stood in this matter. Although my mistress does not realize it, she is much like her mother in temperament. She only hears what she wants to hear. What the *signore* said that day was if the young man didn't suit, she might come home. He did not say if the young man didn't suit Francesca, she could come home. If Rafaello Cesare picks Francesca to be his bride, she will be. He is attractive, good-natured, respectful, and respectable. Father Silvio informed our master of that weeks back, after he had gotten to know the young man. The master wrote back that if Francesca pleased the duke and his son, he would give his blessing to the union."

"Oh, my," Sister Annunziata said softly. "But will she cooperate?"

"What other choice does she have?" Terza responded. "She is not aware that as soon as the decision is made Lorenzo di Medici's men-at-arms will either escort us back to Florence in the company of our own men-at-arms, or the di Medici men will depart immediately, except for the captain and six of his men, who will remain to be witnesses to the union so they may report it to the great Lorenzo himself upon their return."

"When are we to return to Florence?" Annunziata asked.

"You two and the good priest must remain until after the wedding," Terza replied.

"When will it be celebrated?" Benigna inquired. "I have never seen a royal wedding before."

"Probably not until next spring," Terza answered. "*Signora* Pietro d'Angelo will want to have the wedding gown made for her daughter, and she will want to come to see her daughter made a *duchessa*."

"This is so exciting!" Benigna said.

"It is not a reality yet," Terza warned. "We shall know soon enough, however."

And while Terza and the two nuns chatted on quietly before the cozy hearth in the dayroom, Rafaello Cesare was ensconced with his father in the duke's library.

"I have made a decision," he told the older man. "I want the Florentine girl to wife."

"Why?" Duke Titus asked his son quietly. "What is it about the fair Francesca that stands out for you? That makes her more desirable than Aceline or Louisa?" And he was indeed curious to learn why.

Rafaello laughed. "I know. A common merchant's daughter who has taken every opportunity to avoid me and prefers to sit by my ancient father's side."

"Not so ancient that I cannot attract a pretty girl," the duke teased back. "Now, tell me why Francesca."

"I like her independence and her outspoken way. Yet she knows when to be mannerly and charming. Her beauty is extraordinary, of course. She has an inborn elegance that suits a *duchessa*."

"That comes from her mother, who was born a Venetian princess and brought her ways to Florence when she wed the silk merchant," the duke noted. "But I hope perhaps that you feel a small attraction to her. It is better to have love for one's mate than just duty, my son."

"I am attracted by her, yes. I believe that she is sincere in her prayers when we are in church. I like that she traveled with her priest and the two young nuns, although I realize it was probably her mother who made these arrangements. I have seen her with her priest and two nuns, and I see the respect and friendship she has for them. I believe she will make an excellent mother."

"Have you kissed her yet?" the duke wanted to know.

"Nay. She is not a girl a gentleman should disrespect, *Padre*," Rafaello answered.

The duke chuckled, then grew serious again. Rafaello might not realize it but he was falling in love with Francesca. It was just as well he choose her tonight and they return the other two girls to their families, so he might begin to discover it. Hopefully she would too. "Tell me why you decline the other two."

"Aceline du Barry is not to my taste. I find her venal and greedy. In church she appears inattentive and bored. Her eagerness for me stems from her desire to be a *duchessa* more than it does to be my wife or the mother of my children."

Duke Titus nodded. "I cannot argue with your reasoning," he said. "But what of the sweet and fair Louisa, my son?"

"Aye, she is charming, *Padre*, but, alas, the moment she laid eyes on Valiant and he upon her they were wildly in love. There is no loss there for me. Louisa is too fragile to be my wife. But if you would intervene with the Duke of Genoa on Valiant's behalf I know that they would both be very happy. She and Francesca have become great friends."

The duke smiled warmly at his only child. "Your heart is good and you are wise. I have no fears turning over my ducal crown to you once you are wed, Rafaello. Louisa must, however, return home. Valiant will escort her and she will carry my personal recommendation in Valiant's favor. In my opinion he would be an excellent match for her. He is *Signore* di Sponda di Fiume. He possesses both land and wealth. It is an excellent match for a duke's bastard daughter. But it will be up to Louisa and Valiant to convince Genoa, and he's a very wily man. Still, he has the right to meet the man his child would wed, which is why they must both go to Genoa."

"I believe Valiant would go into hell if he could bring her back as his bride," Rafaello said sincerely.

"So you will choose Francesca and announce your choice this evening?" Duke Titus asked. "Good! Good! The others will then have time to return to their own homes before the winter months set in, and you will have time to know Francesca better before the wedding. A December wedding would be excellent. You can spend the snowy month getting her with child. I will see my grandchildren before I die."

"You will not die that soon, you old fraud," his son replied laughing. Then he stood up from the tapestried chair where he had been seated. "I must go bathe and dress for this evening."

"I am certain the young ladies are busy doing the same thing," Duke Titus remarked with a small smile. Rafaello had made him happy. As for his choice of a bride, his son would be quite surprised to learn how very pleased his father was with it. He would have chosen Francesca had he himself been seeking a bride. The girl was stronger in more ways than Rafaello knew. She would not be her husband's cipher.

The fact that he would have to disappoint only the Comte du Barry was a relief. Genoa might be disappointed too, but with Terreno Boscoso sending Louisa back with a possible and eligible bridegroom, along with the lavish gifts she would bring from them for her trouble, it should certainly satisfy her father quite well. Tomorrow he would choose the gifts to be sent with each girl as she departed. The French girl must go first.

Aceline du Barry would not be happy, for he suspected she thought it impossible that anyone but her be chosen. She was too proud by far, and had no idea how many of her cutting and unkind remarks to the other girls he had heard spewing forth from those thin lips of hers. Pouring himself another splash of wine, he settled back in his chair. He would have to go shortly and dress for this evening's entertainment.

Rafaello could not resist slipping into the corridor where the three girls had their apartments. The maidservants were running back and forth from one chamber to another. Footmen carried buckets of steaming water into the apartments. He heard the muffled chatter of the women as they prepared their mistresses for the evening, and he smiled. In just a few hours it would be settled. He would have Francesca, and Valiant would have Louisa. He gave no thought to Aceline du Barry before he walked away.

"The young lord was lingering in the hallway," the little maidservant said to Terza as she came into the apartment, bearing a tray of light refreshments, which she placed upon a table in the dayroom.

Terza nodded her thanks for both the food and the information. Then she went into the bedchamber and woke Francesca. "It's time for you to arise," she said, gently shaking the girl's shoulder. "I have a small meal for you, for I expect the evening will be long, and who knows when the young lord will make his announcement. Best your belly not growl loudly, which will only cause the French girl to make some remark drawing attention to it." Terza helped Francesca from her bed.

Francesca did not protest. She walked into the dayroom,

where she found a small repast consisting of a few slices of warm capon breast, bread, butter, honey, and a dish of stewed pears, along with a small goblet of sweet golden wine. She ate it slowly, then washed her face and hands in a basin of scented warm water that was brought to her.

"I am bathed, rested, and fed," Francesca announced. "Have you chosen what I will wear this evening, Terza? If I do not like it, I will change it to suit myself."

Terza chuckled. "I have not a doubt that you will," she answered. Come and see what will dazzle the hall and fill Aceline du Barry with pure envy."

Stepping back into her bedchamber Francesca gasped at the beautiful emerald green silk brocade gown that was laid out upon the bed. The underskirt was cloth of gold. She could see immediately that the square neckline was lower than she was used to wearing, and it was embroidered in gold braid that also edged the hem of the gown. The bodice was tightly fitted. The sleeves were flared and the cuffs turned back to show a cloth of gold lining. "My breasts will fall out of that neckline," the girl said.

"No, they won't," Terza promised, and then she chuckled. "But they will certainly show to their best advantage, mistress."

The little maid helping Terza giggled and nodded.

"It's indecent. My mother would never allow me to wear a gown like this," Francesca protested nervously. "I don't remember being fitted for this garment."

"Your *madre* chose the design herself," Terza said. "And the materials. You were not fitted for the garment. The seamstress had your measurements. This gown arrived several weeks ago from Florence. I unpacked it and hung it away."

A wicked little smile bloomed upon Francesca's lips. "Aceline will die," she said slowly. "She is certain to have nothing to rival this gown, Terza. Are there shoes to match? What jewelry do I have that will be suitable?"

"Your slippers are covered in the same brocade as the gown. Your silk stockings have a green vine embroidered up their length. And you have a red-gold crucifix decorated with a small diamond lily and hanging from a chain of red-gold, which is also set with emeralds," Terza replied.

"I am ready to be dressed, then," Francesca said, and stood quietly as the two servants completed the task. "How will you dress my hair?" she asked when they were done. "I think a golden caul."

"Nay, you do not want to contain your beautiful hair," Terza said, and the little maid shook her head vigorously in agreement. "I shall brush it out so that it is visible in all its glory, and decorate it with narrow green ribbons studded with tiny emeralds."

When it was finished and she studied herself in the mirror, Francesca was astounded by how absolutely beautiful and so-phisticated she appeared. "I am far fairer than my sister Bi-anca," she said to Terza.

"You are," Terza agreed. "Her beauty is in her face, which you cannot rival, but you wear your clothing better, and com-bined with a beautiful face you are spectacular."

She handed her mistress a beautiful peacock feather fan.

Suddenly a look of concern touched Francesca's face. "What if he chooses me? Perhaps I should not look quite so wonderful."

Terza laughed. "When he chooses you, you will accept with charm and make a marriage that will please your family greatly. You don't particularly care for Florence, my child. Terreno Bos-coso is a lovely place to live. The old duke has already shown his fondness for you and will welcome you warmly into his family. There is no mother-in-law alive to plague you. You have been happy here these past months. Louisa will wed Valiant, and you will have her as a friend."

"No! No! I don't want to wed. I don't want to be constrained by a man's wishes and thoughts, Terza. I would be free!"

"Well, you won't be in Florence," Terza said. "You return a second time to your *padre*'s house, and your *madre* will have you married off to the first well-to-do man she can find. You will end up being the second or third wife of some old man. Is that what you want? Rafaello Cesare is juicy and young. He is filled with passion and he is kind."

Francesca now looked as if she wanted to run. She couldn't, of course. "I would speak with the priest," she said.

Padre Silvio was sent for and came immediately, for he knew how important this evening was. Like Terza, he knew the true lay of the land and that it was most likely that Rafaello Cesare would choose Francesca. He found the dayroom empty but for Francesca. "What is it, my child?" he inquired of her, seeing her face.

"I don't want to be part of this anymore," she said. "I want to go home tonight!"

"My daughter," the priest replied, taking the panicked girl's two hands in his. They were as cold as ice. "I see that you are afraid, but there is nothing to fear." Then the priest lied smoothly as he continued, "You are distressing yourself needlessly. We will return home as soon as the French girl is chosen to be the bride. Now, remember who you are, and draw yourself together so you may enter the hall with the others and enjoy your evening with the rest of us. I understand there are to be dancing dogs." He rose and drew Francesca up with him. "Are you all right now?" he asked her.

Francesca drew a deep breath. She had no choice, and the priest was probably right. Rafaello wasn't going to choose her. She had certainly made her disdain for this whole situation quite plain to him. Certainly he had come to understand that she didn't appreciate being the possible prize in a contest. He did seem a reasonable man. "It was just a fit of nerves, good *Padre*. I am sorry to have troubled you with my foolishness."

He smiled even as he felt the guilt associated with lying to her. Almost everyone in the *castello* suspected Francesca Pietro d'Angelo, the silk merchant's daughter from Florence, had gained Rafaello Cesare's favor even if she hadn't. "Our dear Lord Jesu and his blessed Mother Maria be by your side, my daughter," the priest said, giving her his blessing as he led her from her apartments, followed by Terza, through the hallways, downstairs, and to the door of the Great Hall. There he left her.

Francesca stood a moment in the opening to the hall. Then she stepped past the entry and walked slowly to the high board. She saw Valiant and Louisa by one of the large hearths, speaking quietly. Louisa was gowned in lavender silk, a color that flattered her very well. Her eyes widened at the sight of her friend. She imperceptibly nodded her head to her right. Francesca's eyes followed, only to see Aceline du Barry dressed in deep rose silk trimmed with exquisite cream-colored lace. A fair choice, she thought. The French girl was clinging to Rafaello as if she would never let him go. Well, shortly she wouldn't have to, Francesca thought.

It was at that moment that Rafaello sensed her presence. He turned, and she was everything that she should be. He saw his father join her before he could rid himself of Aceline. His father's eyes met his, and they were filled with humor at the situation.

"You look ravishing, my dear," Duke Titus said to Francesca. "Your poise and your elegance are to be commended, along with your exquisite taste." He bowed low to her and kissed her elegant little hand, noting she wore no rings at all when the fashion was for several rings on each finger, even the thumbs.

"My gown, I fear, is a bit bold, but Terza says my mother sent it to me recently. If she sent it, I imagine I am expected to wear it, *signore*," Francesca told him with a laugh.

A clever woman who best knows how to display the merchandise she has to offer, he thought. "I shall look forward to meeting your *madre* one day," the duke said.

"Ah yes, you must come and visit Florence once you have entered into your retirement," Francesca said.

How charming. She believes the French girl will be chosen, Duke Titus considered to himself. She is proud yet has a sense of honesty, but she is not overbearing at all. She will make Rafaello an excellent wife and Terreno Boscoso a good *duchessa*.

His son now joined them, Aceline still clinging to Rafaello's arm. "How beautiful you look, Francesca," he told her.

"I hope you have said the same to the others," she answered him.

"Oh yes! He was quite extravagant in his praise of my gown," Aceline said.

"The color is most suitable and your lace exquisite," Francesca said pleasantly.

"Well, I should hope so," Aceline responded. "My father consulted with a cloistered convent in Burgundy. The nuns made my lace. I see you have gained a bit of weight since your arrival in Terreno Boscoso. Your bodice is extremely tight. My mama would not approve at all, I fear, but I suppose a merchant's wife has different standards than a nobleman's noble wife."

"We do indeed have different standards, Aceline. We believe in good manners at all times. For instance, right now it would give me great pleasure to smack that look of smug superiority off of your face. I shall not, however, for my mother taught me a lady does not display public anger, except on very rare occasions. You are not a rare occurrence, but an annoying one," Francesca told the French girl.

"Aha!" Rafaello exclaimed with a grin. "I have discovered something else about you, Francesca. The kitten has claws."

Aceline, however, grew red with her embarrassment. When she was *duchessa* of Terreno Boscoso she would see that the Pietro d'Angelos were never allowed to cross her borders. And when Rafaello announced her as his choice this evening she would see that Francesca Pietro d'Angelo was sent packing quickly. "Come!" she said, tugging at Rafaello's arm. "I will not remain here and be insulted." Then she pulled him away.

Duke Titus chuckled. "What a sour wench," he remarked, "and so eager to fault her rivals. I wonder why she believes that my son finds such an attitude attractive."

"She is obviously used to having her own way," Francesca responded.

"As I do not doubt you are too," Duke Titus replied.

"I tried very hard growing up to get my way, but, alas, my mother is the one in my father's house who must have her own way. *Padre* and my siblings danced to her tune. And then my elder sister, Bianca, rebelled, and when widowed ran off with her lover. I do not believe *Madre* will ever recover from the shock."

"Would she not eventually forgive the lovers?" Duke Titus inquired.

Francesca shook her head. "Bianca's lover was the grandson of the Turkish sultan. *Madre* could not forgive the daughter she adored for running away with an infidel, and, believe me, she did all she could to prevent it. It was the first time any of her children stood against her, but Bianca loved Prince Amir and would not be dissuaded."

"True love, my dear, is the strongest of emotions," Duke Titus said. Then seeing the servants were beginning to bring the meal to table, he led Francesca to her place at the high board.

Tonight she found herself seated on the old duke's left while Rafaello was on his right. On her other side was Valiant and then Louisa. Aceline du Barry had been placed next to *Padre* Silvio, who sat on Rafaello's right. Below the high board the trestles nearest were filled with officials from the duchy's capital and important officials from the duke's personal coterie. Beyond them were the men-at-arms.

They were too far from any coast for the safe transport of oysters, prawns, clams, and other seafood, but the fish course, while small, was delicious. There were both salmon and trout from the icy streams that ran through the surrounding forests. There were freshwater mussels in a delicious mustard sauce. Next came a beautiful roasted boar with an apple in its mouth, and haunches of venison. There were waterfowl: juicy ducks in an orange sauce filled with big black cherries; and geese stuffed with smaller ducks stuffed with capons stuffed with onion, sage, and bread. There were roasted lamb, pies filled with larks in wine sauce, and a large kettle of rabbit stew. There were braised lettuces, onions in cream sauce, and green peas. There was but a small amount of pasta in butter and garlic, for pasta was not eaten as much in the north as it was farther south. The array of desserts included pears poached in marsala wine, baked apples, custards, and several cakes, including a small tiered one topped with three female figures fashioned quite clearly in marzipan to resemble the three candidates.

Only Louisa noted that the one representing Francesca was set in the middle. She smiled a secret smile and, catching Valiant's eye, glanced quickly at the top tier of the cake to see if he saw it too. He did and squeezed her hand happily. At that very moment the duke's young page bent between them and murmured low, "Duke Titus will see you both in his library as soon as the announcement is made." Then he slid away.

The tiered cake sat in the very center of the table until the desserts had been consumed, and tiny bowls of candied flower petals were placed before each guest at the high board. There was much speculation and amusement about it. Then suddenly the trumpeters in the musician's gallery above the hall played a grand flourish. Duke Titus arose to speak.

"You all know that three of the most eligible maidens in Europe were asked to our duchy this summer so that my son, Rafaello, might choose a bride among them. He has made his choice, and I thoroughly approve it. He will now remove two of the figures from the cake and present the replicas to the ladies to whom they belong. The figure that remains atop the cake is his choice. She will be joined by a marzipan replica of Rafaello himself. The day after their marriage is celebrated I shall retire, passing my ducal crown to my son, and that of my late wife to his bride." Duke Titus crossed himself. "My son . . ."

The hall was deathly silent as Rafaello rose and plucked the figure of Louisa from the cake and handed it to her. There was a low murmur among the guests. Aceline du Barry smiled a triumphant little smile, which quickly faded as she realized that Rafaello was handing her her own replica. If Francesca had not suddenly been overwhelmed with her own shock, she might have burst out laughing at the French girl's horrified face. The silk merchant's second daughter watched as if in a dream as Duke Titus placed the marzipan figure representing his son next to her duplicate. Then Rafaello said clearly and aloud the words she both dreaded and feared.

"I choose Francesca Pietro d'Angelo of Florence to be my bride!" He pulled her up by the hand to face the hall as it erupted in cheers.

Smile, little fool, she could almost hear her mother saying, and she did, surprised.

Then Rafaello slid his arm about her waist, turning her slightly so she had to look up at him. He tilted her face, and she found herself unable to move as he bent to place a kiss upon her lips. It was not a simple kiss. It was deep and searching. She almost swooned in his arms as the hall erupted in cheers of congratulation.

"I won't let you fall," he murmured now against those lips.

"You don't dare!" she hissed back. "You would look twice the fool I feel."

"We will talk shortly in private," he told her.

"I'm not getting married!"

He grinned down at her but said nothing more.

At that very moment a horrific shriek stunned the hall into shocked silence. Aceline du Barry was standing and in her hands was a sharp dagger pointed towards her heart.

"You cannot marry *her*! A common tradesman's daughter? I have the blood of several great houses in my veins. It is I who is meant to be your wife. I will kill myself if you desert me!" The French girl's eyes were wild. "I will kill you!"

Padre Silvio quickly reached out and disarmed Aceline before she might harm herself. He did not believe that she would really kill Rafaello. "My daughter," he said in his calm voice, "you must accept the inevitable. Come with me now and we shall pray together. God has a reason for everything that happens, and it is not up to any of us to dare to question God's will, my daughter." He led the now sobbing girl off.

"See what you've done!" Francesca scolded.

Rafaello looked surprised. "What have I done?" he said. "I never, not even once, encouraged her to believe I cared for her or was interested in her as a wife. She was the first to arrive, and for five long days until Louisa came I was forced to endure her company. I could quickly see her interest in me was my wealth and the title she would gain by becoming my wife. And nothing she has done over these past months has proven that my instincts were incorrect."

"But why me? Oh, I know Louisa loves Valiant. You know it too, and you are not in love with Louisa yourself. It would appear you have chosen me because I was the only one left you could choose. How flattering that is," Francesca concluded sarcastically.

"I believe you are honest," he surprised her by saying. "You claim to have no interest in me, but do you have a lover back in Florence you would prefer?"

"If you believe me honest, *signore*, then you know that cannot be true. I would not dishonor myself, your family, or mine by being so duplicitous. I simply do not believe I want to be wed," she answered him.

"That is ridiculous," he replied. "You have no religious calling, so you must marry of necessity. There is no other choice for you, Francesca. If your reputation is true, then you have turned away every eligible gentleman who has presented himself to your family, and you did it cruelly by mocking your suitors."

"And my reputation does not deter you?" she demanded to know.

"Nay, it does not! I see a girl of intelligence who possesses a kind heart, Francesca. A girl hiding from hurt who was once refused by a man she thought she loved. He was a fool, Francesca, but I am not. You will marry me, and we will come to love one another, for we are much alike. Independent, eager to have our own way, and yet a love of family and loyalty guides us as well. Now give me a smile, *dolce mia*," he cajoled her.

She couldn't help it. His words had touched her, although she was still not ready to give in to him yet. She smiled a tremulous smile. "I'm not certain we are that much alike," she told him.

He laughed and his dark green eyes lit up. "Yes, we are," he told her. "And now I mean to give you your second real kiss," which he did.

Her head spun a second time and her legs felt weak once more. She liked his kiss, but she wasn't certain she enjoyed this feeling of utter helplessness. But she knew if she let go of him she was going to find herself in a heap upon the hall floor. "Take me to my apartments," she said softly. "I need to think."

"My father would see us before either of us retires for the evening," Rafaello told her. "Now we must make our way through all the well-wishers in the hall to reach him. I know you will draw upon that well of strength within you, and play your part." His arm remained firmly about her waist.

Francesca forced her legs to work, stepping forward slowly and quickly regaining her dignity. All the while his arm pressed her against his side. She smiled as congratulations were offered from the men in the hall she did not know nor had ever seen in her life. His wisdom in choosing her, her beauty, were all discussed as they moved forward and were praised. They were assured by many of those unfamiliar faces that they would create beautiful children. At one point she wanted to scream, but she forced herself to maintain a smiling facade.

Finally they escaped the hall. "I think I am going to be sick," she said.

"Is the thought of being my wife *that* distasteful?" he asked her.

"No!" The word was out before she might think. Well, if truth be told, marrying him wasn't really distasteful. It was just the thought of marriage itself. "Let us see your father first and then I shall be sick," she told him.

A small smile touched his lips, and he led her through the *castello* corridors to Duke Titus's library. There they found Valiant and Louisa waiting. The two young women embraced, and seeing it the duke was well pleased.

"Sit, my children," he invited them. Louisa and Francesca sat upon a small settle by the fire while Valiant and Rafaello stood behind them. The old duke was comfortable in a large tapestried chair opposite them. "I am well pleased by tonight's events," he began. "I understand, Valiant, that you would wed *Signorina* Louisa." Valiant nodded, and the duke continued. "Then you will escort her home to Genoa, and with my blessing and full approval you will ask her father's permission. I cannot guarantee what the Duke of Genoa will say, but I will do my best to see that he agrees to a union between his daughter and Valiant Cordassci, *Signore* di Sponda di Fiume."

"Oh, he will!" Louisa burst out. "My mama taught me that

I should never ask for anything unless I truly wanted it. 'Think before you ask, Louisa,' she would say. 'A man does not enjoy being constantly impugned by the women in his life for one silly thing or another. But he does enjoy giving. Your papa will be generous to you—I know, for he is to me. Ask your father only for your heart's desire.' Valiant is my heart's desire. I have asked him for only one other thing in my life. My mare, Bella."

Duke Titus smiled. A sweet maid, he thought, but a better match for Valiant than for my son. "We shall begin arranging your departure on the morrow. I hope you can be back in time for Rafaello and Francesca's wedding in December."

December? Francesca grew pale. The duke was certainly wasting no time.

Duke Titus now spoke to her and to his son. "I welcome you to the Cesare family, Francesca Pietro d'Angelo. If the choice had been mine to make, I probably would have chosen you my-self for Rafaello. As I have said, we will plan your wedding for December. The day after, you and Rafaello will receive the ducal crowns, and I will gratefully retire, leaving the business of governance to my son." He smiled. "By this time next year I hope you will be close to gifting me with a grandchild, my daughter."

Rafaello winced at his father's words. He didn't have to see Francesca's face to know the old man was terrifying her with this talk of crowns and heirs.

"I am pleased to receive your approval," Francesca said quietly. She even managed to give the duke a weak smile.

"*Padre*," Rafaello interjected, "I think Francesca and Louisa are exhausted by the excitement of this day. Will you excuse us to escort them to their apartments and into the care of their women?"

"Ahh, I am a thoughtless old man," Duke Titus said. "You have made me a very happy man, my son. Yes! Yes! Go! *Buona notte*, my young friends!"

They left him, Valiant and Louisa chattering excitedly to each other about how long it would take them to return to Genoa and if they should travel quickly and leave her baggage train to follow at a more leisurely pace.

"Take my father's men-at-arms. The di Medici soldiers will want to return to Florence quickly," Francesca said. "I'll send two of my own with them so they may carry any messages the duke wishes to send to my father."

"I accept," Valiant said. The hired men-at-arms who came with Louisa were sent back immediately, and it was agreed in advance that if she was not chosen, Terreno Boscoso would arrange for Louisa's protection on her return.

They had reached the corridor where the three girls were being housed. From inside Aceline's rooms they could hear weeping and items being shattered, along with shrieks of outrage. At Louisa's door Valiant bent to kiss his beloved good night while Rafaello and Francesca passed by, reaching her apartments next.

"Good night," he said. "We will talk on the morrow." He didn't kiss her.

"Yes," she agreed, relieved. "Good night, Rafaello." Then she quickly turned to go inside and face her servants, whom she knew would be celebrating her victory.

Chapter 5

She leaned against the door as it closed behind her and drew a deep breath. How on earth had this happened? Why had Rafaello chosen her instead of Aceline? Was it simply because she was the only choice left to him? Louisa was in love with another. He did not like Aceline, although with her noble blood the French girl had been an excellent candidate for a duke's son. Yet it was she, Francesca, who had barely given him the time of day, nor had she encouraged his intentions. It had to be because she was the only one left. How lovely! He didn't love her. She was just convenient. There were days like right now when she wished she were a little girl chasing after Bianca again.

Terza came from the dayroom. "I thought I heard you come in," she said. "We are all so very proud of what you have accomplished. Your parents will be ecstatic. We are all quite tipsy on celebratory wine." Then she saw Francesca's face. "What is the matter, mistress?"

"I don't want to marry. If I marry I am once again caged and, worse, I must answer to a husband for my every action," Francesca said, low.

Terza gave an impatient snort. "In your *padre's* palazzo you answer for your actions, mistress, and more to your *madre* than anyone else. Has this duke's son been unkind to you, spoken harshly, taken liberties he should not?"

"That's the terrible thing of it, Terza. Rafaello is kind and thoughtful of me. What if he lets me run wild? What if he doesn't ever love me?"

"Do you love him?" Terza asked her.

Francesca found herself puzzled. She had not thought about loving any man.

"Marriages among the noble or the wealthy are arranged not necessarily on love. You do not have to be told that, Francesca. You know this young man well enough to have learned he is pleasant and kind. He is handsome, and that is surely a bonus. Is the old duke pleased? I expect he is, for you have quite been his favorite. A duke's son has requested your hand in marriage. You! A Florentine silk merchant's daughter! Not some noble wench with ice water in her veins. You! Francesca Pietro d'Angelo. The so-called marriage of your sister, Bianca, to a Turkish prince cannot be acknowledged. Becoming a *duchessa* is probably the finest marriage any of your parents' daughters will make."

"But . . ."

"You are exhausted, my child, not by this day, but by the past few months you have endured. I am putting you to bed, and you will sleep until the morrow. I shall allow no one to awaken you. Now, do not disappoint the good nuns or the priest or even little Roza, who is almost sick with excitement at your success," Terza said. "When does the duke wish the wedding to be celebrated?"

"December," Francesca replied.

"I must send for your bridal gown tomorrow, then," Terza remarked, and she led her mistress into the dayroom, where the others celebrated. "Here is our mistress to share a sip of wine with us, but she will not remain. She is exhausted, as you can imagine."

Padre Silvio handed Francesca a tiny glass of wine.

"How is Aceline?" Francesca asked.

"Furious and hysterical by turns," he answered her. "She was so certain she would be chosen for her noble bloodline, as if that was all she needed. She is also fearful that her father will marry her to an older but wealthy nobleman of his acquaintance. He was about to agree when Duke Titus's invitation arrived. He took the chance that his daughter would gain Rafaello's approval, but if she did not, he still had the other gentleman who, according to Oriel, quite lusts after Aceline. And the comte would rid himself of the girl, as he has recently taken a young second wife. His older daughter and two sons from his first marriage are all provided for and gone, although his heir lives nearby with a bride of his own. He doesn't want Aceline in the house any longer, but he is a good father and would have her married off and taken care of by a husband."

Francesca took a sip of her wine. "You have certainly learned more about Aceline in this one night than the rest of us have in these past months," she noted.

"Oriel likes to chatter, and when Aceline threw the marzipan replica at her she became quite irritated and turned to me for solace," the priest replied blandly, but his brown eyes were twinkling. Then he said, "I can see how very tired you are, my daughter. You and I will speak in the morning after our devotions."

Francesca nodded and turned to accept the congratulations of Annunziata and Benigna and the little maidservant, Roza, whom Terza seemed to have added to their household. After a moment or two she finally entered her bedchamber, collapsing upon the bed with a sigh of relief.

Terza was immediately there, kneeling to remove her slippers and her stockings. "Stand up a moment," she said, and when her mistress did, she undid the skirts and pulled them down along with the petticoats. "Turn." Her swift fingers quickly undid the laces of the bodice. Terza pulled it from Francesca's torso, and then, gathering up the skirts, she carried them into the wardrobe.

When she emerged Francesca was sprawled back upon the bed, already slipping into sleep. Terza lifted the girl's legs up and rolled her into the middle of her bed. Then she drew up the down coverlet, put fresh wood on the fire, and snuffed the candles. She opened one of the casement windows a little bit, and then departed the bedchamber. The dayroom was empty now. She was pleased to see that everyone else had gone to bed, and with a sigh entered her own small bedchamber. Roza was already sleeping upon the trundle. Terza smiled. She had allowed the little maid the privilege, since it was easier to have her readily available. Terza washed herself and undressed before climbing into her own comfortable bed. Servants here were treated well. She slept.

To her great surprise Francesca did not awaken until late the following morning. Stretching, she lay back in her bed and considered the events of the previous evening. Was it really true? Had Rafaello Cesare really chosen her for his wife? Then her eye caught the graceful glass dome upon the mantel, and within it two marzipan figures. Her and Rafaello. *Madre di Dios!* It was true. He had chosen her, and he had kissed her as well. Twice! For a brief moment she felt a frisson of excitement, but then she recalled that he had chosen her because in the end he actually had no other choice.

Francesca sighed deeply. It wasn't that she really wanted to marry, because now she was quite certain that she didn't. But to be rejected by a man she believed herself in love with in Venice, a man she had once been eager to wed, and in the next breath chosen by a man who didn't really want her but would marry her nonetheless was galling. At least he was no fortune hunter. Rafaello was simply doing his duty, and she could not fault him for that. He was an obedient son who understood the obligations of his position.

Why was it that she chafed so against her similar commitments? Was it that her distrust in men went so deep after the fiasco with Enzo Ziani? She couldn't even recall his face at this point in her life. Her function in life was to be a wife. Her mother certainly hadn't loved her father when she married him and departed Venice to come to Florence. But, like Rafaello, her father had been kind and patient. Still, to be chosen out of necessity niggled at her. He hadn't said he loved her. He hadn't even said he liked her. He was going to marry her because he had to. That is not enough incentive for me to do what my parents, what everyone else, wants of me. I want to be loved passionately, like Bianca.

Give him a chance, the voice in her head said. But he had had his chance. He hadn't even spoken to her before last night about choosing her. He had just boldly announced it. He had made it fact, but it was his fact, not hers. "When the others leave," the voice murmured soothingly. Was it possible that after Aceline and Louisa were gone he would declare some sort of affection for her? Should she give him a chance?

"You're awake!" Terza bustled into the room. "I've sent Roza for some food. Stay right there in bed, mistress." She helped Francesca sit up and plumped the pillows around her shoulders.

"What is all the noise?" Francesca asked. "I think that is what woke me."

" 'Tis Aceline du Barry preparing to leave today. Duke Titus is in an uproar because he has not yet gathered the gifts he wishes to send to the Comte du Barry, but the wretched girl refuses to wait any longer than it takes to pack up her possessions. Oriel will see she isn't ready to go until the morrow, for there is no need to create bad feeling among the French. Duke Titus would be generous to both the girl and her father."

Roza staggered into the bedchamber beneath the weight of a large tray. "Oh, my. What a to-do there is with the French girl," she said, placing the tray upon a table. "When I went by she was beating one of her poor women and screaming at the top of her lungs while she did so. I suspect she was cursing the poor maidservant, but she was speaking her own language."

Terza chuckled. "I suspect that one has never before been denied anything she wanted." She took a smaller tray, and placing two dishes on it set it upon Francesca's lap, and tucked a napkin beneath her mistress's chin.

"Oh, a poached egg in cream and wine." Francesca approved. "And bacon!" She gobbled it down, accepting a slice of fresh buttered bread with plum jam from Terza as well. "I like breakfast in bed," Francesca announced. "I don't believe *Madre* has ever eaten a meal in bed except after childbirth, but I shall do it every day from now on, Terza." She licked jam from the corner of her mouth.

"A habit quite befitting a *duchessa*, mistress," Terza said.

"Is she awake?" Louisa stepped into Francesca's bedchamber. "Oh, good. You're up. Would you like to go riding after you have eaten?"

"I'm going to have my breakfast in bed every day from now on," Francesca announced grandly.

Louisa laughed. "What a wonderful idea!" she said. "Have you heard the ruckus that Aceline is making? It is quite shocking, and she should be ashamed of herself. It does not reflect well upon her family, I fear. Valiant says they will be delighted to have her gone. The old duke has his people scurrying here and there gathering up the gifts he would send with her to placate her father, though she will probably be wed before either of us is, I am told." She giggled. "When I first came she was all sweetness and light until she learned who my father was. Suddenly a duke's bastard daughter was not fit company for a French nobleman's legitimately born child. Well, you and I have both shown her. Haven't we, Francesca?" Louisa wore a smug grin on her pretty face, and her companions all laughed. "Hurry up and finish! The day is gorgeous."

"Roza," Francesca called. "Go to the stables and have Adon saddle the black-and-white for me. Tell him no sidesaddle. I will ride astride today and be comfortable."

Roza hurried out, thrilled to have received a direct order from Francesca.

"You ride astride?" Louisa was surprised.

"I prefer it," Francesca told her. "With the sidesaddle I

always feel like I'm sitting atop the head of a pin. I think it's time Rafaello learned some of my faults."

Louisa laughed. "I think I'll keep mine from Valiant a while longer," she said. "I'll wait for you in the dayroom." She exited the bedchamber.

Terza took the tray away, and Francesca rose from her bed. She washed her face and hands, scrubbed her teeth with a little boar's-bristle brush with a silver handle, and sat quietly as Terza brushed and braided her hair into a single plait. Then she helped Francesca dress in a white silk shirt with full sleeves, and a pair of dark green woolen pants held up with a wide brown leather belt. The pants came just below her knees. Stockings and dark brown leather boots completed her outfit. Terza handed her a pair of leather gloves that had been dyed green.

"You are still pale," Terza fretted, "but perhaps a nice ride in the early September sunshine will bring the color back into your cheeks."

"Have you written to Florence?" Francesca asked.

"It was sent off this morning with two of our men," Terza said. "I sent a pigeon too at *Padre* Silvio's suggestion. I am glad we brought six of them along. They will reach your parents before the messengers can do so. Now, do not worry yourself, and go along with Louisa, mistress."

Francesca joined her friend, and together they walked downstairs and out into the castle yard to the stables. Adon was standing, holding her horse, which was saddled and bridled in red leather. She swung herself up into the saddle. Louisa's gentle mare, Bella, was waiting. She ascended the small set of steps that had been placed by the animal's side and settled into the sidesaddle. Then, to Francesca's surprise, they were joined by Rafaello and Valiant. There had been no talk of the men joining them.

She said nothing, but as the four horses clumped across the drawbridge she turned her head slightly and saw Aceline du Barry glaring down from a window in her apartment, and she could have sworn she heard a shriek. No one else seemed to have heard it, however. The air was sweet with the scent of flowers, and warm. As they rode into the forest Francesca was caught up by its beauty, the sunlight playing among the green trees highlighting branches in shades of dark and light.

"Do you know when you will depart?" Francesca finally asked.

Valiant answered her. "Louisa and I will leave tomorrow. We have decided to not be burdened by her baggage train but ride ahead, giving Elda and her staff time to pack up and follow us. I wish to reach Genoa as quickly as we can so I may gain that duke's permission to marry his daughter. Since Louisa has been born on the other side of the blanket there is not likely to be a gala celebrating our union. We can do it either in Genoa, so both the duke and Louisa's mother may observe the formalities, or if they do not care, come back to Terreno Boscoso for the ceremony."

"The *duchessa* does not acknowledge Mama or me," Louisa explained. "If Mama will come with us, I would bring her back when we return. She and Papa are more friends than lovers nowadays. She has no real influence in Genoa and little family left. My grandfather died last year."

"Then why go to the difficulty of bringing all your possessions back to Genoa?" Francesca wanted to know. "Assume the best outcome with your *padre*. Perhaps your belongings could be sent to Valiant's home to await your arrival."

"My betrothed makes an excellent suggestion!" Rafaello approved. He turned to Louisa. "Your mama will be most welcome to Terreno Boscoso, *cara*," he said.

"Oh, thank you!" Louisa responded with tears of happiness in her eyes. "I was so worried about leaving her behind."

"I should not want *madre mia* living with me," Francesca told them. "Orianna Pietro d'Angelo is a law unto herself. She is beautiful as well, and absolutely convinced that she is always correct. She rarely raises her voice. Just looks at you."

Her companions laughed.

Francesca and Rafaello found themselves riding ahead as the two lovers dropped back to talk privately. For a time they did not speak directly to one another. Then he said, "Did you sleep well, *cara mia*?" he asked.

"Oddly I did," she answered him. "I had not expected to, but I was suddenly overcome by an enormous wave of fatigue." Then, unable to contain herself, she said, "Do you disapprove that I ride astride, *signore*?"

"You may ride as you please," he told her. "But when you are with child you will not ride at all, for I would wish no harm to either you or our infant."

"You are the most irritating man!" she responded.

"I am relieved to see that I am able to engender some emotion in you, Francesca," he surprised her by saying. "Is it not time for you to relieve us both of this petulance? It is no insult that you are to be my wife, *cara*. I shall endeavor to spend the time between now and our wedding day attempting to convince you of your good fortune, but if I cannot it will make no difference. We will still marry on the first day of December."

"My *padre* must give his approval first," she told him.

"He gave his approval when he agreed to send you to Terreno Boscoso as one of the candidates for my hand," Rafaello said. "Messengers are already speeding towards Florence with the news that you are the chosen one. Your priest will sign the contracts in your father's place. They are being drawn up and will be ready in a few days for his signature. He carries one of your father's seals to make it official."

"Well," Francesca said quietly, "if I did not feel like a trapped animal before, I certainly do now." I shall have to steal the seal from *Padre* Silvio, she thought. Without the seal the contract will not be legal.

"Yes, I am the hunter, and I have trapped a little wildcat," he answered her, and she heard the humor in his voice.

"You don't have me yet," she taunted him.

"You will come to love me," he said with irritating certainty.

"I will not!" she retorted.

"You liked my kisses," he teased.

"I am a woman. Of course I enjoyed being kissed by a handsome man. It meant nothing, however," she told him scornfully.

That stung, he had to admit, but he didn't believe her. "You are a maid, and my kisses were the first you ever received," he said.

"And if I marry you I shall never have anything to compare them to, for once the priest has pronounced us man and wife I must, for my own honor's sake, be faithful."

"You are the most outrageous girl!" he said, amused.

"Do you think if I asked Louisa's permission Valiant would kiss me so I might at least have some comparison?" she wondered aloud.

"He will certainly not kiss you, for our friendship's sake, if I tell him no," Rafaello replied, not quite so amused now. "You must be satisfied with my kisses, I fear."

"I shall certainly not be placated until I have a broader knowledge," she said. She kicked her horse into a smooth canter.

His humor suddenly restored by the thought of a dozen young men lined up to kiss Francesca, he followed after her, laughing.

They returned to the *castello* in late afternoon hungry and not just a little tired. Aceline du Barry was not in the Great Hall when it was time for the meal. It was a far simpler repast than the wonderful feast of yesterday. Sliced broiled trout on a bed of cress, a roasted capon stuffed with fruit, a salad of lettuces, bread, butter, cheese and a platter of fresh fruits—grapes, pears, apples, melon. Even Louisa's usually delicate appetite was hearty. The wine was dark and fragrant.

They spent time in the hall that evening, dancing simple country dances together. Then the following morning Francesca and Rafaello bid farewell to their friends as they began their journey to Genoa, surrounded by the men-at-arms wearing the badge of the Pietro d'Angelo family. The di Medici men-at-arms had already departed earlier, at dawn.

Francesca and Louisa hugged one another while Rafaello and Valiant shook hands.

"I wish you good luck," his childhood friend told Rafaello.

"Why do I need luck?" Rafaello asked, laughing. "I have the maid."

"Precisely!" Valiant said with a chuckle. "Charming the Duke of Genoa into marrying his daughter will be far easier for me than you charming the beautiful Francesca to the altar without a fuss."

Rafaello's hearty laughter died and his handsome face grew serious. "I believe you may be right," he responded, "but you know that I never give up, Valiant."

"And so I wish you good fortune," Valiant repeated. "We'll return as quickly as we can," he promised as he mounted his stallion.

The last of the duke's guests to depart was Aceline du Barry. Duke Titus himself saw her off, but he had insisted that Rafaello and Francesca also bid her farewell.

"Is it wise for me to be there?" she asked the old man. "Does it not simply rub salt into her open wounds? I do not wish to be unkind."

"She will never accept my son's choice in a bride if it is not made clear to her," Duke Titus responded. "Certainly the three of us bidding her Godspeed will help."

Francesca didn't think it would. If she had had her heart set on Rafaello and he had chosen someone else, seeing them together would just infuriate her. And she knew it would imply to Aceline that something was wrong with her, and Francesca knew that the French girl believed herself far superior to the Genoese duke's bastard daughter and the daughter of a Florentine silk merchant. "Of course, *signore*," she dutifully replied.

Rafaello listened to the brief exchange between his sire and his betrothed. He thought that Francesca was correct, but was impressed that she was able to accept his father's decision graciously. He gave the dainty hand in his a small squeeze. Their eyes met briefly, but she said nothing.

Aceline swooped into the courtyard. Her baggage train had already departed. Her female servants but for Oriel, who would also ride, were now in the cart that would transport them across the nearby border between France and Terreno Boscoso, back to the Comte du Barry's chateau. Aceline wore a deep blue velvet riding dress trimmed lavishly in lace. A peregrine falcon was perched upon her leather glove. "I am ready," she announced as if they could not see it. She looked angrily at Francesca and Rafaello.

"I thank you for coming, *signorina*. Your presence has enlivened my house these past weeks," Duke Titus said politely. "I am sending your noble father some gifts as my thanks for permitting you to come." He waved his hand languidly towards the gift train.

"You will find a stallion bred from my own horses, two greyhounds, a silk bag of rare tulip bulbs I purchased from a passing merchant this summer, as well as several bolts of rare materials, a dozen silver goblets etched in gold, six gold forks, a silver and gold crucifix blessed by the Holy Father himself, and, finally, a ruby necklace and ring I thought might suit you, Aceline."

"He will give it all to his slut wife," Aceline said meanly. "She will gain the fruits of my failure, *signore*." Turning her head she looked at Rafaello and Francesca. "You have made a mistake," she told him. "Did she sleep with you? Is that how she won your favor, by opening her legs for you? Well, what can you expect from a tradesman's brat? I hope any children she gives you are at least your own."

Francesca gasped, shocked at the vicious words. "I have not slept with him!" she denied, blushing furiously. "I am a virgin! How dare you say such a thing? And I will be faithful to any husband I wed. To say otherwise only shows you do not know my character. Nonetheless I will wish you Godspeed and a safe journey. *Addio!* I hope never to see your face again."

"Then we have found something we can agree on," Aceline responded, "for I never hope to see yours!" Without another word to anyone she turned angrily and mounted her horse and, lashing the beast with her crop, cantered from the courtyard.

Startled, Oriel and the passenger cart followed at a much slower pace.

"Thank God you did not choose that virago," Duke Titus said.

"For all her noble blood," Francesca said, "she had no manners at all. I can understand her disappointment, but there was no excuse for her vile words. I do not envy the man who wants her."

"If her sire is wise he will marry her off to the man quickly," Duke Titus noted. Then he smiled at Francesca. "I have the daughter I want," he told her.

She smiled warmly at him. If she could only bring herself to accept this fate that was thrust upon her, he would be a good father-in-law and, Francesca expected, a very good ally.

"I suspect there will be a number of beatings in Aceline's future. Her temper will not be tolerated by any husband," Rafaello said.

"Would you beat her if she was your wife?" Francesca asked him.

"I'd strangle her," he answered, to her surprise.

The next few weeks seemed to pass very quickly, and the first of October came. The trees in the forest were beginning to change color, splashing their bright hues against the green pines. Duke Titus, along with his majordomo, Piero, began to plan the wedding feast to which all the citizens of Terreno Boscoso would be invited. A calligrapher was brought to the *castello* to write the hundred or so personal invitations for the duchy's officials and important citizens. Larger invitations would be posted in public places for the citizens of Terreno Boscoso.

The wedding gown arrived from Florence on the tenth of the month, along with the Pietro d'Angelo family's personal seamstress, who would remain until after the wedding. If the snows were not heavy by then she would return to Florence and recount everything that had happened during her stay. Greeting *Signora* Sophia, Francesca knew that was the real purpose of her visit. Terza was more than capable of making any alterations on the gown. But Terza would not be returning to Florence.

"Your *madre* is unhappy she cannot attend your wedding," the seamstress told Francesca, then smiled. "But I shall report every detail to her and with enough repeating she will believe she was here." *Signora* Sophia laughed. "I have a memory that forgets nothing. Nothing!"

Duke Titus insisted on seeing Francesca in her gown as it was fitted exactly to her form. "You are outrageously beautiful, my daughter," he said. "After you have delivered your first child, I shall call for one of your famous Florentine painters to come and paint you and my grandson in the manner of the blessed Virgin and her son, our lord Jesu," he told her. "It shall hang in the family gallery."

I can't do this, Francesca thought. I cannot! But what could she do? The invitations were being delivered, the feast was set, the wedding gown was here, and *Padre* Silvio had signed the betrothal agreements. Now the dear old duke was seeing her as the Holy Mother with her child. Panic was filling her, and, worse, Rafaello was paying her proper court. Last night he had drawn her down onto his lap when they found themselves alone in the hall.

She stiffened, but when his lips found hers her body relaxed, unbidden. Francesca found herself kissing him back. After what seemed an eternity, she drew away. His mouth was intoxicating. He pulled her back, shocking her by finding her tongue with his. She made a tiny squeak of protest, but the foraging tongue refused to cease its caresses. Unable to help herself she followed his tutoring softly, stroking his tongue with hers.

A single hand now slipped into her bodice and through the opening in her chemise to cup her breast.

"No!" Francesca gasped.

"Yes," he said, his thumb beginning to rub over the nipple teasingly. "We will shortly be husband and wife, *cara mia*. These are innocent intimacies we now share, and you should be aware of them before we come together in the marriage bed. I suspected, and your actions confirm, that you are truly innocent." He gently squeezed the small breast in his palm. "You are so tender and fresh, Francesca." His lips touched her again as his big hand continued to fondle her.

Her head was spinning. She could hear the beat of her heart in her ears, but his hand and his lips were gentle, giving no indication of rough lust. They were like Rafaello.

Calm, measured in his actions. He wasn't kissing or fondling her out of any need on his part. He was doing it to prepare her for the intimacies they must share after their wedding in order to produce heirs for his duchy. His actions were both dutiful and thoughtful of her own sensibilities. But no matter his reasons, it felt wonderful! But how cold he was to be able to kiss and touch her without any feeling for her at all. "Let me go," she told him.

He immediately ceased his actions. "Have I frightened you, shocked you, *cara*?" he asked her as he withdrew his hand from her bodice.

"I have never been touched in so intimate a manner," she answered him. "I must become used to it, Rafaello."

"Did you like it?" he queried her.

She paused in her thought a moment and then said, "Yes." Nothing more.

"Then we shall conclude tonight's lesson," he responded. "But I shall continue to make love to you, Francesca, at every opportunity I get." And he did. Each night he would take her aside when they were alone.

Francesca found herself becoming more eager for his kisses and caresses. She was filled with a fevered longing as their kisses became more passionate, as she allowed him greater access to her breasts. But what was she longing for? She had yet to figure it out. The night he first took a nipple in his mouth, tonguing it, suckling it, she almost fainted with the exquisite sensation. But never did he admit to feeling any emotions for her.

I cannot marry a man who feels nothing for me. Especially now that he has shown me how delicious making love is. Would it not be even better if he loved me, and I him? Francesca asked herself over and over again. The truth was, she couldn't. But all was being arranged at a rapid clip. There was no other choice. She had to flee. She must depart Terreno Boscoso and find her way home to Florence. And she had to go alone, for Terza would certainly attempt to stop her flight.

Her parents would be furious, especially her mother, but Francesca couldn't be controlled like Orianna, who chafed at her duty but nonetheless did it. And her father, she knew, had loved Orianna almost immediately, even though it took his wife many years to develop her small fondness for him.

Francesca thought of her older sister, Bianca, once hailed as the most beautiful girl in Florence. She thought of how after Bianca's brutal and perverted first husband had died, her sister had defied their world to go with the man she loved. No matter the obstacles they had put in Bianca's path she had prevailed. She had given up Florence, her family, her church to be with the man she adored.

The church had threatened her with excommunication. Francesca never knew if they had carried out that threat. What she did know was that for Bianca, heaven was in the arms of

Prince Amir ibn Jem, grandson of the Turkish sultan. She preferred it to anything anyone else might offer.

Now Francesca wondered, could she be as bold and as brave as her elder sister? Could she flee this lovely prison and the handsome man who was to be her husband? Yes! She could. She had to go, because she could not remain. Accepting this marriage would have been so much easier if he had admitted any emotions towards her. But he had not, and so she must go now. Now, before it became any more difficult, she sent word to the hall that night that she was feeling unwell and would have her meal in her own apartments.

"What is the matter?" Terza asked. She did not think Francesca looked ill, and her appetite that evening had hardly been that of a sick girl.

"I am just feeling out of sorts," Francesca admitted. "'Tis nothing. A quiet meal and a good night's sleep will serve me well."

Terza agreed, no longer concerned.

Later as she lay in her bed Francesca considered what she must do next. The month of October was almost over. In just five and a half weeks the wedding was scheduled to take place. She had to go quickly, but how would she get back to Florence? If she took the open road they would easily catch up with her. But if she hid in the forest for a few days and they didn't find her on the road, they would certainly give her up for lost. Yes! That's what she would do. She would hide in the forest.

The next morning she dressed in her riding clothes, and after her breakfast she sent the unsuspecting Roza to the kitchens for her. "Fetch me some bread, cheese, apples, and a few hard-cooked eggs, if you can find them. I am going to ride out by myself today. Tell no one. I'll give you a silver piece in exchange for your silence when I return."

"Should Terza know?" Roza asked.

Francesca giggled conspiratorially. "No, no," she said. "She would fuss at me like the old woman she is becoming, and send me with two men-at-arms and a groom. Maybe that one you like," Francesca teased Roza, who blushed but giggled too. "I just want some time by myself before I must take up my duties as a wife and your *duchessa*."

"I understand, mistress," Roza said.

"Meet me at the stables," Francesca told the little maid. "Then you'll get to see your friend and visit for a while."

With another giggle Roza ran off.

Francesca picked up her gloves and her cape, for while the day was sunny and bright, the air was growing chillier as each morning dawned. She would have Ib saddle the bay. His color would blend in better within the forest than her showy white with its black mane and tail. She saw no one as she exited the *castello*. This was the morning that Duke Titus and Rafaello sat in the old man's library and did the business of the duchy. They would not come out until late afternoon, and she would not be missed until the meal hour. She would be several hours away by then.

Reaching the stables she called softly to Ib. He came immediately, and with a nod quickly saddled the bay. Then he brought her a small skin of fresh water. "The sun is hot," was all he said. He noted with curiosity Roza stuffing what appeared to be food into the saddlebags as he returned with the water. Francesca put a finger to her lips, and pressed a silver coin into his dark palm. Ib was suddenly uncomfortable, but this woman was his mistress. It was not his duty to question her, yet he sensed her actions would not be approved of by the duke or his son.

Francesca saw the look on his face. "Say nothing until you are asked," was all she told him. "Since it is not your place to question me, you will not be blamed."

Then Francesca mounted the bay and rode slowly from the stables, but not before Ib asked, "I go with you?"

"No," Francesca replied. Then, seeing Roza still standing there, she said, "Go and find your friend. You have my permission."

The bay moved gracefully across the open yard. Francesca smiled and gave the guards at the gates a jaunty wave as she passed beneath the portcullis. Once out on the drawbridge the horse moved into a trot, finally cantering onto the road. Francesca rode him out of sight of the *castello* and its men-at-arms before turning the animal's head into and onto a forest path. She slowed the horse, then rode among the trees for a time. Now and again she would come to a meadow and give the horse its head.

She saw no human, no dwelling. She heard animals—rabbits, foxes, squirrels—in the brush. After several hours she stopped to rest her mount by a stream where it might water itself. Birds called to one another. She ate some bread, cheese, and an apple. Sometimes the birdsong would cease and the crisp air was silent. It was a quiet she had never before experienced in her life. She mounted and rode on until the shadows began to fill the forest. Finding a cairn of fallen stones, she decided to shelter there for the night. She let the bay loose to browse while she ate a supper of bread, eggs, and cheese.

She had sipped the water from the pouch over the course of the day. She heard a brook tumbling over rocks nearby. She had to remember to fill the pouch in the morning. Pouring almost all of the remaining water into a naturally formed stone basin, she led her horse to drink, then tied the beast for the night within her little enclosure. As the dark settled itself around her Francesca regretted that she had no fire and pulled her cloak around herself tightly. A half-moon rose over the forest, and just as she was finally dozing off she heard it.

Hoowlll. Hoowlll.

Could it be wolves? She drew the cloak tighter. The bay nickered nervously.

Hoowlll. Hoowlll.

Instinct told Francesca that they were safer where they were right now. The wolves hadn't necessarily scented them, but they surely would if the horse moved through the forest with her upon its back. She sat straight and listened. But she heard no more howling. The wolves had apparently gone in a different direction, praise God. But she could not sleep again, dozing slightly now and again until the dawn finally lit up the forest, its red and gold rays bringing both warmth and relief.

Francesca slowly got to her feet. She was both stiff and cold. She stretched and moved her aching limbs until the circulation finally began to come back into them. She filled the water pouch at the nearby brook, drank, and then watered her horse. She took the remainder of the cheese and the bread, which was now quite stale, and ate. She would save the last egg and the apple for her evening meal. On the morrow she would leave the forest for the road again. Of course, she would have to find the road, but certainly if she just went back the way she came she would come to it.

She had let the horse off to graze again and now she went to get him. Reaching for his bridle, she was about to mount when a large bird flew out of the trees, startling the beast. The bay reared, whinnying, and, losing her grip, Francesca fell upon her back. For a moment she lay stunned, and then before she might rise the horse took off running. Stumbling to her feet she tried to chase it, but it was gone before she knew it, and so was the path she had been following.

For the first time in her life Francesca Pietro d'Angelo felt fear. She was alone in the forest. With the bay had gone her water, her remaining food, and her cloak, which she had laid across the pommel of her saddle. Even worse, there were wolves prowling the woods. She was going to have to find some way out, or at least an indoor place of safety, before it got dark again. She attempted to seek out the path again, but after an hour or more realized she had lost it. There was no other choice but to keep walking until she came upon shelter or another person who could get her to safety.

Chapter 6

Francesca walked all day. Her feet became swollen and hurt in her riding boots. And now it seemed as if the forest was even bereft of animals and birds. She was very relieved to see a doe eyeing her at one point from the brush. The shadows began to lengthen within the forest and she was fearful now of having to spend another night in the woodlands. She was thirsty and her head was aching.

Then suddenly Francesca noticed that the trees were thinning. She summoned what strength she had left and hurried along, finally coming out into a large clearing. And there, to her surprise, she saw a good-sized building, a sign hanging above its door indicating it was an inn. An inn in the midst of the woods? How could any traveler possibly find it? Was it even inhabited? The answer to her question came to the inn's open door and, stepping outside and seeing Francesca, called to her.

"Come here, girl! You look lost." The woman who spoke seemed ageless. She was short but stocky, yet not plump. Her hair was the gray of a storm cloud and it matched her eyes. "I am *Signora* Alonza, proprietor of this inn."

"Oh, thank the blessed Mother I have found you," Francesca said. "I spent the night in the forest and I heard wolves all about me. Can you help me?"

"I might. I can, if you will help me," the innkeeper said bluntly.

"I have no silver with me, but if I can get home you will be greatly rewarded," Francesca said to the woman.

"I do not need gold or silver, child," Alonza answered her. "The serving wench I hired has run off. I need help in the inn. My busy season is just now beginning and will last until late spring. I need a strong young girl like you to help me cook, clean, and serve my patrons. I cannot do it alone. Help me until spring and I will have my nephew take you to the main road and put a few coppers in your pocket, and you will be cozy and warm for the next few months," the innkeeper offered. "What is your name?"

Francesca paused. She must now reveal her identity. "I am called Cara," she told Alonza. "But I cannot remain with you. I must get home."

"Listen to me, girl, it is obvious to me from the look of you that you have not been out in the world much. You're some lady's maid, to be sure, and because you have a look of honesty about you I will wager you have fled your employer because her husband is behaving disrespectfully towards you. If your employer seeks after you and finds you, you will get a good beating and be forced to accept your master's advances. Remain here and I will keep you safe. By spring you will be able to find your way home in safety."

"But I know nothing of cooking, cleaning, and serving," Francesca said.

"You look like you can learn, however, and I am in difficulty. This inn is not one that is open to passing travelers. This inn is here for the duke's hunters. They eat and shelter with me once the winter sets in. Some will just eat, for they have other places to sleep, but about ten of them live here."

"Perhaps one of these hunters would be willing to take me to the main road," Francesca said hopefully.

Alonza laughed heartily. "Child, they would eat you up and enjoy every morsel of your sweet self. You would be unlikely to see that road, but you would see some good upstanding cocks eager to plant themselves in you."

Francesca blushed a deep crimson at the innkeeper's candid speech.

"Oh, ho!" Alonza said softly. "Cara, child, are you a virgin? Tell me the truth now, for I must know if you need to be protected from my ruffians."

"Yes," Francesca whispered.

The older woman nodded. "I will keep you from harm," she said. "Now come into the inn and have a hot meal. You will watch me tonight as I serve, and learn. Are we agreed, then?"

She really had no choice at this point, but she would ask the hunters when she learned more about them. Certainly they were not as rough as Alonza said. She is just trying to frighten me so I will stay for now, she thought. "Yes," she answered. "I will remain with you."

"*Hola*, Alonza, you beautiful old wench!" Two rough-looking bearded men came out of the forest. They were dressed in leather pants, shirts that at one time were probably white, and sleeveless wool vests, and carried bows over their shoulders with quivers of arrows on their backs. They had rather fierce-looking knives in sheaths tucked into their belts. "Is our dinner almost ready for us? And who is this little flower?" Both men leered at Francesca, who shrank back behind the innkeeper.

"I have just hired her, as Serafina ran away, the bad wench. Now, you will keep your hands to yourself or there will be no supper for either of you. I don't want you scaring this one off. Surely you can see she's a good girl."

The two huntsmen laughed uproariously. "She won't be for long if she works for you, old woman," one said.

Alonza pushed Francesca into the inn and immediately took her into the kitchens. "Sit down at the table," she said. "I'll feed those two first so they'll not bother us. Then I'll feed you. There will be more of my lads coming in soon enough."

Francesca sat down. She realized how very fortunate she was not to have died in the forest. But she had to find her way to the main road. She wasn't a serving girl. She was Francesca Pietro d'Angelo, daughter of a prestigious citizen of Florence. She knew she was intelligent enough to carry plates and mugs, but as for cleaning and cooking? She didn't have the faintest idea how she would accomplish that. Her elegant little hands would be ruined. How Aceline du Barry would laugh to see her now. She put her head down on the table, and was suddenly asleep.

Poor maiden, Alonza thought, looking down at her. Cara. She doubted that was the girl's name at all, but for whatever reason she did not choose to reveal her identity, and Cara was as good a name as any. The innkeeper could see the girl's hands were as soft as butter, but she wasn't stupid. She would learn her duties quickly enough, and when spring came Alonza would keep her promise and have her brought to the main road so she might be on her way. She filled a bowl with a thick soup, buttered a thick slice of bread, and woke her new servant. "Come and eat, dearie," she said. "I've work to do, but when you're through tell me. I have a cozy little room for you."

"Thank you," Francesca said, and she was grateful for the innkeeper's kindness. At least she was safe this night from the wild creatures in the forest. She wondered if the bay had made it safely back to the duke's stable and not fallen prey to the wolves. She hoped so.

Spooning up her soup, she found it delicious. She dipped some of the buttered bread in it and thought it the best thing she had ever eaten. When she had finished she knew enough, having eaten many a time in her family's kitchen as a child too young for the table, to place her bowl and spoon in the big stone sink.

Alonza returned and, seeing her do it, smiled, pleased. This girl might be gently raised, for her delicate hands had attested to it, but she was not lazy. "Those two bears are eating and drinking to their hearts' content," she told Francesca. "Now, while I have a moment let me take you to where you will sleep. You are very fortunate, for the chamber has four walls and a door you may lock for your privacy. It is next to my own room." Carrying a candle to light their way, the innkeeper led her new servant up a narrow flight of stairs from the kitchen. There in a private corridor, walled off from the guest quarters, were two chambers. Alonza opened the door of the first one. It was small, but there was a narrow bed with a little chest at its foot, and a candle stand at its side that held a taper. Next to the candle stand was a single window with a small table under it. It is hardly what I am used to, Francesca thought, but it will have to do until I can leave. And it is certainly better than the forest.

Stepping inside, Alonza lit the taper from her own candle as the light was almost gone. "I'll get you a sheet for the bed," she said. "I expect you are used to such finery. There is a down comforter for you in the trunk and a more suitable array of garments for tomorrow. Sleep well, my child." She departed, returning with a sheet and a pitcher of water so Francesca might bathe. She set the pitcher on the table, which held a metal basin.

"Thank you," Francesca said to the innkeeper as she closed the door behind her.

She could hear more guests coming into the inn from her little refuge. Putting the rough sheet over the straw mattress, she opened the trunk to find a pillow and the coverlet. To her relief there were also two chemises, along with a skirt and two blouses. She wondered if they belonged to the departed Serafina, and considered that servants had very little of their own. She had never before thought of it. Stripping off her clothing, she quickly bathed in the basin and drew one of the chemises over her. It was clean and it was warm, but it was hardly the fine silk she was used to wearing.

She then shook her riding pants out the window to rid them of the dirt and dust they had acquired. She had seen Terza do that. She packed them at the bottom of the trunk, along with the rest of her garments. For the interim Francesca Pietro d'Angelo was gone, and in her place was Cara, a serving girl. Kneeling by her bedside she said her prayers, thanking God for her temporary deliverance. Then she climbed beneath the coverlet and fell into a deep sleep.

Alonza did not spare her, waking Francesca well before the dawn. "Get up, girl. We have bread to get in the ovens," she called, rapping at the girl's door.

"It's still dark," Francesca protested, pulling her coverlet closer.

"I have more than a dozen hungry men to feed," Alonza said. "The bread will not bake itself. Get up and come down to the kitchens."

Francesca struggled reluctantly out of bed. Did Terza and Roza arise this early? Surely not! But she relieved herself in the chamber pot, dumped it out the window, rinsed it with some water, and dumped that too before shoving it beneath her bed. Then she washed her face and hands and pulled on a dark red wool skirt and a white shirt. Yanking on her boots and stockings, she ran her fingers through her beautiful hair before wisely binding it with a scrap of ribbon she found in the trunk. She shook the coverlet and set it to air in the window, as she had seen Terza do. Then leaving the room, she hurried down the back stairs to the kitchen.

"Ah, you're here," Alonza said. "Knead that dough on the board that I have just turned out."

Francesca looked at her, puzzled. "I don't know how," she said.

"Ahh, you've never served in a kitchen. Well, no matter. I suspect you'll learn quickly. Watch what I do, child, and then you'll do it until I tell you to cease." Rolling up her sleeves, the innkeeper demonstrated the art of kneading, then said, "Now you do it."

Francesca followed Alonza's lead, rolling up her sleeves, and began to press the dough over and over again.

"Good! Good," she was told. "I'll tell you when to cease."

Francesca kneaded the dough for several minutes until her hands began to tire, but it wasn't difficult. Finally Alonza bid her stop and spoke once more.

"Now, this is how you shape the loaves," she said, demonstrating as she quickly formed two loaves. When they were done

Alonza put them on a board with a handle. "You try," she told Francesca, and hummed with approval as the girl managed to successfully duplicate her own efforts. "Excellent! You are a quick study," she told her. "Now put them on the board. There is enough dough for two more loaves. When you have shaped them we'll put them in the ovens for baking. Then you will do the dough in the other bowl, readying them for the oven too. We'll mix the rest of the bread to bake after the men have eaten," she told Francesca. "That way we'll have enough for tonight."

"Do you bake twenty-four loaves each day?" Francesca asked her.

"Some days more, for I can shelter twenty men if needs be. Some days less. At the height of the winter we'll be doing forty loaves a day, two for each man. Now, when you've finished with the bread I'll want you to go out to the henhouse and gather the eggs. I'll give you the basket when you're ready."

Francesca went back to shaping the last two loaves from the first bowl. Then dumping out and kneading the second bowl of dough, she shaped the additional loaves and set them on a second wooden paddle. Alonza came, opened the oven doors, and showed her how to slide the bread loaves off the paddle and inside. Then she handed her new servant a willow basket.

"Just pull the eggs from the nest. If the hen is setting, pay no attention to her and thrust beneath her. Bring in all you can," Alonza said, sending her off.

The morning was crisp and the air fresh. Francesca shivered and was glad once again she hadn't spent a second night in the forest. The carefully fenced-in poultry yard was filled with cackling chickens picking in the dirt. She ducked beneath the low door lintel, wrinkling her nose at the strong stench of its inhabitants, and began to seek for the eggs. The nests were empty but for one old hen who glared at her. The creature pecked at Francesca's sleeve as she pushed beneath it to collect its eggs. The girl shooed it away, and it flapped from the henhouse, clucking indignantly.

Returning to the kitchens, Francesca proudly displayed her finds. Alonza quickly counted the eggs. "Twenty-seven!" she said. "I always had to send Serafina back, for she didn't like the stink of the birds and would not stay long enough to get all the eggs."

"It does stink," Francesca admitted, "but you have a large group to feed. The birds were mostly in the yard but for one old hen who pecked at me. I shooed her off."

Alonza chuckled and nodded. "Aye, you can't let them know if you're afraid. Serafina was, and how those hens enjoyed bedeviling her."

When the bread was baked the innkeeper showed Francesca how to use the paddle with its long handle to withdraw them from the ovens. Then she set her to work peeling carrots and onions for the venison stew she would feed the men tonight. Francesca had never peeled anything in her life other than an orange. The knife was uncomfortable. She held it so tightly that it made her fingers cramp. Twice she cut herself, but only slightly. She could hear the men in the dining hall now. Alonza went out carrying trays of eggs, bacon that she had cooked up earlier while Francesca had done other chores, and the round loaves of bread, along with stone crocks of butter.

When the men had eaten and left the inn to hunt in the autumn forest, the innkeeper sent Francesca into the dining hall to retrieve the plates and mugs and leftover food, but there was little of that. Francesca saw there were pots of honey and even salt on the trestles. When she asked about the salt Alonza explained that as the duke owned the inn for the comfort of his huntsmen and he supplied much of what was cooked and served, it was his generosity that brought them the luxury of salt to season Alonza's cooking and be available for the tables.

Francesca had managed to consume a hard-boiled egg and some bread and butter while she completed her chores. She was exhausted by late morning as she helped Alonza get the stew in two large kettles and swing them over the hearth to cook.

"You're a good worker, for all I suspect you've never been in a kitchen," Alonza praised her. "Go and rest yourself, for tonight you will help me as I serve up the meal."

"May I take some bread and cheese?" Francesca asked her. "I am very hungry."

"Of course, child! I do not want to starve you. Take what you want."

Francesca took bread, which she buttered, cheese, and an apple. She went out and settled herself on the edge of the woods to eat. The sun was warm on her back. Finished with her meal, she crept upstairs and lay down. Her comforter had a wonderful fresh smell to it after its morning in the sun and fresh air. Pulling off her boots, she lay down and drew the coverlet over her, and fell quickly asleep.

It was late afternoon when she woke again. Rising quickly Francesca got her boots on, folded the down blanket, and hurried down to the kitchens. The kettles with the stew were emitting a steamy fragrance, and there was the smell of baking apples. Alonza gave her a smile.

"Here you are and just in time. Draw pitchers of ale from the keg and place two upon each trestle. Then put two loaves upon the tables, and half a wheel of good hard cheese on each trestle, along with a crock of butter. Each trestle seats eight, so set twenty places for tonight, and put a trencher of bread and a pewter mug at each place, along with a spoon."

"You have no forks?" Francesca asked.

Alonza laughed. "No, child, I don't. Forks are for fine folk in the big cities and their *castellos*. Spoons serve just as well, and the men have their own knives."

"Where did those trenchers come from?" Francesca inquired curiously.

"I baked them yesterday. I bake a supply of trenchers each afternoon for the following day," Alonza told her. Then I have fewer dishes to wash," she chuckled. "Now, no more questions and get about your work, child. The sun is near to setting, and the men will be coming in from the forest."

When she had finished her chores the innkeeper demonstrated to Francesca how she could carry several mugs at a time. "Some men will come in late, and the first thing they will want is a mug of ale in the taproom. They won't necessarily go directly to the hall to eat. Tomorrow you will serve in the taproom. Tonight you will ladle stew into the bread trenchers. I will give you a small kettle and a ladle. We'll refill it as it empties. Just move quickly from place to place, filling their trenchers. I'll tell you now that you're bound to be pinched. These men are fierce, but actually quite good-hearted. However, you'll have to put them in their place if you're not to end up black and blue all over, child. Do what you must to keep them civil, or they will never cease plaguing you."

Francesca was terrified of the evening ahead. She had never served food in her entire life. She had had servants to perform such a chore. How could she stand to avoid the abuse that Alonza predicted would be visited upon her? If she was serving one man, her back of necessity had to be to another. Men were not permitted to accost her rudely. She was a maiden and delicately raised. Yet she doubted the men visiting the inn knew anything of gently raised maidens, but she had never been required to stand up for herself, defend her honor. She would ignore their advances, Francesca decided. She would move quickly, not speak to anyone, and do just what was required of her.

The men began to enter the inn, and Alonza went immediately into the taproom.

Francesca filled the smaller pot the innkeeper had laid out with a ladle, and peeping into the hall saw several men taking their places at the trestles. Picking up her container she now hurried into the hall to fill the trenchers of the men already seated. Fortunately the earlier diners were more interested in their food, and she was not accosted. But shortly more hunters began to pour into the hall, seating themselves.

"What's old Alonza cooked up for us tonight?" one asked her as she began to ladle food into his trencher.

"Venison stew," she answered politely, and then jumped as she felt the sting of a pinch. But Francesca ignored it. More pinches and leers followed as she moved about, serving them. She ignored them all until, to her horror, a big hand slid beneath her skirt and fondled a cheek of her bottom. Unable to help herself, Francesca shrieked, dropped her almost-empty kettle, and burst into tears.

A horrified silence descended on the hall and then a loud voice boomed, "Now, see what you've done, Pippino! You've gone and made the maiden cry. Did Alonza not warn you she was not to be harmed? A friendly pinch is expected, but you put hands on the maid and without her permission." The speaker was a huge man, well over six feet in height with a large body to match. His long hair was pulled back and tied.

"I didn't mean to do harm, Bernardo," Pippino defended himself, "but the maid is so pretty I couldn't help myself." He was not small but appeared so before Bernardo.

"Apologize to the maiden, and take your meal into the taproom," Bernardo ordered. "Ye'll eat there for the next few days. The morning meal too." Bernardo then went over to where Francesca stood sobbing and picked up her kettle and ladle, saying, "Get yourself back into the kitchen now, Cara." He handed her the pot, the ladle now in it.

Francesca managed to stop crying. She took her equipment from him and said, "*Mille grazie, signore,*" and bobbed a little curtsy.

Bernardo was not used to receiving such courtesies. Nodding his head at her, he growled gruffly, "Go on, now."

Francesca fled gratefully, not waiting to hear Pippino's apology.

Alonza, who had come from her taproom at Francesca's sound of distress, was waiting for her. "I'll fill the pot, child, and serve the rest of the supper."

Francesca sniffled but then said, "I'll get the bowls with the baked apples."

Alonza nodded, pleased by the girl's recovered strength.

October turned into November. Francesca grew surer of herself around the huntsmen. Bernardo seemed to have taken it upon himself to be her protector. The chastised Pippino was allowed back into the hall after two days because of Francesca's intercession to her self-appointed guardian, who, it turned out, was the duke's head huntsman. She was learning how to twist and turn herself as she made her way through the taproom, carrying several mugs of ale for Alonza's guests. She didn't avoid all the pinches aimed at her, but she did escape most of them now.

She knew the names of all the huntsmen now, and had begun to banter back and forth with them as she worked. To her distress, her hands were becoming rough with all the work she was doing. Alonza had set her to certain chores she herself was no longer able to do because her joints, she told Francesca, ached too badly. The silk merchant's daughter found herself scrubbing the floors. She also did the laundry. As the days and nights grew colder she developed chilblains on the knuckles. I never realized how hard other people worked to make my life so comfortable, Francesca thought. Well, at least if her parents refused to have her back, she could hire herself out as a housemaid or cook's helper. Then she smiled to herself. Her mother would be horrified, which would probably make Orianna forgive her or at least take her back.

But did she want to go back to Florence? To that insular life that she had lived until now? She could always remain here with Alonza. Her life had become interesting, even if every bone in her body ached each nightfall. She sighed. Of course she had to go back. She was Giovanni Pietro d'Angelo's second daughter and meant for greater things than being a serving wench in a forest inn. Briefly she thought of Rafaello, but dismissed him with her usual practicality. He hadn't loved her, and she wasn't going to spend her life without love.

Then one blustery evening at the end of November the inn door swung open, and a tall bearded man stepped into the taproom. Bernardo was the first to spot him. "Carlo!" he said. "I wondered if we would see you at all this winter. Come in and get warm. Alonza! Your favorite is here," he called out to the innkeeper.

She bustled out from the kitchen with a cry of delight. "Carlo, *amore mia*! It has been forever since you have come.

Have you any news, good or bad, to report to us?" She gave him an enthusiastic hug.

"The wedding of the duke's son has been postponed," the tall huntsman reported.

"The blushing bride did not think there was enough time to prepare the wedding she had always dreamed of, and she wanted her parents to come from Florence. So we must wait until springtime for this great event," Carlo told them with a laugh. "Duke Titus is not pleased, but the *Signore* Rafaello will indulge the maiden. It is said he is madly in love with her. So instead of a ducal alliance on December first, the wedding of Valiant Cordassci to Louisa di Genoa will be celebrated quietly and privately. He is the lad raised with our Rafaello since the time they were four. He is always at Rafaello's side. Oh, and France is sounding as if it would go to war again, and 'tis said the Venetians have made some sort of secret alliance with the Ottoman sultan. The pope is furious, but Venice denies it."

Those in the taproom all listened avidly, but none more so than Francesca. So they had postponed the wedding. She would wager that her parents were indeed coming from Florence in the spring. She had not requested their presence in December. Orianna would be intolerable with her victory. She had hoped to keep them away from the wedding. She realized now that the bay had returned to its stables, and her whereabouts were being sought. Even after two months. Poor Terza and little Roza. She knew they would be worried, but Terza would not give her up until they laid Francesca's dead body before her faithful servant.

Carlo went on giving them the latest gossip. He took the mug of ale she handed him but didn't even bother to look at her. That was all to the good. "Who is he?" she murmured to Pippino.

"He hunts in the farthest part of the forest," Pippino said. "Sometimes he comes in for the winter, and other times he remains. They say he has his own cabin. We see him now and again but not often. He's like a shadow in the night, but old Alonza has a soft spot for him, for when he comes he brings her the finest game," Pippino answered her.

"When you go back into the kitchen you will find something that he has left for her."

Pippino was correct. Returning to the kitchens, Francesca found a string of six fat rabbits already skinned, gutted, and cleaned, ready for roasting. There were also three plump ducks and a goose. Alonza was going to be so very pleased. She jumped at the sound of a deep male voice.

"I've hung a carcass of venison in Alonza's cold pantry. Who are you? Certainly not Serafina, who had a crooked nose and a slight limp," he said.

Francesca turned about to face the huntsman known as Carlo. "I am called Cara," she answered him. His beard was quite lush and full but neatly barbered. His eyes more dark than light.

"You do not look like a serving wench," Carlo noted.

"And yet I am," Francesca responded. "I am only Cara, who was lost in the forest and found the inn just after Serafina left. Alonza took me in, and now I toil for her in exchange for my food and pallet. I am really nobody, *signore*."

"You are beautiful, Cara," he told her. "Would you consider sharing your bed with me tonight?"

"No, she would not!" Bernardo said, stepping into the kitchen. "Alonza has told us that Cara is a good maid and not to be trifled with, at peril of losing our private parts," he explained. "Do not attempt to seduce her with your charming ways," the big huntsman said with a chuckle. "You would relinquish Alonza's favor if you did."

"Ahh," Carlo said with a small grin at the duke's head huntsman. "And you have taken it upon yourself to be her knight, old man."

"I have," Bernardo answered good-naturedly. "And I am not so old that I cannot take you in a fair fight, my fine young friend. You are barely past being a stripling."

Alonza came from the taproom, and seeing the two men and hearing the last of the conversation, she said, "Get out of my kitchen, the two of you. It is time for bed. Cara and I have much to do before we may find our rest." She shooed them out, flapping her apron at them, but noting the game she called to Carlo, "My thanks for such fine bounty. But Cara is to be left in peace, or you will have to go."

"You would value a serving wench above your old friend?" Carlo teased her.

"I have many old friends," Alonza said. "But it is not easy to get and keep a good serving wench in the heart of this forest, *dolce mio*. Now get out!"

Both men departed, laughing.

"Harmless, all of them, but some a bit more daring, like Carlo," Alonza told Francesca. "He won't give up attempting to seduce you. If he becomes too troublesome, just tell me and I will straighten it out."

"He's handsome," Francesca replied, "and used to having his way with women, I have not a doubt. But I am yet a virgin, and will save myself for marriage, as I should."

She is such a sweet innocent, Alonza thought to herself. Still, something compels me to protect her.

Francesca then went about cleaning up for the night in the

kitchen, the hall, and the taproom, while Alonza prepared the dough for tomorrow morning's baking. She covered each of her big bowls with a warm, damp cloth, leaving it to rise and for Francesca to knead and bake come the morrow. Francesca swept the hall and then the taproom. She hummed as she worked, thinking that several months ago she would have never considered such menial work. But this was how ordinary folk survived, and for now at least she was ordinary folk. In the spring she would attempt to regain her own world. A world where Francesca Pietro d'Angelo had soft, delicate hands and beautiful clothing and jewels. A world where she would begin to reconsider carefully any suitor who came calling.

She knew now she had made a great mistake in fleeing Duke Titus's *castello*. What had possessed her to want to be like Bianca? Her sister had not sought a great love. It had simply come to her, and, wise enough to recognize what she had, Bianca did not let that love escape her. In doing so, however, Bianca had given up her family. Francesca didn't think she could be that brave.

Rafaello Cesare was a kind man. He probably would have made her an excellent husband. Just because he chose her out of convenience was no reason for her to run away. Most honorable unions began that way, and often, as in her own parents' case, love or genuine affection eventually came. He had offered her marriage and a *duchessa*'s crown. What had been the matter with her that she could not have simply accepted him?

I am a fool, Francesca decided as she finished her sweeping. She had disappointed her family, but, worse, she had disappointed and possibly offended Lorenzo di Medici, who had made it very plain that her duty in Terreno Boscoso was to win the duke's hand and bring glory to Florence. Hopefully Duke Titus would cover up any embarrassment for his own sake, and she could sneak back to Florence, quietly hiding behind the excuse that she was not chosen.

"You appear to have deep and serious thoughts," a voice said from the darkness of the taproom. It was the deep, rough voice of the huntsman Carlo.

"Because I serve does not mean I cannot consider something other than cooking and cleaning," Francesca answered him.

"You were not born to serve," he replied.

"Who knows what we are born to do?" she responded.

"You are a philosopher," Carlo said.

"Today I am a woman who has worked hard from before dawn until now," Francesca told him. *"Buona notte, signore."*

"Dream of me, Cara," he teased her, "for I shall surely dream of you."

"I hope I dream of nothing, for I just want sleep," she responded. She could still not see him in the darkness, but she sensed he was smiling. Turning, she reentered the kitchen and climbed up the back stairs to her little bedchamber. Alonza had gotten into the habit of lighting Francesca's bedside taper when she came up each night, for these days she was always ahead of the younger woman. It flickered madly as the girl entered the room, closing and locking the door quickly behind her.

Her evening habit had become routine. She relieved herself, bathed, scrubbed her teeth with a small piece of willow, and disrobed but for her chemise. Then, brushing the garments she had worn that day, she set them aside for the morrow. She said her prayers by the side of her bed and climbed into it and blew out her taper. Some nights she slept quickly, for the quiet at the inn, even with guests in residence, was amazing. Some nights the cold wind kept her awake for a time as it blew frostily through her shutters.

Tonight she was kept awake by her thoughts of Carlo, the huntsman from the deepest part of the forest. There was something very mysterious about him, an air of danger that attracted her, and she was not certain it should. He got on well with the other huntsmen, yet she thought him perhaps more civilized despite that danger. She liked the way he respected Bernardo, and how he had spoken to her from the dark of the taproom. Not like she was some servant girl to be seduced, but as an equal. Still, even Francesca was wise enough to have heard there were many roads by which seduction traveled. If she thought any further she didn't recall it when she awoke in the morning, for sleep had come suddenly and claimed her.

Carlo was not there the next day, nor for several days after, but then he returned, announcing to Alonza that he intended to spend the winter months at the inn. "I'm not of a mind to be solitary when the snows come this year."

"Is that where you disappeared to?" the innkeeper asked him.

Carlo nodded in affirmation. "I've cleaned it up and made it tight for the winter. When I return in the spring it will just need a good airing."

Francesca had lost track of the days. She was surprised when a friar appeared at the inn one afternoon. He was of indeterminate age, dressed in brown robes and sandals.

Alonza greeted him, delighted. "Brother Stefano! You have come just in time for Christmas." She hugged him, and then brought Francesca forward. "This is my new serving girl, Cara. She has truly been a godsend to me."

Francesca bobbed a little curtsy, and Brother Stefano smiled broadly, giving her a blessing. "I decided that you needed a wee bit of God this year, Alonza. How many are you caring for this winter?"

"Fourteen," Alonza told him. "Six of the men went home to their families."

"And you supply the family for the others," Brother Stefano said. "You're a good woman, Alonza. God bless you for it!"

"And Carlo has come for the winter this year," the inn-keeper said.

"Has he? I find that interesting. Do you know why?"

"Ask him yourself," Alonza said. " 'Tis not my tale to tell."

"I will," Brother Stefano replied.

The hall was livelier that evening with the addition of the friar. The men laughed, ate, and drank, but most important to Francesca, they kept their hands to themselves. She received not a single pinch. Alonza laughed when she said so. Her day ended as she swept the taproom and talked with Carlo in the darkness. He had made it a habit, and Francesca had to admit that she looked forward to their talk, even if he never revealed himself.

He was just a shadow in the concealing dimness, and it was their secret, for he rarely spoke to her before the others. She liked the idea of having this clandestine time with the handsome hunter. She would not admit it, but she found him and the air of mystery about him exciting. But should she? Still, being a serving wench lowers many barriers for me, Francesca thought. Cara might do what Francesca ought not. But should she? She suspected not, and yet this air of freedom was too intoxicating to ignore.

Chapter 7

Brother Stefano said a Mass each morning he was with them. He heard confessions, but Francesca did not make one, smiling and refusing him when he asked.

"Next time, then," the friar said calmly. "No one should be forced to God."

"I have no great sins, I promise you. I am a maid, and mean to remain a maid until I wed a good man," Francesca told him.

"I believe you, my child," Brother Stefano responded, and he blessed her. He departed after the Feast of the Nativity. There had been little snow up until then. His small friary was three days' walk from the inn, and he wanted to reach it before any storms came and prevented his passage. His timing was foreknowing. The first big storm began on the last day of December.

It had been a strange Christmas for Francesca. She was used to being surrounded by her family, exchanging lavish little gifts with her parents and siblings, feasting in her father's *sala da pranzo* on hard-to-find fruits and hazelnuts, among other special foods.

Instead she gave Alonza a small potpourri she had made in the late autumn, and the innkeeper gave her a new chemise she had sewn for the girl. They feasted in the hall with the hunters, pushing the trestles together so that Alonza sat at one end and Francesca at the other end.

It was the last night of the year, with Alonza in her bed and the hunters in theirs, that Francesca slipped into the taproom to sit before the fire. There was no wind tonight, and she could see the snow falling silently outside. She was going to be sixteen in this new year that was coming. It seemed so old when you had neither mate nor child.

You could have been married, the voice in her head said.

"You are pensive tonight," he said from the darkness, but he sat next to her upon the settle by the fire. "What do you think?"

"Of nothing, of everything," she replied, surprised, for she thought him abed.

"Here," he spoke again, and he shoved something into her hand. "It is for you."

"What is it?" she said, and looking down saw a beautifully carved pear wood comb in her hand.

"Hair as beautiful as yours needs a comb. I carved it for you, Cara," he told her quietly. "I hope you will like it."

Francesca was both touched and amazed, but then, distressed, she said, "Alas, I have no gift for you, Carlo. It does not seem fair that you give me a New Year's gift, and I have not one for you."

"Give me a kiss," he said. But there was no suggestive tone to his voice.

"I think, perhaps, I should not accept your gift," Francesca told him. "Bernardo has warned me that you are a seducer. Is this the first step in your plan of seduction?"

He laughed softly. "I suspect that you are worth far more than a poor man's gift of a pear wood comb, Cara. And the value of your kiss far exceeds the worth of the comb."

"Oh, my," she replied. "How flattering you are, Carlo. And dangerous too, I fear."

Then, leaning over, she kissed him upon his bearded cheek. "I hope that you will accept my little kiss in return, *signore*."

"I do!" he replied. Indeed she had taken him quite by surprise. Daringly he put a light arm about her shoulders, and she did not flinch away. "Shall we sit and enjoy this peace as the New Year begins?" he asked her.

She said nothing in reply, but relaxed against him. A new year, Francesca thought. So much had happened since the last New Year had been celebrated. Two years ago she had been in Venice, living with her grandfather, and they had watched the fireworks display brought from China that had been sponsored by the doge for the enjoyment of the populace. And last year she had been back in Florence with her family, celebrating together with wine and cakes and sugar-coated almonds.

Her mother had worried that Francesca's behavior would end up costing her a good husband. Her father had assured Orianna that their daughter's dowry and her beauty would overcome any and all alleged faults. Her brothers had teased their parents by saying they agreed with Francesca. The suitors coming to pay her court were not worthy of her at all. Lucianna bragged that she would make the finest marriage of all, and little Giulia fell asleep before the bells tolled the midnight hour.

Francesca's eyes grew misty. She missed her family. She

missed Venice. She was even willing to admit to missing Florence. As this new year was about to dawn, she was not home with those she loved. She was not Francesca Pietro d'Angelo, the privileged second daughter of the head of the silk merchants' guild, living in an elegant and civilized city. She was Cara, a girl with red hands who served a coterie of rough huntsmen in the midst of a winter forest.

She trembled but barely, and then hot tears began to roll down her pale cheeks.

She had callously thrown away the life she was meant to have as the young *duchessa* of Terreno Boscoso. She had scorned the good man who would be her husband. Could she really return to Florence and her family in the spring? What was the matter with her that she had allowed her pride to overwhelm her good sense? What did it matter now why Rafaello Cesare had chosen her?

Carlo had felt the tiny tremor that had gone through her. "What is the matter?" he asked gently. He caught her face between his thumb and his forefinger and tilted it up, surprised to see that she was crying. Without thinking he bent his head and placed a tender kiss upon her mouth.

She didn't scold him or even push him away. His kiss was comforting and gentle. Eyes closed, she held her lips up to him for more. He complied, at first careful not to alarm her, but his desire was quickly aroused. Carlo's arms wrapped about Francesca. She did not resist. His kisses deepened. Her lips parted slightly for him. His hand slipped first past the neckline of her blouse, and then between the opening of her chemise. His fingers slid deeper, deeper until his hand was cupping a small but very full breast within his palm.

She murmured a faint protest.

"Don't forbid me this sweetness," he begged against her swollen lips as he began to stroke the silken skin.

Francesca sighed. *I shouldn't let him, but it feels so good,* she thought, as she sensed her nipple pucker as if it had been touched by frost. She couldn't speak. She didn't want to forbid him, nor did she want him to cease.

Skilled in the art of passion, Carlo immediately recognized that Francesca was enjoying his touches. He also noted that she wasn't crying anymore. He stroked the breast slowly, slowly, squeezing it slightly, rubbing his rough thumb over the nipple again. "Does this please you, *amore mia?*" he whispered in her ear.

She was silent a moment, but then she said softly, "Yes." She sighed deeply. "Still, I cannot permit you to go further with your seduction because of my melancholy, Carlo. I am a virgin, and must save my virtue for the man I will one day wed."

Reluctantly he withdrew his hand from her warm flesh. "Will you die a maid if no one suitable comes along? I suspect you are a maid who will not accept just any husband, Cara. What do you seek in a husband?"

"A man who will love me, who chooses me because I am the only one who can fill his heart. I have a sister who ran away for that kind of love. I have a friend who merely looked upon a certain man and knew he was the one with whom she wished to spend her life. I suppose I am foolish to want this kind of love, but I do."

"You are not foolish," he told her quietly. "You are a maiden who holds to her ideals. I hold to my principles too, so I understand you. Now go to your lonely bed, Cara, for if you remain I fear we shall both be tempted despite our good intentions." He stood, pulling her up behind him, and gave her a small push towards the taproom entrance. "Good night, *amore mia.*"

Francesca did not argue with him or even look back. He was correct, and she knew it. Her first taste of passion had been delicious. She was beginning to understand why people found forbidden fruit so tasty. Hurrying up the back staircase, she quickly found her bed. Soon enough Alonza would awaken her to begin her morning's chores.

But when she awoke it was already daylight. Francesca jumped from her little bed, wincing at the icy floor beneath her feet. She quickly washed and pulled on her clothing, then went in search of Alonza.

But the innkeeper wasn't in the kitchen. Francesca hurried back upstairs and crept into the old woman's bedchamber. Alonza lay in her bed, and at first glance Francesca knew she was very sick. Her wrinkled brow was dotted in beads of sweat, and when the girl touched her, she found, as she had suspected she would, that Alonza was burning up with fever. *Madre di Dios!* What was she to do?

Alonza croaked from her bed. "Cara, you must take care of the inn's business today without me. I have caught the winter flux."

"You need to be taken care of," Francesca said.

"No, no! First feed the men. Then return to me." She waved the girl away with a limp hand.

Francesca debated a moment before nodding and hurrying out of Alonza's bedchamber. The old woman was very sick, but she did not appear anywhere near to dying. Reaching the kitchens, she uncovered the bowls of dough, kneaded them, shaped them, and got them into the ovens. Their meal would be late today, but she suspected their guests were also sleeping late, for it was as quiet as a tomb. Outside the snow was still gently falling and all was silent. Pulling on her cloak, she made a quick trip to the henhouse and gathered up every egg she could find. The snow was already above her knees. She found Bernardo in the kitchen when she returned.

"Where is Alonza?" he inquired of her.

"Sick with the winter flux. I'll get the meal ready for the men as quickly as I can before I return to nurse her," Francesca told him.

He gave her a short nod. "What can I do to help?" he asked her.

She gathered up the bread trenchers, got a tray, and handed it to him. "Put the trenchers, the mugs, and spoons at each place," she told him.

"Most of the lads are still sleeping," Bernardo told her. "Managing this all by yourself won't be easy, but we'll all help out where we can. You just make certain that we are all fed, Cara."

"They'll want hot food, so when I tell you to fetch them please do," she answered him. "Then they can sleep the rest of the day away until the dinner hour."

He nodded and took the trenchers into the dining hall.

She paid no attention to him after that, boiling up eggs for the meal and taking the bread from the ovens. As it was New Year's Day, she took a small ham from the larder, sliced it, and lay the slices upon a platter. A pot over the hearth cooked a grain cereal. When it was done she added bits of chopped apple and stirred honey into the pot, setting it in the coals to keep warm.

Bernardo came into the kitchen. "Shall I fill the cups with ale now?" he asked her.

Francesca nodded, adding, "Then fetch the men to the hall."

As he went off to follow her instructions, she began bringing the food into the trestles. She added crocks of butter and cheese to each table. Bernardo had quickly filled the mugs and gone off to rouse his companions. They began to straggle into the hall, sleepy-eyed, but smelling her good meal they became more awake. Francesca came from the kitchen, managing to hold on to the pot of hot grain. She filled each trencher full as the benches at the trestles quickly filled. Bernardo had explained that Alonza was very sick and still abed. They had hardly expected the bounty they received from the serving wench, and were therefore both surprised and grateful. The food was consumed quickly and they thanked her.

"We'll have to help today as Cara's duties include nursing the old woman, and seeing that we are fed again will take all of her time," Bernardo told his huntsmen. Then he turned to Francesca. "What will you need done?"

"We'll need a path shoveled from the kitchen door to the barn and the henhouse. The animals in the barn will need feeding. Break the ice on their water. The two goats and the cow will need milking. The chickens need food too. They can hardly go out to scratch in their yard in all this snow. Scatter grain for them on the henhouse floor. I'll need firewood brought into the hearths, and charcoal for the braziers in the sleeping chambers. And several buckets of water for the kitchen from the well. If it is frozen hit the ice with the bucket until it breaks. And the trestles must be cleared so I can wash the mugs, spoons, and dishes. I cannot think of anything else now," Francesca concluded.

She was relieved that having heard her instructions Bernardo now began assigning the required tasks to his men. She returned to the kitchen and went upstairs to check on Alonza. She found her awake but still filled with fever. "I've fed the men," she said, giving the innkeeper her menu.

Alonza nodded, pleased. "When I took you in, child, I honestly did not believe you could be of much help to me, but even an inept servant is better than none. But you have learned quickly and become most valuable to me. You did well."

"I've set the men to most of my chores so I can cook and see to your care." And Francesca explained what she had asked of them, concluding, "Have I forgotten anything? If I have you must tell me, and I will see to it."

Alonza listened and then shook her head. "You have forgotten nothing."

"What can I do to ease your fever?" Francesca asked. "I do not know the herbal arts. If you will tell me, I will do it."

"Go into the cold larder," Alonza began. "You will find a supply of marrows. Take a fat one, mash it well and smooth, removing its seeds. Then mix it with olive oil and honey. Warm it slightly, and bring me some in a dish. This will help my fever. A cup of mint tea with honey will soothe my belly cramps, child."

Francesca left the innkeeper briefly to follow her instructions. When she returned with the required items, she spoon-fed the weak woman the paste of marrow, oil, and honey, then held the cup of mint tea to her dried lips. Then she settled her back in her comfortable bed, for she could see Alonza was going to fall asleep again. "I'll keep your brazier lit," she told her, gathering up the dish with the marrow but leaving the tea and creeping from the bedchamber.

Back in the kitchens she found Carlo bringing in wood, which he piled carefully by the large hearth where she cooked. He then brought her several buckets of water. "How is the old woman?" he asked Francesca.

"Sick, but I don't believe in any serious danger," Francesca said.

Bernardo came in with the mugs and spoons. There were no plates, as most of their morning meal had been eaten out of the trenchers. She gave him some heated water and he quickly washed the items in question. "The taproom and the hall need more wood," he said to Carlo, who with a nod left the kitchen.

"Is that young villain bothering you, Cara? Tell me and I will deal with him," the big man growled.

"He is most respectful and courteous," Francesca told him. And his kisses are almost too delicious to bear, she thought.

"Good! Good! I'll go help with the wood, then." And Bernardo stomped out.

She mixed more bread dough and set it aside to rise. She considered what she would feed the men later. Foraging in the dry pantry, she found a surprisingly large supply of spaghetti. She decided to cook it up and serve it with vegetables, the left-over ham, cheese, and oil. Enough of it would fill their bellies until tomorrow morning. She sautéed the onions, which she had finely cut. She washed and thinly sliced the carrots. There had been peas until the great snowfall. She found them in a bowl in the cold pantry, and a wedge of Parmesan cheese. She quickly cooked the vegetables, then minced some drying basil and parsley that had been hanging in the dry pantry. That along with more bread, butter, and a hard cheese would make a satisfying meal. Because it was the new year she stewed some pears and set them in a large bowl of sweet wine.

Francesca kept checking on Alonza during the day. She attempted to feed her some chicken broth, but the innkeeper was not quite ready for nourishment. Alonza listened intently as her servant girl explained what she would feed the men for their main meal that day. She nodded her approval.

"We do not eat as much pasta here in the north," she remarked, "but they will enjoy it because it is different and you have made it festive. I had quite forgotten about that pasta. I never quite know what to do with it. You have obviously been raised farther south than Terreno Boscoso. And the sweet is a good touch. 'Twill soothe any of our lads who are disappointed at not getting a haunch of venison to chew upon." Then she gave a weak cackle. "You have learned quickly in my kitchen, Cara. I hope you will consider remaining with me come spring."

Francesca shook her head in the negative. "You are good to me," she said, "but I must go, Alonza, and you did promise me I could."

"I will keep my promise," the old lady told her, "for you have certainly kept yours, my child." She gave her young companion a weak smile. "I need to rest again," she said.

Francesca left her, first emptying the chamber pot, which was filled with a noxious substance. The rest of her day remained busy, and only when everyone was fed and the hall emptied did she feel at ease. Her trenchers were baked for the morning; the bowls that had contained the food washed and stacked. Alonza was settled, hopefully for the night, her fever much abated. Finally Francesca was able to creep into the taproom, dark but for its blazing hearth.

"I will not remain long," she told him, knowing he was there in the shadows. "I understand now why it takes more than one to manage this inn."

He chuckled. "You were not used to hard work before coming here, were you?"

"Nay, I was not," she answered without thinking, and then said nothing more. Those four words had already revealed too much.

"I am astounded by all you and Alonza accomplish together," he told her, and now he came to sit by her side on the little settle.

"Most of it you and the lads accomplished today. All I did was cook and tend to the old woman," Francesca told him. Without thinking again, she lay her head on his shoulder and he slipped his arm about her waist, drawing her closer.

He had never believed that she could be this vulnerable, but in her exhaustion she seemed to let down her barriers. So easy, he thought. It would be so easy to seduce her right now here by the fire. He sensed she would resist initially, but then would yield herself to him in all her innocence. He felt his cock begin to tighten with his need for her. With effort he said to her, "You must go to bed, Cara. Tomorrow will be no easier for you." Standing up, he gently pushed her away. *"Buona notte."*

"Buona notte," she responded, surprised by his thoughtfulness.

For the next ten days she managed the inn by herself and cared for Alonza. Carlo no longer met her clandestinely in the taproom when everyone else slept. She dared not ask him why. Now and again when he was certain no one would see them, he would catch her unexpectedly in a pantry or the kitchen and kiss her most soundly.

Once, as she stood kneading bread dough, he pressed himself against her, his large hands cupping and fondling her breasts. When he did that she could not think, or rather her thoughts took a lascivious direction. She wondered what it would be like to lie naked with him, touching him as he did her. She felt her buttocks, unbidden, grind themselves into his groin, and flushed bright red with the realization of what she was doing.

He laughed softly. "I see that you have the potential to be very wicked," he said.

He pressed his lower body hard against her.

Francesca felt a sticky wetness coming from her most private place. It was a sensation she had never before experienced. Her legs felt weak. "Oh, stop!" she begged him. "I don't really understand what is happening."

"You are feeling desire," Carlo explained. "Passion can be stoked at any time or in any place, Cara." He pinched her nipples lightly.

"I do not understand," she said low, shuddering slightly.

His hot lips touched the nape of her neck. "I know," was all he said.

Francesca was relieved when Alonza was finally able to leave her sickbed, even if at first it was only for a few hours of the day. There was less opportunity for Carlo to be near her. She was puzzled by her reaction to him. No man, not even the man she had imagined Enzo Ziani to be, had spoken to her so freely and directly. He did not treat her as if she were a delicate flower, a witless fool, or a child who needed to be indulged. Many times Francesca thought they spoke together as her parents did, with respect for one another.

As for his gentle lovemaking, the truth was she had never permitted any man to really court her with kisses and tender touches. She could not help but consider what it would be like if she allowed him more liberties. She wasn't even certain she knew what those liberties would consist of, but she realized she wanted to know. Was this the kind of thing a respectable maiden asked a man? Again she did not know.

The snow was finally gone, though patches of it remained on the hillsides and along the deeper forest paths. The huntsmen were becoming restless to return into the forest but it was still too chill and damp. They bided their time, however. She had locked up the inn for the evening. Alonza was already snoring as Francesca entered her bedchamber.

"Do not scream," she heard his voice say.

"What are you doing here? Alonza will surely hear you," Francesca said calmly.

"Alonza is well enough to have entertained Bernardo in her bed," he said.

"What?" She was startled by this bit of information.

"They have been lovers for years," Carlo told her. "He'll remain until you have gone downstairs. He'll sneak down when you go to the henhouse. It is their habit."

"Oh, my!" was all she could manage to say.

"I want you," he told Francesca suddenly.

She was stunned by his frank speech. "I don't know what to say, Carlo."

"Say you'll allow me the privilege of your bed, the gift of your innocence!" His voice was almost hoarse with his longing, his need.

"I cannot," she told him. "My virginity is the only pure gift I can give the man I wed one day. I cannot squander it, although these feelings that you engender in me are surely borne of my need for you and tempt me greatly."

"I have fallen in love with you," he surprised her by saying.

Her eyes filled with tears. "I don't know what that sort of love is," she responded.

In response he pulled her into his arms and kissed her deeply, his tongue sliding into her mouth to stroke her tongue sensuously. His hands held her heart-shaped face. Lifting his lips from hers he said, "What do you feel, Cara?"

"Joy!" she answered without hesitation. "Utter joy!"

"Then you love me too," he told her triumphantly.

"You say it because you want your own way," Francesca accused him.

"Aye, I want my own way! I want you naked and in my arms. I want to kiss every bit of your beautiful body. I want to hear you cry out in pleasure each time when I fill you full of myself." He looked deep into her eyes, and Francesca struggled with herself.

"No," she said. "You must go. Now!" And she pulled from his embrace.

With a groan he quickly departed her chamber, leaving her considerably shaken.

Sitting heavily upon her bed, Francesca wept. She hadn't wanted to send him away. She longed for the warmth of his arms, for his body, for that mysterious joining she had never experienced but suddenly desired. What had happened to her? She had been courted by men of power and wealth but had scorned them all. Yet she was drawn to a simple huntsman. A lowborn man who set her heart thundering and her pulse racing. What was the matter with her?

You are in love, the voice in her head said.

I will not even acknowledge such a possibility, Francesca considered. I cannot be in love with him. I don't even know what love is. This must be what they call lust. She quickly undressed and climbed into her bed, but she did not find sleep easily.

The winter was waning away and signs of spring were beginning to appear. The birds now sang in the mornings. The buds on the deciduous trees began to slowly swell.

Tufts of greenery began to emerge from the dark earth, and Carlo's eyes followed her everywhere. Francesca began to contemplate departing the forest, but she could not quite yet leave Alonza, who was still weak from her winter flux.

The days began to linger longer. In mid-April some of the huntsmen began to depart for their own places in the forest. The hall now sat eight men at mealtimes. It was easier taking care of eight as opposed to twenty. Three came to her one morning and politely asked if she would wash their garments. One of the men was Pippino.

"We would leave in a day or two," he said.

"And your clothing will not be washed until you return next autumn," Francesca said, laughing. "Very well. You shall begin the summer months free of fleas and the other vermin who manage to attach themselves to you during the winter."

He grinned at her. "I'll wash my clothing once or twice before I return to my shelter by the lake," Pippino protested.

"You'll be wearing them into that lake, I have not a doubt. 'Tis not the same as a good scrubbing," she told him, and as she laundered their rough garments, Francesca chuckled. A year ago as she prepared to come to Terreno Boscoso as a candidate for the hand of Rafaello Cesare, she would not have imagined herself playing the serving wench over a tub of hot water, scrubbing someone else's garments. She didn't know whether to laugh at herself or weep at the position in which her own foolishness had placed her.

She thought about Rafaello, and wondered if they had obtained another bride for him and if he had been quickly married to cover the embarrassment of her desertion. She had treated him badly. She had treated all her suitors badly. Until recent events she had not thought seriously that courting was not a game. Every time she had been cruel to one of the young men who sought to marry her, she realized now that she had been striking out at Enzo Ziani and his refusal to have her for his wife. How childish and how silly she had been. She had probably ruined her chances of ever marrying at all. And the truth was, Francesca now understood that she did want to marry. Marry and have children and be with her family once again. Family was all, and she had been too selfish to realize it.

She climbed the stairs to her bedchamber, entered, and prepared quickly for rest.

Outside a full April moon filled the little room with silver light. With a sigh Francesca closed her eyes and slept. It was the sound of boots hitting her floor that awakened her. A dark shadow loomed, the window behind it.

"Don't scream," Carlo said in his now-familiar deep, rough voice.

"You shouldn't be here," she scolded, but already her nipples were tingling with excitement.

"I love you," he said simply.

"A seducer's words," Francesca replied.

"No!" He sat on the bed next to her. "A lover's words. The words of a man who loves, needs, and wants you."

"For how long?" she taunted him. "Until you return to your forest lair in a few more days, Carlo? What do you need me for? To satisfy your lust? How many women have you spoken those three words to in order to have your way with them?"

"I have never spoken those words before to anyone else except my mother," he told her.

He stunned her into momentary silence. Oddly she believed him. "I am afraid," she admitted to him, sitting up.

His eyes filled with the beauty of her breasts, which he could see beneath the thin fabric of her chemise. He put an arm about her shoulders. "What do you fear, *amore mia*?" he asked her.

"How I feel about you," she half whispered. "I should feel nothing, and yet I do."

"You love me," he told her without any sense of conceit.

"I think I do," Francesca admitted shyly, and felt heat suffuse her cheeks.

"This cot you sleep upon is too small for us both, and I would lie by your side," he said. "Let me put your coverlet upon the floor so we may be together."

She nodded. She wanted to lie fully in his arms, and she could feel the bed suffering beneath his weight. If it broke they would surely be discovered.

He pulled the down coverlet off her and spread it upon the floor, where it touched the wall, for the room was not large. Then removing his boots, he drew her down to join him, and wrapped his arms tightly about her so that they were almost fused from chest to thighs. Her soft body against him was the most comforting yet arousing sensation he had ever known. He undid the ribbon holding her plait and spread out her hair, burying his face in the red-gold curls, becoming dizzy with the fragrance of it. "I adore you!" he whispered into her ear.

"And I you, though I should not," Francesca confessed, wondering how this could feel so right and yet be wrong.

"Why should you not love me?"

"Because I have an obligation to my family to return to them unsullied so they may make another match for me if they can. I foolishly ran away from the last arrangement they had settled. I was wrong to do so. He was a good man."

"Ahh," he said. "So that is why you were lost in the forest."

"Yes, that is why," Francesca admitted.

"If he was a good man, why did you flee him?" Carlo asked her, curious.

She thought a moment before she answered him. "With the example of my elder sister before me, I decided I wanted what she had. It is not the usual way to make a marriage among our kind, I know. But I wanted love. He did not love me. He barely knew me. He was ready to wed me because there was no other choice for him," Francesca said. "Bianca's behavior cost her everything but the man she loved. She has no family but him and no country to call her own. But that is not really what I want. I want my family. I want to have babies. I want to gather together with them when it is possible and see my parents delight in the children I have given my husband and his family.

"But I spoiled all that with my arrogance and my ignorance, Carlo. Now I will creep home and beg their forgiveness. I pray they will not disown me, and that they are able to find another good man I may wed when the scandal of my latest offense dies away. If they do not, I do not know what I will do, for I shall truly be lost then."

"Marry me," he said simply.

Francesca was very surprised by his suggestion, but she shook her head. "Nay. I am not who you believe me to be. Marriage to me could easily cost you your life. Ask me no more, I beg of you, for I have already said too much. I must leave Terreno Boscoso."

He was stunned by all she had told him. "And tonight?"

She lay back, looking up at him so she might speak more directly to him. "Tonight I will belong to you because I love you. You will have my special gift." Francesca then kissed him passionately and let him take the lead in their love play.

He actually debated with himself for a long moment as they kissed. He could have her now, all of her, as he had dreamed for many nights. But she was really so innocent of passion that it seemed better to him that he introduce her slowly to the delights of true love. There would be time for them now that she had confessed to him of her love. He had always believed that beneath her pride there was a warm and loving heart beating within Francesca.

She quivered with anticipation as his rough hand began to caress her full, round breast. His touch was so tender, so gentle, yet it set her afire with longings she had never before experienced. And she wanted more. She nuzzled his neck, nipping at his ear. He growled low against her warm flesh, and then his mouth fastened upon a nipple.

Francesca gasped with the sensation, then gasped again as he began to suckle on her. Unable to help herself, she reached up to tangle her fingers in his dark hair, holding him close against her as his tongue and lips awoke her newborn lust.

When he raised his head from her breast she whispered frantically, "No! Don't stop, my love. Please, don't stop!"

In response he transferred his attentions to her other breast and she pressed herself up against him. There was absolutely no space between them. She could feel every inch of his lean body against hers. She fumbled to loosen his leather breeches, but he stopped her, taking her hands in his, holding them firmly so she might not use them. "Carlo!" she protested. *Madre di Dios!* She could feel the hard ridge of his manhood pressing itself against her through the fabric of his clothing.

"So eager. So eager," he groaned against her ear. And he wanted her every bit as much as she wanted him, but he would not take her now, tonight, without the benefit of a marriage between them. She just wasn't some servant to be used and discarded. She was the woman he loved. He fought down his own raging needs.

"Yes!" she whispered back. Her tongue licked his ear provocatively. "Yes!"

"I want you more than I have words to tell you, Cara, my love, but I must be true to the lesson my mother—may God have mercy on her sweet soul—taught me. I will not give myself the full pleasure of your body until our wedding night," he explained.

"But such a thing cannot be!" she cried out to him, and those beautiful green eyes of hers began to sparkle with tears.

"Then I shall never have you, Cara. You are simply not a woman to be taken and then discarded, even by so rough a fellow as I am." Jesu! She could have no idea of what this gallantry was costing him, but with a final caress to her breast he forced himself to his feet. His male member was aching with his need for her, but his mind was made up. He did not imagine she expected her huntsman to play the gallant.

She began to weep as she lay curled upon the floor. She had wanted him. She had offered herself to him freely without conditions, and now suddenly he was refusing her generosity. She swallowed back her sobs. She would not let him know how much he had hurt her by crying with her disappointment. Perhaps it was better this way. Francesca scrambled to her feet, pulling her chemise closed and about her. "Get out!" she said to him, but he was already half-gone, slipping out the window through which he had earlier entered her small chamber.

Bending down, she gathered up the quilt that had been spread upon the floor, wrapping it about her as she lay back down again upon her small cot. She could smell the woodland fragrance he always had about him on the fabric. Certain she was alone once more, Francesca wept. So this was how it felt to be scorned and refused by the man you loved. Only now did she really understand the cruelty she had demonstrated to her many suitors over the past two years. She was alone and bereft.

Francesca suddenly realized that it didn't matter to her at all if she ever married. Now that she knew what love was, how could she give herself to just any man? But when she managed to find her way back to Florence and her parents' house, there would no longer be any choice left to her at all. If they could find a man to wed her, she would be wed. At least her husband would have the gift of her virginity. But even that was not her doing. Her virginity remained intact because a rough huntsman had had more honor than she had. How shameful was that? But it was a shame she would keep to herself.

Her eyes burned from her tears. There was no more time left to her. The summer was almost upon them. She could not linger here with Alonza at the inn in the forest. She had kept her part of the bargain she had made with the innkeeper. Francesca knew that once she told Alonza she was ready to leave, the older woman would keep the rest of the bargain, for she was every bit as honorable in her own way as was Francesca Pietro d'Angelo. It was time to face the consequences of her own foolish actions.

Chapter 8

Making certain that Alonza's health was fully restored, Francesca broached the subject of her departure several days later. She had discovered the
morning after Carlo's visit that he and the other huntsmen had
gone in the early light even before the dawn. The inn was empty
now, and would remain so until the autumn came, when the
duke's huntsmen would once again come in from the cold
weather of winter.

For the next few days the two women cleaned the inn from
top to bottom. The chambers where the men had slept were
emptied, their floors and windows scrubbed before the rough
furniture was returned to be stacked against the walls until it
was time again for them to be occupied. Alonza announced as
they cleaned the kitchens that she would be spending the summer with her sister near the city.

"My nephew, Alonzo, will be here in a few days to take us out of the forest, my girl. I hope you'll return with me next autumn, for you have been the best serving girl I have ever had, Cara."

"I cannot," the younger girl said, truly touched by Alonza's words. "I must go home to my family, and make my amends for running away."

Alonza nodded. "Aye," she said. "I understand, child. But I will miss you."

"And I you," Francesca said, unable to help herself as she hugged Alonza. "You have taught me so much, and I am grateful."

Alonza shook her off but she was smiling. "Well, you were quick to learn, which is more than most of them are. Perhaps I'll bring back my sister's ugly daughter with me. They'll never find the poor girl a husband, so if she enjoys the inn perhaps the duke will allow her to have it when I have grown too old for all this hard work."

Alonza's nephew arrived two days later just after dawn. He was a good-natured lad about fifteen years in age. "I know you, Auntie, and you are eager to go, but first you must feed me. I left my mother's after supper last evening, and traveled by moon-light most of the way. Hello! And who is this pretty maid?"

"I'm Cara, your auntie's servant, and you are much too young for me to flirt with, boy," she told him, laughing.

"A pity," he said. "I'm in the market for a wife, and if your work pleased my auntie, then you would probably make me a good wife." He grinned winningly at her.

"Give him a wife, now," Alonza said laughing, "and he'd wear the poor lass out before he was seventeen. The food is on the table. Eat quickly, for Cara and I are ready to be quit of the forest for now. I've packed food for our journey, but we should reach our destination by sundown if you hurry."

The boy gobbled down the loaf of fresh bread, the half-dozen hard-boiled eggs, and half a cooked chicken. Francesca washed the few dishes quickly, looked about the inn a final time, and joined Alonza. The innkeeper carefully locked the front door of the inn, hanging the key on a large decorative hook by the door.

"Will you not take it?" Francesca asked the older woman, surprised.

"It's unlikely anyone will disturb the inn before I return in late summer," Alonza said. "It is hardly on the beaten path, but someone like yourself, child, might find themselves lost in the forest, and could shelter here. Best they have the key and not break in. There is little to steal. The livestock comes with us now."

"The duke doesn't mind?" Francesca said.

"He is a kind man," Alonza told her.

Aye, Francesca thought to herself, he was a kind man. She remembered him well and hoped he did not think too badly of her. Well, it doesn't matter any now, she thought.

The little party departed the inn yard, and, riding upon the mules Alonzo had brought with him, they followed him through the forest. Francesca could not clearly see the path they traversed, but it was obviously there, for the boy and his beast moved along at a brisk pace, undeterred, as they followed along behind him. Gradually the way became more obvious, but Francesca realized that she would have never found her way out of the woodlands without their guide. And then in late afternoon they emerged from the trees onto a more obvious narrow roadway that finally led to a larger road, which was crowded with people.

"Where are they all going?" Francesca asked Alonzo.

"To Castellocitta. The duke's son is being married tomorrow, and everyone wants to go to the wedding. There will be wine and food for everyone. None in Terreno Boscoso will miss this wonderful event," Alonzo explained to them.

"Oh, how exciting!" Alonza said. "You would think your mother would have sent me word of such an event."

"She knew you would be home in time," the boy said.

Francesca was silent. So Duke Titus's son, Rafaello, would finally take a bride. She wondered who the girl was. Her mother was really going to be furious at her for the dreadful mess she had made of what had been a marvelous opportunity.

"How exciting!" Alonza said again, enthusiastically. "We'll get to see the spectacular event all of Terreno Boscoso has been awaiting. By this time next year, God willing, we will have another heir! You will come with us, Cara!"

"No, no!" the younger woman said. That was all she needed to do. Stand in a crowd of happy citizens and cheer Rafaello and his new bride. "I must find my friend if she is still in the town, and then we must be on the road south as quickly as we can."

"Well," Alonza said, "you'll miss a wonderful day, but I can understand your need to return to your native city and your family. I'm sure they will be happy to see you."

Francesca almost laughed aloud at Alonza's words. If she hadn't already been disowned, her mother would probably kill her where she stood when she was announced at Palazzo Pietro d'Angelo.

They arrived at Alonza's sister's cottage in early evening. Both older women insisted that Francesca remain the night, and the girl was too tired, if truth be told, to argue.

But when the morning came she was prepared to depart into the city. With the crowds still filling the road, she wondered if she might make her way to the castle. Would Terza still be there? Or had she been sent back to Florence with the priest and two nuns who had accompanied Francesca last year? As she considered what to do there came a loud knocking at the door of the cottage.

Alonza went to answer and found herself facing a small contingent of the duke's guardsmen. "Good morning," Alonza said. "What is it you want?"

"We've come for the girl who calls herself Cara," the spokes-man for the group said. They wore red uniforms with fine gold-colored buttons decorating the jackets.

"What?" Alonza was very surprised. "What has she done? She is a good girl who worked hard for me all winter in the duke's forest inn. Why do you want her?"

"If you are employed by our master, the duke, I will not chastise you for questioning me," the guardsman said. "Is the girl here? If not, where has she gone?"

Alonza's sister, Barbetta, now hurried forward. "Cara is here," she said.

Then she called, "Come, girl, you are wanted by the duke's guard. Come quickly! I'll have no trouble in my house this happy day."

Young Alonzo half dragged Francesca forward. "Here is the girl who calls herself Cara," he said. "Is there a reward?"

Alonza cuffed her nephew upon his head.

"I have done nothing," Francesca said, frightened.

"I have orders that you are to come with us," the head guardsman said. "I want no trouble. Just come quietly."

"You don't have to go with them!" Alonza said. "I'll speak with the duke myself. They cannot just come to our door and demand to take you away without cause."

"My orders come from Duke Titus himself," the guardsman said. "Just come with us, girl, and do not place these good people who have sheltered you in jeopardy."

"I'm coming with her!" Alonza said in a firm voice, her hands on her hips.

"If you wish," the guardsman said. "No harm is meant the girl, mistress. I have simply been instructed to bring her to her people at the castle."

"It's all right, dear Alonza," Francesca told her protector. "I believe they mean me no harm. Stay here with your family." The girl turned to the guardsman. "I will come with you," she said quietly. Her fear had suddenly evaporated as she absorbed the man's words. He had come to bring her to *her people* at the castle. Somehow the duke had learned she was in the city, but how? Francesca shrugged to herself. Does it matter?

She gave Alonza a quick hug and then followed the guardsman outside. He mounted his horse and then, holding out a hand to her, pulled her up before him on the saddle. The mounted party moved away from Barbetta's cottage and into the traffic on the road, where the guardsmen urged their mounts at a brisk speed into the town itself and then onto the road leading up to the castle.

Francesca remembered her entry into the duke's home a year past when she had come dressed in a beautiful gown, her jewelry sparkling in the summer sunshine, her great and impressive train causing immediate jealousy on the part of the arrogant Aceline du Barry. Had the duke recalled her to wed Rafaello? No. Rafaello would have never married Aceline under any circumstances. She thought suddenly of Louisa. Had her father, the duke of Genoa, given his permission for her to wed her beloved Valiant? They would hardly recognize the proud and beautiful Francesca Pietro d'Angelo in the girl she had become. The servant with tangled hair, and her hands with their broken nails, rough from doing laundry.

Francesca felt a tiny surge of her old pride, and kept her head low so that no one would recognize her. She had hoped to reenter the castle quietly, pretending to be a serving wench hired for the day. Then she might have sought out news of her own servants and departed quietly amid the excitement of the celebration for Rafaello's wedding. They crossed the oak drawbridge and Francesca was shocked to see Terza standing with Sister Maria Annunziata and Sister Maria Benigna. Her tiring woman's face lit first with joy and then distress seeing the condition her young mistress was in.

"What was done to you?" she exclaimed as the guardsman lifted Francesca down from his horse. "Mother of all mercies, come quickly! I need to get you at least in a tub before your *madre* sees you." She grasped Francesca's hand, and, almost running, the two nuns by her side, hurried the surprised girl from the courtyard and into the castle.

"Where are we going?" Francesca asked Terza. "And are you telling me that my mother is here in Terreno Boscoso? How? Oh, *Madre di Dios*, are my parents forced to pay the duke an indemnity for my bad behavior? I just want to go home, Terza!"

"You are home," her serving woman said in a stern voice as they entered what Francesca remembered was her old apartment. "You certainly took your time returning from the forest, and everyone was terrified when your horse returned to the stables without you. They thought you might have been eaten by wolves, but no sign of remains could be found. Roza! Here she is, and not a moment too soon. Is the tub ready for her?"

"Yes, Mistress Terza," the servant girl said. "Welcome back, my lady."

If Francesca had been confused before, she was even more confused now. They practically tore off her clothing and hustled her into the large steaming tub. The hot scented water brought tears to her eyes as it covered her from neck to toes. The warmth seeped into her, and without even realizing it she sighed gustily. It had been months since she had had a decent wash. She could hardly move, it felt so good.

Terza was fussing with her hair, undoing the thick plait, searching through her tresses, and finally pronouncing in a satisfied tone, "No nits! Praise the blessed Mother for small favors!"

Francesca gasped as a pitcher of hot water was dumped over her head. Then Terza began scrubbing the girl's head vigorously. "You've not had your hair properly washed in months. Have you?" she said, not waiting for an answer. "It will have to be clean considering the work I must do to make you look respectable today."

"I just want to go home," Francesca said. "I only came back for you on the chance you had not already been sent home."

"Foolish girl!" Terza said fondly. "Why would I go back to Florence when you are here?" She rinsed her mistress's hair, washed it again, rinsed it a second time, and then wrapped it in a hot towel to begin drying. "Roza, see to her fingernails, dearie, will you? Her hands look like that of a common servant wench."

"I've been a servant," Francesca attempted to explain. "How do you think I survived all these months?"

They paid absolutely no attention to her. The two nuns prayed, smiling, while Terza and young Roza saw to Francesca's toilette as they chattered away. A servant she didn't recognize hurried in with a tray, and the girl realized that she was hungry. She was taken from the tub, dried, massaged, creamed, and finally, in a clean chemise, allowed to eat. The soup was hot and flavorful. The bread was still warm from the ovens, and it dripped with butter. Francesca couldn't ever recall having eaten anything that good. She was so concentrated on the food, she hardly realized her toenails were being trimmed and buffed.

The door to the bedchamber opened, and Orianna Pietro d'Angelo entered the room. She stared hard at Francesca. "You have caused more difficulty for us than even the other one, and I did not believe such a thing possible," she said in a cold voice. "But you are back, and the duke assures me you were safe all winter and are unscathed. I am astounded he still wants you for his daughter-in-law, Francesca. At least we have kept this scandal from Florentine society and protected your sisters' reputations from any taint of your willfulness, and that of the other one. I pray the blessed Mother that Lucianna and Giulia—or Serena, as she now styles herself, preferring her second name, but no matter—will be easier to marry off than you have been."

"Is my father here too?" Francesca asked quietly.

"Aye, he is," Orianna answered. "Your behavior has aged him, Francesca."

"I am sorry," the girl replied.

Her mother snorted as if she did not believe her daughter. She turned to Terza. "Can she be prepared to look her part this day?"

"Yes, mistress, she can. The grime is gone now. Her hair is clean. It is just her hands that will take months to be repaired, but for today we will cover them in lace," Terza said cheerfully.

"Then I will leave you to your task," Orianna said, and without another word to her daughter she exited the girl's spacious apartment.

"Well, the worst is over now," Terza said with a grin.

"It was not as bad as I anticipated," Francesca said with a show of her old spirit. She was beginning to feel more like herself again with all the cosseting they were giving her. "Am I really to marry the old duke's son today, Terza?"

"He was distraught when you disappeared into the forest," Terza told her. "He led the searchers himself until he learned you were safe at the inn his father maintains for his huntsmen. It was decided to leave you there, for the duke believed if you were forced to return you would run away again."

Francesca was very quiet with this knowledge. So they had known all along where she was and they had left her there. Briefly she felt anger, but then she laughed to herself. Duke Titus was a wise old man. He had understood her when no one else had.

She would eventually thank him for it. But not today. Today she must wed his son, Rafaello, and make her peace with him. She would never love him, for her heart had remained in the forest with Carlo the huntsman. It was he she loved, and she would always love him. He would never know what happened to her, and it was quite unlikely they would ever meet again.

But she had been given a second chance when the truth was she didn't deserve it at all. But she would take it, and she would make her husband a good wife. In the end it didn't matter if a woman loved her husband. Such a thing was rare. A woman loved her children. It was to her children she gave her all. Orianna had certainly shown her that. Her desire for her children's happiness did not mean it always turned out as she wanted it, but Bianca had been happy with her choices even if her mother had not been. And Francesca knew her mother would enjoy returning to Florence and bragging of her second daughter's marriage to the young duke of Terreno Boscoso.

She was bathed and fed. Terza saw that her mistress's hands and face were cleansed of her meal. Francesca brushed her teeth with a real brush for the first time in months. Her mouth felt wonderful as she rinsed. She chewed the small mint leaves Terza gave her to make her breath even fresher.

"There is no time for you to nap," Terza said. "Your wedding is set for high noon in the cathedral. We just have time for you to dress."

"I understand," Francesca replied. Then she stood quietly as they dressed her first in silk stockings that were rolled up her legs and fastened with garters made of white rosettes, a fresh chemise, and an underskirt of the finest cream-colored silk brocade, its center portion beautifully embroidered with tiny gold and silver stars settled over the underskirts. An overskirt of cream silk fell away over it, leaving the underskirt's embroidery visible. Now came her fitted bodice, the neckline low and square, edged in tiny pearls and delicate lace embroidery. Her sleeves were simple, long and fitted with graceful wide cuffs turned back to reveal more embroidered gold and silver stars.

"Your mama carried this gown all the way from Florence," Terza told her.

"It fits perfectly," Francesca marveled, turning to preen slightly in a full-length glass that had come with her from Florence a year ago and been the envy of both Aceline and Louisa. "Where is Louisa?" she asked Terza as she thought again of her friend.

"Wed to her Valiant and with a big belly now. You will see her soon, child, for once they returned from Genoa she would not leave the castle until you were returned safely and wed to Rafaello," Terza told her mistress.

"Oh, I am glad!" Francesca exclaimed.

There was a knock upon the apartment door, and Roza hurried to admit Master Pietro d'Angelo.

"*Padre!*" Francesca cried and hurried to catch up his hands and kiss them.

"You gave us quite a fright, daughter." He greeted her with a smile. "But all is well now and you shall shortly be wed, to your *madre*'s relief."

"I realize what a fool I've been," Francesca admitted to him. "I am fortunate to have this second chance, *Padre*."

"You are," he agreed. Then he offered her his hand. "Come and I will escort you to the church."

"Wait!" Francesca said suddenly. "I need just a moment alone, and then we will go." She turned quickly and hurried back into her bedchamber, shutting the door behind her. What was happening to her? Was this a dream? From the moment she had awakened this morning in Barbetta's cottage until now, the time had raced by. Her appearance after several months' absence seemed to have surprised no one except possibly Francesca herself. They all behaved as if she had gone for a prenuptial retreat and nothing more.

Everyone except her mother had behaved as if she had hardly been gone at all. If it had not been for Orianna's sharp tongue reminding her of her faults and the condition of her own hands, Francesca might have believed she had dreamed the past seven months.

And what of her betrothed, Rafaello? She had not seen him yet. Was he going to behave as if her disappearance was nothing? Why hadn't they found another bride for him? Why did it have to be her?

A gentle rap sounded upon the door. "Francesca," her father's voice called.

"I am coming, *Padre*," she answered. Aye, why her? And could she ever love this man they insisted on marrying her to today? Would she ever feel for Rafaello the longing that Carlo had engendered within her maiden breast? She silently thanked her huntsman now for leaving her virginity intact. Rafaello would have no complaints about that, nor could there be any doubt as to the legitimacy of any heir she produced. Her mother's practical nature was suddenly blooming within her. Reaching out, Francesca turned the handle on her bedchamber door and opened it. "I am ready, *Padre*," she told her father.

Giovanni Pietro d'Angelo escorted his daughter through the corridor and down the wide staircase outside to the courtyard, where the two horses awaited them. Francesca was carefully boosted onto a snow-white palfrey; the lead line was handed to her father, who had quickly mounted a fine roan-colored gelding as his daughter was assisted. It was but a short distance to the little cathedral in the town. As they rode surrounded by guardsmen in deep blue and gold uniforms, the silk merchant spoke to his daughter.

"You were obviously not mistreated during your time away from us," he said carefully. He knew little of what had transpired.

"I was fortunate to come upon the duke's inn," Francesca explained. "He keeps it for his huntsmen to shelter in during the winter months. The innkeeper took me in, and I was her servant."

Her father looked briefly incredulous. "*You*? A serving wench? I cannot believe it. Surely you told her who you were, daughter."

"Look at my hands, *Padre*," Francesca said, holding one out. "Beneath these delicate lace coverings Terza has put on me are the hands of a serving girl. Rough and able. I will never again treat a servant with scorn, *Padre*. I know now how hard they toil." Then she laughed. "Only a few days ago I was scrubbing the garments of a huntsman who was shortly returning to his post in the duke's forest. His name was Pippino, and he was most grateful to go back to his part of the forest with garments no longer infested with fleas. I learned to cook too, and nurse ailments less delicate than those I was taught by my *madre*."

Giovanni laughed in spite of himself. It was unthinkable that his beautiful daughter had done the things she was telling him, and yet he knew she did not lie. "What can you cook?" he asked her, very curious.

"I make an excellent rabbit stew," she told him proudly, "and I can boil pasta without overcooking it."

The silk merchant shook his head, half-surprised, half-proud at this little list of her accomplishments. "I think we will keep this knowledge from your *madre*, who would be horrified to learn you are able to cook such hearty fare, but one day I should like to taste your pasta if you will prepare it for me with oil and cheese. I do not like these new sauces that are becoming so fashionable in Florence and Rome."

Francesca smiled warmly at her parent. "One day, *Padre*, I promise," she said, but she wondered if she would ever again help to prepare a meal as she had with Alonza.

Suddenly the sides of the roadway were filled with cheering citizens, more and more of them as they drew closer to the cathedral itself. The flowerboxes of the buildings lining their way were overflowing with June blooms that actually scented the air about them. People hung from the windows and leaned from rooftops to get a glimpse of the bride they had waited so long to see.

Francesca wondered as she rode slowly towards the cathedral what they would think of their new *duchessa*. Did they know she had run away after having been chosen as Rafaello's bride late last summer? Or had her escapade been kept secret? Didn't they wonder why it had taken so long for the wedding to take place? Or perhaps nothing had been said at all, and the citizens of Terreno Boscoso had only been informed recently of the wedding to take place.

They reached the cathedral square. The church was not, by Florentine standards, particularly large. Francesca thought Santa Anna's was larger, but the stone building had impressive wide steps leading up to the open cathedral doors. She sat quietly as her father dismounted. Then a guardsman lifted the bride carefully from her saddle. Giovanni Pietro d'Angelo escorted Francesca up the stairs into the cathedral, where Terza was already awaiting them.

The serving woman quickly brushed her mistress's hair so that the red-gold curls flowed in ripples down the bride's back. Then, to Francesca's surprise, Terza set a circlet of pearls and small sparkling diamonds upon her head. "The old duke wanted you to have it," the servant said. "His late wife wore it at their wedding."

Francesca's eyes filled a moment with bright tears, which Terza quickly brushed away. "How kind he is," the girl said.

"Aye," Terza agreed, "and very fond of you despite your behavior."

There was a flourish of trumpets, and Master Pietro d'Angelo took his daughter by the hand, leading her down the cathedral's center aisle to where the duke and his son awaited her. Francesca swallowed hard as she focused her eyes on the two men. The older was smiling warmly, his eyes twinkling with his pleasure. The younger, standing by his father's side, was solemn. Not a hint of a smile touched his handsome face. Oddly Francesca understood his demeanor. Her flight last autumn had been a rejection of sorts of his decision to wed her. And obviously his father had forced him to await her return.

It was obvious he was not pleased, although he would do the old duke's bidding because he was a dutiful son.

As Francesca walked slowly towards Rafaello Cesare, past the church filled with the small nobility of Terreno Boscoso, and perhaps some near neighbors, she wondered what her life would have been like if she had wed Carlo, her beloved huntsman, and gone to live with him deep in the forest. His face would not have been grim with a duty to be done if she had walked up a church aisle towards him. He would have been smiling at her, and her heart would have soared with happiness, knowing she would soon be his wife and they would be together forever.

Francesca knew now she could have left her old life behind as her older sister, Bianca, had so easily done. Left it behind for love. But it was too late for love. She had a duty to do, and she would do it. As she passed her mother she could see Orianna was delicately dabbing at her eyes with a dainty linen and lace handkerchief. But when their gazes met Francesca saw the triumph in her maternal parent's fine eyes. Orianna had finally gotten her way, and her second daughter would shortly become the new *duchessa* of Terreno Boscoso. Lucianna and Giulia would not be undervalued in the marriage market now. She nodded slightly at her mother in acknowledgment.

They had now reached the marble steps below the beautiful altar where the duke and Rafaello awaited them. Without a word Giovanni Pietro d'Angelo placed his daughter's hand in that of her bridegroom's, then stepped back to join his spouse. The old bishop of Terreno Boscoso, with the assistance of Father Silvio, performed the marriage ceremony. Rafaello's strong voice answered the holy queries. Francesca's voice was as firm. She was not going to whisper her vows like some simpering fool. If she was to wed him, then let the whole world hear her replies. It pleased her to see the brief surprise upon his handsome face as she spoke in a sure voice.

Finally, to her relief, the ceremony was completed. Bride and groom rose from the gilded prie-dieu with their red velvet kneelers. The cathedral bells began to ring out a joyful peal, to be joined by the few churches in the town and the nearby vicinity. The bishop had unwrapped their two hands after the blessing, and now Rafaello led Francesca back down the aisle. He had not yet spoken a word to her, and she had no intention of speaking to him until he did so.

They descended the steps of the cathedral to where the troupe of guardsmen waited with their horses. He mounted his own animal, leaving the surprised captain of the guard to lift Francesca back onto her white palfrey. She thanked him softly, and the captain flushed shyly. Their horses moved off surrounded by their ceremonial guard, which wended its way through the town and the deliriously happy crowds, who called out their good wishes to the young man about to become their new duke and his bride. Francesca could not help but smile and wave her acknowledgment in return.

Now and again the crowds pressed them so closely they were stopped momentarily in their passage. Several small children pressed flowers upon Francesca, their small grubby hands touching hers. She smiled at them, patted their heads, and blew kisses to them, which set the crowds about her to cheering louder. It seemed to her that there were more people in the streets now than there had been earlier. They filled the road right up to the castle's drawbridge, where their horses finally came to a stop.

Rafaello dismounted, leaving the captain of the guard to once again help Francesca from her animal. She was beginning to be angry. Why was he being so damned rude to her? But then he was offering her his hand to lead her inside to the Great Hall, where the wedding guests were now crowding about, waiting for the bride and bridegroom to come and begin the feast. Francesca heard a squeal of delight, and turned to be embraced by her old friend, Louisa di Genoa, now married to Rafaello's best friend, Valiant.

"Francesca! Ohh, I am so glad you are back and safe!" Louisa cried happily.

The bride stepped back apace. "Look at you, Louisa!" she exclaimed, staring at her friend's enormous belly. "When is the child due?"

"Any minute," Louisa said laughing. "Valiant wanted his heir born on his estates at Sponda di Fiume, but I refused to leave the ducal castle until you were back and wed. Now I can't go until the child is born, but that is all right, since I want you to be his godmother. Will you? Oh, please say you will!"

"Of course," Francesca replied. "I am honored that you would ask me."

"You will introduce me to your friend, Francesca," Orianna Pietro d'Angelo said, coming up to stand next to her daughter.

"*Madre*, this is Louisa Maria di Genoa. She is married to my husband's best friend, Valiant. That is why Rafaello chose me. He would not take the maiden his dearest companion had fallen in love with, and the French girl was a perfect bitch. He had no other choice but me," Francesca told her mother bluntly. "So be careful when you boast on my marriage once you have returned to Florence. Rafaello did not choose me for my beauty or my wealth or even my charm. He had no other choice."

Orianna flushed, embarrassed at her daughter's words. "Francesca!" was all she could think of to say.

"Mama is very proud of this marriage I have made, Louisa," the bride continued.

"You see, when my older sister was widowed she ran off with a very unsuitable man, a Turk. We no longer speak of Bianca. Do we, *Madre*? So my marriage today to Duke Titus's son is quite a coup for her. Isn't it, now, *Madre*?"

"Do not be cruel, Francesca," Orianna replied, startled by her daughter's boldness. "It does not suit you at all, and especially on such a happy day."

"Happy for whom?" Francesca persisted. "Have you seen Rafaello smile once yet?"

"Oh, he is just nervous," Louisa said cheerfully. "You should have seen Valiant on our wedding day, with my papa looking so sternly at him and threatening him with all manner of punishment if he made me the least bit unhappy." She laughed at the memory.

"You hope for a son, of course," Orianna said, attempting to add to the change of subject. "Marco was easy to birth. All my sons were. It was the girls who gave me difficulty," the older woman said. "Even when I had the twins. There was Luca born before I barely had time to reach the birthing chamber, but his sister, Lucianna? It was hours before she finally came, but she has proven the most obedient of all my daughters."

"We'll see what happens when you attempt to wed her off, *Madre*," Francesca said with a knowing chuckle.

Orianna paled slightly, but then recovering, said, "Lucianna is too young yet to even consider marrying off. It is to be hoped in a few years, when she is ready, any memories she may have of you and the other one will have gone from her head."

Rafaello was suddenly by her side. He led her to the high board, seating her between himself and his father.

Duke Titus greeted her warmly, saying, "Did you enjoy your winter in the forest, my dear?" His eyes were twinkling at her.

Francesca laughed. "Actually I did," she admitted. "Alonza was very good to me, my lord. Did she know who I was?"

He chortled, but then said, "No, she did not. All she was told was that you were of importance to us and to keep you safe until spring, when I would tell her when to bring you to the castle. She is here in the hall today with her family to help us celebrate your marriage to my son. I have known Alonza for many a year. I knew I could entrust her with your safety. I am sorry you felt it necessary to run away, Francesca. If your parents' decision upset you, you might have come to me. Whatever happens in the future, remember that Titus Cesare is your friend. I will help you solve your problems, for I knew the moment I set eyes upon you that you were the one for Rafaello."

"You are kind, my lord," Francesca answered him, "but we both know Rafaello chose me to be his wife because Louisa was obviously in love with Valiant, and the du Barry girl was a shrew. I was all he had left."

"You are wrong, my dear," her father-in-law told her, "but I will allow you and Rafaello to discover the error of your ways," he chuckled. "Old men have sharper eyes than do the young." He patted her hand, then said, "Ah, I see Alonza did not spare you any hard work, did she? No matter, a few months and those beautiful hands will heal."

"I found I did not mind the work," Francesca admitted to him. "For the first time in all of my life I felt useful and very happy."

The duke nodded, smiling. "Having a purpose in life other than one's self will do that to a person," he told her. "Now, I know you will make Terreno Boscoso a fine *duchessa*, Francesca. There is much to be done."

"Will you guide me, my lord?" she asked shyly.

"Gladly!" he answered her. "Gladly!"

A fine feast was served to all in the hall. Roasted boar, fish from the waters of the forest streams and lakes, venison, stuffed geese, roasted ducks, and capons. There were salads with lettuces and new peas; pastas in many shapes with olive oil, black olives, and the fresh grated Parmesan that was made in a town just outside of Terreno Boscoso. Within the town, bread, meat, pasta, wine, and ale were offered to every citizen. There were marzipan sweets for everyone, and in the hall cakes soaked in wine with fresh strawberries and fresh cream. The duke did not stint his guests, and served them only the finest wines from his own cellars and vineyards. Those who preferred ale could fill their mugs from the casks scattered about the hall.

There was a musicians' gallery above the entry to the hall, and soft music was played throughout the meal. The men got up and danced for the entertainment of everyone. And while they were thus engaged, Francesca and several women quietly departed the hall. Led by Terza, the bride was taken not back to her maiden chamber, but to the apartment she would now share with her new husband. Once there Francesca sent all of them but Terza away. She was tired, and not in the mood for the usual loud and slightly vulgar merriment that could be part of a bride's bedding.

Orianna protested. "I must tell you what to expect from your bridegroom," she said to her daughter.

"*Madre*, I think I should prefer to have my husband instruct me in these matters," Francesca answered.

Orianna would have protested further, but she saw immediately that her daughter's speech had found favor with several of the older noblewomen of the court who had accompanied them. They nodded in agreement, and one of them said aloud, "The young *duchessa* shows great wisdom in her decision." Then the women all curtsied to Francesca and backed from the bedchamber. Orianna had no choice but to kiss her daughter and bid her happiness before joining them and departing the apartment.

"That old biddy was the chancellor's wife. She'll be an important ally to have here at court," Terza said as she and Roza undressed Francesca.

When the bride was naked she bathed in a basin of lightly scented warm water, and then clothed herself in a clean light silk chemise. Terza took the pins and jeweled décor from Francesca's beautiful hair. She brushed the girl's tresses, asking, "Will you leave it loose, or will you have me braid it?"

"Leave it loose," Francesca said.

They helped her into the large bridal bed, and then both servants bid their mistress good night. Terza had made certain there was a nice fire in the little fireplace, for though it was June the evening was still chilly. They had drawn the curtains for privacy's sake.

Francesca lay quietly in the big bed. She could hear the faint murmur of sound from the hall below. Outside a nightingale began to sing. But her bridegroom did not come. She tried hard to remain awake, but she could not. Sleep overtook her, and her heavy eyelids closed. She attempted to force them open, but they only closed again. Whatever fault she had committed that had kept Rafaello silent this day would surely be compounded by his finding her asleep on their wedding night instead of waiting for him. But, damn him, it had to be at least an hour since she had left the hall. If he found the company of his guests and the wine more inviting than his bride, then it served him right if she sought her rest. Francesca gave herself up to sleep.

Chapter 9

She awoke suddenly, realizing as she did that there was someone else within her bedchamber. The fire in the hearth had died to embers, and darkness surrounded her. But there was someone here. Was it Rafaello? Would he continue to remain silent as he had this past day? "Who is here?" she asked in a slightly shaky voice.

The curtain from one of the windows moved and the shadow of a large man revealed itself. "Cara, my love," the deep rough voice said.

Her heart almost exploded within her chest. "No! It cannot be you! It cannot!"

"Have you forgotten me so quickly, then, my love?" he murmured as he came and sat upon the bed.

"*Carlo! Carlo!* Is it really you?" she half whispered. She reached out to him.

"It is me, my love," he told her. "Surely you didn't believe I could desert you."

"You cannot be here!" she told him, sitting up in her bed. "I am a married woman. Wed this day to Duke Titus's son, Rafaello. You must go! Go quickly! Even now I am awaiting my bridegroom."

"He is drunk in his father's hall, my love," Carlo said. "He will not come to you."

"But I am his wife, no matter," Francesca said, and she began to cry. "Why did you not come this morning, before the guardsmen came and brought me to the castle? If you had come then I should have gone with you, no matter what. But you did not come. When they came to get me I was afraid. I thought surely Rafaello was to wed another. I had no idea the old duke had known all along where I was. That I was still meant to be his son's bride." She gave a little sob. "If only you had come first," she repeated.

"Does he want you as I want you?" Carlo demanded of her. "If he did he would already be here, so now I must do what he has not." He pulled her up from the bed, his arms wrapping about her as he bent to kiss her.

At first Francesca melted into his arms, her lips eagerly accepting his passionate kiss. *Yes!* This was what she wanted. The man she loved and who loved her. Carlo. Her beloved huntsman. His kiss deepened. Her response equaled his. And then the reality of her situation slammed into her. With a little cry she pushed him away. "No!" she said in a shaking voice. "No!"

"My love . . ." he began, reaching for her again.

She ducked away from him, scooting to put her marriage bed between them. "I should not have allowed you to kiss me now," she began.

"I love you," he told her.

"I know," Francesca answered him, "and I love you. But I will not sully the vows I took today in the cathedral to be a good and faithful wife to Rafaello Cesare. Tomorrow we shall again go to the cathedral, where Duke Titus will turn over his authority to my husband. The bishop will then make Rafaello the new Duke of Terreno Boscoso, and I, as his wife, will be designated the new *duchessa*. I will not soil the honor of the Cesare or the Pietro d'Angelo families by any dishonest behavior. The time for us is past, Carlo."

"You are sending me away?" he said softly.

"Reluctantly, but aye," Francesca answered him.

"Can you really live without love, *cara mia*?" he queried her closely.

"If I must, I will," she told him. "It would seem I am my mother's daughter after all," Francesca said with a wry smile. "She left the man she loved in Venice and made the marriage to my father that her parents wished her to make. Hopefully Rafaello and I will become fond of one another as she and my father have. I will bear my husband's children without complaint, as she did hers. I will teach my offspring honor and respect as my mother taught me." Reaching out she put a hand on his arm. "My mother never forgot the man she loved in Venice. I will always love you, my beloved huntsman. Now go before we are discovered. I cannot allow my reputation to be challenged, and if you were caught here they would kill you without hesitation."

"Kiss me farewell at least, Cara," he said, but she shook her head.

"Go," she said, turning her back on him. Then she waited wordlessly until she sensed he was gone, and, turning, saw she was again alone. Francesca climbed back into her bed, where she lay restlessly for several hours before finally falling asleep once again.

She felt drained of all emotion and could not even cry, with the mixture of anger and frustration that she was feeling that she must send away the man she loved while the man she had married but several hours back could not be bothered to come to her bed.

Terza woke her an hour after the dawn had broken. Puzzled, she looked at the unsullied bridal bed, as neat as it had been the night before but for the side where her young mistress had obviously slept undisturbed.

"No, he did not come," Francesca answered her servant's unspoken question. "He obviously remained in the hall, drinking himself into oblivion. Keep my mother away from me, if you can, for she will certainly have questions that any mother would ask her daughter the morning after her wedding. What can I possibly say to her that will not set her into a fury, should she learn I spent my wedding night alone?"

"*Madre di Dios!*" Terza groaned. "You are correct."

"And I cannot have my father-in-law distressed by his son's lack of action," Francesca said. "He has been so good to me and so patient with my behavior."

Terza nodded. " 'Tis true. He is a kind man, Duke Titus." Then she clapped her hand to her mouth. "The bedsheet! They will want to fly the bedsheet to prove that your husband did his duty."

"We'll strip the bed and burn the sheet in the hearth. I will tell them I consider such a thing undignified. Certainly Rafaello will not disagree with my attempt to hide his neglect of me, and the old duke will go along for my sake," Francesca said.

Before even little Roza arrived with her mistress's breakfast

tray, Terza and Francesca tore the sheet from the bed and saw
it devoured by the flames of the newly revived fire in the hearth.
Rafaello Cesare's lapse was now their secret. The bride bathed
quickly in a basin and began to dress for the ceremony at the
cathedral, which would be held in late morning. She ate her
meal in her chemise before being dressed. The gown she would
wear to be crowned the new *duchessa* of Terreno Boscoso was
the sea blue and gold colors of the duchy flag. The underskirt
that showed between the two panels of the divided overskirt
was cloth of gold. The rest of the gown was sea blue. The low
square neckline was heavily embroidered with gold, diamonds,
and pearls, as was the hem of the skirt. The sleeves were close-
fitted to the wrists but had deep turned-back cuffs with embroidered edges.

"You must now wear your hair in a more elegant style, as it
is assumed you are no longer a maid," Terza said softly to her
mistress. Then she brushed out the long red-gold hair and affixed it into a chignon that sat low on her mistress's neck.

Francesca stared into the mirror. She suddenly looked older.
And seductive, she thought. "I like it," she said.

"We'll just put this jeweled band on your head, and a wisp
of veiling," Terza suggested, and her mistress nodded in agreement.

Roza was giddy with excitement as she held open Francesca's jewel chest for her mistress. The gemstones sparkled in the
morning sunlight coming through the bedchamber windows.

"What would you choose?" Francesca asked the girl.

After a moment of initial surprise Roza immediately drew
out a pair of sapphire and gold ear bobs. When Francesca nodded, the girl affixed them in her mistress's ears.

"What else?" Francesca said.

"Pearls," Roza replied. "The bodice of the gown is heavily decorated, my lady. The elegance of a long strand of pearls is more than enough."

"Indeed, girl. You have a good eye for this," Francesca approved, ducking her head slightly as Roza dropped the long creamy length of pearls over her lady's head.

Terza nodded her own approval, and Roza beamed proudly. She very much wanted to serve her new *duchessa* the best she could. Being chosen by Terza to help the upper servant with her mistress had been quite a coup for the younger woman.

Francesca slipped her feet into a pair of deep blue sollerets that had been made in Florence for her. The leather was soft and comfortable on her feet. She stood reaching out into the still-open jewel case for several rings she slid onto her fingers. Holding out her fingers, she looked and was satisfied. Even after a day, the cream Terza rubbed into her hands seemed to be helping to ease the roughness.

Roza ran to answer a knock on the outer apartment door. They heard her say, "Tell him that she is ready and will meet him in the courtyard." Then she hurried back to tell her mistress, "Your noble husband sent his serving man to see if you were ready."

"Of course," Francesca said as she walked from her apartment with Terza and Roza in her wake. The arrogant dog, she thought, irritated. He could not be bothered to come himself. Probably still suffering from the excesses of his overindulgence. She walked proudly down the stairs leading to the courtyard and stepped out into the morning. Terza handed her a pair of gold-colored leather gloves when she had been helped up onto her mount. Francesca glanced about and saw her husband.

Rafaello did not look like a man who had spent the night

drinking. Indeed he looked quite healthy. His color was good. His hands did not shake. He nodded curtly at her in greeting. Francesca nodded back. He was garbed in blue and gold, as she was.

Duke Titus came from the castle, and, mounting his horse, put himself between them. "Good morning, my children!" he said cheerfully. "I am happy to finally see this day come when I may lay down my duties, and you, my son, may take on a burden more suited to younger, stronger shoulders. And you will have your good wife by your side, which is a true blessing, and now we have the hope of heirs as well."

"I am honored that you would entrust me with even the small responsibility of being the *duchessa* of Terreno Boscoso," Francesca said before her husband might speak. "And with God's own blessing we will give you grandchildren all in good time, my lord."

She turned her head as she spoke to smile sweetly at Rafaello. "Is that not so, my lord?"

He is a worthy opponent, Francesca thought, as her bridegroom nodded at his father.

"In time, Father," he said, "it is hoped we will be blessed with children."

"Especially considering my mother's fertility," Francesca added. The wily dog must certainly do his duty by her tonight. If he avoided her bedchamber much longer, the whole castle would know, and they would talk. She had sent the man she loved away so she would not compromise her new family's good name. Her husband would get children on her if for no other reason than he did not want to disappoint his sire.

Francesca almost laughed aloud at the absurdity of the situation. She was young, beautiful, and came with a more-than-plump dower portion. The serving girl she had been was desperately desired by a simple hunter, yet the *duchessa* she was about to become was obviously not desired by her husband. What on earth was the matter with him, and why would he not speak to her? Certainly tonight he would rectify his omission of last night.

They rode again through the cheering crowds in the small town and ascended the steps to the cathedral once again. Inside Titus Cesare abdicated his ducal crown in favor of his son, Rafaello Titus. The red-gold headband was moved from the older man's snow-white head to the dark head of his only child. Prayers of thanks were given for the peaceful and prosperous reign of Duke Titus. Prayers of hope were offered that Duke Rafaello's reign would be as auspicious and pacific. And then Francesca was crowned as Rafaello's wife, his *duchessa*. Prayers were offered for her fertility that the house of Cesare would prosper and continue.

Francesca appeared demure and dignified as the old bishop with shaking hands set the smaller crown upon her veiled head. She rose and, turning with her husband, faced the crowded cathedral. Both of them were smiling upon their guests and subjects.

"*Long live the duke! Long live the* duchessa!" The cries rang out first inside, and then as they came outside again to stand at the top of the cathedral steps, the shouts and good wishes echoed from all the people crowded into the square. Without even being instructed to do so Francesca raised her hand and acknowledged the cheers with a wave of her elegant gloved hand. There was applause now along with the cheers.

"You know how to play to the crowd," Rafaello growled low at her.

She turned a dazzling smile upon him, and, reaching up, touched his face. "I was born to be your *duchessa*," she told him.

He caught her hand and kissed it. "I can play the game too, darling."

The crowds below them went wild with their delight at this show of affection between the newly wed and now newly crowned duke and his *duchessa* bride.

"If you do not come to me tonight I shall complain to your father," she told him sweetly. "He wants grandchildren, and it will be difficult to give them to him without some cooperation on your part, *darling*," she purred at him. "Give me a half-dozen or so of sons and daughters and you may go back to your mistress or whatever it was that kept you from our bridal bed."

"And you may go back to your rough woodsman, then, for all I care," he answered her coldly, though his lips were smiling for the benefit of the populace.

Francesca gasped with her surprise, but then she said, "I am no wanton, my lord. You will find me a virgin if you will bother to get into my bed and do what you should. I never betrayed you with another man, nor would I even, given the opportunity. Like you, I have my pride. I will never allow doubt to taint your heirs. If you had taken the time to know me instead of just choosing me because the French girl was such a bitch and Louisa was in love with another, you would have known it. But you picked me for your bride only because I appeared to be the only unblemished fruit in the basket you were offered!"

He led her down the cathedral steps, setting her back upon her palfrey before mounting his own animal. Her words stung him because they were true. His father had forced him into choosing a bride because God only knew Rafaello wouldn't have himself, for he was having too much fun as a bachelor. A man without a wife could hunt and wench and drink until dawn. A man with a wife could hunt as long as he brought home game for dinner, and before dusk. He couldn't wench with anyone but his wife unless he was a complete cad, which Rafaello wasn't. And as for drinking with boon companions until the sun came up, well, a married man had to bed his wife and beget heirs.

Born late to his parents, he had been spoiled and indulged. When his mother had died he and his father were even closer. Rafaello was glad of that, for Duke Titus was an intelligent man and a great wit. It had pleased his son to emulate him. But his father knew him too well, which was why he now found himself with a beautiful wife who hadn't wanted to marry him at all, much to his surprise. Girls always wanted to marry him. Francesca hadn't, however. She had even run into the forest to escape him and their shared fate. Only good fortune had kept her from a wretched end, and she had come upon the huntsmen's winter inn. As they now rode through the town returning to the castle and another day long feasting on too-rich foods and too much wine, Rafaello Cesare considered what had followed when they had learned Francesca was safe.

"She doesn't want to wed me," he had told his father. "Send her back to her family. I'll find a wife eventually."

"Hah!" his father had said scornfully. "I know you better than that, Rafaello. No, we made a mistake in rushing the girl. She is proud and strong, but like all women she wants to be appreciated for her finer qualities."

"I appreciated her pretty breasts and sweet lips," he had answered his sire, only to receive a cuff to his head.

"She is like any other girl, my son. She wants to be courted and perhaps even fall in love. But if she doesn't fall in love, at least let her know you like her, you enjoy her company, you are proud to take her as your wife."

And it was then Rafaello Cesare had taken it upon himself

to spend the winter months at the inn in a persona he had sometimes affected since his late teens, when one day he had joined a party of his father's huntsmen as Carlo, who usually lived so deep in the forest he was more legend than truth. Now and again over the years that followed Carlo would appear among the woodsmen, always welcome, for he easily fit in with them. He could bring down a deer with a single arrow, a skill they all admired. He paid his small gambling debts with them and was an honest friend to all.

Only Alonza knew his true identity, for she had once been a castle servant and had tenderly cared for Rafaello's mother when she lay dying. Duke Titus had been grateful to the faithful Alonza and had offered her anything she desired. On her suggestion he had seen the inn in his forest constructed to shelter his huntsmen in winter, and because she asked it of him, Duke Titus had put her in charge of the inn. Alonza explained to her master that she had had an older brother who had once been one of the duke's huntsmen. Caught in a bad winter storm with no shelter to be found, he had died, his decaying body not found until the following spring. But thanks to Alonza, the duke's huntsmen now had a safe shelter for the winter months.

And last winter the mysterious Carlo had joined them at the inn, where Alonza had a pretty new servant helping her. Rafaello had been fascinated to see the proud Francesca he had so briefly known shed her lofty persona as she learned to cook and clean. She even seemed to enjoy what she was doing. He was particularly impressed when Alonza had fallen ill and without any complaint Francesca had nursed her while managing the inn by herself. And his companions, always eager to bed one of Alonza's helpers, had shown only respect for the feisty girl, while he had fallen in love with her.

He might have considered himself fortunate, for she had returned his affections, but he had not been able to decide how to reveal his identity without drawing her anger.

And she would have been angry at having been tricked. Women, he had learned, did not enjoy having their delicate emotions toyed with by anyone, let alone a man.

The Francesca who had wed him so dutifully yesterday did not love Rafaello Cesare, her husband. She loved Carlo, a poor huntsman, and the new Duke of Terreno Boscoso couldn't figure out a way to reconcile the two for her. He had thought to reveal himself when he had crept into her bedchamber last night in his disguise, but instead he found a dutiful woman who would not betray her lawful husband even for the man she loved. Part of him was well pleased at her sense of honor, but as he exited her chamber through the window to get back to his own chamber, he found himself also disappointed. He had considered making passionate love to Francesca, revealing himself at the crucial moment as he captured her sweet innocence. But then he actually considered the sense of shame and betrayal she would feel at having yielded to her would-be lover only to discover he was actually her husband. Jesu! What was he to do?

They clopped over the castle drawbridge and into the courtyard, where a servant had Francesca down from her saddle even before Rafaello could dismount his own stallion. He helped his father instead. Inside the hall his new mother-in-law was preening as if she had been crowned *duchessa* and not Francesca. He wondered how soon they would leave Terreno Boscoso to return to Florence. It would be rude to ask, of course. He suspected that Francesca would not object to seeing her parents depart.

The days seemed to drag, unlike their wedding day, when everything had gone so quickly. At one point Rafaello had slipped from the hall and found his way into his father's gardens. To his surprise he saw his wife sitting quietly upon a marble bench near a small fish pond. He quietly joined her, saying, "The hall is too noisy and full of stinks."

"I like the smell of the gardens better too," Francesca answered him, "but I think I liked the forest best of all. The air is cleaner, and the sounds natural, purer."

"I suppose while we are so newly wed no one would mind if we went off to be by ourselves for a short while," he told her. "My father could manage for us. Don't you think? He certainly has the experience."

Francesca turned her head to look at him. "You like the forest?"

"Very much," he replied. "I have been running off into it ever since I was a boy. I like the freedom of it."

"As duke you will not have much freedom now," Francesca noted.

"I know, which is why I believe we should take this opportunity," he said.

"Run away?" Her green eyes twinkled with humor.

"Why not? I am the duke. Can I not do as I please?"

"I'm not sure," Francesca admitted. "I've never been wed to a duke. I think you must first consider what is good for the duchy before you act upon your own impulses."

Rafaello laughed aloud. "I think it would be a very good thing for our duchy if you and I slipped away after our long separation. My father has a little hunting lodge deep in the forest. We might go there for a few days. Just you and I. No servants."

"How will we eat?" she asked him.

"I will hunt. You will cook," he said.

Now it was Francesca's turn to laugh. "Perhaps we can

bring some food with us. Bread, cheese, meats already roasted, wine. Enough for three days and nights. Would you not rather spend your time with me than out in the forest, hunting our supper? Would you leave me alone by myself?"

"Let us go now while all the rest of our guests are more involved in eating our food, drinking our wine, and gossiping," he said. "And when we return they will all be gone. Perhaps even your mother and father."

"Oh, especially my mother," Francesca said. "My father I can tolerate, but my mother must return to Florence, where she may regain her strength and then begin to consider an even richer and more important husband for my next sister, Lucianna," Francesca said mockingly. Then she continued, "We must tell your father that we are going so he will not worry about us, and we must arrange for the food to sustain us in the next few days, and we must dress appropriately, for I have no intention of going into the forest in my coronation gown. As for any beasties you would hunt, they would laugh themselves to death at you in your fine blue and gold ducal garments. How near is this hunting lodge? It is already afternoon."

"If you can dress quickly, my *duchessa*, then we shall just be able to reach it by sunset," he promised her.

Francesca rose from the marble bench where they had been conversing. "I will meet you in the stables," she said. Then, turning, she hurried away from him.

Rafaello remained on the bench, considering what had just happened. Perhaps all was not lost. Was it possible that alone together in the forest, they might reach some sort of détente? Or would she be thinking of her huntsman? Was that the real reason she wanted to return to the woodlands? In hopes of finding her lover? But of course Carlo hadn't really been her lover at all, and he was Carlo. How was it he was jealous of himself? It was ridiculous. If he daren't tell her of the ruse he had played on her, then he would simply have to turn her girlish passion away from Carlo and to him. Rafaello laughed aloud at the ludicrous position in which he found himself. There is no fool, he thought to himself, like a man in love.

Returning to the castle he avoided the noisy hall and hurried upstairs, calling to Fidelio, his manservant, so he might change his clothing. He signaled to Matteo and when the servant came quickly to his side, he said, "Go and find my father in the hall. Tell him I would speak discreetly with him now. Then escort him back to me."

"Yes, my lord duke," Matteo said, and Rafaello looked startled briefly. Matteo grinned cheekily at him.

Rafaello laughed. "I am, aren't I?" He chuckled as Matteo ran off. Fidelio was awaiting him, and said nothing when his master asked for hunting clothes. "My bride and I are going to the forest lodge for a few days before we take up our duties," he said. "Pack lightly. There will be no servants accompanying us."

"Of course, my lord duke," Fidelio responded, as if this were an everyday request. "Shall I send Piero to notify the stables you will want two horses saddled and ready?"

"Yes, and tell them not to put a sidesaddle upon my wife's horse. She will want to ride astride," he said, hoping that he was right, for when she had run off into the forest she had been astride. The forest was no place for a woman to be dainty. Even as good a horsewoman as he knew Francesca to be.

He dressed quickly in woolen breeches, a chemise that served as a shirt, a sleeveless leather doublet. He pulled on his boots over woolen socks. Tucked a sharp knife in the leather knife case attached to his belt.

Fidelio handed him a cloak. "It could rain," he said. "Piero has taken a saddlebag with your essentials to the stables."

The apartment door opened and Duke Titus appeared. "My wine is so good that your absence has gone unnoticed, except by *Signora* Pietro d'Angelo, who has complained to me that she did not raise her daughter to be rude to her guests," the older man said.

"Francesca and I have decided to go to the forest lodge," Rafaello said. "We will remain a few days."

"Have you told her?" Duke Titus asked his son quietly.

Rafaello shook his head. "No, and I don't really know how to tell her. She fell in love with Carlo, and now I must turn her love from the huntsman who doesn't really exist to me, because I love her."

Duke Titus nodded, chuckling. "I must tell you, Rafaello, that I find your situation quite comical. Even I know if you tell her the truth right now she will be furious with you for perpetrating such a jest upon her. I think it is better you make her fall out of love with Carlo and in love with Rafaello. Francesca was ripe for seduction when she ran off last autumn, and a rough hunter certainly offered her something different than a civilized and proper suitor. Perhaps you need not be so mannerly with her now that she is your wife. Overwhelm her with the passion you feel for her. Push aside her maidenly fears, for despite her Florentine sophistication Francesca is still a virgin, my son."

"You know women far too well, Father," Rafaello teased his parent.

"And now that it is you who are the duke of this wee country, I shall again indulge my taste for variety. Discreetly, of course, but I am not dead yet, by any stretch of the imagination, my son. I will give you a week—no more. Then you must return and pick up the reins of your government, Rafaello, so I may have the time to enjoy my old age." Duke Titus bowed to his son, and then, turning abruptly, departed his presence.

The young duke laughed. He had seen his father eyeing the ladies of their small court these past few days. There were some very toothsome widows he had no doubt his father would soon be approaching for companionship. They were ladies of means who would understand what the duke sought of them and be quite willing to share themselves with such a virile and charming gentleman.

Rafaello bid his servants a brief farewell and went directly to the stables, where he found Francesca awaiting him. She was garbed in tight leather breeches and a silk shirt. "No, not the white palfrey," he heard her say. "I want the storm-gray gelding with the black mane and tail. Ah, here is my good lord. Quickly now!" She turned to greet him.

"They wanted me to ride that sweet dainty creature I parade through the town on, but she is not for the forest, my lord."

"I agree," he said. "The gelding is sturdier and will not suffer in the rougher terrain, madam." Out of the corner of his eye he saw that the stable boy was hesitating, waiting for his master's approval. "Did you not hear the *duchessa*, boy?" he said sharply.

"Do not dally. Fetch the gray. When your mistress gives you an order, you obey it."

"Yes, my lord!" The boy ran off to quickly restable the white mare and saddle the big gray gelding Francesca wanted.

"Thank you," she said.

"You are to be obeyed in all reasonable matters," he told her.

"What if I am unreasonable?" she teased him.

"We will thoroughly discuss any unreasonableness on your part, madam," he said to her seriously. "I prefer discussion. I do not want to have to beat my wife."

Francesca looked genuinely startled by his declaration. "You would beat me?"

"You will never, I am certain, drive me to such uncivilized behavior," he said with a wicked smile. "Will you, Francesca?"

She found herself shaking her head and saying meekly, "No, my lord, I will not drive you to barbaric behavior, for then I might have to respond in kind."

Rafaello found himself laughing at her response. He had forgotten how quick-witted she could be, and remembered the many times she had bested the poor Aceline du Barry. He wondered briefly if her father had found a husband for her. She was a girl who needed a man's guidance, unlike his new *duchessa*, who would have her own way, he suspected, in all she did.

The gray gelding was brought from the stables, and Francesca quickly, without any help, sprang into her saddle. "How much easier it is without all those skirts," she said, gathering the reins in her hands and urging her horse forward.

Together they clopped across the thick wooden drawbridge, and cantered into the forest upon a narrow but quite visible path. Francesca remembered that was how she had come last autumn when she had impulsively run away from an impending wedding she hadn't wanted. It had made no difference, however. They had just waited for her temper to cool, and now she was wed to the young duke.

They rode together for some time within the forest, the dappled sunlight pushing through the trees to enhance the beauty of the nature surrounding them. She followed Rafaello without asking questions, realizing after a time that they seemed to be going uphill. Ahead all she could see were trees. Behind them the forest seemed to close itself so that the path they traveled was no longer visible.

"How do you know where we are going?" she finally broke the silence to ask him.

"I've come this way ever since I was a boy," he replied. "I was five the first time my father brought me. My mother was not fond of the forest. It frightened her. She preferred the open spaces of the land around the castle, where she might easily see the sky," he explained. "I hope you aren't afraid."

"I don't think I am afraid," she answered him, "but having been lost in this place I have a healthy respect for your forest. Is it much farther?" They had been traveling for at least two hours now, according to the position of the sun, Francesca noted. The duke's huntsmen had taught her to tell time by the sun the previous winter when she lived among them. It was, she decided, a good skill to possess.

"No, it is not far now," he told her. Then the trees began to thin just slightly, and they found themselves upon the shores of a lovely lake. "Look on the far side of the lake, nestled in the hills. Can you see it, Francesca?"

She peered carefully, and then the lodge became visible to her eyes, but had he not told her where to look, Francesca wondered if she would have ever seen it at all. The construction of the small building was such that it blended in to the landscape around it.

They rode around the lake and then up a barely visible narrow path to where the lodge stood upon a promontory jutting out from the hillside and over the lake itself.

"There is smoke coming from the chimney," Francesca said.

"A pigeon was sent to advise the caretaker of our coming," he explained. "We do not leave this place unattended. One of my father's former huntsmen watches over the lodge with his companion. We will not see them, but they will have prepared the lodge so it will be comfortable for us. First, however, we must stable our horses. It may be summer, but there are still beasts that will seek and attack a horse not stabled."

Francesca slid down from her gelding, and, following her husband, led the beast into a small stable. She unsaddled it, rubbed the horse down, and then set him in a secure stall to eat and drink after his long journey. Her saddle and bridle she put neatly into a small alcove that seemed for that purpose, for Rafaello had set his gear there first. Then together they secured the stable door and found their way to the lodge.

Francesca didn't believe she had ever been in so small a dwelling. It was simply a large room with a big hearth now blazing with a fire, an ample supply of wood set nearby.

There was a table, two chairs, and two benches. A small oven in the wall next to the fireplace; two black iron kettles, one large, one small; a shelf for their supplies; and a large bucket of water. In one corner was a large bed with red linen curtains that could be pulled about it for privacy. The bed was freshly made.

"Are you hungry?" Francesca asked him, and then answered her own query. "Of course you are. Sit down, my lord, and I will prepare us a small repast."

He sat down and watched as she prepared a plate for him with half of a roast chicken, some buttered bread with a wedge of hard yellow cheese, and a peach she sliced for him. Then she filled the stoneware cup she had found with the pewter plates with some red wine for him. "Is it enough?" she asked him before she joined him.

"Aye," he said shortly, and set about to eating the simple meal. And after the meal?

What then? He was going to have to woo her into the bed if their married life was to begin in earnest. He could not leave her as he had last night. They both knew this escape to the forest was for the sole purpose of consummating their union in the privacy that this isolated place could give them and that the castle filled with curious guests could not. Will she compare me to Carlo? he wondered jealously.

But what had Carlo done that he could not do the same, since they were the same? No! Carlo had been gentle, but had his conscience not overcome him he would have taken Francesca quickly to satisfy his own lust. Rafaello would not. No. He would arouse her slowly, slowly, until she was burning with her own desire and begging him to take her. He smiled wolfishly at the thought. Aye! What better way to show her that he was the master of their bedchamber.

"Why do you smile?" she asked him innocently.

"I am thinking of you naked in that bed," he said, candidly enjoying the flush that suffused her pale cheeks. For all her sophistication she was still an innocent girl.

"Did you think of me naked last night when you did not come to our bridal bed?" she surprised him by asking. "I waited for you."

"You fell asleep," he countered, "and I allowed you to sleep, for I knew how tired you must be after the last few days."

"I thought you were marrying someone else. I returned to see if my servants were still here so that we could return to Florence. I would not leave them behind. The priest belongs to my father's household. The nuns are from a convent whose head is my mother's kinswoman."

"And of course Terza," he remarked. "Oh, how she scolded us for your disappearance. She attempted to go into the forest to find you herself, but we stopped her. Then came word you were safe at Alonza's inn, so we left you there to cool your temper, Francesca, but the entire winter she nagged us for not bringing you back immediately. She loves you dearly, my wife. Such loyalty in a servant is commendable."

"So knowing I was in an inn of rough men, you left me there," Francesca said to him. "What if one of them had seduced me? What if they had all seduced me?"

He laughed at her. "Alonza warned them—did she not?—that you were not to be touched. And I am told they all fell madly under the spell of your sweet charm, treating you as if you were a precious daughter and not some itinerant serving wench. Nay, you were perfectly safe the whole winter long, for your duties gave you no time to cause mischief even had you wanted to do so."

"Certainly you do not think me some wanton?" Francesca said, a slight edge to her voice. Her green eyes glittered, narrowing as she glared at him.

"Wanton? Never!" he replied. "You have too much pride in both your father's name and in mine to bring shame to any of us, Francesca." He rose from the table, his meal now concluded. "Let me fetch some water to heat so we may wash the dishes up. There is a small well out back."

"And after the dishes are done and put away?" she demanded of him.

"Then I am taking my wife to bed, as I should have done last night," he told her. "My father wants grandchildren. Surely you do not want to disappoint him, Francesca. Do you?" Then reaching out, he pulled her to her feet and drew her close. His lips brushed hers lightly. "Remember that you swore before God to obey me, my beautiful wife, and so we will not dash my father's dreams. Will we?"

"Nay, we cannot," she agreed breathlessly.

Chapter 10

"Then I shall go and fetch the water for washing up," he said, releasing her.

Francesca quickly reached out to place her hand upon the table lest she fall. Her knees were weak, much to her surprise. Rafaello was not her Carlo, but there was something about him that excited her. Since he was her husband it was certainly permissible that she indulge her curiosity. And the sooner, the better. She barely heated the water he returned with, then quickly washed the two plates, the stone cups, and the knives they had used. Then she washed her hands and face in the remaining water.

When she had finished and turned to find him, she saw he was already in the big bed. His clothing was neatly piled on one of the chairs. He had obviously undressed while she attended to the dishes. Certainly he did not expect her to undress before him, did he?

"Pull the bed curtains, my lord, and leave me a modicum of privacy, I beg you," she said.

"Tonight," he said in a quiet voice, "because it is our first night together. But never again. I don't want you ever hiding yourself from me, Francesca." The brass rings holding the curtains rattled as he drew the red material about the bed, shielding her from his sight.

Francesca undressed slowly, placing her garments neatly upon the other chair and leaving on her chemise. She had no hairbrush to skim through her hair, and debated undoing her tresses. She reached up, pulling the pins from her hair and unfastening the elegant chignon Terza had styled earlier. She would use her fingers to comb her hair, and braid it come the morning. She had not put a lot of thought into spending a few days away from the castle, smiling at herself for always expecting that everything she needed would be available to her. Even Alonza had supplied her with what she needed when she had spent time at the inn. I am obviously very spoiled, Francesca thought to herself with a little smile.

"Wife! I am waiting for you," Rafaello's voice called to her.

"I waited for you last night," Francesca heard herself say sharply, and heard him laugh. "A woman needs time to prepare herself."

The curtains on one side of the bed were pulled back. "Get into bed," he told her.

"Is this how you speak to a maid?" she demanded of him, realizing that she was suddenly very nervous. This was not the wedding night she had envisioned. Actually did any maiden really think of her wedding night except with trepidation? Rafaello

Cesare, duke of Terreno Boscoso, was her husband, but the truth was she barely knew him but for a brief time they had spent together almost a year ago. Now he expected her to get into bed with him and give his family babies as quickly as possible.

He saw the look on her face. It was not fear but rather nervous consternation. Of course! What in the holy name of Jesu was he thinking? This was not some woman of experience. For all her quick tongue and Florentine sophistication, she was still a girl. A virgin who had refused to betray him or his family to his alter ego. He held out his hand. "I forget how young you are," he said. "How innocent."

She stared at his outstretched hand. "I know what is expected of me," she said proudly, her whole body stiffening with resolve.

"Of course you do," he agreed, "but nonetheless the first time is frightening." Sweet Maria. She stood like a little soldier ready to go into battle. He swallowed down his urge to laugh. "If I promise not to devour you in a single gulp," he teased her gently, "will you share this bed with me, Francesca?"

"Now you are making fun of me. If I flung myself upon you and demanded you do what must be done, would you find that more to your taste, my lord?"

"Nay. Actually I find your reticence charming and quite appropriate given the circumstances. But certainly you are getting cold standing there in your chemise and bare feet, Francesca. What needs be done will eventually be done. Make no mistake about that, for we both understand our duty to our family and to Terreno Boscoso. But we have a great deal of time in which to accomplish what may now seem onerous to you, and I believe by the time we are done I will have changed your mind as to the nature of bed sport between a husband and a wife," Rafaello told her gently. "Come now, and take my hand, Francesca."

She could avoid him no longer without leaving their shelter. Her curiosity was niggling at her. From all she had heard or overheard in her life, making love was not really so terrible once a girl rid herself of that troublesome thing called her virginity. Did she really want to continue to avoid this marital obligation? Was she that much of a coward?

Her mother did not complain about her bed sport, and her elder sister had certainly been eager enough to partake of it with her Turkish prince. Reaching out, Francesca took the hand he offered her and allowed him to draw her into the big bed.

He kissed her gently and then slowly undid the small ivory buttons holding her chemise closed. Pulling the fabric away from her, he gazed with rapt delight at the two round young breasts revealed to him. Though she made no attempt to stop him he could see her pale cheeks grow pink. At first he did not touch her. He just looked at the seemingly flawless twin spheres. Their perfection was broken only by their rosy nipples.

Briefly Rafaello considered their child nursing upon those sweet teats, but then he considered that before any baby tasted her flesh he had to, or he would expire with his own longing for her. His dark head bent to kiss the plump sweet flesh that tempted him. As his lips neared their goal he could actually see the fluttering of her heart in the small valley between them. He stopped and looked up into her face.

Francesca had shut her eyes tightly in her embarrassment as he stared at her bosom. She didn't know what she had expected, but this slow and measured behavior was not at all what she believed he would do. She wasn't certain of what she had thought him capable. She wasn't certain she was even breathing right now. Then his voice startled her in its demand.

"Open your eyes, Francesca," he said.

"I can't if you continue to stare at my breasts," she told him.

"But your breasts are beautiful," he replied, smiling at her shyness. She had not been quite so shy with Carlo, as he recalled it. But then she had fancied herself in love with the huntsman. She was not yet in love with him. "As your husband it is my right to admire you, and I am certain that you know that."

"It is our duty to make a child, my lord. The church tells us that the coming together of a man and his wife is solely for that purpose so that we may perpetuate the holy Catholic faith," Francesca said primly.

He refrained from swearing. Certainly her mother had said something of the delights to be had when a man and his wife made love. He couldn't believe that Orianna Pietro d'Angelo had dutifully bore her husband seven children without a modicum of pleasure. But perhaps she hadn't spoken to Francesca. Mayhap she had believed that keeping the girl totally innocent was better.

"Making love," he said to Francesca, "can be whatever you make of it, Francesca. It can be dutiful without emotions of any kind, as the church would have it. Or the coming together of a man and his wife can be a joyful time, with each of us admiring and appreciating the other's finer points."

"You believe my breasts to be my finer points?" she asked him, and she actually giggled at the thought.

"I do! I do!" he told her. "So much so I would worship them with kisses and caresses if you would but allow it."

"Will I then be rid of my virginity?"

"Ohh, we have a bit of a ways to go before we unburden you of your virginity, Francesca, but enjoying your breasts is a fine start," he told her.

"What else must we do?" she asked him bluntly.

"It is difficult for me to explain such a process, but if you would simply trust me I will show you all you need to know," Rafaello promised her.

"You are my husband," she pondered. "I suppose I really have no choice but to allow you to have your way with me."

"Some men would not argue the point with you, Francesca. With some men you would have already been most cruelly unburdened of that virginity you protect, without a care for what you wanted. I will be gentle with you, Francesca, but by morning's light you will be a complete woman. Make no mistake about it. I will have your virginity, and more by the dawn. You belong to me, wife."

"I will not be any man's mere possession," she said spiritedly.

"Nay, you will not. You are, I have seen, a woman of independent spirit, which is one reason that I chose you. You think I picked you because I had no other choice, but that is not so. If I believed that Louisa would have suited me I would have picked her, despite her girlish longing for Valiant. But Louisa would have withered beneath my hand.

"As for the French girl, we both know her eagerness to be my *duchessa* was not enough, despite her beauty and her plump dower. Her sharp tongue towards everyone made her unsuitable. Who wants a shrew for a wife? But you three weren't my only choices. If I had asked him, my father would have sent you all home and found other maidens from which I might choose.

"But it was you, Francesca Pietro d'Angelo, who caught my eye. I liked your wit, your intellect, and your manners. I saw through the veil of disinterest you affected to a maiden who did not wish to be caged by either church or husband. But you would be forced in the end to choose one. I chose you to prevent you from making a mistake, because it was obvious to me that you were meant to be my wife. I had no intention of allowing you to return to Florence, where your parents would have finally forced a marriage on you out of their desperation. So now you are mine. And I yours. And tonight is our wedding night."

She was stunned by his speech. Finally she said, "You might have told me this before, Rafaello."

He laughed. "You say that now, but had I confessed my desire for you earlier, you wouldn't have believed me. You are everything I want and need in a wife, Francesca."

"I'm not certain I believe you now," she responded tartly. "And just what is it you wanted in a wife that made me the one? I don't think you are so shallow that only beauty was what drew you to me. The others were fair enough."

"I wanted a woman with whom I could talk on matters other than children and her unsuitable allowance," he began. "What if I were called from the duchy? I would want my wife to rule in my stead. Do you honestly think either sweet Louisa or the ill-tempered Aceline du Barry could manage by themselves? But you could, Francesca. I could see that you were self-assured and able to make decisions unlike the others."

"So you chose me not just for my beauty but because you believed I could manage something other than a household," she said, not knowing if she should be offended by his confession. Was his reasoning flattering? Or just plain sensible? There was nothing particularly romantic about any of it. But marriages such as hers were not necessarily romantic. They were practical, and his words seemed truthful enough. "Shall I believe you or not?" she said, and looked directly at him.

"Of course you believe me," he said in an assured tone, his eyes meeting hers without flinching. "The ice about your heart is melting, Francesca. You know that I speak truth to you." He bent down and kissed one of her nipples. "Now can we please get on with the business at hand? I will be happy come the morrow to discuss this further, if you feel the need to do so. But for now there are other matters to which I would eagerly attend." He kissed the other nipple.

Francesca found herself speechless now. She could find absolutely no reason to prevent him from his determined course of action, which was to make love to her. He hadn't said he loved her, and yet certainly his honesty could be construed as love. His mouth closed over a nipple and he began to suckle upon her. She gasped with surprise, for rather than being unpleasant, his action was beyond exciting. *"Rafaello!"* she said.

She should stop him. Shouldn't she stop him? Surely she should, but she didn't want to. She wanted his mouth on her breasts making her feel. . . . Sweet Maria! What was she feeling? She wasn't certain, but it was wonderful and she wanted more. Her fingers tangled in his dark hair. The tips of them caressed the nape of his neck. She was unable to prevent the soft moan of distinct pleasure that escaped her lips.

He was dizzy with the taste of her, the clean, slightly fragrant scent of her skin. He felt her fingers in his hair, on his neck, and shuddered with the simple pleasure her touch gave him. He had known many women in his life, but he had never before experienced the sensations of pure enjoyment now filling him. Her sweet moan left him almost helpless with the voracious need he suddenly had for her.

Releasing the nipple, he let his tongue lick the smooth flesh between her breasts. He was unable to keep his tongue from moving downward, from caressing her smooth torso. Rafaello wondered if a man could die from just the anticipation of wanting a woman. His member was already hard with his need to plunge it deep into her virginity, taking away that girlish obstacle so they might enjoy one another without further impediment. But right now she was stiff with dreaded anticipation. He took the very tip of his tongue and tickled her navel with it.

Francesca giggled in spite of herself.

"Are you ticklish, then?" he asked in what she recognized as a dangerous voice.

"No!" she prevaricated in what she hoped was a sure and certain tone.

"Liar," he purred in her ear, and his fingertips found her weakness.

"No! No!" Francesca cried, trying to squirm away from him, her helpless laughter filling the room. "Stop! Ohh, stop!" She was breathless with his wicked torture.

Then his mouth was on hers, and they were kissing passionately. His kisses were hungry. She both felt and sensed the need. But for what? Francesca realized she didn't care. She just wanted him to go on kissing her like this forever. *Carlo.* His name flitted briefly through her mind, but was as quickly gone. Her huntsman had been a girlish fancy. This man now kissing her with such heated kisses so filled with desire was her husband, and Francesca realized she wasn't at all unhappy about her situation. She kissed him back with equal fervor until they were both breathless.

Francesca caught his hand and kissed it. Her eyes met his once again. "How is it," she asked him softly, "that you know me better than I know you?"

He smiled. "Someday I will tell you my secret," he murmured to her, catching at her hand and pressing a kiss upon its palm. Then he pulled her chemise up over her head and off of her. "Now we are both as God fashioned us."

She hadn't noticed until this very minute, for he had been hidden as she had been by the coverlet, but he was as naked as the day he was born. "Oh, my!" she said, and he was genuinely amused by her blushes.

"Are my kisses that intoxicating then that you did not notice my state of undress?" he asked her. "It is usual for a newlywed pair to sleep nude," he told her.

"How would you know that? Have you been wed before? I had not thought so, my lord," she replied sharply.

"You talk too much, wife," he replied, and pressing her back amid the pillows, he began to once again kiss her.

Francesca wanted to learn from where he obtained his knowledge of marriage, but his kisses were too delicious. She eagerly returned his tribute kiss for kiss, until she was dizzy. Warm lips. A tongue that played mischievously with her tongue. It was simply too delicious to ignore. She slid her arms about his neck, but he caught her hands, holding them in his own so he might move once again from her lips to her throat and what lay beneath.

His lips paid homage once again to her breasts, but then moved on across her torso, her belly. The warmth of his mouth against her skin was the most exciting thing Francesca could ever remember having experienced. How could a pair of lips engender such wild emotions within her? She wanted to ask him, but he put two fingers across her mouth and murmured, "Shh, my love. Just enjoy the sensations of passion."

His body was half atop hers. She let her hands smooth down his long back again and again. Finally unable to help herself, she cupped his buttocks in her palms. The flesh was soft yet tight against the pressure of her fingers. He encouraged her, whispering, nibbling at her ear teasingly, licking her nipples until she thought her breasts would explode, they felt so swollen with need. But a need for what?

His thighs pressed against her thighs. His legs were far longer than hers, and well muscled. His belly rubbed hers, and then their two mons pressed one another.

"Ohh!" It was only a small gasp, but he did not address it. If he did she would begin to talk again, to ask questions, to engage him in some sort of discussion. His male member was burning. It throbbed with his patience, but it could be patient no longer. She made a slightly louder sound as he slowly and deliberately rubbed his length against her cleft. He could already feel the heated moisture from her. Whether she realized it or even understood it, his bride was ready to taste deep passion.

He took his length in hand and rubbed hard enough with it so that it pushed between her nether lips. The tip of it found her most sensitive spot and rubbed against it. She made a sound, but he couldn't tell if it was concern or encouragement. He kept grazing it against her until she shuddered with a small frisson of pleasure. While she reveled in this new sensation he began to enter her body slowly, fighting back his desperate need to plunge deep inside her.

As her first pleasure melted away Francesca was suddenly aware that Rafaello was pushing himself slowly, slowly, into her body. Her first reaction was pure panic. She knew what he was about, but she had never before experienced a man filling her. She stiffened with her nerves, but he spoke softly to her as if she were some wild creature that needed gentling.

"Don't be afraid, my love. It is time for this, and I will be as gentle as I can, for the first time is not always easy for a virgin.

If you will trust me, Francesca, I will try to add to your first pleasure." He kissed her lips, caressing her beautiful face briefly.

"I . . . I know what must be done," she told him. "I just . . ."

He kissed her hard to quiet her, but said nothing else.

Francesca felt his length moving a short distance back and forth within her. The motion was actually very exciting, but then suddenly his thrusts were stronger, and deeper. She felt a sudden sharp pain, and he seemed to sheath himself entirely within her. She cried out and tears slipped down her cheeks. He gave her a moment's respite, but then he began to move very quickly back and forth within her. To her great surprise, for the quick pain had taken away any thought of pleasure, Francesca was suddenly aware once again of a small pleasure that began to fill her, but before she might fully enjoy it, he groaned loudly. His body shook for a brief moment and she actually felt herself being filled with his seed as he released it into her body.

He did not withdraw from her immediately. The wee delight she had been taking was gone and she felt bereft. She was no longer a virgin. She was a woman now. Francesca considered as he lay atop her that she had actually enjoyed his attentions. Would she have felt the same with Carlo? Or would it have been better? Thank God her huntsman had been gentleman enough to leave her intact. Better she not have to make any comparisons.

"Are you all right?" he asked softly after a short time had passed. He rolled from her.

"Sore, but I imagine 'tis expected, my lord," she answered him.

"I sensed you gaining pleasure," he said.

"Aye, I was beginning to, but then it faded when you released your seed."

"I apologize," he responded, "but taking you for the first time was very exciting for me, my love. I want you to sleep now, and tomorrow we shall enjoy ourselves again not once, but several times, I promise you. One of the advantages of being here alone with you is that there is no one to disturb us or our bed sport. Get some rest now, Francesca."

Several times? Francesca had honestly thought now that he had filled her with his seed, they would wait to see if he had gotten her with child. She hadn't realized a husband would want to sport with his wife so often. She thought that was why a man kept a mistress. Why hadn't her mother said something? Or Terza? What else didn't she know that perhaps she should? Still, coupling again with him was not really an unpleasant thought. She had very much enjoyed the little bits of pleasure that she had experienced tonight. She would certainly enjoy more if she might gain it.

But considering her little dalliance with Carlo, did she deserve pleasure from her husband? She had to tell him of the huntsman. Her husband might be jealous and he should be, but he knew her for an honest woman, for he had had her virginity this night. She had not really betrayed him, and there was no need for him to know how deep her feelings for the huntsman had been. She was Rafaello Cesare's wife and *duchessa*. They both knew she would never betray him or herself.

He awoke her with kisses, his manhood already hard with his lustful longings. Francesca took her husband into her arms eagerly, spreading herself for him, and wincing only slightly when he eagerly thrust himself deep into her with a sigh of delight. The soreness evaporated as he used her. He encouraged her and helped her to her own enjoyment before he took his own this time.

"In time we will learn to take our pleasure together at the same time," he told her.

"Will it make it even better?" she asked him.

"Aye," he said with a smile.

"Then I would learn how," Francesca told him, smiling up into his face. "Teach me, my lord!"

"It is a learned skill, my love, but we shall work together to master it," he promised her, smiling back.

They spent half the day in bed, enjoying each other. He taught her how to caress him and which touches could bring him pleasure. She gave him the freedom of her body, and thereby learned quickly what pleased her. They finally took the time to feed themselves, eating the second chicken that had been packed for them, along with some bread and cheese. They drank wine and became half-drunk before sleeping. When they awoke it was to make love again and sleep again. It was a rhythm they practiced until well after midnight, when they finally slept soundly.

He awoke to find her up and dressed. "I did not say you could leave our bed," he complained to her sleepily.

"We must return today, my lord," Francesca told him. "We have had two nights to ourselves. Your father will surely send someone after us if we do not go back on our own." She smiled at him. "Besides, we are just about out of food, and we have drunk all the wine. "Get up! When we get back to the castle I shall give you a bath and take one myself. The stink of passion surrounds us both."

He grinned. "I cannot help it if you are so delicious, Francesca, my wife, that I cannot resist you."

She laughed. "Get up! And when you are dressed I would speak with you."

"About what?" he asked, making no move to exit the bed. "Come and give me a morning kiss, my love."

"No! I can see what you are about, my lord. You will not lure me back into that bed. You may come to me tonight."

"Come to you? Oh no, my love. We will share the marital bed each night. I do not believe in a happily married couple having separate bedchambers. We are happy. Aren't we, Francesca?"

"Aye, I believe we are," she agreed softly. "Come and get up now, Rafaello."

He wanted to stay where he was. He wanted to lure her back into bed and strip her shirt and pants from her so he might make love to her again, but she was correct. If they remained at the ducal hunting lodge his father would send someone for them. He was, after all, now the duke of Terreno Boscoso. He had a government to manage. Rafaello arose reluctantly, washed lightly in the basin of cold water she brought him, and dressed quickly. Then, going to the table, he sat down to eat the bread and cheese that she had placed there for him.

"I will speak with you while you eat," she said. "While I was at Alonza's inn last winter I became fond of one of the huntsmen, a young man named Carlo. I believe he fell in love with me, Rafaello. On our wedding night while you remained drinking in the hall, he somehow gained entry to the castle and came to our bedchamber. I sent him away, of course, though he begged me to go with him."

"Did you love him?" he asked her, wondering what she would say.

"I think I may have if briefly, but never did I betray our name, my lord. You know I was a virgin when you had me first the other night. I will not see him again."

"How can you be certain?" he asked her, fascinated that she had confessed to him. He wondered if he should take this opportunity now to tell her that he had actually played the role of Carlo. That he had done it so he might learn to know her better.

"I am certain because I told him not to come back. If he truly loves me he will accede to my wishes, my lord. I have told you the truth of this matter because I would have no secrets between us now that we are truly husband and wife," Francesca said.

He nodded as if in concord with her. No. He would not tell her of the ruse he had played upon her, even if his intentions were good. Perhaps one day, but not today. Francesca was not apt to see it as he did now that she had confessed her girlish indiscretion to him. Indeed she would feel quite foolish. No. Better to let this lie for the interim. "I trust you," he told her quietly.

"I shall not discuss this matter ever again," she said.

"No," he agreed. "*We* will not speak on it, nor will there be a need to, Francesca."

"Thank you, my lord," she answered him.

He finished his small meal, and then they departed the lodge. The two caretakers would come from their own discreet cottage and put everything back to rights. Their horses were well fed and well rested. They had a good half-day's ride ahead of them.

Once again Rafaello found the narrow path that would lead them from the forest and back to the castle.

They arrived in midafternoon, and went immediately to Lord Titus so he would know they had returned home. The former duke greeted them warmly. One look at his son and Francesca told him they had resolved the difficulties between them. "My children, I see your brief stay at our lodge has done you both well. I am happy to see it. While you were gone, however, I received a rather disturbing letter from the Comte du Barry. You need not be concerned, Francesca, my dear. This is something Rafaello and I must discuss and resolve."

"If it is ducal business, my dear father," Francesca surprised both her husband and father-in-law by saying, "then I believe as *duchessa* of this little territory I should know what is happening. Especially as I shall eventually mother the heir to Terreno Boscoso."

Rafaello's first instinct was to send her from the chamber, as he knew his father would if he were still the duke. Wives, he had been taught, were to be protected from any unpleasantness. A quick look at Francesca, however, changed his mind. She was his *duchessa*. If she were kept in blissful ignorance she would be unfit to rule if he grew ill or found himself away for some reason. How could she protect the children they would have if she didn't know what was going on in their small world? "Francesca will remain, Father," he told his parent. "There could come a day when I need her to speak for me. She cannot protect Terreno Boscoso or its people or our children if she is kept in ignorance. She cannot just be my wife, or the mother of our children. She is my *duchessa*, and as such her position must be reasonably equal to my duke."

"It is a modern concept, my son," Lord Titus replied.

"There have been women who have ruled, my lord father," Francesca told him. "I sat hidden in my brothers' schoolroom and learned much of history. A wise woman must partner her lord husband, especially when there is territory involved."

Her father-in-law chuckled. "What were you supposed to be doing when you listened to your brothers' lessons?" he asked her.

"Oh," Francesca said, "a variety of things women are expected to know. How to sing sweetly, play an instrument, candy violets and rose petals. But I never heard it said that a woman was chosen to wife any man because of her abilities to sing or candy flower petals. Minstrels sing, and a lady's serving woman can make sweets. It was far more interesting to listen to adult conversations and a tutor lecturing on history. And after my sister, Bianca, ran away with her Turkish prince, I thought it even more important to know more of the world and less of the meaning of flowers."

Lord Titus laughed heartily. "If you give this family sons who are as spirited and as curious as you are, my daughter, I will be quite content."

"I will do my best to please both you and my husband," Francesca said with a mischievous smile. Then she grew serious. "But tell us what the Comte du Barry had to say to you. Certainly he was upset that you sent his daughter home, but he surely understood, as my family did, that she would be returned if not chosen."

"Therein lies the problem," Lord Titus said. "It should have taken the French entourage no more than two weeks to return to the du Barry estate. But she did not return home for almost six months, and then with only her maidservant. She was great with child, and has only recently given birth to a son. She claims the infant is your son, Rafaello, and the rightful heir to this duchy."

"She lies!" the young duke said.

"The bitch!" the *duchessa* said.

"Of course she lies," Lord Titus said. "But, having spoken the lie, we must now disprove the falsehood. The comte is outraged. His daughter claims you seduced her, and for six months hid her away from everyone as your mistress until you were ready to marry Francesca. Then you sent her back to her father with nothing but a big belly."

"But I didn't," Rafaello said. "The girl's arrogance and ill nature had me discount her as a possible wife almost immediately. And while she was fair, I never found her enticing enough to seduce. Especially as I was so intrigued with Francesca from the start. How in the name of heaven are we to discredit the wench's claim?"

"By telling the Comte du Barry what you have just told your father, and me," Francesca said. "He won't want to believe you, for it is his daughter, but he knows the kind of girl she is. How could he not? And if you refuse to acknowledge the child what can he possibly do? The blessed Mother only knows where Aceline managed to get her bastard, but he is not yours, my lord, nor will he take the place meant for my firstborn son," Francesca declared fiercely. Then her old arrogance surfaced, causing her husband to smile. "How dare she even think her beauty could surpass mine and win your heart?"

"With no marriage or promise of one," Lord Titus told them, "Aceline du Barry has no hope of foisting her bastard upon us. But we cannot keep writing letters back and forth. The Comte du Barry must be invited to Terreno Boscoso so we may settle this face-to-face. And I wish to know where all the rich gifts we sent with Aceline have disappeared to. Perhaps Aceline will have a clever answer for us."

"You are surely not considering asking her to come with her father?" Rafaello said. "This will become an open scandal, especially given Francesca's disappearance into the forest last autumn."

"We knew where Francesca was," Lord Titus said. "We

knew she was safe with Alonza. And when she returned she was not carrying another man's child. Besides, it was not common knowledge when we postponed the wedding. It was assumed we did it because your bride wanted her family to come from Florence, and we acceded to her wishes."

"Yet if anyone in the castle is asked, none saw her the entire winter long," Rafaello pointed out. "How do you explain that without telling them my bride ran away?"

"Why, my son, Francesca being the devout young woman she was, she spent her winter in isolation with her priest and the two nuns who were her companions. She prayed for the success of her marriage to you and for the healthy children we all desire," Lord Titus said, the lie coming easily to his lips.

"What of Terza's distress? Everyone in the castle knew of it," Rafaello said.

"And everyone in the castle will remain silent if I say Francesca was here, choosing solitude from all, even Terza," Lord Titus replied.

"I will speak with Terza and explain the situation," Francesca said. "She is clever, and will know what to do if questioned. The priest and nuns have returned to Florence with my parents. I am assuming, of course, that they are gone?"

Her father-in-law chuckled again. "Yes," he told her. "I saw them off myself the morning after you two left. They were all but your mother anxious to go, for the journey is a long one. As your father pointed out, however, they needed the di Medici men-at-arms that had escorted them here early this spring, and the captain of those soldiers was quite insistent he needed to return to his master in Florence. Your mother was not pleased, but when reminded of the two daughters still in need of husbands she decided perhaps it was time for her to go."

"It will be a few more years before Lucianna is ready to wed. While Bianca is not spoken of, the fact that her marriage exists cannot be denied. Now *Madre*'s second daughter is a *duchessa*. She will seek carefully for Lucianna and Serena. It is hoped that neither of them gives her the difficulties Bianca and I did."

"I do not find you difficult," Rafaello said with a grin.

"We are but newly joined, my lord," she answered him with a wicked little smile. Then she grew serious again, and turned to Lord Titus. "You truly mean to ask the Comte du Barry to Terreno Boscoso?"

"I see no other choice," the older man answered. "We need to face this lie, and disprove it before Aceline du Barry causes more difficulties."

Francesca nodded. "I understand," she said.

"I will write the letter myself," Rafaello said. "Now that I am the duke it should come from me. I will deny the wench's charge, but I will insist the comte come to Terreno Boscoso so we may settle this face-to-face. It would seem there is no other way."

Chapter 11

Rafaello Cesare, duke of Terreno Boscoso, wrote to the Comte du Barry. He denied Aceline's charges but invited the comte to come to his castle so they might discuss the matter face-to-face as gentlemen of honor would do. A month later Raoul, Comte du Barry, arrived, his daughter and her offspring in tow. The Frenchman didn't want to believe his daughter was a liar, but one look at Rafaello Cesare and he knew his grandson had not been sired by the young duke.

Lord Titus came to look at the infant. It was big-boned and large. It was unlike any Cesare in the former duke's memory. The child had a full head of dark brown hair and dark eyes. Even swaddled in silk and lace it was obvious this baby had not been sired by any lordling. It was a peasant's child.

"Here is your son," Aceline simpered to Rafaello, holding the infant out to him.

"He is not mine, madam," Rafaello said coldly. "Why would you even attempt to pass off this boy as mine? He is nothing like me, or for that matter nothing like you. Your lover was a big man, and your child takes after him." He turned to the Comte du Barry. "Do you still believe I sired this child, my lord?"

"I do not," the comte admitted, flushing, embarrassed. He turned angrily to his daughter. "Slut! What have you done that you would shame your family?"

"When your daughter was not chosen as my son's bride," Lord Titus said gently, "I returned her home to you, my lord, last September, with a train full of valuable gifts."

"She came home to me in April with naught but her servant to keep her company," the comte responded. He said again to the young mother, "What have you done?"

"So," Rafaello said, "the question remains, Where was Aceline during those seven months, and what happened to the gifts we sent with her? Where is the maidservant, Oriel? If she was with her mistress she will know the truth. Did she not return with her?"

"I sent the wench away," Aceline said. "She no longer pleased me."

"It is obvious that the maidservant knows the truth of this matter." Francesca, who had been silent until now, spoke up. "Perhaps she sent her away, or perhaps she had her killed to insure her silence. I would put nothing past the bitch."

"You are just jealous of me," Aceline said irrationally. "You were always jealous of me. I don't know how you got him to choose you, but he would have chosen me had you not bewitched him or told him lies about me."

Francesca looked at her former rival. "He chose me because

I was more beautiful than you. He chose me because my manners are flawless and my character better."

"You were the scandal of Venice!" Aceline replied angrily. The infant in her arms began to wail. "Someone take this brat!" she almost shouted, handing the squalling child to a nearby female servant, who looked both terrified and horrified.

"He sounds as if he's hungry," Francesca said. "Take your son and nurse him, Aceline." She signaled to the servant to give the baby back to his mother.

"Nurse upon me?" Aceline looked horrified. "He would ruin my breasts. I have a wet nurse with me. Have your woman take him to her."

"Clarinda," Francesca said. "Take the poor mite and find the wet nurse."

"He is not a poor mite. He is the heir to this duchy," Aceline said. "*My* son, not *yours*." She smiled, and when she did Francesca realized that Aceline du Barry had gone mad. She had not been so in that summer she and Louisa along with the French girl had been brought to Terreno Boscoso so Rafaello might choose one of them as his bride. But she was mad now. What had happened to her that had brought this condition on? Francesca caught her husband's sleeve and whispered her concerns to him.

"See how she plots and schemes!" Aceline cried. "She means to harm my son!" She spun about. "Where has your servant taken my baby? Where have they gone?"

"Your daughter is not of sound mind, my lord," Rafaello said to the comte. "We must learn the truth of what happened to her after she left Terreno Boscoso. Her maid, Oriel, is the answer to this puzzle. We must find her, and pray she is not dead."

The Comte du Barry nodded. His mistress had told him when his daughter returned to him that Aceline was not of sound mind. He hadn't believed her. He had even beaten her for saying so. Now seeing his daughter in her current state, he realized it was true. And only the maidservant, if they could find her, would be able to tell them the truth of the matter. "Both she and Oriel returned together. The servant was frightened and spoke little. Then suddenly she disappeared, and Aceline's old nursemaid was looking after her. I asked my daughter where Oriel had gone, and she simply shrugged. I was afraid to press her, for fear of harming her unborn child. Only when it was born did she claim it yours, my lord," the comte said, looking to the young duke.

"I took no liberties with any of the maidens my father brought for my consideration," Rafaello said. "Louisa di Genoa had fallen in love at first sight with my best friend, Valiant, *Signore* di Sponda di Fiume, who was with me and my party of gentlemen when we rode out to greet her arrival. His reaction to her was the same, although he sought to conceal it from me on the chance I should choose her. We greeted your daughter the same way. Aceline, however, was arrogant and rude from the moment we met. She seemed to believe I could not possibly have any other choice than to choose her. I mean no offense, my lord, but your daughter never appealed to me in any way. But if she had I should certainly not have dishonored her virtue."

"But you were quick to visit your whore wife's chambers at night," Aceline said.

"How dare you!" Francesca said angrily. "My husband did not have my virginity until we were wed. Not having your noble French blood, I knew I must be particularly careful of my reputation."

"The court of Lorenzo de Medici is known for its debauchery," Aceline snapped.

"I would not know if that were true or not," Francesca said, although she did. "I was not a member of that court, being the unmarried daughter of a respected citizen."

"Your sister was a known whore!" Aceline said viciously.

"If it is my elder sister to whom you refer, she was respectably wed to a famous lawyer of the city. Widowed, she remarried. How dare you spread such nasty lies!"

"Remarried?" Aceline screeched. "To an infidel?"

Madre di Dios, Francesca thought. She had not imagined the scandal would have spread as far as France and the house of an unimportant noble in an isolated region. She must write this information to her mother, who would shortly be seeking a wealthy and titled husband for her next sister, Lucianna, who had just turned thirteen. Such news would not please Orianna at all. "My sister, Bianca, lives under the rule of the Ottoman sultan, and under his laws she is happily wed to his son, Prince Amir," Francesca calmly answered Aceline. "Again you speak with no knowledge of the truth, just as you have lied in claiming that my husband fathered your son. Had he visited any of us privily while he considered his decision to marry, you may be certain the servants would have known about it and gossiped so that everyone in Terreno Boscoso would have known. Rafaello's choice of a wife was important to our citizens."

"Ah, how high and mighty you have become, *duchessa*," Aceline sneered.

"Where did you go, Aceline, after you were sent home?" Francesca asked her.

Aceline looked slyly at her imagined rival. "Every time he

fucked me he would say to me, 'I am Rafaello, your secret lover.' "

"We must find the serving woman," the young duke said. "She surely can enlighten us as to what happened to her mistress to drive her mad, and hopefully give us the identity of the father of this infant."

"Where is Oriel?" Francesca asked Aceline.

But Aceline just laughed. "Gone away," she sing-songed. "Gone away."

"We'll retrace the route Aceline took last September," Rafaello said. Then he turned to the comte. "Perhaps you will remain to aid us, my lord. I must send your daughter back to your home, for I cannot have her here spreading her lies and putting in doubt the legitimacy of the child my wife will bear me."

"Gone away," Aceline said smiling.

"I will stay," Raoul du Barry agreed, "and tomorrow Aceline will be returned home with her child. There is little hope of finding a husband for her now."

The hunt for Aceline's maidservant began in earnest. Word was spread along the route that had been traveled when Aceline was sent home the previous autumn.

It was several days later when old Duke Titus remembered something that had happened in the few days Rafaello and Francesca had been away and while he had ruled for those last days of his tenure. Embarrassed, he told his son what he had learned. "I meant to tell you, for it is something we must correct, but alas my mind is not what it once was, and I have grown forgetful, which is why I resigned in your favor."

"What is it, then, you should have told me?" the young duke encouraged his parent.

"Bandits!" Duke Titus said. "The High Road that Aceline took to reach her father's home last autumn is being plagued by ferocious bandits. Because it is the shorter road into both France and Switzerland it is more traveled, but a complaint came to us from an innkeeper along that road about these bandits who are ruining his trade because few people will take the High Road now. They also come into his establishment, eat, drink, use the servant girls, and do not pay. This part of the road as far as the French and Swiss borders is our territory, and therefore our responsibility. You will have to go and drive these thieves away, my son."

Rafaello told Francesca what his father had reported to him.

"Interesting that the complaint should come only now. I wonder if these robbers are the ones responsible for the disappearance of the gifts your father sent with Aceline last autumn. And possibly her condition. It is obvious her *bastardo* is not your child, but someone fathered it. She was gone for months and returned with only a full belly. Then her serving woman who was with her disappears once they are home."

"Whatever the truth may be," Rafaello said, "I must go and drive these bandits back to from wherever they have come, be it France or Switzerland."

"No," Francesca said. "If you drive them away they will eventually return. You must kill them all, my lord, so that there is no chance of them returning, or, worse, becoming mercenaries of some other lord."

"Now, here is a side of you I had not imagined, wife. You are a warrior, and obviously unforgiving," he said.

"Women of my class are schooled to be wives and mothers, but some of us are also educated to understand the complexities of ruling. A few even know the intricacies of battle and weapons, although I do not. I mean you no disrespect, my lord husband, but I can be of more help to you, for I am not simply a pretty ornament like my dear Louisa. That sort of wife suits Valiant, but I think it would not please you entirely, else you would not have chosen me to be your wife," Francesca told him.

She surprised him. He had chosen her because she seemed intelligent. He had just not considered she might be aware of it. As he was not a man who was afraid to ask a woman's opinion, he said, "You are probably correct when you say we should kill these bandits, but first we must learn if they had anything to do with Aceline du Barry."

"Someone took her and kept her for those seven missing months," Francesca said. "And it is obvious she was robbed of her virginity during that time. The question is, Was it simply one man who had her, so we may know the boy's sire, or was she given to many?"

He was shocked she would even contemplate such a thing, but she was not stupid.

It was the only answer to the mystery of what had happened, but no one except the maid, Oriel, could tell them the truth of the matter. Aceline's wits had been weakened by what happened. Whether she would ever again be sane was a matter of speculation.

"I am going with you," Francesca said to Rafaello, and before he might protest she told him, "If you find the maidservant among these bandits, she is not apt to speak to you for fear of punishment and being held responsible for her mistress's condition."

"Yes, you would be useful, but these men are dangerous, my love. I do not want you falling victim to them as Aceline may have," the young duke told his wife.

"Aceline's train was small, with not many men-at-arms to protect her. We will travel with a great group of soldiers, for if these bandits have dug themselves in to the mountains above the High Road you will need a strong force to root them out. I will remain safely under guard at the inn of the innkeeper who sent the complaint."

"No, you will stay here," he told her, but before she might complain he continued, "If I find the serving woman I will send for you to come, for if I return her here and she sees Aceline or her father she will be intimidated. If she is to speak freely without torture it must be in a place in which she feels safe," Rafaello said to his wife. "You will oversee the return of Aceline and her child to her father's house."

"The woman has been rendered mad by whatever happened," Francesca said. "I would speak to her father and suggest that Aceline be placed in a convent to be cared for by the nuns. A convent is a safe environment for a madwoman. She can raise her son in peace, preparing him for the church when he is older. The French are not as liberal about bastards as we Florentines, Milanese, Venetians, Romans, and others in our land. Our families consider such children useful. Daughters can be used for marriage alliances, and sons for the church and the military. The wife of an important man can have just so many children. His mistresses give him others."

"So," he answered her, "if I took a mistress you would be content that I gave such a woman children?"

"You are not important enough to have children other than by me," she told him sweetly.

"Not important enough? I am the duke of Terreno Boscoso," he reminded her.

"We are a tiny duchy edged by the Swiss Confederation and

France, and obviously carved out of a tiny scrap of what was once Savoy," she told him. "I am competent to read a map, my lord. We could be absorbed by any of these if they chose to attack. You will have to be content with your wife alone, I fear, my lord."

He wanted to be offended, perhaps even angry, but there was nothing that Francesca had said that wasn't true. Still . . . "Yet you married me," he remarked.

"My *madre* loved the idea she would have a daughter who was a *duchessa*. She does not recognize Bianca's marriage to Prince Amir, which made her eldest daughter a princess. Besides, my sister is not known as Bianca now. She is said to be called Azura, or so my brother, Marco, told us, for he was allowed once to visit her. So having me become a *duchessa* was pleasing to Orianna Pietro d'Angelo."

"I might not have chosen you," he reminded her.

"What choice did you have?" she said, laughing. "Louisa was in love with Valiant, and Aceline was an ill-tempered bitch."

"I might have had my father send you all home," he told her. "I might have requested three more respectable virgins be brought to Terreno Boscoso. Or I might have gone and visited other houses in Milan and Florence who had marriageable daughters."

"Hah!" Francesca responded scornfully. "You fell in love with me, and no other would do."

"But you were not in love with me," he reminded her. "Instead you ran off into the forest and developed a *tendre* for a rough huntsman. I am surprised you returned."

"I came back for my servants," she said. "If I was going home I was not going to abandon them. And the moment I reached the main road I was told you were to be wed to another, husband."

"Another? Who said anything about another woman? You assumed it," he replied.

"What was I to think?" she demanded of him. "Every citizen in Terreno Boscoso was on the road for the castle to see you married. How was I to know you were marrying me and not some other? I did not know you knew where I was all along and meant to bring me back."

He laughed. "You said yourself that I loved you. Since I declared it not, how could you understand that I did?" he asked her.

"I knew by the way you looked at me," she told him. "Besides, a man not in love would not have gone searching for me or waited for me, or planned a wedding for me."

"These are matters we have never before discussed, my love, but it has taken us away from the problems we have. Bandits on the High Road. I like your idea of a convent for Aceline and her child. I am certain the comte can find one."

The Comte du Barry, while approving of the young *duchessa*'s idea to place his mad daughter in a convent, had no knowledge of one, for his own home was so isolated.

"If you would consider placing her far from you, there is a convent outside of Florence where my mother's kinswoman is in charge. *Madre* Baptista is kind but firm. Two of her younger nuns accompanied me when I first came to Terreno Boscoso," Francesca said to him. "Santa Maria del Fiore is a good place. My own sister stayed there once for a short visit. It is peaceful, and beautiful. If your grandson is meant for the church it is far nearer Rome and the church's power than your home. The boy might even be educated in Rome, my lord."

"It is a long way away," the comte considered, "and yet

perhaps it would be better if Aceline and her child were not near us. I must think on this."

"If she left from here the journey would be shorter," Francesca said. "If you would like to accompany your daughter I would send a letter with you. Of course, you will have to forfeit Aceline's dower portion to the convent for her care."

"Of course," the comte said, wondering if he might stint a bit on the amount and save himself a coin or two. Then he thought better of his parsimony. Better he be generous, for taking in a madwoman and her infant would not be an easy thing for the nuns, no matter how kind and competent they were. Having survived childbirth, and with a future that would not allow for more babies, Aceline was apt to live a long time, as did his grandmother's maiden sister, who had lived to the unheard-of age of eighty-four. "I think I must thank you for your kindness, my lady *duchessa*. My daughter is not deserving of it. Had your positions been reversed I doubt Aceline would have been as generous towards you," the comte said truthfully. "Yes, I need no more consideration of the matter. I shall take my daughter and her child to the convent of Santa Maria del Fiore outside of Florence. It is the best solution."

"And we will find the maidservant and ascertain the truth of what happened," Rafaello said. "Stop on your way back, and perhaps then we shall have the answers you need to know."

Several days later the Comte du Barry departed Terreno Boscoso with his daughter, her son, and servants, for Florence. The roads south were safer, and his party of men-at-arms would suffice. The young duke and his wife were relieved to see them go. Now they would turn to the business of ridding the High Road of the bandits troubling it.

Although Francesca was not pleased to be left behind, she

had her husband's word that he would send for her when he had found the missing serving woman.

"You and my father will rule in my absence," Rafaello told her before he rode out surrounded by at least one hundred men-at-arms. Bandits in the region were not good for anyone. Eventually they would move farther south down the High Road until they were at the very gates of Terreno Boscoso. That could not be allowed to happen.

"Be careful," Francesca said, not knowing what else to say to Rafaello as she looked up at him upon his horse. "Keep warm." These were things her mother said to her father and brothers when they went off.

He laughed at her obvious distress at not knowing exactly what to say. "I will," he promised her. "It will not take long to rout these fellows, my love."

But he quickly found it was not as easy as he had thought it to be. The bandits had obviously been victimizing the High Road for more than a year, but until the innkeeper had complained everyone else living in that area had been too afraid to speak up. Rafaello introduced himself to the innkeeper and made the establishment his headquarters while he and his men sought out the bandits' hideaway. Once he discovered it, he would kill them all. Driving them into another place would be no favor to the residents of that area. Several weeks passed as the young duke and his men played cat and mouse with the bandits.

Francesca was fretful with her husband's absence, and her father-in-law suggested one day that she go into the little town below the castle.

"We do not cloister our womenfolk," he explained to her. "As long as Terza or another servant accompanies you it will be fine."

"I have never walked about a town," Francesca admitted to the old gentleman. "In Florence the only women on the streets were servants or those not considered respectable. Now and again my parents would be invited to someone's house, and my mother would travel in a closed litter or sedan chair. Once or twice I was invited with them to the di Medici palazzo, which is quite grand, but only because Lorenzo wanted to help my parents find a husband for me, and I was on display."

"Visit the open-air market in the town," Titus Cesare suggested to her. "Our people will be delighted to see you. Take a purse with you so you may purchase anything that catches your eye."

Francesca had never gone out on her own. An exciting adventure lay ahead.

Finding Terza, she told her what the old duke had suggested.

"Oh, can I come too?" Roza asked. "My aunt sells the soaps she makes in the market. She lives on a farm just outside of the town."

"Of course," Francesca agreed.

"Notify the captain of the guard," Terza told Roza. "We will need two men-at-arms to accompany us."

"Is that necessary?" Francesca wanted to know.

"It is expected of you," Terza said. "You are the *duchessa*."

The three women walked from the castle courtyard and across the drawbridge, then down the hillside into the small town. People passing them once they were in the street bowed or curtsied when they saw their *duchessa*. She acknowledged them with a smile. Francesca couldn't stop looking about her. She had ridden through the town on horseback, but it was entirely different on foot. The neat houses were pleasing to the eye, with their window boxes filled with bright summer flowers.

Reaching the market, she was delighted by all the stalls and colorful awnings beneath which farmers and small merchants without shops sold their goods. There was fresh farm produce from the outlying farms. Fruits, vegetables, and newly slaughtered meats hanging from metal hooks for the purchaser to inspect and buy. Roza's aunt greeted them warmly, delighted that her niece had come with her mistress. To have the custom of the *duchessa* would only be good for her business.

Francesca bought several bars of the woman's soaps in both rose and lily fragrances. "If you do not do bath oils to match these scents you really should," she suggested. "Do you think there would be a market for them?"

"For ladies, yes, I believe so," the farmer's wife said. "It is not a large market, but it is there. My husband thinks such little luxuries are foolish, but he is wrong. The serving girls often save up their coin so they may purchase a single bar of soap from me. I have saved quite a bit with my little business."

Francesca was delighted with her purchases, handing them to one of the men-at-arms to carry. As she turned to do so her eye caught that of a woman selling eggs. "Terza!" she said urgently. "Look over there! The egg seller! Is that not Oriel?"

Both Terza and Roza looked at where their mistress indicated. "Yes!" they chorused. "It is! She has seen us, my lady, and is trying to leave."

Francesca turned to one of the men-at-arms. "Fetch that egg seller to me," she told him, and pointed. "Do not let her get away!"

"At once, my lady," he replied, and pushing through the crowded market sought his quarry.

Oriel saw him coming and attempted to evade the soldier, but he was quicker than the woman. His big hand closed about her arms. "Just a minute there, woman. The *duchessa* wishes to speak to you." And he half dragged her over to where Francesca stood with the other women. "Here she is, my lady," the man-at-arms said.

Oriel looked terrified. "What do you want of me?" she managed to say.

Francesca replied, "I mean you no harm, Oriel, but you will come back to the castle with me now."

"I can't leave my stall!" Oriel protested. "My master will beat me if I do not sell all his eggs. Please, my lady, please!"

"Find the egg farmer," the *duchessa* instructed the soldier who had Oriel's arm. She handed him a coin. "Tell him that is for all his eggs, and bring them with you for the cook. And tell him that the *duchessa* has taken his servant with her to the castle. She will be returned shortly."

The man-at-arms went off to do his mistress's bidding, while his companion escorted the four women back through the town and up the hill to the castle. Once they were settled in the day-room of Francesca's apartment and Oriel had been given a small taste of wine to calm her, Francesca began her questioning.

"How is it you came to be the servant of an egg farmer?" she asked Oriel. "You are a trained lady's maid."

"My mistress gave me a choice. Either go, or remain and she would kill me, for she said she could no longer trust me," Oriel said.

Francesca nodded. "At least the Frenchwoman remembered your past loyal service," she noted. "Now tell me, Oriel, what happened after you departed the castle last September? Why did you and your mistress not return home until seven months later? It is a brief journey from Terreno Boscoso to the Comte du Barry's home."

Oriel looked unhappy at the question.

"You must tell me," Francesca said. "Your mistress came with her father and attempted to convince us that her child was my husband's child. It is not so."

"She is mad," Oriel said. "What happened drove her mad."

"You need to tell me what happened, Oriel," Francesca insisted.

"Where is she now?" the former maidservant asked, nervously looking about her.

"She is on her way to a convent outside of Florence. Her father is escorting her, and her child is with her. My own *madre* is a patron of Santa Maria del Fiore, and the superior is her own kinswoman. Aceline du Barry and her child will be safe there and well treated. Perhaps one day her sanity will return."

"I hope not," Oriel said. "If it did she would remember what happened, and I do not think she could bear to relive it." The Frenchwoman's eyes filled with tears, which spilled down her cheeks.

Terza and Roza looked uncomfortable.

"What happened?" Francesca asked once again.

Oriel sighed deeply as she wiped her tears with her hand. "Two days into our journey our little caravan was attacked by bandits. They were fierce, and slew everyone in our party but for my mistress and me. Those killed were the lucky ones. They were delighted with the horses and all the rich gifts that Duke Titus had given Aceline. We were brought back to their encampment high in the hills.

"My mistress, once she managed to recover from her initial shock, immediately began telling their leader who she was and how important she was, and how unless they returned her and her belongings to her father, she would have them executed. She had no thought for those in our party left dead on the road for the crows. As always she thought only of herself. I tried to get her to be silent. I could see immediately the kind of men these were. They were desperate fellows with no care for anything except the moment in which they were living.

"But my mistress would not stop talking. She told their leader how she would have been the new *duchessa* of Terreno Boscoso had it not been for a Florentine bitch—your pardon, my lady—who had stolen the duke's son from her. She babbled on about how important she was until their leader, a brute who called himself Bruno, hit her across her face. Then he told her he intended fucking her because he had never fucked a lady before. He said he wanted to know if fucking a lady was different from just fucking any other woman."

"*Madre di Dios!*" Francesca whispered.

"Must I continue, my lady?" Oriel asked. "It is not a happy tale I have to tell."

"Continue," the *duchessa* said. "I would hear it all."

"He raped her," Oriel said tersely. "He had his men hold her down while he used her. When he discovered that she was a virgin he decided to keep her for himself and not let his men have her. He gave me to the others. And every time he mounted her he would say to her, 'It is the lord of Terreno Boscoso fucking you, bitch.' Then he would laugh uproariously. She quickly lost her senses after that, but Bruno did not care. He was a vicious man who enjoyed despoiling a lady, and there was hardly a day he did not use her several times. I was not surprised when I realized she was with child.

"That knowledge briefly brought her back to herself. She suddenly said she had to escape and return home. Her father would want to know she carried the heir to Terreno Boscoso.

When I attempted to explain to her that her child was that of a bandit, she hit me. How stupid I was, she said. She knew it was the lord of Terreno Boscoso who lay with her each night. He told her so.

"The bandits had grown used to leaving us in their camp whenever they went off. There were only a few other women. Two old women who cooked for them, and three farm girls they had taken for their pleasure. Bruno told one of the old women whom he particularly trusted that they would be gone for several days. I had always been pleasant to her, and so she would gossip with me. When I learned what Bruno had told her I took the opportunity to help my mistress escape."

"How were you able to manage to get her back to her father?" Francesca asked.

"I learned that our camp was actually just over the border in France. I had learned from the men who used me that there was a path just a short distance from the camp. As soon as Bruno and his men had gone we left. I got my mistress to the path and started walking. We reached the High Road a day later, when I begged help from the first party of travelers we met. They were grateful of our warning about the bandits and took my mistress to her father via a less-traveled road nearby," Oriel finished.

Francesca nodded. "Were you with her when the child was born?" she asked.

Oriel nodded. "Once the infant was birthed its origins were obvious. When she insisted upon telling her sire and his wife that this was the young duke's son they wanted to believe her. I told the comte's wife it was not possible, and she told me to keep my mouth shut or she would have my tongue pulled out. It was then my mistress looked at me and said that I had a choice. To remain and wait for my death, or to go. I did not linger, my lady. I fled the house of du Barry that same day and hour. Not knowing where to go, I begged for work from the egg farmer. His wife had just died and he needed my help, as they were childless."

"Do you want to go back to him?" Francesca asked her.

"What else is there for me?" Oriel asked bleakly.

"You are a house servant, not a farmer's woman," Francesca said. "I will employ you if you will be loyal to me."

Oriel nodded. "I am a lady's servant," she said. "You have two women to serve you. What would I do?"

"The castle's majordomo will find a place for you," Francesca told her. "Or you may return to the farmer or go wherever you please. I will give you a few coins to ease your way. The story you told me is tragic, but I shall be able to ease my husband's mind and the old duke's now that I have learned it."

"I'll stay," Oriel said. "I'm a hard worker, and here I know that I am safe."

"Very well, then. I thank you, and you are welcome to Terreno Boscoso. Roza, take Oriel to Matteo. Tell him I would have him find a place for her."

"Yes, my lady," Roza said, and escorted Oriel from the *duchessa*'s dayroom.

Terza shuddered when the woman was gone. "What a terrible fate for the Frenchwoman," she said, and crossed herself. "As unpleasant as she was to you, I should not have wished it on her. And what will happen to her poor child?"

"If he can be taught he will probably end up in the priesthood. If not he will be a soldier," Francesca said. "That is the usual fate of male convent bastards."

"I hope when the young duke catches this bandit, Bruno,

and his evil crew, he shows them no mercy at all," Terza said angrily. "No woman deserves to be mistreated as those wicked men did to the Frenchwoman and her servant."

"I will send a messenger to my lord telling him that we found Oriel by chance," Francesca said. "He need have no worries over her. All he need do is punish the bandits."

But catching the marauders was not as easy as Rafaello had anticipated. Bruno was not a fool. There was nothing the young duke and his men had that he wanted. They were robbers, plain and simple. They did not engage soldiers by choice. Once he understood that the duke wanted him dead, Bruno and his men, like hunted animals, went to ground, hiding in the uninhabited hills, moving daily so that they could not be caught.

Rafaello didn't want to just drive the bandit chief from his territory. Why force the problem on Milan or Savoy, who were his nearest neighbors? No, better to rid the world of the monster who had tortured and raped poor Aceline du Barry, causing her to retreat into madness.

After a few weeks of playing cat and mouse Rafaello and his men withdrew to the inn where they had been headquartering to formulate a better plan of attack. "We need to lure him out," the duke told his captain, a man who went by the name of Arnaldo.

"As long as we are anywhere in the vicinity he won't be fooled," Arnaldo responded. "This innkeeper, for all his complaints, is playing both sides, my lord. We cannot trust him."

"What if we withdrew back to the town and then sent what would appear to be a wealthy wedding party onto the High Road? I think it might be too rich a prize for Bruno to resist," the duke suggested as he walked across the chamber to yank open the door into the hall. "Ah-ha! What have we here?" he asked as a serving man fell into the room. He looked to Arnaldo. "Take him out and cut his throat," the duke ordered.

"My lord! No! Please, I beg of you, do not slay me," the servant said.

"You were spying," the duke said quietly. "For whom?"

"My master, the innkeeper," the man babbled without hesitation.

"Why? Did your master not ask me to rid the area of these bandits?" the duke asked the frightened man.

"My master is a careful man," the servant responded. "He expected you would come, and quickly catch Bruno and his men. When you did not he grew frightened that the bandit king might punish him for bringing you here and sheltering you. He planned to send to Bruno word of your latest plans in hopes of saving himself."

Captain Arnaldo shrugged. "This is what you can expect of these peasants, my lord. We must return to the town, I fear, and leave the High Road to the bandits."

"I think I am inclined to agree," Rafaello said, "which means I will spare your life," he told the serving man. "Tell your master all you heard was that we will depart back to the town tomorrow."

"Yes, my lord," the man said, and with a bow almost ran from the room, while behind him the two men laughed heartily.

Chapter 12

*F*rancesca was surprised to see her husband return so quickly. A few weeks were hardly time enough to rid an area of bandits, she thought. "I wanted you to be able to tell the Comte du Barry that you had rid the High Road of these robbers and avenged his daughter's mistreatment."

"Bruno is a far cleverer fellow than I anticipated," Rafaello told his wife. "Come and kiss me, damnit! This is hardly a warm welcome, Francesca."

They had not been wed so long that she was yet comfortable with him. "Not before the servants, my lord," she said.

"Why not before the servants?" he half teased. "I think it would reassure them to see their master and mistress showing affection for each other. Come here!"

"My parents never made a display before their servants," Francesca insisted.

Rafaello chuckled. "Perhaps if your father had been more determined handling your mother, you would have had a better example," he told her, reaching out for her.

Francesca sidestepped him. *Handle my mother?* "How old fashioned you are, husband. My parents respect one another, and we must follow their good example and do the same. A marriage cannot be happy if a wife does not support her husband's strengths and safeguard his weaknesses. And a husband must do the same for his wife."

"Do you think I have any weaknesses?" he asked her, offended.

"I do not know you well enough to answer that," Francesca said.

"Did Carlo have any weakness?" he demanded of her. "Other than, of course, for another man's betrothed." The moment the words left his mouth he regretted them. What was the matter with him? How could he be jealous of himself? But what was it about Carlo that had attracted her love when Rafaello could not?

Francesca drew herself up to her full height, saying coldly, " 'Twas you who insisted upon this marriage, my lord. I should have been happy to return to Florence, but no sooner had I come from the forest where I had been hiding from you than you rushed me to the altar that very day. Yet I was honest with you in every way. 'Twas obviously a mistake to be so, for you will never allow me to forget my girlish sin. Will you?"

"Francesca!" He was very contrite. "I apologize, wife. I do."

"You need have no fear, my lord," she answered him. "I will be a good wife to you, and bear your children without complaint. I hope you will honor me with the knowledge of your plans for the bandits, if you intend to go back to the High Road and rid it of that scurrilous plague so people may travel in safety. It is worrisome for a woman not to know when her husband would put himself into danger."

"Will you never forgive me?" he asked her.

"There is nothing to forgive, my lord. You have your manner, and I have mine."

"I am a great fool," he admitted.

"Yes, you are," Francesca answered him, but a small smile touched her lips.

"Come and kiss me," he cajoled her. "I have returned from a dangerous mission and need a warm greeting from my wife to sustain me."

Now Francesca laughed, but she slipped into his embrace, sliding her arms about his neck. "How can I resist such charm?" she said, offering him her lips.

He kissed her slowly, his mouth exploring and tasting her. There was yet a shyness in her kiss that reminded him of his days in the forest with her. His kiss deepened with the memory. He had come to know and love her as Carlo, the huntsman. He knew that she had been falling in love with that persona. How could he tell her they were one and the same without engaging her outrage for having deceived her? Lifting his mouth from hers he said to her, "I could love you, Francesca, if you would just let me. Is not a loving marriage better than just a respectful one?"

"We are only newly wed, my lord. I have not the answer to your question," she replied slowly. "I wonder if love lasts. Do you know? From the way he speaks of her, I can tell how much your father loved your mother. Perhaps we should ask him, husband."

"I was a party to that love," Rafaello told her, kissing her brow lightly, his arms still about her. "I think their love deepened and changed with time. Nothing, Francesca, ever remains the same. They were happy together, and that's what I would have us be."

She kissed him softly. "Welcome home, my lord," she said sweetly. She had to resign herself to her fate, Francesca thought to herself. He wasn't Carlo, but she believed him to be a good man, and he was her husband until death.

"It is good to see you two so affectionate," Duke Titus said with a smile as he rose from his place by the family hall hearth, where he had been dozing. It seemed that ever since he had re- signed his responsibilities he had grown frailer.

"Rafaello tells me the bandits on the High Road are clever, my lord. He has come home to formulate a plan to rid us of them," Francesca told her father-in-law.

The old man perked up at this. "What do you intend to do?" he asked his son.

"I haven't quite decided yet, sir, and when I speak to you I think it would be better in a more secluded setting. I don't want my plans trumpeted about. This Bruno is a clever fellow. For tonight, however, I would be content for a good meal and the company of my bride in our bed."

The old duke chortled. "If I were your age, my son, I think I should prefer my wife's company first and then a good meal. Passion is good for the appetite," he told his son with a broad wink.

Francesca blushed, then she laughed. "You are a wicked old man," she told her father-in-law.

"I simply wish to see my grandchildren before I die," he told her.

"We will do our best, Father," the young duke replied, look- ing at his wife.

With only the family and their retainers about them, they ate a simple meal as the day began to wane. There was broiled trout from a stream in the forest; a roasted capon stuffed with little green onions, bread, and sage; a dish of small pasta dressed with butter and a local Parmesan cheese that was grated over it right at the high board; peas; and a green salad. The wine came from the vineyard owned by Francesca's family in Tuscany.

When the meal had concluded Duke Titus settled down by the fire once again to play a game of chess with Piero, the castle's majordomo.

Francesca excused herself from the hall and retired to her bedchamber, where Terza was waiting. A tub had been set up, and to Francesca's surprise Rafaello said he would join her. She had never shared her tub with him before, but she also knew it was her duty to bathe him, and it was easier to do so in the tub itself. First, however, she dismissed Terza, who smiled as she went, catching Roza by the arm as she was about to reenter the chamber.

"We are dismissed for the evening," Terza told the younger maidservant. "Our mistress is bathing several days of travel from the young master."

Roza nodded. Such intimacy as bathing could lead to a passionate encounter, and as a loyal citizen of Terreno Boscoso, Roza was as anxious as the old duke for another heir. "Well," she said, "if she doesn't need us I'll take this time to visit my mother in the town. Would that be all right, Terza?"

"Go along," the *duchessa*'s senior serving woman told the younger woman. Then she hurried to her own chamber, where she knew a pile of mending awaited her attention.

Francesca had turned her head away when her husband casually shed his clothing and climbed into what was to have been her tub. She had seen him naked in their bed, but not like this. He was so big and bold, standing straight and then climbing into the tall oak tub. She retained her chemise as she slipped into the water to join him, picking up the washing cloth and soaping it as she prepared to bathe him.

"Take off that silly garment," Rafaello said. "Wet, it clings to your body in a most suggestive manner. If you thought to be modest, you are not." He leered wickedly at her.

"The nuns who chaperoned me last year bathed with their chemises on," she told him as she rubbed the soapy cloth over his broad smooth chest.

"You are not a nun, Francesca," he replied to her logic. Her nipples were more visible, it seemed, beneath the thin wet cloth. Reaching out, he rolled up the chemise. "Either you help me get this off of you, or I will be forced to rip it," he told her.

"You cannot wantonly destroy this garment, my lord," she responded to him.

"I cannot?" He pulled it tighter.

"It is wasteful!" she cried to him, raising her arms so he might draw the garment over her head.

"Your frugality is pleasing," he remarked as he squeezed the garment free of excess water and tossed it on the floor. "Now, madam, you may continue washing me. When you are finished I will bathe you."

He makes me nervous, Francesca thought. Then she wondered if her own mother and father had ever shared a tub. She couldn't imagine Orianna doing so. She was far too fastidious. Had Rafaello's parents bathed together? She doubted if he would know the answer to that question even if she asked it. She continued to wash him. His chest and arms. His handsome face. She turned him about and scrubbed his back.

"There is more of me beneath the water," he said mischievously.

Francesca handed him the washing cloth. "Then you must bathe those parts yourself, for I cannot dive beneath the water and do it," she said sweetly.

Laughing, he took the cloth from her and finished his cleansing ritual. Then he looked to his wife. "I will now bathe you," he told her.

"I am capable of washing myself," Francesca said quickly. "You must leave the tub and dry yourself. The water is growing cold, and I do not want you to take a chill."

"Your concern is touching, wife. Stand still now so I may serve you as nicely as you did me." Turning her about he used his hands to soap her breasts slowly, rubbing her nipples teasingly, making her squirm. Her buttocks brushed against his groin. His manhood stirred strongly. Unable to help himself he bent and kissed the tender spot between her neck and her shoulder. He licked her shoulder, but his hands never left her breasts. Instead his thumbs began to stroke her nipples, causing her to shiver. "Are you cold?" he purred wickedly in her ear.

"You are distracting me," Francesca complained. "You are not washing me. You are teasing me. A tub is for bathing, my lord."

"I should obviously not go away from you, for you have grown shy in my absence," he said, releasing her breasts and scrubbing her back with the soapy cloth.

"I never imagined a tub could be used for any other purpose than bathing," she responded.

He chuckled. "Lovers can make love anywhere and at any time," he assured her.

"Lacking practical experience, I must take your word on it," Francesca told him.

He rinsed her back and then, turning her about, gave her a slow sensuous kiss. "I'm glad you can accept my word on such matters," he said, his hands sliding beneath her buttocks to lift her up. Their lips met again as his hard length slipped into her warm body and he began to move himself back and forth.

Francesca's head spun with the deliciousness of his tender assault. "Ohh, my!" she gasped. "Ohh, Rafaello, it is so good!"

His hands crushed the plump flesh of her bottom in his passion. He had known enough women in his life to understand passion, but never had he felt with any woman the way he felt with Francesca. With every stroke of his cock he felt fulfilled. Her little cries of pleasure, her whimpers of delight sent a thrill through him. Could his alter ego, Carlo, have wrung those sweet sounds from her had he taken his pleasure there in the forest inn? No! No! He couldn't have. Francesca was his and his alone!

"Rafaello! *Ohh, Rafaello*!" She cried his name in her passion. Her arms tightened about him. Her legs squeezed his torso hard. She felt a fierce stirring within that threatened to overwhelm her entirely. "Oh! Oh! *Ohhh*!" She shuddered as the pleasure rose to overwhelm her entirely.

He cried out, feeling her completeness in the act, his own lust releasing itself so that they shared each other totally.

Her legs fell away from him, but Francesca continued to cling to his neck because she knew if she let go she would collapse and sink beneath the water of the tall oak tub. They held each other tightly, until finally Rafaello asked her, "Can you stand if I leave the tub? Or shall I help you out first, my love?" His lips brushed her brow.

She didn't answer him immediately. Then she said, "That was totally delicious, husband. Anytime? Any place? If that be so, then I am eager to try." She relaxed her hold on him. "I won't fall and drown," Francesca assured him.

He climbed from the tub and, having wrapped a drying sheet about his loins, reached to lift her out of the cooling water and enfold her in a second, warmed cloth. Tenderly he rubbed her shoulders, her neck, and her arms. Seating her upon their bed he dried her feet, making her giggle as he slipped the towel between her toes.

"My old nursemaid used to do that when I was a child," Francesca said.

"Mine too," he admitted.

"Rafaello?"

"Yes, Francesca?"

"I asked you that morning at the lodge if we were happy, and you said you were. Now I would tell you that I am happy too, my lord husband," Francesca admitted shyly.

"Would you mind if I fell in love with you?" he asked her almost boyishly.

"Have you?" she countered as her heart skipped several beats. *Love.* She hadn't considered marriage would bring her love. She wasn't her elder sister, Bianca, giving up everything she had and knew for a man. She had left those illusions behind her in Venice, when as a silly little girl she had believed herself in love with Prince Enzo. To be loved by one's husband was a wonderful dream.

"I'm considering it," he teased her. "If we lived in your Florence it would be considered very unfashionable, I know, but here in Terreno Boscoso we make our own rules, wife. Yes! I believe I shall fall in love with you, Francesca."

She suddenly felt shy of him again, but she had to admit that the idea of having her handsome husband fall in love with her was a pleasing notion. She stood up and her drying sheet fell away. "I had best get a chemise," she said.

"No," he told her. "We will sleep as God fashioned us, my love." Drawing back the coverlet of the bed, he invited her into it. Then he said, "Would you mind?"

"Mind what?" she asked him as she slid beneath the coverlet.

"If I fell in love with you," he said softly as he joined her and wrapped an arm about her. Drawing her close, he began caressing her breasts.

"N . . . no," Francesca answered him as softly. "I would not mind if you fell in love with me, my lord husband."

"Do you think you could love me?" He bent and kissed a nipple.

"Oh yes!" Francesca said, blushing at her own eagerness. To love and to be loved. She was suddenly overwhelmed with a burst of happiness. She could not see the smile that touched his lips at her answer.

"I am glad," Rafaello said. The shadow of Carlo the huntsman was banished now, and he was relieved. She would love him alone, and it was comforting. He was surprised to know how much that meant to him.

During the next few days the young duke considered a way to ferret out the bandits troubling the High Road. It was obvious that their leader was a trifle smarter than most robbers, for he could not be lured by too big a party of travelers, who would be very well guarded. He had not the men for such a venture, and they had not the skills of trained soldiers. The bait would have to be something inviting but not obviously dangerous. He discussed the matter with the old duke.

Listening, Francesca had an idea. "A wedding party," she said. "Wedding parties are not generally considered risky to thieves."

"We could not put some poor girl at risk," Rafaello said.

Francesca laughed. "It doesn't have to be a real wedding party. The bride in her closed litter can be a young man dressed like a woman. The men-at-arms guarding the wedding can appear older than they actually are, which should reassure the bandits of their superiority. Those accompanying the bride, both male and female relations, will actually be soldiers."

Duke Titus chuckled. "Your *duchessa* has a devious mind," he approved.

"A Florentine trait," Francesca answered him pertly with a grin.

"What if Bruno and his robbers do not take this very tasty bait that you are suggesting?" Rafaello asked his wife.

"Oh," Francesca answered him, "you cannot simply send your faux wedding party down the High Road without laying your groundwork first," she explained. "First you must go to the innkeeper who brought the complaint about these villains. You have told me he is not trustworthy, for he fears you are not strong enough to root out Bruno and his ilk. He plays both ends against the middle.

"So send Captain Arnaldo to this man. He will be impressed by that. The captain will tell the innkeeper that a wealthy merchant from Milan is bringing his daughter to wed her cousin in France. The captain will tell the innkeeper that your men will do a sweep of the High Road the day before the wedding party is to come. That if he hears that Bruno is near he must let us know. He will, of course, send to the bandit in order to ingratiate himself with him. He will not realize you are on to his dangerous game.

"I guarantee there will be no sign of these robbers when your men patrol the High Road. But the next day when the wedding party goes on its way it is sure to be attacked, especially if we make it tempting enough. The bride is a virgin. She is attended by six pretty maidens. Her dower, which will travel with her is very, very rich. Bruno is a man who violated a noblewoman and took pleasure in the deed. He gave her serving woman to his men. There hasn't been a prize like this wedding party on the High Road in months. It will be too good for him to resist. Gold and women. No bandit could eschew such a treat. Could he?" Francesca asked.

"It is a good plan," Rafaello said, looking at his young wife with growing respect.

"An excellent plan," old Duke Titus agreed. "I liked Francesca from the start for her common sense and her kindness. But when you chose her for your wife, my son, you gained a serious helpmate."

"I will send Captain Arnaldo to the innkeeper in a few days' time, after we prepare our trap for the bandits," the young duke said.

"Let me choose the bride," Francesca said, giggling.

"We will let our captain do that, my love," her husband replied. "The young man chosen will be embarrassed enough."

"And he will fight harder to prove his manhood once the enemy is engaged," Francesca remarked wisely. "But Terza, Rosa, and I must help to dress the ladies of the wedding party, my lord."

"That seems fair," her father-in-law agreed. "After all, my son, this clever plan is Francesca's. She should have some part in it."

Rafaello nodded.

During the next few days they put together the appearance of a prosperous wedding party. Captain Arnaldo visited the innkeeper and told him of its imminent arrival. He watched with half-closed eyes, a mug of the inn's best ale half-empty in his hand as the innkeeper surreptitiously spoke with a stableman whom the captain watched leave the vicinity. He allowed the duplicitous taverner to believe all was well. The next day he and his men swept the road from the inn to the nearby border with France and back with much noise and saber rattling.

"Your bandits appear to have gone," he said to his host on his return. "I shall tell my master the road is safe for this wedding party. It would not do for us to have an incident. You know how sensitive Milan's rulers are right now, even with the peace. They sent to our duke to make certain this bride and her family reached their destination safely." Then with a nod he departed with his men back to the castle.

Reaching his destination, he sought out the young duke. "It's done, my lord. The innkeeper, as we suspected, sent a man off to notify Bruno of the impending riches coming his way in a few days. We traveled the High Road to the border with much noise and flourishing. It was as quiet as a tomb. I saw deer and I saw wildflowers, but not one sign of the bandits. They know how to hide, although I doubt not they were spying on us as we rode the entire way," the captain reported to his master.

"We'll depart in two days' time," Rafaello said.

"Surely you aren't going. Are you?" Francesca asked.

"I am the Duke of Terreno Boscoso," Rafaello replied. "It is my duty to go."

"But there will be fighting!" Francesca cried.

He and Captain Arnaldo both grinned. "Aye, my love," he said. "There will be! And it will be glorious. The rulers of small duchies like this one rarely get to engage in any sort of battle. My father and I kept clear of the altercation between the French king and the Italian states. We showed no partiality to either side but avoided the conflict. This little adventure, rooting out these bandits, will give me an opportunity to use the skills I spent my youth learning."

"Why is it that men never grow up?" Francesca said to no one in particular. Then she looked at Captain Arnaldo. "I charge you with his safety," she said. "If you fail me I will be ruthless in your punishment. Do you understand me?"

"My love," Rafaello chided her, "do not be so harsh."

"You are this duchy's only heir right now, my lord," she reminded him, "and we are but newly wed."

"She is right, my lord," the captain said. Then he turned to Francesca. "I will personally see to his safety, my lady."

While the *duchessa* and her two serving women had a great deal of fun dressing the soldiers who would pose as the women of the wedding party, they were also careful to see to it that the colorful robes they wore could be quickly and easily discarded to reveal the fighting men. The men involved looked uncomfortable, as Terza and Rosa couldn't resist teasing them, especially the young man who would play the bride, a fresh-faced lad whose head they covered with a butterfly headdress—a generous length of transparent linen that was wired and draped to effect the shape of a butterfly.

Much hilarity ensued once the head covering had been donned. The red-faced bride was escorted to her open litter.

"I'm almost tempted by such a lovely wench myself," Captain Arnaldo chuckled, seeing the results of the women's labor.

The false wedding party departed the castle. The soldiers that would be shadowing them blended into the landscape, but for a token force escorting the merchant and his family. Traveling slowly along the High Road they passed the inn, the innkeeper watching them.

"I wonder who he is more afraid of," Captain Arnaldo murmured to the duke. "You or Bruno."

"I suspect we are equally dangerous," Rafaello replied, "but I am this duchy's ruler. Having complained to me of these bandits our innkeeper friend would have done better to trust in my authority instead of playing both ends against the middle. I will have to punish him when this is over. No one must be allowed to believe that I am not aware of everything happening on my own lands."

"I agree," the captain responded.

The false wedding party moved along. The bride was clearly visible in her open litter.

Half a dozen richly garbed ladies upon their horses surrounded her, escorted by several prosperous-looking gentlemen. There were three carts full of what appeared to be a rich dower, and eight men-at-arms. To anyone seeing the train it appeared to be a wealthy wedding party. Nothing more.

They were at least two miles past the inn when the bandits struck, rising from the side of the High Road, weapons in hand. The travelers stopped, the false ladies shrieking as it was expected that women surprised by robbers would do. The man chosen to play the bride's father shouted in an outraged voice.

"How dare you stop us? Move aside!"

The bandit chief called Bruno stepped forward. "That is a fine horse you are riding, sir. I will have it! And I will have your pretty daughter for myself, while your ladies entertain my men. As for you and your gentlemen, you are all dead men!"

It was then that the duke and his men appeared, surrounding the bandits from behind.

"I think not," Rafaello said in a hard voice. "It is you who has earned a quick trip to hell! You are sentenced to death for the kidnapping and rape of Aceline du Barry last year, and for your boldness in impersonating me while you used the poor woman."

Bruno's mouth fell open with his surprise, but, recovering quickly, he lunged at the duke, who was still ahorse. Rafaello Cesare was an excellent horseman. His stallion responded to the rein and reared up, knocking the bandit to the ground. The duke then jumped from the animal's back, dagger in hand, flung himself atop the robber, and slit his throat. Standing up he told his men, "Hang the rest of them, and leave them hanging as a lesson to any who would steal from travelers along this road." Then, turning to Captain Arnaldo, he said, "We have an innkeeper to punish."

The two men rode back to the inn, where they found the innkeeper in his taproom. The man looked up, surprised, as the duke and his captain entered. "My lord!" he exclaimed, and hurried to bring them wine.

The duke waved his hospitality aside. "You came to me for justice, and then you betrayed me," he said without any preamble. "Know that Bruno is dead and his men as well. The High Road will be kept safe where it runs through Terreno Boscoso as long as I am this duchy's ruler. The wedding party that passed by your inn several hours ago was a trap conceived to draw Bruno and his men out into the open. When we realized your duplicity we knew if we told you of such a rich prize you would be certain to get word to the bandits. You did not disappoint me. Bruno and his men have paid for their crimes with their lives. Now I must decide how to punish you."

"My lord, have mercy!" the innkeeper begged him.

"Are you aware that your bandit friend kidnapped and assaulted a young noblewoman who had been a guest of my father's last summer as she traveled home to France? She bore his child, and the horrendous experience rendered her mad. She now resides in a convent with her bastard, being cared for by the nuns."

"My lord, I did not know!" the innkeeper babbled.

"No, you did not. But you did know this bandit and his men would ruin your trade if word got out that the High Road was not safe. So you came to me, and I promised you that I would take care of the matter. Yet before I might, you betrayed me by going to the bandits. Why?"

"My lord, my stableman is kin to Bruno. He told the robber of my complaint to you. Bruno came and threatened to burn my inn to the ground and slay me if I did not cooperate with him. I had no other choice!"

"Aye, you did," the duke said. "You might have sent to me again telling me of this threat, but you did not. I would have protected you. What if I had not sent this decoy wedding party along the High Road to trap this man? What if they had been a real group of travelers? The men in the group would have been killed and the women violated. You must accept a certain responsibility for this, innkeeper."

"No harm was actually done," the man whined.

"Find his cache," the duke told Captain Arnaldo. "And confiscate it."

"No, my lord!" The innkeeper's eye went to the fireplace in his taproom.

Seeing it the duke said, "Check the fireplace wall for loose stones. His cache will be there. Let us see what he had hidden away."

Captain Arnaldo quickly found the innkeeper's hiding place, and drew forth three small chamois bags. They held a variety of coins including gold, silver, and copper.

"Take them," the duke said.

"My lord, 'tis all I have!" the innkeeper cried. "It has taken me years to save these coins! How will I survive in my old age?"

"You are young enough yet to save more. I do not want what I take from you this day. I shall send it to the convent that shelters Bruno's child, so that when the boy is grown he will have a small inheritance. He did not ask to be born under such circumstances as he was. Whether he becomes a priest or a soldier he will have your coins to give him a start.

"I will not burn down your inn around your ears, nor will I slay you, innkeeper. I will leave you with your livelihood and with your life," the duke said. "I am generous. Another man might not be. You should be grateful. If the Frenchman whose daughter was so brutalized knew of your association with Bruno, he would have slain you without a qualm. But should you ever be disloyal to me again you will suffer long and painfully." Rafaello looked sharply at the now-shaking man. "Do you understand me?"

"Y-yes, my lord! Yes!" the innkeeper said. His face was drained of almost all color in his fear.

The duke turned away from the man and strode from the

inn. He would see that a sharp eye was kept on the innkeeper, for the man's inn was the only one between the castle and the French border. And then a smile touched his lips as he swung himself into the saddle. A chuckle escaped him.

"What is it, my lord?" Captain Arnaldo asked him.

"I have had an idea how to keep our innkeeper friend honest and on the straight-and-narrow path," the duke told his companion. "The man has no competition. I shall commission another inn to be built along the High Road. Then I shall hire some of Alonza's family to manage it." He chuckled again.

"Who is Alonza?" Captain Arnaldo asked his master.

"She is the woman my father hired to run the little winter inn he built in the forest so his huntsmen might have a place to shelter in the cold months," the duke said.

The captain nodded. The old duke had a kind heart, he thought.

Returning to the castle they found Francesca waiting for them in the courtyard.

"Has he been injured in any way?" she demanded of the captain. "Remember, you promised to keep him safe for me."

"There is not a scratch on me, my love," the duke assured his wife. "It was all rather anticlimactic, with virtually no fighting once I had killed Bruno. Then we hung the rest of them, leaving their bodies for the crows and as a warning to any who might consider taking up where Bruno left off."

Francesca suddenly shrieked and pointed at him. "There is blood on your doublet!" she cried. "You have been injured!" She turned on Captain Arnaldo. "You swore to keep him from harm!"

"Madam, the blood is Bruno's, not the duke's," the soldier assured her. "Your husband cleverly used his horse to knock the bandit to the ground, then quickly jumped down and cut his throat. Considering the thickness of the man's neck it was masterfully done, my lady, but it is difficult to avoid blood after a kill," Captain Arnaldo explained.

"The doublet is ruined," Francesca said to no one in particular. Relief was pouring through her at the knowledge Rafaello was safe and had not been hurt.

The duke felt a rush of warmth fill him. She loved him! Oh, she had not admitted to it in so many words. But would she have been so concerned if she didn't love him? Putting an arm about her waist, he suggested, "Let us go into the hall and tell my father of our success in clearing the High Road of the bandits." Then, turning to Captain Arnaldo, he said, "See that all the men return safely and that they have an extra measure of wine tonight for their trouble."

In the hall the old duke was delighted to see his son had safely returned, and even more pleased to learn the task of clearing the bandits had been easier than anticipated. When Rafaello suggested building another inn along the High Road, Duke Titus concurred. "An excellent idea, my son. Yes! A bit of competition will be good for that villain who now runs the only inn along the road."

"You must write to the Comte du Barry and tell him his daughter's honor has been avenged," Francesca said. "He should know that you personally killed the bandit chief. It will not return his daughter to him or make her child legitimate, but the Frenchman must know that Terreno Boscoso did not take this matter lightly. Shall we pay him an indemnity?"

"No," her husband said. "Aceline du Barry was returned to her father's house as she had come. It was the comte who was too tight with a coin to provide his daughter with a proper escort. She arrived safely. It was to be expected she would return safely. We had no knowledge of the bandits early last autumn when she left us."

Francesca nodded. "I understand," she said.

"To pay the Comte du Barry an indemnity would suggest that we were aware of the danger on the High Road and allowed Aceline to go anyway. We did not know. If we had we would have sent her home another way and provided her with a stronger escort," the duke explained to his wife. "When the comte returns from Florence I will tell him what transpired. A letter might not reach him for I doubt he will remain there. He will want to return to France as quickly as possible."

Again Francesca nodded. "Nothing can change what has happened, but at least your actions in punishing those who so cruelly harmed the comte's daughter may ease his pain."

Chapter 13

Raoul, Comte du Barry, returned from Florence alone. He thanked the young *duchessa* for her kindness in suggesting the convent of Santa Maria del Fiori as a shelter for his mad daughter and her bastard child. The nuns, he said, had been very kind, and he had left his daughter's dower portion in gold for her care with them. He looked relieved of the burden of Aceline, but sad as well.

Francesca recalled that Aceline had said her father had little interest in her. He would see her well married because her late mother would have wanted it; but he found his current wife more intriguing than his only daughter. But more interesting to Francesca was all the news the Frenchman brought of what was going on in the world outside of Terreno Boscoso.

A great deal had happened since Francesca had left Florence, and her mother's few letters had said little other than that the wool merchants were having difficulties, as England was now weaving its own cloth. Orianna had also mentioned that Milan was now manufacturing silk in competition with Florence, although she said the weave of their own silk was tighter, which made the material softer. But Milan's silk was less expensive. Orianna wrote nothing of politics.

Before Francesca had returned from her grandfather's house in Venice and prior to her journey to Terreno Boscoso, a rival family to the di Medici, the Pazzi, encouraged by the pope, had attempted to assassinate the di Medici brothers in Florence's cathedral. Lorenzo's younger brother, Giuliano di Medici, had been killed. Lorenzo was wounded but fought off his attackers. The archbishop and several priests were involved. The Pazzi had been certain the Florentine population would rise in support of them. Instead the citizens of the republic turned against them as the great bell, the *vacca*, was tolled in the Palazzo della Signoria. The di Medici family was popular with the people of the city. They identified with them. The Pazzi, however, were descendants of an ancient noble family, and they never forgot it. Florence sided with Lorenzo di Medici.

The archbishop and all those considered part of the conspiracy or sympathetic to it were caught and hanged from the windows of the Palazzo della Signoria. There was very little mercy shown to them. Some were sentenced to prison. Lorenzo's own sister was married to a Pazzi, but her husband had had no part in the conspiracy and was merely confined to his villa for a brief time. All evidence of the Pazzi family was removed from Florentine history. They were totally disgraced. The pope's involvement in the plot was made public.

The utter defeat of the Pazzi family roused total fury in their Roman enemies. Florentine bankers and merchants in Rome

were arrested, but then released, for the pope had been reminded of his kinsman, Cardinal Riario, who lived in Florence.
But it did not stop the Holy Father from taking all the di Medici
assets, both property and gold, that he could find in Rome.
Then the pope forgave the enormous debt owed by the Vatican
to the di Medicis.

In Florence the di Medicis grit their teeth at this economic
blow. But the pope was not finished with his revenge. He sent
his nuncio with an order of excommunication against the di
Medici family, Lorenzo in particular, and the entire elected Florentine government. They were to be turned over to papal justice; their homes were to be destroyed and their properties
confiscated. Of course, none of this was enforceable, and the
arrival of a Turkish force in southern Italy brought all the Italian states together again to fight the infidel who was their common enemy. A delegation of important Florentine citizens went
to Rome, muttered an apology to the pope that no one could
hear, and were forgiven in equally muted tones. The Turks withdrew with the death of their sultan, and peace came to Italy.

In Terreno Boscoso these things became known only when
Raoul du Barry returned from Florence and told them. The
duchy was so small that no one had ever paid a great deal of
heed to it. It had been at peace for centuries with its more powerful neighbors. It had no army, and nothing anyone else would
want unless they sought more territory. But before the Frenchman departed for his own home he mentioned that the di Medici
banking system appeared to be failing.

"I am not surprised," Francesca told her husband. "Lorenzo
is not the man for business that his grandfather was."

"It is fortunate we have never used their bank," Duke Titus
said. "We are too small for the di Medici to bother with, al-

though I must one day remember to thank Lorenzo de Medici for sending you to us, my daughter."

"If the di Medici banking system is failing," Francesca said worriedly, "my father's business will be involved. He has always kept his monies with them. I hope he will not lose by his loyalty to the di Medicis."

But like many in Florence, Giovanni Pietro d'Angelo found it difficult to believe that the always-reliable di Medici bank was having difficulty. The di Medici banking system had always been there for Florence's citizens. Unfortunately not having a brilliant business mind at its head had taken a toll. Its branch managers had been allowed too much latitude. The general manager of the di Medici banking enterprise had not been chosen wisely. He was a man who was afraid to speak frankly to his master and always delayed bad news, thereby making the problem worse than it would have been.

Too much money had been loaned out to England's King Edward IV, causing the London branch to fail, as well as the one in Milan. The branches in Naples, Lyon, and Rome were all in jeopardy. There was too much incompetence on the part of those picked by Lorenzo to direct his family business. Lorenzo admitted to not understanding a great deal about his family's financial empire. Hearing that, Giovanni Pietro d'Angelo withdrew his remaining monies from the di Medici bank and placed them with a smaller but more conservative bank owned by a Jewish goldsmith, Jacobo Kira.

The di Medici bank in Florence could not refuse to give the silk merchant his monies. As head of his guild Giovanni Pietro d'Angelo was an important man in his own small way. His actions affected only himself. He made no public display of his decision. The di Medicis had always been generous to his family, but he could not allow Lorenzo's attitude to destroy their security. He still had two daughters to marry off.

As it was, the economic climate was no longer a particularly prosperous one for the silk trade. Even his wealthy clients were spending less and less. Removing his monies from the failing di Medici banking system had been his way of protecting his family as times grew harder. Orianna was instructed to make changes in the way she spent her household allowance. Fortunately he had previously purchased his son Georgio's place in the church. His second son had been educated for the priesthood and only recently been ordained. At nineteen he was a secretary to a cardinal. It had been an expensive position to obtain, but the silk merchant was glad he had done it. His second son's future was now secure, for which he was glad. With the silk trade becoming less lucrative there was room only for his eldest son, Marco, in his business. Some of this Orianna wrote to Francesca, but not all.

"My *madre* is afraid," the young *duchessa* told her husband. "The world is changing around her and too quickly."

"The world does not change here in Terreno Boscoso," Rafaello answered his wife. "We remain the same no matter what happens around us."

"That is comforting," Francesca responded, "but I think perhaps now we cannot help but be affected as everyone else around us is. If Florence changes, then so does the rest of the world."

He laughed at her. "You are so serious, my love," he said. "You must not be."

But Francesca worried. Her husband did not see things with a woman's eye. He settled fairly and equitably the small disputes brought to him by his citizens. He hunted. He played chess with his father. His *duchessa*, however, saw that the harvest that summer was not as bounteous as in past years. She heard the rumors in the marketplace of the French incursions on their far border. So far, however, that had been nothing more than a patrol or two straying across the invisible line between the two countries. She mentioned it to Rafaello, but he did not appear concerned.

"The borderlands are porous," he told her. "The French and the Savoyards stray across the boundaries. They mean no harm."

Francesca was surprised by his words as she realized how sheltered in his little duchy her handsome husband was. No one had ever attacked or coveted Terreno Boscoso, but Francesca knew that larger powers did not encroach upon the territories of smaller ones by accident. If Francesca had learned one lesson from her mother it was to be aware of anything that would affect her life. Unlike her charming husband and his dear father, she was suspicious of French activity.

Old Duke Titus realized her concern and sought to allay it. "Over the years the French and Savoyards have encroached on our lands, but they never remain. There is nothing here for them."

"There is land," Francesca replied. "King Louis recently inherited Anjou. He has secured it, and appropriated not only Anjou, but Le Maine and Provence as well," she explained to the elderly man. "His wife is a Savoyard. Adding Terreno Boscoso to his possessions would give the French an easy passage into the Italian states. If the French invade us from the north and west, the Milanese would feel threatened and would come up from the south to protect themselves. Caught in the middle between these two powers, Terreno Boscoso could be destroyed."

"We must trust in God and the fact that we have never threatened our neighbors," Duke Titus said. He turned to his son. "What think you of this, my son?"

"I agree with my father," Rafaello replied, to Francesca's frustration.

"Autumn is here," her father-in-law said, "and winter will be upon us before you know it. No one goes to war in winter."

Francesca had to take their word on this matter, but she was still concerned. Growing up in Florence she had learned the lessons of history and political maneuvering well. But her father-in-law was correct when he said most wars did not begin in winter.

As the days grew shorter and the winds blew from the north, the young *duchessa* recalled her adventures of the previous year in the forest. She assumed Alonza was now at the woodland inn, and that the huntsmen were beginning to slowly come to their winter shelter once again. Francesca wondered if the inn-keeper had found a suitable serving wench to help her this season. She was almost tempted to suggest they visit the inn, but knew that would but raise suspicions in her husband's mind about Carlo. Still, she could not help but wonder about the huntsman who had so briefly been her almost-lover.

The winter holidays came, and they had been wed for six months. Francesca was concerned because there was yet no sign of a child on her part. Rafaello's childhood friend, Valiant, had visited the castle briefly. Louisa had given him one child and was already expecting another. Even poor Aceline du Barry had quickened swiftly after her assault. Her mother had borne seven healthy children, a rarity in their world. Yet Francesca seemed unable to conceive. She felt guilty, because she knew one of her assets as a bride had been the fertility shown by her mother. What if she were barren? It was unthinkable! She confided her fears to Terza.

"You are barely wed," her faithful maidservant said. "Besides, it took old Duke Titus almost ten years to produce his only child. It is always the woman who is blamed, but what if the man's seed is not fertile?" Terza asked practically.

Terza's words, however, did little to reassure Francesca. Her duty was to produce an heir for Terreno Boscoso. Her seeming inability to conceive was very disturbing.

The winter deepened and was extremely hard. The north winds blew steadily. It seemed to snow every day until everything was white. The mountains beyond the castle, the tower roofs, the town. The courtyard was being constantly shoveled so that the stables could be reached and the animals fed. When two chickens froze in the night, the birds were brought into the kitchens, penned there for their own safety.

Everyone seemed to be suffering from the weather, sniffling and sneezing. Keeping warm was difficult, and then Duke Titus began to cough. At first he seemed no worse off than everyone else in the castle, but his cough would not go away. Indeed it grew worse, deepening and sounding thick. Francesca dosed him as best she could. She fed him hot soup and rubbed his chest with a mixture of goose fat and peppermint. She kept him dressed warmly, and when he was strong enough to sit in the hall she saw that he was wrapped in a fur coverlet.

But the old duke grew worse despite her nursing diligence. He was suddenly quiet and would not eat. It reached a point where even Francesca could not get hot wine and herbs into her father-in-law to ease his cough. His body grew frail and shook so hard that she feared he would injure himself. "He is dying," she told Rafaello. "I can do no more, my lord husband."

The young duke nodded. He had eyes. If he had one regret it was that his father would not live to see a grandchild. "How long do you think he can survive?" he asked his wife. "If he could live until spring perhaps he would grow strong again."

Francesca shook her head. "Terza says he will die at any time now. He is not strong enough to last much longer, and certainly not until spring, which is two months away, my lord. I am sorry. I have done my best."

"I know you have," Rafaello replied, his eyes filling with tears as he looked at her.

Her own tear-filled eyes met his, and it was in that same moment that Francesca got the oddest sensation. Her husband's wonderful dark green eyes with their golden lights reminded her of something or someone, but she could not put her finger on it. Shaking off the strange feeling, she put her arms about Rafaello to comfort him. "We will do our best by our father, my lord," Francesca said softly.

Duke Titus died several days later. Before he closed his eyes that final time, he had called his son and Francesca to him, giving them his blessing. The bells in the little town's cathedral tolled his passing, and Duke Rafaello ordered a mourning period of two months. The old duke was interred in the family vault, which was located deep in the bowels of the castle itself. Francesca was thankful they had not had to dig a grave, for the frozen earth would not have yielded easily until the spring thaw.

And eventually winter began to release its hold on Terreno Boscoso. The snows melted slowly from the nearby hillsides, although the high mountain peaks beyond remained white.

There were patches of green here and there. The winds began to come again from the south some mornings. The sun shone more and more each day. And then when the danger of snow seemed past, word came from travelers along the High Road that the French were moving a small military force into Terreno Boscoso.

"I knew it!" Francesca said. "Last year's incursion was to see if there would be any resistance, and of course there wasn't, because this duchy has never been threatened."

"There has to be a mistake," Rafaello insisted.

"There is no mistake. The French want something of you. They know we have no armies to contest their incursion. You will have to wait to see just what it is they want. We cannot wait too long, however. If you do not at least protest their incursion they will believe the duchy is theirs for the taking."

"Perhaps they will withdraw," the young duke suggested.

Madre di Dios, he is so trusting of the world, Francesca thought. Well, she would be patient. After all he had not been raised in her father's house in the city of Florence. He could not imagine the machinations that went on among the powerful. "First," she said to him, "we should learn who has ordered this force to invade our territories. If it is some minor lord we will protest to the French king and send to Milan for aid. But if it is King Louis himself we have a greater problem, and Milan must be notified, else they believe we are in collusion with the French. Remember that Milan's duke is a child. His mother and uncles are quarreling among themselves for his authority. News of a French incursion will not please the Spanish either."

"How are you so knowledgeable in such matters?" he asked her.

"If you had grown up in Florence, my lord, you would know

these things too," she told him. "The world is a hard place, but you have been so sheltered here in your little duchy that you are not aware of such matters. Men of wealth and power always seek more wealth and more power. We will set a watch on the High Road and wait to see what will happen. Remember, my lord, that nothing ever remains the same. The world is always changing, and changing whether we will it or no."

They did not wait long. Several days later a small party of French arrived. It was led by the Comte du Barry, which surprised Francesca. What mischief was this man up to? She thought their kindness of the previous year had been accepted. Obviously it had not.

Francesca spoke privily to her husband before they greeted the Frenchman and his party.

"Do not accuse, but ask him what purpose he has encroaching upon our lands," she said. "He should know you are aware of the French presence and disturbed by it."

Rafaello nodded, and then together they went into the castle's hall to greet their unwelcome visitors. "My lord du Barry," the duke said by way of greeting.

The comte bowed. "I bring you greetings from King Louis, my lord duke."

"While I am flattered, I am puzzled as to why France's king would trouble himself with me," the duke responded. "Certainly I hold no importance for King Louis."

"There you are wrong," the comte answered him. "Terreno Boscoso is of great interest to the king."

"Why?" the duke asked.

"It offers an easy gateway into the Italian states where Spain is interfering. King Louis would like to have your fealty, my lord duke. He needs to know his armies may pass through your little duchy unimpeded if needs be," the Comte du Barry responded.

"Terreno Boscoso has never taken sides in any conflict between the larger powers. If I swear fealty to France, then Milan will feel threatened. France will not come to my aid if that be the case. My duchy will end up being menaced from all sides. If your king invades the Italian states again as he did several years ago, let France's armies pass the same way as they did before," the duke told the Frenchman.

"The northern route takes longer, and time could be of the essence," the comte protested. "France needs to come through Terreno Boscoso if necessary. You cannot be permitted to refuse King Louis!"

The duke signaled his servants to bring wine, hoping his hospitality would cool the Frenchman's rising temper. The foreign delegation accepted the goblets offered.

"I am amazed that King Louis even knows of our existence," Francesca murmured. The duchy had been left in peace for centuries. They had never taken sides in any of the disputes that arose between larger powers. How had the French king even come to know of Terreno Boscoso?

"King Louis is very well informed on all matters," the Comte du Barry replied in answer to her query. Then he turned back to the duke. "I have with me a document for you to sign, my lord. In return for your fealty King Louis will defend your rights and that of your heirs to rule this duchy in perpetuity."

Rafaello burst out laughing. "The Cesare family is descended from the Caesars, and have held this territory since ancient times. Times before your king's original ancestors even came into existence. The first ruler of this duchy was a Roman general, Titus Flavius Caesar. I do not need King Louis's permission to rule, nor for my descendants to rule. We have held this land for centuries, my lord. I will not permit my people to be put in danger by the squabbling of great lords and kings."

"You have no armies," the Comte du Barry pointed out.

"We have never needed any," Rafaello responded. "We are neutral."

"If you do not cooperate with King Louis we will take Terreno Boscoso from you in his name," the Comte du Barry threatened.

"I will protest to Milan and to Florence," the duke said, his temper beginning to rise with every passing minute.

"Neither will aid you," the Frenchman replied smugly. "Milan's duke is a child caught in a power struggle between his uncle and his mother. As for Florence, the di Medicis are too busy attempting to salvage their crumbling banking empire to be bothered with an unimportant duchy that holds nothing of value for them."

"If it is explained that your king wants my lands so he may invade the Italian states easily, both Florence and Milan may think better of my plea for help," the duke said.

The Comte du Barry shrugged. "There is peace between us right now. King Louis considers the future. Both Milan and Florence are too far away to be bothered with you. Sign the document I have brought you, and you will continue to remain at peace."

Francesca murmured something to her husband, and the duke said, "I must think on it, my lord. I am content to offer you and your delegation hospitality for the night, but tomorrow you must be gone."

The Comte du Barry bowed politely in response.

Francesca excused herself from the hall. She didn't like being stared at by some of the comte's companions. They had been eyeing her as if she were some prize to be gained. This is a dangerous situation, she thought. She spoke to Piero as she departed, telling him to see that their guests were well fed and housed in the hall overnight, even the Comte du Barry. "Take care for your master's safety. I do not trust these men," she warned him, and the servant nodded. Francesca hurried to her own apartments.

"What is happening?" Terza asked her. "Roza said she saw that the Comte du Barry is among those men now in the hall."

"He is," the *duchessa* answered her serving woman. "King Louis has sent him to demand that the duke swear fealty to France."

"How did an unimportant fellow like that become a king's messenger?" Terza asked aloud. "And how did the French king learn about our little duchy? And why would he seek the duke's fealty?"

"I do not know the answers to any of your queries, but these are questions that will need answers, and quickly," Francesca said. "When my lord has fed and settled these unwelcome guests he will come to me so we may discuss it." She did not tell Terza that the French wanted easy access into the Italian states and would come through the duchy if there was war again.

Francesca dismissed her serving women and waited for her husband to join her. When he did his handsome face was grim. She poured them both some wine from the tray on the sideboard in her dayroom. Then together they sat by the hearth and talked.

"Not only do the French want easy access to our neighbors to the south," he began, "they want to quarter troops here as well. Terreno Boscoso has never in our long history been occupied by a foreign power," Rafaello told her. "I cannot allow it, yet if I forbid it they will force themselves upon us. Du Barry even hinted that our lives are at risk if I refuse them. I do not understand the French king's sudden need for my duchy."

"We might have hidden from public knowledge the fact that you signed an agreement with France and swore fealty to King Louis, but we cannot keep secret an occupying force," Francesca said. "Because we have no army of our own we are at a huge disadvantage with all of our neighbors. You will refuse this demand, of course."

He nodded. "Du Barry cannot force his king on me now, for he has not enough men with him. If I call King Louis's bluff he may let this go. The truth is that if he wanted to move his armies through the duchy we could not stop him. I do not understand this need to gain my fealty," Rafaello said.

"Perhaps this was not King Louis's idea. Perhaps it was du Barry who brought us to his attention and has convinced him of the wisdom of having Terreno Boscoso in his purview. I remember Aceline bragging to Louisa and me that her father was a cousin of Louis's queen, Charlotte of Savoy. This kinship would give him a certain easy access to the French court."

"But why is he doing this?" Rafaello asked his wife. "Can you divine his reasoning?"

"He seeks revenge for what happened to his daughter. I believed the knowledge that you were not responsible for her child and our kindness in arranging for Santa Maria del Fiore to give Aceline and her infant a home would have contented him. But he is angry, for his daughter had value to his family as a marriage prize. If you did not choose her, he had another man eager to take her to wife. That was another thing she bragged about. Her father sent her here at your father's invitation in the hopes of gaining a duke for a son-in-law, but the other man was very wealthy, according to Aceline.

"The Comte du Barry has a guilty conscience because he did not send enough men-at-arms to guard his daughter in her travels here to Terreno Boscoso. He requested of your father that he feed and house these men until a decision was made one way or another. Duke Titus appreciated the comte's practical side. But having so few men escort his daughter home in early autumn was the cause of her unfortunate tragedy. Raoul du Barry knows this on one hand, but on the other he wants to hold Terreno Boscoso responsible for what befell his daughter. It is not our fault, but du Barry is unable to see that now. Revenging himself on us will not change what has happened, but regretfully you will not be able to convince him of that."

"I will refuse him, refuse King Louis. I have no choice in the matter. We are a sovereign nation. I will not permit the troops of another nation to occupy us," Rafaello said. "I must take the chance that having said no the French will permit the matter to drop, and we will hear no more of it."

"And if they don't?" Francesca asked her husband. "What will you do then? Have you considered it, my lord?"

"I don't know what I will do," he admitted to her. "I could keep a pact of fealty between me and the French secret, but there is no way I can keep it secret if French troops march into my duchy and remain."

Was he correct in his assessment of their situation? Francesca honestly didn't know. What she did understand was that this was a dangerous situation in which they now found themselves. She had no experience in governing, and so she could offer her husband little advice. However, she did realize that whatever he did, Rafaello was taking a chance when he defied the French. Yet du Barry was correct when he said that neither Milan nor Florence would come to their aid, being too involved in their own difficulties right now. Silently she damned Raoul du Barry, whose parsimony had cost his daughter so much misery and would now cost them.

Neither the duke nor his *duchessa* felt like making love that night. They slept restlessly in each other's arms, waking with the dawn. Freshly bathed and dressed they descended together into the castle's Great Hall. Rafaello had wanted to go alone, but Francesca insisted her place was by his side at all times.

"It will not be pleasant," he said.

"But we will stand together," she replied.

Their guests were already breaking their fast. The Comte du Barry rose from his place at the high board as the duke and *duchessa* joined him.

"Have you made your decision, my lord?" the Frenchman said, and reseated himself as they sat.

"I have," Rafaello answered him.

"And that decision is?" the comte persisted.

"You already know," the duke told him. "I cannot in good conscience sign a treaty of any kind with France, my lord. Terreno Boscoso has been a sovereign realm since the days of Titus Flavius, its first lord. The key to our survival has been our neutrality, and so we will remain. We will not favor any side, as we have done all these centuries. I would not offend King Louis, but neither can I offend my other neighbors. If your king needed to access my lands in time of war I could not prevent him from doing so. Yet the French have always taken an even more northern route into the south. Your king has my respect, but I will not cede my duchy to him."

"I beg you to reconsider, my lord," the Comte du Barry said with false courtesy.

"You ask the impossible of us, my lord," the duke replied. "When you have finished your meal I will expect you and your men to depart."

The Comte du Barry acknowledged this request with a polite nod, but then he turned to Francesca. "Tell me, madam. Do you agree with your husband's decision?"

"I do," she answered, "and if I may speak frankly, my lord, I find it ridiculous that King Louis would attempt to take our little duchy from its rightful ruler. Terreno Boscoso has never been a threat to any of its neighbors." She was surprised that he would ask her such a question, as if he expected her to publicly disagree with her husband.

"My king consolidates his own rights, madam," the comte answered her. "He has already this year annexed Burgundy, and will soon possess both Artois and Franche-Comté. With the death of his brother, King Louis has also seen Guyenne revert into his hands. France is a mighty power."

"So mighty it must bully a peaceful neighbor?" Francesca asked him sweetly.

"Your wife shows intelligence and spirit, my lord," the comte said to the duke. "What a pity you do not have an heir yet."

"We Cesares are slow to produce, but when we do our sons are strong," Rafaello answered. He did not miss the suggestion that if the young duke had chosen Aceline du Barry instead of Francesca he would now have a son. "As you may or may not be aware, my wife's mother birthed seven healthy children for her husband." Then, seeing his guest's plate empty, he continued. "You will want to be on your way now, for the day is new and you have several days' travel ahead of you. You will, of course, give King Louis my respectful felicitations."

The Comte du Barry had no choice, having been so firmly dismissed. He arose from his place at the high board, bowing to the duke and Francesca. He signaled his men, and Rafaello couldn't help but notice that the comte traveled with more men-at-arms than had escorted his own daughter last year. The duke gestured silently to Matteo, and the serving man hurried to his master's side.

"Make certain that the Comte du Barry departs the castle quickly," he said. "And send Captain Arnaldo to me."

"Very good, my lord." Matteo hurried off.

"Why do you want the captain?" Francesca asked her husband.

"I want the comte shadowed for a few days. I would make certain he leaves my lands with all possible speed," Rafaello answered her. "I do not trust him."

"Should you perhaps send a missive to King Louis, asking if the Comte du Barry is actually acting in his name?" Francesca asked him. "Perhaps this attempt to usurp your authority was not King Louis's idea. Perhaps Terreno Boscoso was brought to the French's attention by the Comte du Barry. As a distant cousin of Queen Charlotte he has access to the court. He may have suggested the king acquire your lands, as he is acquiring so many others right now. To destroy your family and our duchy's sovereignty is in his mind a supreme act of revenge for his daughter's shame. Du Barry would, of course, say nothing to you in that regard. Such an act is unworthy of a man of honor."

"If he has indeed done as you suggest, then he has no honor," Rafaello replied. "To attempt to steal another's man's birthright lacks integrity. He is unworthy of our sympathy and our scorn."

"I cannot disagree, but it does not change the fact that Terreno Boscoso is threatened by outside forces," Francesca responded. "You need to learn if it is the French king behind this maneuver or the Comte du Barry."

"If I send to King Louis with this tale and it is untrue, I risk attracting the attention of an acquisitive man," Rafaello told her. "Du Barry is correct in one thing: France has become a power with which to be reckoned."

"What will you do, then?" Francesca asked him.

"We will wait to see what will transpire. If it is indeed the French king behind this matter I do not see how I can fight such a takeover," the duke told his wife. "But if this has all been Raoul du Barry's doing, then we will hear no more of it."

Captain Arnaldo arrived, and the *duchessa* left her husband to speak with him.

Rafaello explained what the Comte du Barry had wanted of him, and his refusal to yield to such a demand.

The captain listened intently as his master gave him his instructions.

"I will want the comte and his men shadowed right to the border, so I may be certain he is gone. Send only one man, for I do not want him seen."

"I have just the man for such a task," Captain Arnaldo said.

"When he is certain that the comte is gone he is to return to us with all possible speed to make his report," the duke instructed his captain.

"Very good, my lord," was his reply, and with a smart bow the man-at-arms hurried from his master's presence.

At that moment Matteo returned to report. "The comte and his men have gone, my lord. I followed them through the town and saw them gain the High Road."

"Excellent!" the duke said.

A number of days later Captain Arnaldo's man returned to tell the duke that the Comte du Barry had gone over the border without incident. The duke now waited to see what would happen. If the French king was indeed attempting to take Terreno Boscoso from its rightful rulers it would be weeks before they would learn anything. A watch was set up at the border between the two countries so that the duke could be warned in advance of any aggressive action towards his duchy. They could do nothing now but wait.

Chapter 14

*T*he duke called a rare meeting of his advisory council. They had not met since the late Duke Titus had brought them together to announce that as soon as Rafaello married he meant to abdicate in his son's favor. The council was made up of the town's three most important merchants, the heads of the three families who descended from the three tribunes who had come to what was now Terreno Boscoso with Titus Flavius Caesar, and Terreno Boscoso's bishop. He told them of the visit he had had from the Comte du Barry, and his claim that King Louis wanted the duke's fealty and to quarter troops in the duchy.

"I have refused both requests, my lords, madam, and good sirs. However, if King Louis does indeed request these things of me it is possible my rejection of his demands may cause him to act in a hostile manner towards the duchy. He could send his troops to force his will upon us." Rafaello looked down the council table at the six men and one woman who were gathered. "I realize that I have put us all in possible danger, but I could not yield to such a request. If Milan learned that the French had put troops in our duchy we would make an enemy of a friend and a trading partner. I regret that I must bring you this news."

The council murmured among themselves. And then the bishop said, "The sovereignty of this duchy must be preserved at all costs, my lord." His companions nodded in agreement.

"Is it possible, my lord, that the French may attempt to force their will upon us?" The question came from the only woman on the council, a merchant who exported beautiful gold and silver jewelry to the Italian states. Her wares were in great demand. "Soldiers have a habit of stealing from the local population when they occupy a country. And as you are aware the artisans in my employ are all women. I would not put them in danger, my lord. Certainly you can understand."

"I do," the duke answered her, "but I have no certain answers to give you. I can tell you that it will take weeks before we know what is to happen. The Comte du Barry must report to his king, and King Louis must then decide if Terreno Boscoso is worth the trouble he must go to in order to force us to his will. Whatever I learn I will communicate with you as soon as I know it. I ask you to have faith in me, and not to gossip and frighten the townspeople."

"We can ask no more of you, my lord," the bishop said. "I shall pray for us all."

The council was dismissed.

Rafaello sought out his wife and told her what had transpired.

Francesca was concerned. "You cannot expect the council

to keep silent about this," she told him. "They will seek to move their families out of harm's way, and you cannot blame them. I have written to my parents, asking them to tell the di Medicis what is happening here. I do not know if Florence can help us."

"It is not likely," Rafaello answered her, "and I dare not seek aid from Milan. If they should learn of our difficulties it is entirely possible that their duke's uncle would seek to take my duchy for himself. He would excuse himself by saying he could not have French troops on his nephew's borders. We had best pray King Louis decides we are not worth the time or trouble."

"And if he does?" Francesca asked. "What will we do then? We have no army to defend us, my lord, nor influence with our more powerful neighbors. What will we do if the French march into Terreno Boscoso?"

"I do not know," he admitted.

"And yet you refused King Louis's request," she said.

"I had no choice," he told her proudly.

"We have to defend ourselves," Francesca replied. "We cannot simply allow a foreign power to force their will upon us. You must hire mercenaries. The di Medicis do it. All the important families do. My dower was paid you in gold; let the important families and merchants pay as well."

"We have never had the need to impose a tax on our people," he said.

"If they wish to be defended they will pay," Francesca replied simply.

"My father was correct about you," the duke told his wife. "You are clever."

"It is obviously better you wed a merchant's daughter than a French nobleman's," Francesca told him with a smile. "I know how to be practical, my lord. If you do not wish foreign troops to be quartered in Terreno Boscoso, then you must defend it."

"Where can we find mercenaries?" he asked her.

"We must ask Captain Arnaldo," she answered him. "He is a soldier and will know. I do not, but I do know if we present a strong front to the French we can drive them off. They will not depart without a fight, of course."

"I love you," he said quietly.

"And I love you," Francesca replied. "We must not be driven from our duchy. At least not without a fight."

Captain Arnaldo was sent for, and when he heard the duke's idea of hiring mercenaries to defend the duchy he nodded in agreement, then said, "If you will permit it, my lord, I will go to Milan to seek the men we need. I have a cousin in the service of the Duke of Milan. He will direct me and advise me. It will be better if I choose them myself, for mercenaries are not loyal by nature except to the highest bidder. To obtain the best fighters you will have to pay very well indeed."

"I have no choice," the duke told his captain. "If we are to defend the duchy from the French we must obtain the best mercenaries we can find. You will have your hands full with these men."

"There will be one among those I choose who is a natural leader, and he will be the man I appoint as my secondary," the captain said. "I will depart today, my lord."

The duke nodded. "Offer what is fair, perhaps a bit over the going rate, and hold out the promise of a bonus when their term of service to me is completed and the French are successfully discouraged," he said. "Your kinsman will know."

"I will, my lord," Captain Arnaldo agreed. Then, bowing smartly, he turned and left his master's presence.

"He will do his best," Francesca said to her husband when

the man-at-arms had gone. "We can ask no more of him than that. Let us pray his cousin is willing to help."

"Mercenaries are not known for their delicacy of behavior," the duke replied in a worried tone. "Bringing that many armed foreigners into the duchy could prove as dangerous as being invaded by the French. They will have no loyalty to Terreno Boscoso as their motherland. I had hoped to keep this unfortunate possibility from my people because I did not wish to frighten them, but the mercenaries we need cannot be hidden from them. While I can house them in the castle, their numbers will attract attention, and some of them may get into the town to cause havoc. I am damned without protection, yet I place us all in an equally dangerous position with this protection."

"You must decide, then, which are the lesser of the two evils we face. You can stop Captain Arnaldo from going, and we will take our chances that the French threat from the Comte du Barry is a hollow one. An attempt on his part to curry favor with his king by delivering the duchy into his hands. Or we can believe Raoul du Barry, and take precautions to defend Terreno Boscoso from an invading force."

He had never in his life been faced with such a decision. Either way he risked the peaceful life they had always enjoyed here. They had avoided the recent wars between the Italian states that fought with each other and with the French. Those altercations had come to an end with the clever diplomacy and bravery of Lorenzo di Medici. But who would look after Terreno Boscoso if its own duke didn't? Who would keep it safe from the invading French? He had not aided his neighbors, nor had they even considered his duchy enough to ask. Many were not even concerned with its existence or aware of it. They should have made alliances with other countries, but it had never been necessary. Now they had no one to turn to for aid or support. The French king, however, had become acquisitive during his reign. Now that his troops were home he was obviously looking about to see whose lands he might acquire, and his eye had fallen on Terreno Boscoso. Should he have sworn fealty to Louis XI and permitted him to quarter troops within the duchy? Rafaello questioned himself again as he had these past few days, but the answer that always sprang into his mind was a resounding *no*.

Fealty alone he might have managed for necessity's sake. Who would have known? It was not something that King Louis would have publicly bragged about, because Terreno Boscoso was really of no great importance to anyone save its duke and his people. And the French ruler would have wanted to have a certain hidden advantage over the governments in the Italian states. But the quartering of troops would have been untenable to his larger neighbors. It would draw attention to them. Milan would not have been contented at all by such a turn of events, nor would they be pleased to learn what had happened. Now Rafaello wondered what they would do when they learned that the French were attempting to force their will on the duchy and might very well succeed.

They waited as early summer moved to late summer and then early autumn. Captain Arnaldo had returned with at least two hundred mercenaries. Among them one man seemed to be a leader, and the duke's captain had wisely appointed him as his second in command. If the French meant to attack it would not be before much more time had passed. Armies did not like battling in the winter months.

The duke had stationed men on the border to watch. It was a wise precaution and would give them a tiny bit of warning, as the border was at least several days from his castle. Poor Aceline du Barry had been only a few miles from France when her party had been attacked. An army, even a small one, would take a few days to reach Terreno Boscoso. Rafaello had no choice now but to warn the townsfolk. The great bell in the little cathedral was rung, an age-old sign that the duchy's citizens were required for an important public announcement. Surprised, for it was rare they were called, they came to learn what it was their duke would say.

The duke's council had been called in to a short session just prior. They had been unhappy, but not surprised, to learn the French were preparing to attack the town. "I will send the small defensive force I have had brought from Milan to meet the French before they reach us, but I can guarantee nothing with regard to our safety."

"You will do your best for us, my lord," the bishop said. "The Cesare family has never failed Terreno Boscoso."

"The duchy has never before faced such peril," the duke answered the cleric.

Now Rafaello faced the anxious men and women of his duchy. Francesca had insisted upon being at his side. It was her duty as their *duchessa*. She believed that while the news would be extremely frightening to the people, for in their own history Terreno Boscoso had never been faced with the danger of invasion by a foreign power, nonetheless their united appearance would hopefully do something to allay the citizens' fears, if only briefly.

The hum of voices died as the duke and *duchessa* arrived in the town's main square. Rafaello, seated upon his stallion, with Francesca on her own horse by his side, began to speak. "Citizens of Terreno Boscoso, it is with great regret I must bring you bad news," Rafaello began. "Several months ago the French sent a demand that I give their king my fealty and that I permit them to quarter their troops in our duchy. I refused, for never have our dukes been subject to a foreign power."

A small patriotic cheer arose from the assembled.

"Quartering French troops here would have caused Milan concern, but more important, I thought the French demand bold. I was threatened by their emissary with armed retaliation if I did not accede to King Louis's demands. I might have reluctantly given my oath of loyalty to this king and then pleaded that no troops be quartered within our borders. I could not for honor's sake. Now, however, the French have sent their forces over our borders. They are approaching the town slowly. I have sent the mercenaries that I hired in Milan this summer to meet them. We will do our best to defend the duchy, but if you can, take yourselves and your families south quickly, for safety's sake. I am sorry to have put you in danger like this."

"Will the *duchessa* Francesca be going south too?" a voice from the crowd called out, and expectant faces looked to her.

Before Rafaello might answer, Francesca spoke up for herself. "No, I will not go south. I will remain here by my husband's side, good folk. It is my duty as your *duchessa*, and I cannot do otherwise. We will be secure in the castle until we can solve this unhappy situation, but your homes and shops provide little protection against a marauding army. You must do as my husband says and go until it is safe once again to return."

They cheered her wildly, and a few voices were heard saying, "If the *duchessa* doesn't go, then we won't either!"

"But you must protect your families," Francesca said. "Your loyalty to us is wonderful, but I know my husband agrees with me."

"For my sake, for Terreno Boscoso's sake," Rafaello told the people gathered below them, "you must do what you believe best for yourselves. But be warned that those soldiers in the employ of the French are not known for their mercy. These men will come no farther than the town itself. Once they hold it, they hold all of my duchy. We will either drive the French back or we will be forced to yield to them. If that happens I cannot protect you. They will steal what they can from your houses and your shops. Your wives and your daughters will not be safe from rapine. I beg you to consider my words seriously. Go now while you have the chance, my good folk. I will never question your loyalty in this matter, but my heart would break if any of you suffered on my account."

Then the duke and his wife turned their horses to return to the castle. Behind them they heard a cacophony of voices arise as the townsfolk began to loudly and publicly discuss what they had just been told. Rafaello knew that some of them would go, but some would remain to take their chances with the possible French occupation and protect their homes and shops. Most would send their women and children to safety. He understood the men, but the duke knew he would be extremely unhappy if the women and children suffered on account of his decision.

The castle was well fortified to withstand a siege, although never in its history had it been forced to do so. There were wells for water within its walls. They had food. They had men-at-arms to guard them. The drawbridge was now drawn up per-manently. When they had done so it made a great creaking noise, for it had been years since it had been raised. They could do nothing but wait.

Francesca had sent a long letter to her parents, telling them of the current situation and asking that they bring the French demands and incursion to the attention of Lorenzo di Medici. She had asked them to shelter her messenger, a young boy who had been so proud to be given his *duchessa*'s trust. She explained to her mother that she did not feel comfortable having the lad come back to Terreno Boscoso under the current circumstances. She knew they could expect no help from Florence. It was too far away, and the interests of the duchy were not the concern of the di Medicis or the Florentine government. If their mercenaries could not drive the French back over the border, Francesca did not know what they would do.

King Louis didn't really need her husband's fealty. She realized now it had been a polite gesture, and explained that to Rafaello. "The French only want one thing of us: to quarter their troops here for their future forays into the Italian states. Your fealty would have given them the right."

"And without my fealty," Rafaello said, suddenly understanding, "they will simply seize the duchy for their own purposes. What arrogance!"

"It is the nature of the French to be arrogant," Francesca replied. "They cannot help themselves, I fear."

"But we must pay the price for their overweening pride," he responded. "I have never before in all my life felt so helpless."

"Thank God your father is no longer with us to see this," she answered him.

He nodded in agreement. "Nonetheless I somehow feel as if I have failed him, our ancestors, and Terreno Boscoso," Rafaello admitted.

"You have not, my lord," Francesca assured him. "You have done your best. You have done what is best for the duchy and for your people. No one can fault you."

"I should have pledged my fealty to King Louis," he said.

"It would have done no good. What the French wanted was to quarter their troops here. It is a veiled threat to the Italian states, and they are aware of it. With or without your permission they were determined to do it."

"I pray we can stop them before they reach the town," Rafaello said, but she heard the hopelessness in his voice.

"I hope so too," Francesca agreed, but she knew it was unlikely. She had read the first dispatches sent by Captain Arnaldo from the front line. There were more than 500 French troops to their 225. Unless a miracle occurred it was likely that the French would reach the town in a few days.

Most of the women and children, along with the elderly who were mobile, departed the town. The goldsmith and jeweler who served on the council took her female artisans and departed for Milan. She had friends there, and they would welcome her and her workers. A silence such as Francesca had never known surrounded the castle now both day and night. The town boasted no lights once the night set in. It felt like they were the only people left upon the earth itself. Francesca did not know which was worse: the empty silent days, or the dark and silent nights.

The facade of the castle's inhabitants was calm, but Francesca knew that they were as nervous, frightened, and concerned as she was. It was almost a relief to have the French troops march into the town. Captain Arnaldo and a few of his men had managed to return a few hours ahead of the invaders, gaining entrance to the castle by a hidden back entry that opened into the cellars and dungeons beneath. The doorway by which they gained admission was then barred by an iron rectangle that was screwed into the stone walls. It would be difficult if not impossible to get into the castle by that door now. It could be unlocked only by removing the iron barrier from the inside.

Captain Arnaldo immediately sought his master. Finding him in the hall with the *duchessa*, he gave his report. After a brief fight some of the mercenaries had switched sides, and the rest not killed had fled. He and his own small force had fought on until he realized that future deaths would accomplish nothing for the duchy. He had given the order to the remaining few survivors to retreat. "There is no hope, my lord, and I can only beg your forgiveness," the soldier said, hanging his head.

"You did your best," Rafaello replied. "We could ask no more. And I am glad that you brought those who remained loyal to us home."

"The French?" Francesca asked him.

"With nothing to impede them now, my lady, they will arrive in the town within a few hours," he answered her. "We have but to wait."

"Do they carry heavy artillery with them?" the duke wanted to know.

"No, there is only the small French force. The Comte du Barry leads them," was the captain's answer.

"He is no soldier," Rafaello said.

"He is the official face of his king, but the soldiers are directed by another man. I do not know who he is, my lord."

"They want the town," Francesca said softly. "They expect they can easily take the castle, for it has always been open to all visitors."

"Even du Barry could not expect me to keep my drawbridge down under such circumstances," Rafaello said, disbelieving.

"Of course not, but he does not realize how thick the drawbridge truly is. He believes it will be easily breached because there has never been any sign of this castle being defensive. We have men-at-arms, but only a few patrol the heights of the castle. And we have no army. For the Comte du Barry and his king, taking Terreno Boscoso is like picking a ripe plum from its tree. Or so they believe. They will discover the plum has a rather tough stem, and it is not easy at all. They may have the empty town, but the castle will remain inviolate."

"Once they have discovered that, they may send for cannon," Rafaello replied.

"Then we must flee," Francesca said quietly. "We cannot allow ourselves to be taken prisoner. As long as the duke is free his people may have hope."

He was astounded by her calm bravery, her logic. He had learned in the year that they had been wed that his wife was not just beautiful. She was clever and intelligent. Still, when she spoke as she had just done it came as a surprise to him. "I never meant for you to be caught in such turmoil," he told her. Your life should have been as sweet and peaceful as the *duchessas* before you."

"I would have been truly bored," Francesca said, "although to confess I should have preferred my life to be slightly less exciting. However, I have never before been involved in a war," she remarked.

Rafaello burst out laughing, and he caught her to him and kissed her hard. "I cannot see Louisa or Aceline taking this situation in such good stride," he told her.

"They did not love you as I do. Louisa did not love you at all," Francesca replied. "As for Aceline, who is to say if she had been your wife that her father wouldn't have prevailed upon you to allow the French to have a garrison here? Refusing your father-in-law would have proved awkward."

"I could have never married Aceline du Barry," he said. "Not if I had never met you, Francesca, my love. She was a shrew."

"But you might have had a son by now," Francesca said softly. "Your father might have known an heir was due before he died."

This was the moment, Rafaello realized. He would never have one so perfect again. "Perhaps if you had succumbed to Carlo we would have," he said quietly.

"*Carlo?*" Francesca blushed, but then she said, "I could not betray you, my lord husband, even if we had not been formally betrothed."

"A pity," he said with a small grin. "I did try so hard to seduce you. That one night . . ."

"What one night?" she demanded, and then she said, "*You tried to seduce me? My lord, what can you mean?*"

"Jesu, Marie, was I that good that you do not realize that Carlo and I were one and the same, Francesca?"

"No!" she replied, disbelieving.

"Yes," he told her. "I was terrified when you ran off into the forest, but when word came you were safe at the inn with Alonza, I grew angry. What could I have possibly done to offend you, to send you fleeing me? I could not at first understand, and then I realized that I did not really know you. That I had been delighted by your extraordinary beauty, and how kind you were to my father, and how you and Louisa had become friends, but I really knew nothing more of you. I thought perhaps if I might understand you better we could make a good marriage. I had frequently hunted in the forest using the name Carlo. It is one of my Christian names. Were you not paying attention when the bishop asked at our wedding if I, Rafaello Titus Eduardo Carlo, would have you to wife?"

"No," Francesca said in a little voice. "I was too overwhelmed by all that had happened that morning." She still wasn't quite certain she believed him.

"What is it that puzzles you?" he asked her

"Carlo was bearded. You are clean shaven," she answered.

"He was," Rafaello agreed. "Shall I grow my beard again to convince you that your romantic huntsman and I are one and the same, Francesca Allegra Liliana Maria?"

She stared at him, surprised. "You remembered all of my names. I think I am impressed. Yes! Grow your beard again. It makes you look older, which might not be a bad idea when you must face the French leader of these forces. You are much too handsome and youthful, which makes people who do not know you believe you are easily overcome."

"I shall take your suggestion, but now we must return to the subject of Carlo," Rafaello told her.

"Why? If you were Carlo, then you know I am truthful when I say we were not lovers, although, my lord, it is not that I was not tempted. I was. Why could you not have been yourself with me when we first met? If you were not the duke, is Carlo the man you would prefer to be?" Francesca asked perceptively, and she looked closely at her husband.

"You are too clever by far, my love," he told her. "It is not that I am not proud to be who I am, but it brings with it too many responsibilities. Now we are faced with a French invasion, and shortly the Milanese will come filled with righteous indignation over the fact that the French are in Terreno Boscoso. None of the previous dukes had to deal with a situation like this. I do not like it, and I do not know if I am strong enough to handle it," he told her. "Yes, I should rather be Carlo, the huntsman right now."

He looked so miserable at his admission that Francesca took him in her arms to comfort him. There was no doubt that his peaceful ancestors had never found themselves in a position like this. He hadn't been trained to manage a problem such as now faced him. "If I agreed to offer my fealty to the French king and host his troops willingly now, would he still accept my loyalty? I did what I believe was right, Francesca, but it was wrong for my duchy. My people have had to flee. There is no business being transacted. How can the duchy survive without its people and its commerce? In one noble and proud gesture I have destroyed my country."

"Do you forget Milan, my lord?" she asked him. "They would not help if we asked, yet they would cry to the heavens had you willingly allowed the French here," Francesca reminded him.

"I should have put Terreno Boscoso first. I realize now there was no way I could have pleased everyone," he said unhappily.

"Had you admitted the French willingly, Milan would have attacked their soldiers and made a battleground of our duchy," his wife said.

"They will probably do it anyway," Rafaello replied.

Francesca didn't know what to say to him after that. She had never had any experience with a difficulty such as they now found themselves in. She had been raised to be a good wife, a perfect ornament, and the mother of her husband's male heirs. Now, however, she was relieved that there was no child in her womb. Worse, she was not certain exactly what was going to happen to them, or to Terreno Boscoso, now.

Rafaello disappeared within the castle for the next few days. He needed to consider any options that they might have, and he was very concerned for his wife's safety. So far in the town be-

low there had been no chaos. The French quartered themselves
in the houses of his citizens. He could imagine the irritation of
the ordinary soldiers. There were no women to rape. The few
that had remained were ancient crones who kept to their beds,
and cursed them beneath their foul breath anytime they saw
them.

There was virtually nothing to steal, and soldiers relied on
booty to fill their pockets, as their masters were usually slow to
pay them for their services.

The French made no effort to speak with the duke at first.
Seeing the strength of the raised drawbridge they realized that
only cannon could force it down and allow them admittance to
the castle. They could see no other way that would admit them
into the castle. But truthfully there was little need to speak with
the duke immediately. They had the town, which they had
wanted first and foremost, and took time to settle themselves.

An envoy from Milan came to speak with the duke. The
invaders had no orders to stop anyone from entering, if indeed
they could. The French laughed heartily to see the pompous
envoy forced to row himself across the moat and then wrap a
rope about himself so he might be pulled up to a place where he
could be hauled into the castle.

Even from the ground across the water they could hear the
Milanese sputtering his indignation at such treatment.

"I suppose if we wish to speak with the duke we must enter
the castle the same way," the military commander said with a
chuckle.

"Nonsense!" the Comte du Barry responded. "They will
surely lower the drawbridge for us. The young duke is not unreasonable."

"If he were reasonable," the commander said sarcastically,

"we should not be living in the town, but rather be his guests in the castle. We will question the envoy when he returns. It is our right."

"We cannot harm him," the Comte du Barry said. "King Louis wants no fuss with Milan right now. He is not a well man."

"Why on earth did he want this tiny bit of land to add to all the great inheritances he has gained?" the commander asked the comte. "We do not really need to garrison soldiers here at all. You would know the truth of this matter, my lord comte, if you would but tell."

Raoul du Barry smiled. "I see no harm in you knowing, although you must keep the secret for now. France has enough land for successful agriculture, but unlike the Spanish, we have no source of precious metals. Terreno Boscoso has in the far north of the duchy gold mines. They are small, for the dukes of this duchy have never wanted to bring attention to their good fortune. They mine what they need for themselves and their little economy. France could expand those mines and have a goodly supply of gold for the king if the duchy was ours. But if it became publicly known that these mines exist, then there would be others who would want them too. King Louis hoped to have this wealth peacefully by gaining the young duke's fealty. That is why I offered my daughter to the young duke for a bride. He rejected her in favor of that merchant's daughter from Florence."

"I am told the *duchessa* is very beautiful," the commander said.

"I cannot deny it," the comte admitted. "Her maternal grandfather is a Venetian prince, it is said, and one of her brothers, a priest, is secretary to a cardinal in Rome."

"You have quite a knowledge of the *duchessa*'s family," the commander noted slyly. "Do you resent her being chosen over your daughter?"

Raoul du Barry smiled tightly. "Wouldn't you if it were your daughter?" he said bitterly. "Aceline told me that the merchant's daughter showed lascivious behavior, which is what attracted the duke."

"And you believed her?" the commander said boldly.

"Not after I met the *duchessa*," the comte admitted. "Like all in our family my daughter is proud. She did not like being passed over for a silk merchant's daughter."

"And so now we have both the duke and his beautiful wife at our mercy," the commander said slowly. "Do you believe the duke will relent and offer King Louis his fealty now?"

"We no longer need it," the comte said coldly.

"And the envoy from Milan? Do you think he brings word of the little duke's aid? We will have a fight on our hands if the Milanese come."

"King Louis has soldiers enough to contain the Milanese. I do not believe they will offer any aid. The duke of Milan's guardian uncle probably believes that Terreno Boscoso is in league with King Louis, and seeks to warn their duke of such folly." The comte chuckled. "Duke Rafaello has probably destroyed his duchy with his overweening pride."

"If he relents and swears fealty to King Louis we must honor his promise," the commander said. "We are honorable men. The French are not barbarians."

"I carry with me an order signed by the king himself. Remember it is the duchy's gold mine he wants. Duke Rafaello and his wife are to be disposed of in order to prevent the duchy from rallying about him. The *duchessa* has not yet given him an heir, for even I should be reluctant to kill a child. We are to gain the duke's trust. Then we are to gain entry to the castle with just a few men, our servants. They will see the job done quickly and quietly," Raoul du Barry said.

The commander nodded slowly. He could not refuse his royal master's orders, but he did not like this trickery. It was murder. The murder of a consecrated ruler and his wife. No. He didn't like it at all. But he would do it because those were his orders, or so the comte said. The commander decided he would want to see the king's order before he acted. I don't like it, he thought once again. And he didn't like Raoul du Barry either.

A sudden shout of outrage, and then a splash turned his attention just in time to see the Milanese envoy being pitched into the moat. Sputtering with fury, the man swam to the far side of the water where the two Frenchmen stood. He scrambled out and, turning, shouted, "My master, the duke, will hear of this outrage!" He shook his fist upward.

"Fuck your master," someone on the battlement shouted down angrily.

The French commander hurried to help the wet Milanese envoy. "Let us aid you," he said. "France has no quarrel with Milan. Why were you thrown into the moat?"

The Milanese looked at the Frenchman and then decided it didn't matter at all. "My master, the duke, sent me to demand from Duke Rafaello an answer as to why you French have come into Terreno Boscoso. The duke had sent to him for help."

"I think your duke must be mistaken. Duke Rafaello has sworn fealty to King Louis. Granted, we did march into this duchy without permission, but the duke's barring his castle to us is a simple misunderstanding. We will straighten it out shortly." The comte smiled at the man. "Now, sir, we must see that you have dry clothing for your return to Milan. Your master will certainly want to know what you have learned." He smiled again.

"Clever, my lord, very clever," the commander said to the comte when the Milanese envoy had finally gone on his way. "But to what purpose?"

"Simply to cause consternation among the Milanese and any others they will share this knowledge with," the comte said. "Now, who will help the duke of Terreno Boscoso? There is no one, I will wager." He smiled his cold smile again.

The commander suddenly realized that all this man was doing came from his need for revenge. Revenge on the young duke who had refused the comte's daughter's hand in marriage. But King Louis would be lured by the knowledge of gold. He would not care even if he were told the truth. The commander was glad he was a simple soldier.

Chapter 15

"Was it really politic to toss the Milanese envoy into the moat?" Francesca asked her husband. She was trying hard not to laugh.

"Pompous fool!" Rafaello said. "How dare he speak to me as if I were a dishonest and naughty child. I knew asking the Milanese for aid was a lost cause. At least he was able to bring you a letter from your mother. Is all well with your family?"

"My mother writes that the di Medici cannot help us. Terreno Boscoso is too far away for Florence to have any real interest in it. Lorenzo sends his regrets," Francesca responded quietly. "What are we to do, my lord? Milan believes we have betrayed them. It would seem we have little hope at all. I realize we have not the strength to drive the French out of our duchy. What, then, can we do?"

"I am realizing now that there is more to this than just the need to quarter troops here," the duke said slowly. "But I cannot imagine what else they would want of us."

"The Comte du Barry wants revenge," Francesca replied. "He is a fool, of course. We are not responsible for Aceline's plight. He is."

"He is a proud man, my love. He will never admit to that, but it is more than just his need for revenge. You do not get the king of France to aid you in your revenge when you are an unimportant man. No. King Louis has been told there is something here that he has decided he wants. But what is it?"

The autumn came and with it a request shouted from below the castle walls for a meeting with the duke. The desire was relayed to the duke, who gave the man-at-arms his reply. The answer was shouted down.

"The duke says he will speak with anyone but the Comte du Barry."

Hearing that, Raoul du Barry was infuriated, but the commander chuckled. "You, like your daughter, du Barry, have not endeared yourself to the duke," he noted. Then he turned to the soldier who had brought the answer. "Say that Commander d'Aumont will speak with the duke at his convenience."

The soldier nodded and hurried off.

"Are you mad, treating this fellow as if he mattered?" the comte demanded.

"I would remind you, my lord," the commander said quietly, "that this small troop of King Louis's soldiers is mine to direct. You have a history with this duke, and he obviously does not like you, so he will not treat with you. But of necessity we must gain the duke's trust enough to get a few men into the castle so the duke and his wife may, as distasteful as I find it, be disposed of. Once that is done Terreno Boscoso and its wealth are King Louis's. I would be remiss in my fealty if I did not do my duty by my king."

The comte grew silent, but then he said, "Before the *duchessa* is killed I want her raped before her husband's eyes."

"*What?*" The commander was not so much disgusted as surprised by such a request.

"I will tell you something I have told few others, d'Aumont," the comte said. "When Rafaello Cesare chose the silk merchant's daughter to be his bride, my daughter was sent back to me. But Aceline was not sent with enough men-at-arms to protect her. Her little train was set upon by bandits. She was raped and held captive for several months. When she and her serving wench managed to escape and reach home it was discovered she was enceinte by her captor. She birthed her bastard and was rendered mad by the shame of it all. She and the boy now reside in a convent. I want the *Duchessa* Francesca shamed in the same way before you cut her throat. I want her raped and killed first so her husband may suffer the same tortures of the damned that I have over the loss of my daughter. I want him to hear her cries as she is violated by one of your soldiers, and then another and another, at least a dozen men. I want this duke to hear his wife's screams and know that he is helpless to aid her. Then he is to be whipped until his back is raw and he is screaming with his anguish and pain. Finally he will be hanged."

"And this is all in King Louis's directive to you, my lord?" Commander d'Aumont said dryly.

"They are to be killed. The manner in which they die is left up to me," the comte said shortly.

"King Louis is not a man for wanton cruelty, Comte. We will execute them as quickly and as mercifully as we can," the commander said. "With no other heirs to Terreno Boscoso the duchy is ours. That is all King Louis desires." *Mon Dieu!* This Comte du Barry was a vengeful man, but what he proposed to do to the duke and his wife was intolerable. Their demise must be swift and without undue cruelty.

The soldier returned from the moat to say that the commander would be granted an audience with Duke Rafaello the following morning. He could row across the moat and would then be hauled up to the battlements. Once there he would be taken to the duke. The drawbridge would not be lowered. Commander d'Aumont had to admire the duke's caution, but then considering the French had invaded the duchy without cause, why wouldn't Duke Rafaello be wary?

He was spared the comte's company this evening and was relieved. Commander d'Aumont might have sought out the nobleman and told him of his meeting on the morrow, but he did not. When morning came he broke his fast and then rowed across the moat. Anchoring the small boat, he waited for the rope to be lowered, and when it was he skillfully tied it about his waist, indicating he was ready to be slowly and carefully drawn up. Once over the battlements he was taken to the duke.

Rafaello Cesare greeted the Frenchman by offering him a goblet of wine.

"Thank you, my lord duke," d'Aumont said. He raised the goblet. "To King Louis!" he toasted. He then introduced himself. "I am Jean-Paul d'Aumont, a commander in his majesty's armies."

Without hesitation Rafaello raised his goblet. "To King Louis," he agreed. Then he said, "Come and sit by the fire, Commander. You will tell me why you sought to speak with me." He took a deep sip of the wine as he sat and waved his companion into the high-backed tapestried chair opposite him.

The Frenchman sat down and drank from his goblet. "I am told you refused to give King Louis your fealty," he began.

"I might have given it, but I could not countenance French troops in my town," the duke replied. "And yet now I have them." He smiled wryly.

"King Louis merely wishes to ensure that Milan and the other Italian states remain peaceful. It is easier to intimidate them by garrisoning a few of his troops in Terreno Boscoso," the commander said smoothly.

"Nonsense!" the duke replied. "It is obvious to me that my duchy has something King Louis desires, although I cannot imagine what that is. But, then, I am new to my position. I might have asked my father, the former duke, but he has died." Rafaello crossed himself piously.

"I cannot help you there," the commander lied. "I am just a soldier and I was given my orders."

"What is the Comte du Barry doing among your little army?" the duke asked.

The commander considered the query, and then decided truth was a better weapon in this case than a lie. "He seeks revenge upon you for his daughter's misfortune."

"So my wife said, but I could not believe it. Aceline du Barry's mischance was not my fault, but her father's fault. My father, the late duke, invited Aceline along with two other maidens to Terreno Boscoso in hopes that I would choose one of them as a bride. I did not choose Aceline. She was an overproud shrew. She was returned home, laden with rich gifts from my father, Duke Titus, and guarded by the few men-at-arms her father had sent with her when she came and who remained until it was time to return her home. Her own father should have sent more men to guard his daughter, but he did not. Her tragedy was not the fault of Terreno Boscoso.

"When she claimed her bastard was mine, the innocent child's very appearance gave lie to the assertion. Her maidservant told us the truth. My wife arranged for Aceline and her infant to be cared for by the gentle nuns of a convent my mother-in-law favors. It was not our responsibility to help the comte, but he was so distraught at the time that Francesca felt sorry for him."

" 'Tis not exactly the tale he tells, but no matter," the Frenchman said.

"So King Louis's only interest is in protecting his borders by invading Terreno Boscoso," the duke repeated slowly.

"I know nothing more, my lord," Commander d'Aumont replied.

"So even if I offered to give your king my fealty now he would not withdraw his troops," the duke said. "What have we to talk about then, Commander? France has invaded my duchy. It is well known that Terreno Boscoso is peaceful. It is also known that we have no army with which to defend ourselves. We are at your mercy. There is more to this than is being spoken aloud. If that were not so my fealty would be enough for you to withdraw your troops from my duchy. Your loyalty must lie with your king. But mine must lie with my citizens. They are my responsibility."

"You have few folk that I can see in your many-housed town," the commander noted with a small smile. "I can only assume they were made aware of our coming and fled for more peaceful climes."

"Soldiers are known to pillage and commit rape," the duke answered.

"Believe me, my lord, there is little to take in those many houses, and no women but ancients who grudgingly cook for those now housed in your town," the commander told the duke. "You may have no army, but you have nonetheless protected your people."

The duke acknowledged the compliment with a nod. "I suppose, then, that we are finished, Commander d'Aumont." He rose from his chair.

The Frenchman stood as well. "Might I beg a boon of you, my lord duke? It is said that your wife is very beautiful. Would you permit me to present my compliments to her? I am bold to ask, I know, but . . ." He shrugged.

Rafaello laughed good-naturedly. "Matteo," he called to a servant. "Go and ask the *duchessa* if she would attend us in the hall."

"My lord, thank you for satisfying a bold man's curiosity," the Frenchman said.

Matteo hurried to the *duchessa*'s apartment. Terza admitted him as Francesca came forward. "My lady, Duke Rafaello requests you attend him and his guest in the hall."

"What did you overhear?" Francesca asked the servant. She knew Matteo to be intelligent and he could not help but eavesdrop.

Matteo shook his head. "Nothing has happened or will happen. The French claim they but desire to protect their borders by invading us. This commander is pleasant, but if he has any knowledge other than that he will not reveal it. The duke has asked if he offered King Louis his fealty, would the French withdraw their troops. The commander says no. The duke says then the French desire something else of Terreno Boscoso, but the commander says he knows nothing about such a thing. Of course he lies."

"What does the duchy have that would be of value to the French?" Francesca wondered aloud. We are forests and fields and a single town where normal commerce is carried on. There would seem to be nothing more."

Then Terza spoke up. "What of *Signora* Donatella and her artisans? Where does the gold come from to fashion their wares?"

"There is a small old mine in the far north of the duchy," Matteo said, "but no one has taken so much as a single nugget from it in years. There is no gold left to my knowledge. I didn't think anyone even remembered its existence."

"*Madre di Dios!*" Francesca exclaimed. "Surely that is it!"

"My lady, the duke is waiting," Matteo said, reminding her of Rafaello's request.

Francesca nodded. "Let us go," she said, and followed him down into the hall.

Commander d'Aumont leapt to his feet as she entered the chamber. *Mon Dieu*, he thought silently. The rumors are truth. She is beautiful. If she came to France she would rule the court.

"You sent for me, my lord," Francesca said to the duke in deceptively meek tones, and she curtsied deeply before him.

There was a twinkle in the duke's eye as he said, "Commander d'Aumont, madam, and his manners are decidedly better than the Comte du Barry's. Hearing of your charms he wishes to view them for himself."

Francesca turned her beautiful green eyes on the Frenchman and held out her hand to be kissed.

He did so, unable to hide his admiring glances. "Madam *la duchesse*, I am honored that you would agree to greet me."

"Thank you," Francesca said sweetly. "Is it the gold mine in the north, Commander, that your master wants from us?" she asked him innocently.

Commander d'Aumont's mouth fell open with his surprise.

"The northern mine?" Rafaello repeated. "There's nothing in it. It hasn't been worked in more than fifty years! King Louis has invaded my country for a mine that no longer produces? Who the hell told him we had a working gold mine?"

"Our dear and good friend the Comte du Barry," Francesca answered her husband sarcastically. "Is that not so, Commander?"

The Frenchman quickly overcame his surprise. "My lord, I can neither confirm nor deny such a suggestion."

"Commander, you are more than free to send someone to the mine and see for yourself," the duke told him. "The mine is useless. It has not been worked in half a century. Du Barry has put his king in an embarrassing position by invading my duchy on a foolish pretext."

"I will send someone to your mine," the commander said. "And then, having assured myself that the mine is useless, I will send to King Louis."

"We tell all who will listen that the comte told his king that the duke of Milan's guardians were threatening France by planning to march through Terreno Boscoso. It was therefore natural that King Louis would protect himself by making the first move. Your king's reputation will be saved and the comte's ruined, and when your troops withdraw all will be well again," Francesca said. "After all, your men have done little damage," Francesca told her two companions.

"Your wife is most clever, my lord," the commander said admiringly.

"Yes, she is," Rafaello agreed.

"I will take half a dozen men and visit this mine myself," d'Aumont said. "Then I shall send a report to King Louis." He bowed to them both. "Do you suppose I might be lowered by your rope conveyance back to my boat in the moat rather than tossed into the water below?"

Rafaello chuckled. "Your charm and good manners have certainly earned you that small respect. I shall accompany you myself to the battlements."

Commander d'Aumont bowed to Francesca. "Madam, it has been my pleasure," he said. Then, turning, he followed the duke from the hall.

When Rafaello returned she awaited him. "How did you know about the mine?" he asked her.

"Matteo told me as we tried to consider what King Louis really wanted," she answered her husband.

"It was a masterful stroke, my love, and you may very well have saved the duchy," Rafaello told her. "Thank you."

They thought, they hoped, that in a few weeks it would be over. The French would learn the single small gold mine in the north of the duchy was worthless at this point. But then Matteo came to them with troubling news. His grandmother had been one of the elderly who had remained in her home, and that home had been confiscated by the Comte du Barry. Neither the comte nor those Frenchmen surrounding him paid the old woman any mind, and so it was she had learned that du Barry held an order of execution for the duke and his wife.

Matteo's grandmother had overheard the comte planning to act upon this order while the commander was away. She had heard him arguing with d'Aumont about it before he left the town to investigate the old mine. The order, it seemed, was only to be acted upon if the duke refused to cooperate with the French. Commander d'Aumont had argued that his meeting with the duke had been productive and the duke had invited the French to inspect the mine themselves, claiming it was worthless now. The comte, however, while pretending to reconsider, was even now arranging for assassins to enter the castle and slay Rafaello and Francesca.

"She sent me word that she must see me," Matteo said, "and then told me all of this when I visited her yesterday, my lord."

"Du Barry wastes his time," Rafaello said. "No one can get into the castle with the drawbridge up. It is not possible."

"There is the hidden door to the cellar," Francesca reminded him.

"And it is well hidden," Rafaello said. "Few are aware of it, and no one is permitted to use it. Even Matteo must be lowered to the moat and a small boat to visit with his grandmother. He went and returned before dawn so that no one saw him."

"Nonetheless," Francesca told her husband, "we must be wary. We can trust few, my lord. Even a loyal heart can be tempted by a rich bribe or a wicked threat against a loved one."

"Which is why I sent almost all the servants away before the French arrived. Only the cook, Matteo, Piero, Fidelio, Terza, and Roza remain. I do not question the loyalty of any of these few," Rafaello told her.

"There are Captain Arnaldo and those few men-at-arms who remain," she reminded him. "Can you vouch so assuredly for them, my lord? I do not like this at all."

"Do you believe that I do?" he demanded, irritated.

"We cannot remain," Francesca said to him. "We have to go where we cannot be found until the French depart. Until the Comte du Barry and this threat on our lives is gone for good.

He wants revenge, but he would find if he took it against us he would still not feel at ease. He knows his parsimony is what is responsible for his daughter's tragedy. If he had given her more men-at-arms to watch over her the bandits would have not attacked her train, or have been driven off if they did."

"Go where?" he asked her. "We are more at risk outside the castle than in it."

"Are we? I wonder," she replied. "I must think on it." She would not allow that arrogant Frenchman to ruin her life. Not now. Especially not now. Despite Aceline's terrible lies against Rafaello, Francesca felt sympathy for the girl. How could she not when Aceline's life had been ruined while hers had flourished and been filled with love?

"You have that look on your face," Terza said to her mistress later.

"What look?" Francesca asked her.

"The look that says you are planning something that perhaps you should not," Terza replied.

"We are in danger here in the castle," Francesca told her serving woman. "The French comte has his king's permission to murder us. Rafaello says we are safe because the castle is inviolate, but we are Florentines, you and I, Terza. We know better."

Terza nodded. "What are we to do?" she asked. "Can we go back to Florence?"

"If we deserted Terreno Boscoso the people would be heartbroken. The French are sure to withdraw once they learn there is no gold to be had in the northern mine. But we cannot sit here while we wait for King Louis to realize his error."

"Kings do not acknowledge their errors," Terza said wisely. "And what if the French refuse to depart despite the lack of wealth? He is certain to look the fool for being persuaded by the

Comte du Barry to this folly. He could simply decide to retain this little duchy rather than appear a greedy dupe. To do that he needs its ducal family gone, my lady. The duke has refused to give the French king his fealty. Therefore he must be eliminated. I believe that we must flee for our lives, but it is unlikely the duke will be able to regain his position. There can be no continued loyalty to the Cesare family if King Louis would rule here peaceably," Terza explained. "This Comte du Barry will have his revenge against you and the duke after all, and there is nothing you can do to stop it but save yourselves. But where can you go where you will not be known?"

The terrible truth of their position hit Francesca as she listened and absorbed her faithful Terza's words. At first she didn't want to believe what she had heard, but then she realized her serving woman was correct. She saw their situation through a different eye. It would be difficult to explain it to Rafaello. He would not believe her. He was not a strong man, but, then, the men in his family had grown less like their founding ancestor as the centuries had passed. They had lived in peace even when there was war all around them. They were not weak, for they had governed their little duchy well through the years. They were simply naive in thinking it would always remain the same in Terreno Boscoso while all about them the world had been changing.

For a brief moment Francesca was overwhelmed by fear, but then she pushed it back. It was up to her to see that they survived. That the Cesares survived even if it wasn't as rulers of this duchy. Rafaello was her husband. She loved him. She would not allow the Comte du Barry's insane desire for revenge to hurt them. *Madre di Dios*! How much I have changed, Francesca thought. Her desire for survival for herself and her family suddenly far outweighed her need to be important. If they must lose the duchy, then so be it. Convincing Rafaello of this, of course, would take more time than they had right now. The important first step must be taken. To escape their own castle and hide themselves where they could not be found.

"Where can we go?" Terza asked her mistress.

"The forest," Francesca said without hesitation. "The French will not seek us there. They will assume we are attempting to make our way to Florence."

"But how will we live?" Terza queried.

"We will secrete ourselves at the huntsmen's inn," Francesca told her. "Alonza fled with her family before the French arrived. She had told Duke Titus before he died that she was too old to care for his huntsmen any longer. She would go one more winter, and then he must find someone else. He gifted her for her time and agreed. But then his life came to an end, and with the French threat Rafaello did nothing, although he meant to do so. It is autumn, and in a few weeks the huntsmen remaining will seek their winter shelter. They will find Alonza's former serving woman has taken over, along with a huntsman known as Carlo. Those remaining among our personal servants may join us or seek their families. We must go quickly, for it will be several weeks before Commander d'Aumont returns. The comte will attempt our end before he returns. D'Aumont is a reasonable man. He is loyal to his king but not unfair. Matteo's grandmother heard him arguing fiercely with the comte and forbidding him any action against us, but once he departed for the north the comte began his treachery against us."

"When I think of how kind you were to his wretched daughter," Terza said indignantly.

"He failed Aceline, causing her misery. He believes by revenging himself on us he has restored himself as her paternal champion."

"It will change nothing," Terza said angrily. Then she calmed herself. "What shall we take with us?" she asked.

"Wait until I have discussed this with the duke," Francesca replied.

"He will not be easy to convince if indeed you can convince him at all, my lady."

"I know," Francesca said. "But convince him I must."

"Are you mad?" Rafaello said when Francesca broached the subject of fleeing. "I will not desert my people!"

"Oh, I see," Francesca said. "You will leave them with the memory of a martyr instead. The last duke whose enemies will probably not even have the courtesy to bury him in the family crypt. They will murder you and then hang your handsome body in the town's main square for all to see and the crows to feast upon. One day they will cut you down and bury you in an unmarked grave. You will be forgotten. At least hidden away you keep the hope of your people alive, though it will make no difference, really. The French cannot leave the duchy as if nothing has happened. King Louis will look the fool."

"What are you saying? That I will never have my birthright back? That the French will retain this land?" He was both angry and confused.

Francesca sighed. Her husband was passionate and he was sweet. He had been a good ruler as long as there had been peace, but the rulers of Terreno Boscoso had lived a charmed existence for centuries. They did not know how to deal with a situation requiring them to act decisively. But, then, she was being unfair. Rafaello had managed to get his townsfolk to safety. He knew not what else to do. Francesca knew that swearing fealty to the French king would have done no good. Louis believed there was an endless supply of gold to be had in Terreno Boscoso, and that was what he really wanted. He could not simply accept the duke's allegiance and then take his gold. He would have to absorb the duchy into his own territories, using the excuse that he needed quicker access into the Italian states, should they attack him. It was an impossible situation, and she wasn't certain she could make Rafaello understand.

"The French have put themselves in an untenable position, my lord," she began, "and great kings do not like being publicly embarrassed. Remaining here puts us in great danger from the Comte du Barry. Fleeing where he cannot find us gives us the chance of survival and when King Louis learns there is no gold, that he has been misled in the comte's effort at revenge, we have at the least foiled and disgraced du Barry."

"Small compensation," Rafaello grumbled.

"We can eventually see him dead," Francesca murmured. "He is not a nice fellow, and it is very possible he will eat or drink something that does not agree with him."

He looked sharply at her. "Poison?" he said.

"Did I say such a thing?" she responded, smiling. "Nay, my lord, but badly treated servants will sometimes revenge themselves."

"Especially if they are bribed to do so," he chuckled. She suddenly amused him. He would never have expected his beautiful and passionate wife to even consider such a thing, but, then, she was a Florentine, and her mother did not lack intelligence. Though she would deny it Francesca was much like her mother. Devoted to her family and willing to do what she must to protect that family. He doubted, however, that his mother-in-law had ever been faced with such a difficult situation. "I don't like the idea of going into hiding," he said quietly.

"It is for your people. We must survive, Rafaello," Francesca told him, thinking even as she spoke the lie that they must live for themselves, for the children they would eventually have, please God. It was unlikely he would ever rule Terreno Boscoso again. It would become part of France, but for now the first step was getting them safely from the castle and to the inn.

"Where can we go?" he asked her. "Even if we got to Florence we would be highly visible exiles."

"We will not leave Terreno Boscoso," she said, knowing that would both surprise and please him. "We will seek refuge in the forest. You never appointed another to run the huntsmen's inn. Alonza's former serving girl will run it along with her husband, Carlo. We will be safe there, and it is unlikely the French will find us even if they look."

"Are any of the huntsmen still there?" Rafaello wondered aloud.

"Surely there are, for the efforts we made to stop the French did not concern them. They live year round in the forest, coming into the town to sell their skins and other wares in the early summer, then returning to the woodlands. They need only the inn's shelter in the winter months. The autumn is deepening, and it is that time of year when Alonza returned to make their habitation welcoming. They will be relieved to find the inn still available to them. None of them, I will wager, has ever seen the duke. How many years did you play at being Carlo, my lord? Since you were a boy?"

"Only Bernardo suspected my identity, though he never asked me directly."

"He will not betray you," Francesca said. "He is a good man."

"I suppose the forest is as good a place as any, then. Soon it will be winter and we will have a safe place. Who will we take with us?"

"Those who have remained in the castle, if they choose to go. If they prefer to seek refuge with their families, then so be it. We will let them go. They are the loyalist of the loyal. Captain Arnaldo must know, but, then, he is free, as are his few remaining men, to offer their skills where they choose. No one can know where we are going. Those who come with us must trust us."

"Can you cook?" he asked her, smiling.

"Enough to feed the huntsmen this winter. We must take as much of the castle's supplies with us as we can carry. I believe the cook will come with us. She has no family remaining. No one will go hungry," Francesca said.

"When do you want to go?" he asked her.

"Today! Tomorrow! As quickly as we can escape. The longer we remain, the more danger we face," Francesca said.

He was not certain that they really faced that much danger from the Comte du Barry, but a man-at-arms was caught lowering a rope to two men in a boat below the walls. Called to the battlements, the duke sent the traitor over the walls into the water below. Then, without a word, he left Captain Arnaldo, who was grinning broadly, and the remaining men-at-arms, who after a minute or two burst into laughter to see their former compatriot splashing in the moat below. On their captain's command the men-at-arms took their bows and aimed down at the three men, and loosed their arrows, killing two of the trio. The survivor clambered up the moat embankment and ran for his life.

Francesca spoke with the remaining servants one by one. Piero, the castle's majordomo, and the duke's valet, Fidelio, decided that they should prefer to return to their families. The cook, Roza, and Matteo decided they would take their chances with the duke and his wife. Terza, of course, would remain with her mistress, although Francesca offered to fund her passage back to Florence.

"And what would I do there?" Terza demanded to know.

"My mother would take you back into her household," Francesca said. "Our life is going to change, and perhaps not for the better."

"I would rather toil for you, my lady, than for your mother. Besides, the *signora* does not need another mouth to feed with things the way they are these days in Florence. At least if one is to believe her letters."

"Very well, and bless you for remaining with me." Francesca said.

"Where will we go?" Terza asked her mistress.

"I will tell you, but only you shall know before we reach our destination. The huntsmen's inn in the forest. The duke did not replace Alonza when she departed with her family. Few know of the inn's existence and we should be safe there. The huntsmen will come in from the woodlands soon for the winter. We will feed them and care for them," Francesca explained. "I know what is required, having spent a winter there."

"The men did not know you were the duke's bride," Terza said slowly. "So they will not know you are the *duchessa*. But what of the duke?"

"The winter I lived at the inn he masqueraded as a huntsman called Carlo. It was a persona he had used since he was a boy. Carlo was in love with Alonza's serving girl, Cara," the *duchessa* explained to her servant. "It is not likely anyone will consider it odd that he wed her and together they now manage the inn. Carlo can hunt with the others this fall and winter. Come spring we will know better what our final fate is to be."

Terza nodded. She already understood, and she knew that Francesca comprehended that their fate would be to remain in the forest or eventually, when the French felt secure in Terreno Boscoso, to make their way to the Pietro d'Angelos in Florence. No one had helped the young duke, and it was unlikely that anyone would now. Especially when he and his wife disappeared from the castle. She wished there was another choice, but Terza knew that the Comte du Barry, like his daughter, was vengeful. He wanted Rafaello and Francesca dead. His family had been insulted when the young duke had refused the comte's noble daughter in favor of the daughter of a Florentine silk merchant. Aceline's subsequent tragedy had insulted the du Barrys further, and the duke of Terreno Boscoso must be held responsible. Terza sighed deeply.

"Why do you sigh so?" Francesca asked her.

"Alas, mistress, there is no hope," Terza replied gloomily.

"There is always hope," Francesca told her softly. "Now call Roza, and let us pack what we can."

For the next few days the three women carefully went through Francesca's wardrobe. Other than her undergarments, night garments, and stockings, there was little they might take. The clothing of a *duchessa* was hardly appropriate for that of an innkeeper's wife. Her riding breeches would be worn, and fortunately she had only one cloak that was much too fancy. Two others were good, plain wool lined in rabbit fur. They divided the task among them now. Terza and Roza set to work fashioning and sewing several skirts, blouses, and one plain gown in the event such a garment would be needed. Her plain leather slippers and her boots would do for her feet. She had ribbons and two simple veils for her head, as well as a few pairs of gloves. Within a few days they had a proper amount and style of garments for the *duchessa* in her guise of an innkeeper.

"What are we to do with your jewelry?" Terza asked.

"I will take it with me and hide it at the inn. I will not leave it here for the French to find and rob," Francesca said as they packed the soft saddlebags that would carry their personal belongings. "Has Fidelio seen to the duke's clothing?"

Her husband's valet and the majordomo would not leave the castle until after the duke and *duchessa* had departed. Since there were no French inside the castle it was unlikely anyone would even realize they were missing for several days. Captain Arnaldo and his men-at-arms would remain for at least a week, and then disappear in the dark of a moonless night. The drawbridge would remain up. When their enemies finally realized that the castle was empty, it would take a great deal of cleverness on their part to get in.

The night set for their departure was colder than previous nights had been. The duke invited Captain Arnaldo to dine with them in the hall at the high board. A simple hot meal was served of a vegetable and meat soup, venison, a simple pasta dish mixed with butter and herbs, the last of the autumn peas, bread, and cheese. There was a good red wine to drink. When they had finally satisfied their appetites the duke spoke quietly to his captain.

"You will find a bag of coins in my library with which to pay the men when they are dismissed. I know they were paid at St. Michael's for the year they just served. This will be my gift to them for the year ahead, though they will seek places elsewhere. There is a smaller bag for you, my friend. We are grateful for your steadfast loyalty over the years. Make certain that the men depart in the dark of night. You are safe within the castle as long as you can keep the Comte du Barry's assassins out. He will not, I suspect, attempt to breach these walls again soon after his last experience, but one cannot be certain. He must act before Commander d'Aumont returns."

"My lord," the captain replied, "I know that the men will be grateful for your great kindness to them. I will not ask you even now where you go, for I am no fool, and know that even I could be broken under torture. If I know nothing I can say nothing."

"Do not get caught by the French, then," the duke advised wryly.

"I am going north to the Swiss states," the captain said. "I will find a plain-faced daughter of some family willing to take an old man for a husband, marry her, and settle down. I am forty now, my lord, and have spent my life soldiering. I want children and a warm hearth. The Swiss are a peaceable folk."

The duke nodded. "I understand," he said. "I wish you good fortune, my friend." The two men shook hands.

"When will you go, my lord? It threatens rain later tonight."

"So much the better," the duke replied. "The French will keep to the town and not concern themselves overmuch with the castle. Have the horses brought to the secret door for us. Use only the most trustworthy men. There will be six of us and a packhorse."

"What hour?" Captain Arnaldo asked.

"Midnight," the duke replied.

"They will be there when you come," the captain promised. He bowed to the duke and said, "I wish you and our beautiful *duchessa buona fortuna*, my lord. God go with you. The blessed

Virgin protect you." Then, turning, he stepped down from the dais and hurried off.

The duke went down into the kitchens, where the cook toiled alone now.

"My lord!" she greeted him.

"We go tonight, Balbina. Come to the hall at the midnight hour," he told her. "Leave your fires banked as you normally would."

"The rope will be strong, my lord, will it not?" she asked him. "I am a very sturdy woman, I fear. What if it breaks with my weight and I am pitched into a dark moat?"

" 'Tis true you are as plump as an Easter goose, Balbina," the duke teased her, "but we will not be leaving in that manner. There will be no chance of you getting wet unless it rains. You must trust me. Are you still certain you wish to go with us?"

"Oh yes, my lord!" Balbina the cook exclaimed. "I am not young any longer, but neither am I old. I think I might have at least one adventure in my life before I die."

He chuckled. "Aye, every woman should have at least one adventure," he agreed. "With God's blessing on us this will not be a big one, and within two or three days we will reach safety." He gave her a grin. "Midnight!" he repeated, and left her.

Balbina watched him go, surprised by the conversation that had just passed. The young duke had always been polite, but tonight he had seemed almost friendly—nay, he had seemed most companionable.

Rafaello found the hall empty when he reached it. He hurried upstairs to his wife's apartments and found Francesca alone in her dayroom. Bending, he put an arm about her and kissed the lips she offered him. "We will leave at midnight," he told her as he sat down next to her on the settle before the fire.

"In the dark? How will we find our way?" she asked him.

"We will light our way by a small lantern. It will be slow going, but we will be deep in the forest and several miles from the castle by daylight," he explained.

She nodded. "I understand. How do we get across the moat in the dark?"

"It is not known, but the moat was dug very shallowly in one spot so anyone using the hidden door could cross easily. But it is only four feet in width, so you must guide your horse cautiously, being careful not to stray from the easy depth, or your mount will find himself swimming. I shall have Matteo lead Balbina, for she is the least skilled of our riders. Crossing water in the dark is a dangerous business."

"I understand," Francesca said. Then she began to cry softly.

"My love," he exclaimed. "What is it?" He tightened his arm about her shoulders.

"Nothing," she said. "I am being foolish, of course. I suppose the reality of our situation is finally making itself known. But we must survive! I will not allow that arrogant Frenchman to see us dead! He has cost us our duchy, our home, but he will not cost us our lives, Rafaello. We will live and triumph despite him! And I will have my revenge upon him one day for this injustice. I will! If I did not repay Raoul du Barry in kind I should not be my mother's daughter. *But I am.* He will live to regret this."

Chapter 16

The midnight hour came, and the duke's little party met in the hall. They were all dressed for travel. With a final glance about his family's home Rafaello Cesare led them into the deepest cellar, down a corridor, and finally into a small passage, a lantern held tightly in his hand to light their way. They followed him quickly, silently until they reached the little door in the castle wall. Reaching up, the duke took down a key from an alcove in the wall. He unlocked the door. Neither the key nor the hinges made any sound. They stepped out into the dark chilly night to find Captain Arnaldo waiting alone with the seven horses needed.

The duke looked questioningly at his captain, and the man shrugged, nodding his head slightly. The duke nodded, knowing that somewhere in the dark on that small bit of dry land was the body of the man-at-arms who had helped bring the horses.

Captain Arnaldo had taken no chances, making him the only one to know that the duke and his family had gone. The horses were quickly assigned, and they mounted. The duke handed his captain the key, said a soft "*Mille grazie*," and then led the way across the narrow moat passage to the other side.

Sadly watching them go, Captain Arnaldo reached into the darkness and finding the body of his late man-at-arms, dragged it slowly and quietly into the passage. Then stepping in himself, he locked the door and replaced the key in its wall alcove. Without another glance at the dead man-at-arms he returned through the narrow passage to the cellar and barred the entry to the secret passage with a large, tall chest.

Outside a soft but cold rain had begun to fall. The duke slowly led the way to the barely discernible path that led them into the forest. No one spoke. They rode very slowly and cautiously along the narrow track. The rain continued to fall, but it fell lightly. It was uncomfortable but not unbearable. After several hours the sky began to lighten, revealing a gray rainy morning. Finally they stopped to rest the horses.

Balbina offered them bread, cold meat, and cheese to eat. Both men and women took the opportunity to relieve themselves before remounting and continuing along their way.

By midafternoon the skies were brightening. Only the duke knew where they were. His companions could only follow trustingly. Reaching a small clearing as the sun began to set, Rafaello Cesare signaled his little party to a stop. "We will spend the night here," he told them as he dismounted. "We can have no fire, for I do not wish to attract attention. Fix your bed spaces now, and we will eat. Once the night sets in we must be silent again. Matteo, help me secure the horses. You will have the first watch, and at the midnight hour I will take the second, until dawn," the duke told the serving man.

The horses were eventually fastened tightly to two trees in the center of the clearing. The riders would sleep about them on one side. Their saddles had been removed, and they were taken to the little stream bordering one side to drink, then fed before they were made fast. The travelers sat upon their saddles, which had been set on the damp ground so they might eat. Balbina brought out a large roasted capon and more bread and cheese for their meal.

"There is only bread and cheese remaining for the rest of our journey, my lord," she told the duke. "I could carry only so much."

"You've done well," he praised her. Then he looked about the little group. "Now I must speak to you about where we are going and how you must behave from now on." Reaching out, he took Francesca's hand in his and kissed it, smiling faintly at her. "Deep in this forest my grandfather had many years ago a small inn raised so that his huntsmen would have shelter in the winter months. It was available to the men once the cold weather set in, and then was shut up each spring," he explained. "The old innkeeper, Alonza by name, is no longer able to take care of her responsibilities. Before he died my father let her return to her family, and I never managed to arrange for another inn-keeper.

"The French, as you know, wish the *duchessa* and me dead and gone. If we survive I may live to retake my duchy one day. But if I cannot retake the duchy, then my wife and I will survive. You have chosen to survive with us. The duke's huntsmen know me as Carlo, one of them. They have no idea I am Duke Titus's son, or that the man they have always known as Carlo is now their duke. But until the French leave Terreno Boscoso there is no duke. Carlo and his wife, Cara, will manage the inn this winter. What will happen in the spring I cannot say.

"From this moment on you will not address my wife and I as *my lord* and *my lady*. We are Carlo and Cara, even to you, as you are Matteo, Balbina, Terza, and Roza to us. The inn is not the castle. Our identities must remain a secret from any seeking shelter at the inn. Do you understand, my friends?"

"But what will we do at the inn?" Matteo asked. He couldn't quite address the duke yet by a Christian name.

"You and I will hunt until it becomes too cold. We will care for the horses. Alonza's nephew usually brings a cow, so we may have butter and cream. He will hopefully do so this autumn, having not been told otherwise. We have my wife's dogs with us to help with the hunting." Reaching out, he patted one of the greyhounds' heads. "The women will do what women do. Balbina will cook and Francesca will help her. Terza and Roza will keep the inn clean. Francesca can tell you how Alonza managed, for it was at the inn she hid from me before our marriage."

"We will be safe," Francesca said to them. "Only the hunters know of the inn, and there is no real road traversing this forest."

The night had set in now. They could barely see one another. The women lay down to sleep. The duke dozed, and Matteo kept watch. Near midnight the moon broke through the clouds. Rafaello rose and told Matteo to sleep. He kept watch through the rest of the night, though it was not easy. He was chilled and damp. In the first gray of the new day the moon had disappeared and it was beginning to rain again. He roused his companions. They ate their bread and cheese, and began on their way again.

The next night was as uncomfortable. No one spoke for fear of complaining, and the situation they faced couldn't be changed. The bread was stale now and the cheese dry, but it was all they had to eat.

Finally in the early afternoon of that third day they reached the inn. It was silent and it was obvious that they were the first to arrive since Alonza had departed that previous spring. Francesca looked upon the inn with surprisingly fond eyes. She had certainly never expected to see it again, much less come to manage it. She smiled to herself as she dismounted her horse, wondering what her elegant mother would think of this situation that her second daughter, the *duchessa*, found herself in now. Orianna would not be pleased. One daughter a Turkish prince's third wife, and another a fugitive. Francesca knew her mother had wanted, nay, had expected, better things for her children.

"Matteo, you may find some critters have taken up residence in the stable. Could you clear them out for us, and then settle the horses?"

"Yes, m— Cara," he answered her uncomfortably.

She laughed, seeing his chagrin. "You will get used to it, Matteo," she told him.

Then she turned to the three women. "Come along and let us see the condition the inn is now in. But Alonza usually left it neat." Going over to the front door of the building, she bent and lifted a flowerpot by the door and slid out a key. Then, fitting it into the inn's main door, she ushered them inside. "We need to freshen the rooms. Open all the windows. Balbina, come along and I will show you the kitchen. It isn't as big as you are used to, but you will find it does nicely."

Rafaello stood watching her admiringly. "What shall I do?" he asked her.

"We will need wood for the fireplaces," she told him. Then she turned away to rejoin the other women.

By nightfall the horses had been stabled and were fed. There were fires in the inn's fireplaces. Terza would have Francesca's old chamber. Balbina and Roza would share a small windowed chamber off the kitchens. Matteo had an alcove with a cot off the large dining hall. Francesca had allotted Alonza's old chamber to her husband and herself. It would require refurbishing, but for tonight it would do. The bed, while not as large as the ducal bed, was commodious enough for the lovers.

"I always wondered what this chamber looked like," Rafaello murmured to her that night as they snuggled together.

"We will have to make a new mattress for it as soon as possible," Francesca said. "I cannot help but remember Alonza and Bernardo pleasuring each other in this bed. The walls are not so thick that vigorous and noisy lovers can't be heard," she giggled. "We must remember that Terza is now in the little chamber next to us."

His answer was to pull her night garment down and fasten his mouth onto her breast, suckling hard.

"Rafaello!" she gasped.

He lifted his head and she saw the passionate lust in his eyes. "How many weeks has it been since I have had the pleasure of your body?" he asked her softly.

"I was always there for you," she murmured, her fingers in his dark auburn hair.

"Be truthful, my love. Neither of us could feel passion given our circumstances, our fears for our people, for the duchy, for our own lives," he replied low. His hand was sliding along her leg as he pushed up the fabric of her garment. "We are safe now, however, and I find my appetite for you has but increased. Take this damned thing off before I tear it off."

"Do not, for I have nothing to replace it with, Rafaello, my love," she said. Her heart was beating wildly as she pulled off the garment. She liked it when he was less civilized, and the beard he now wore made him look older, fiercer.

"*Carlo*," he reminded her. "Rafaello no longer exists for you, Cara. It is Carlo. Only Carlo who kisses you, who takes you in his arms, who will fuck you." Then he was kissing her a wicked deep kiss, his tongue running along lips that opened eagerly to him so he might plunge into her warm mouth and taste her.

She met his hot probing organ with her own dancing tongue. They fenced, she caught him and sucked hard, her hands caressing his naked back and buttocks. He groaned, and, escaping her, began to kiss her eyes, her face, her throat. He placed his palm over her mound and squeezed it. "Oh, Carlo!" she gasped.

Satisfied that he once again had the upper hand he let a long finger slide along her hot wet slit. "Shameless. Shameless," he whispered in her ear as he took a brief moment to nibble the lobe. She pressed up against the finger. "I know what you want, Cara. But of course I might be wrong, so you must tell me in your own words what it is that would please you, my love." The finger slipped easily between her nether lips to find the tiny nub of flesh that when stroked properly could send her to heaven.

"Yes!" she gasped.

"Yes, what?" he teased as he found what he sought and began to worry it.

Francesca closed her eyes and just let the deliciousness of his touch there fill her with pleasure. "Yes!" she repeated, "and yes again!"

He ceased the delicate torture. "Naughty one, you must tell me what it is you want before I will continue further."

"Do not be cruel, my Carlo," she purred at him.

"Tell me!" he insisted.

"I want you to play with me until I am filled with a lust that only your cock can cure. I want you to fuck me and fuck me and fuck me until I am mindless with my pleasure. But I want you to know pleasure too, my Carlo," Francesca told him. "I am not entirely greedy. Just a little bit."

"I think my finger will not be enough tonight," he told her. Then he was between her legs, drawing her open to him, his tongue finding her.

"*Madre di Dios,*" Francesca gasped, as his tongue touched her in that sensitive secret place again and again and again. "Ohhh! It is too much! Too much!"

His tongue continued to torture her with wicked little flicks, slow, slow, and then faster and faster. Her female fragrance filled his nostrils, rousing his lust even more.

"I will die of this!" Francesca gasped.

"Shall I stop?" he asked her.

"Yes! No! No!" Her whole body shook in a fierce spasm.

Satisfied she was more than ready, he ceased, slid between her soft thighs, and slowly pushed his manhood into her now fevered body. "Is this better, my love? Is it?"

He began to move in her slowly at first, causing her to moan with her excitement, then faster and faster until she was half sobbing with the pure pleasure with which he filled her. He watched her face, and the joy he saw in it almost caused him to spill his seed too soon. She needed just a bit more tonight. It had been so long since they had had the pleasure of each other's passion.

"Carlo! Carlo!" she sobbed to him. Then as he gave her his

remaining passion, she found herself in a magical world of divine satisfaction, her body shuddering with the pleasure of his passion, the wonderful sensation of his hot seed filling her womb.

Briefly Francesca lost consciousness.

He groaned with the incredible release they had just shared, his own body relaxing with relief. *His!* She was his for always. He kissed her gently, bringing her back to consciousness.

Francesca opened her eyes and smiled up at her husband. "I love you by whatever name you choose to affect," she told him.

"I think perhaps Carlo, a simple huntsman, can offer you more than Duke Rafaello, who finds himself beset by so many problems," he told her.

"I think you were always happier here in the forest than in the castle," she noted wisely. "But your responsibility to your family guided you. For now that choice is no longer yours. And as for the spoiled daughter of the Florentine silk merchant, I think her winter as a maidservant changed her as well."

"You are not afraid of this life, then," he said.

"I am not afraid. Besides, I have it much better than poor old Alonza did. I have Balbina to cook, and Terza and Roza to help me with the rest. It will not be so difficult once the men come in from the cold."

"I think they will welcome us," he replied. "They know us both, and the others are easy to get along with."

"But there is much for us to do before our huntsmen arrive, and we do not have much time," Francesca reminded him.

"Tomorrow, my love," he answered her. "Tonight is for us." Then he kissed her again, and Francesca sighed with her happiness.

During the next few days they worked to prepare for the

arrival of their guests. To their relief Alonza's nephew arrived with a rather scrawny-looking cow. He recognized Francesca at once. "Why, hello, my beauty. You have come back, have you?"

"I was appointed to take your aunt's place, as she no longer wishes to do it," Francesca said. "Could you not have brought us a fatter cow and more chickens?"

"Alonza died," the boy said matter-of-factly. "She wouldn't leave when the French came. She cooked for them, and then one morning they found her dead in her bed. I had remained with her, and once she was buried, that same day they sent me from my home. When the bastards slept I crept into the barn and took the cow and the remaining chickens. There's been little food for the folk who remained, let alone the animals. I thought the cow might die before I got her here, but I knew the duke would not forget his huntsmen. At least that's what my old aunt said." He climbed from his cart.

"Do you want to remain with us?" Francesca asked him. "I brought some friends from the town to help. We can always find room for another."

"Thank you, my beauty, but I'll go back. I'm leaving Terreno Boscoso to find my fortune elsewhere in the world. The townsfolk are now scattered throughout the countryside. They'll not return as long as the French occupy the town. The duke has barricaded himself in the castle. There is nothing left. I don't suppose you'd come with me, my beauty? I'm a man of some property now, with my donkey and cart." He grinned.

Francesca laughed. "I have married Carlo the huntsman. I do not believe he would like it if I deserted him."

"Well, good luck to you, then," Alonza's nephew said. "I'll remain the night if you will have me. I like the smells coming out of the kitchen." He grinned.

"You are more than welcome to remain," Francesca told him. "My thanks for the cow. We'll fatten her up somehow. Let the chickens loose in the yard."

"She's better here now than in the town," the boy said. "The French are eating everything and leaving those who remained to starve. The Terreno Boscoso we knew is gone, I fear, but I do not understand how it happened, Cara. Why did the French invade us? Our ducal family is a peaceful one. They always have been. They kept us from the wars and other conflicts between the Italian states and France."

"I have heard that the French king is amassing more and more land," Francesca answered Alonza's nephew. "I suppose because Terreno Boscoso was peaceful it seemed an easy conquest."

"A warm hearth, a hot meal, and a good woman should be enough for any man, or so Alonza always said to me," the boy replied. "Oh, well. I must simply find my fortune elsewhere. My aunt is dead, my mother gone to her brother's farm."

Rafaello, who would now be known as Carlo, listened to the boy. In his entire life he had never felt so helpless. He was Terreno Boscoso's hereditary ruler, and yet he had been unable to protect his own duchy. Rather than frittering away his youth and enjoying himself while his kindly father ruled, he should have been looking to the future. He should have considered the possibility of one of their larger neighbors coveting the duchy.

The constant wars in the Italian states and between the French and those states would have convinced a wiser man that the world was changing. Nothing, after all, ever remained the same. He should have thought to convince his father to allow him to raise and assemble an army. Despite the mercenaries they had been helpless to defend themselves, and now his people were suffering for his lack of foresight.

Alonza's nephew departed the following morning. The new innkeeper, however, had hardly spoken since the previous evening when he had listened to the boy. He climbed into the bed he now shared with Francesca and lay awake most of the night. If she was surprised by his lack of interest in lovemaking, Francesca said nothing. She had had a busy day and was content with the opportunity to sleep. In the morning, however, she saw that his mood was no better. "What is the matter, my love?" she asked him, concerned.

"I should have known," he said bleakly. "I should have known that the French would seek to have Terreno Boscoso. It is well-known that King Louis is acquisitive."

"Nonsense!" Francesca said, surprising him, for she rarely disagreed with him so strongly. "It is not likely that King Louis knew anything of us until the Comte du Barry told him of a gold mine and a wealthy duchy he might easily have for the taking. Du Barry knew how to stoke his king's greed, and he did."

"We should have had our own army," he told her. "I should have made alliances."

"Yes, we should have," she agreed. "But from the time your noble Roman ancestor founded the duchy those of his descendants who followed him have lived in peace with their neighbors. Terreno Boscoso was peaceful and prosperous, nothing more. It did not threaten anyone, so none felt threatened by it. But once King Louis learned of that mine we were lost, my love. Even when he learns there is no longer any gold in the mine he cannot simply withdraw and reveal his avaricious greed to the rest of the world. He will retain it, and your duchy will be no more. He will use the excuse that Milan constituted a threat to France, and when you would not swear your fealty to France he had no choice but to take the duchy from you, for he feared you were in league with Milan."

"Then all is lost," Rafaello said bitterly. "I shall never be able to regain my duchy. Our family's castle will remain empty of the Cesares."

"We are alive," Francesca said.

"To what purpose?" he asked. "I am the duke of Terreno Boscoso yet I have no home, can rule nothing any longer."

"We are alive," Francesca repeated. "We will make a new life for ourselves here in the forest of Terreno Boscoso."

"I am not an innkeeper, Francesca!" he said, suddenly angry.

"Nor am I," she countered. "I am the daughter of a wealthy man. I was raised to be cosseted and waited upon. Every wish I had was granted. I was destined to a life of privilege, to be the wife of a duke, a prince. But when I ran away from you, when Alonza took me in, I learned to serve others, and in doing so found myself happier than I had ever been in my life, Rafaello. I did not think you a weak man who could not change given the opportunity. Do not dare to prove me wrong, *my lord*! We have survived our enemies, and we will continue to survive them. Now, it is almost sunrise. Get out of bed, for we have much to accomplish today. It will not be long before the huntsmen begin coming, and we must be ready for them."

She got up, washed in the cold water she poured into the basin, and dressed quickly. Then she left him, silently praying that she had roused him before he fell into a melancholy. Francesca realized as she considered the words she had spoken to him that she would rather toil in the forest as the innkeeper's wife than live in exile in Florence on her father's largesse as an object of pity. I should be surprised with myself, she thought, but she wasn't. Two winters ago she had learned a valuable lesson in humility. She hadn't forgotten it. Now her husband must learn that lesson.

Reaching the kitchen even before Balbina, she added wood to the hot embers and soon had the kitchen hearth blazing. Seeing the risen dough in a large bowl, she kneaded it into several loaves and tucked it into the ovens to bake, just as the cook hurried into the kitchen, Roza behind her.

"Oh, my lady," the cook exclaimed, but before she could continue, Francesca held up her hand.

"Who?" she asked. "I see no lady here, Balbina."

"It is difficult to address you in what seems a disrespectful manner," the cook said. Then she added, "I apologize for oversleeping, Cara."

"Our trip was long and fraught with danger," the younger woman replied. "Do not apologize, Balbina. I will usually be up before you each day now that I am responsible for this inn. Be aware that Carlo is suffering regret at having been unable to defend the duchy from the French. The lad who brought the cow and chickens gave him news from the town. Barricaded in the castle, we had had none in weeks. The plight of our people troubles him greatly."

"If it hadn't been for the duke's warning," little Roza spoke up, "the town wouldn't have been able to evacuate and take its wealth with it. At least the French got little, and if our folk do not come back they will be able to begin anew somewhere else. Duke Rafaello was a good ruler. He looked after us as best he could under the circumstances. How many might have been killed resisting? How many women shamed by lustful soldiers, Cara? It is the people who made Terreno Boscoso, not the land. And our duke saved the people. He should feel no regret. He thought first of his people, which is more than most of these great lords do."

"Thank you," the duke said, stepping into the kitchen. He had been entering the kitchen, but curious to hear the women talking, he had stopped to listen. His despair lifted.

"Oh, sir!" Roza cried, blushing.

"Will no one feed me my breakfast?" Carlo the huntsman said with a smile and a wink at Roza.

"Go and gather the eggs," Francesca ordered him. "Despite their uncomfortable trip the hens may have laid a few."

"How does one *gather* an egg?" he asked her.

"Come along, Carlo, and I will show you. You will not sit about while the rest of us work to be ready for our guests," Francesca said briskly as she hurried from the kitchens with her husband in her wake.

Roza giggled. "She is more a *duchessa* here than at the castle," the girl said.

Balbina chuckled. "The castle was his, and he adores her. He treated her like a precious possession," the cook noted wisely. "But this inn is hers already. She might have been raised in luxury, but I can see she knows how to work."

Over the next few weeks they toiled to ready the inn for the huntsmen. The days were growing shorter, the winds blowing more from the north and west now. The bedding had been aired in the cool sunshine, the rooms swept free of dust, the windows washed. Matteo and the duke chopped wood each day, filling a woodshed. Then they built a second shed and filled it as well. Repairs were made where necessary. Gathering the eggs first thing in the morning was now a chore assigned to Roza. Carlo seemed to break more eggs than he brought. And then late one afternoon as the sun was setting, two rough-looking men emerged from the forest.

Alerted by Matteo, Francesca hurried to the open door of the inn and immediately recognized Bernardo and Pippino. "Welcome back," Francesca greeted them with a smile, and was immediately enveloped in a bear hug by Bernardo.

When he released her he asked, "Alonza?"

"Gone to God," Francesca said, crossing herself, as did her two companions. "The duke appointed me to replace her on Alonza's advice. I have brought a few friends from the town to work with me, and I have married Carlo. Come in, come in! The wind is coming up, and I smell rain in the air. Roza, ale for these two thirsty guests of ours."

"When did you come?" Bernardo asked her.

"About a month ago. Alonza's nephew managed to bring us a cow and some chickens. I hope all is in order for the men. Do you know how many have survived the French? How many will be coming to shelter with us?"

"The few with families in the town and about it left to take them to safety just before the French came. Half came back to the forest once that was done. You may have a few empty pallets, Cara, but those of us who shelter with you will be grateful."

"We brought with us what stores we could find that escaped the French's eyes," she told him. "And, of course, there were things already here, but we must be careful if we are to get through the winter. And then we shall hope to be able to find what we need for next season. Tonight, however, you will eat well, and not my cooking," Francesca teased him. "I have a fine cook, Balbina by name. Come, and I will take you to the kitchens to meet her. Balbina appreciates a man with a good appetite. Pippino, if we leave you here, can I trust that Roza will be safe from your randy behavior?"

Pippino chuckled. "She looks like a warm armful, Cara," he

said eying Roza lasciviously and grinning. "But I'll try to behave myself."

Francesca took Bernardo off to meet Balbina, who eyed the
big huntsman approvingly. "He looks like he enjoys his food,
Cara," she said. Then she turned to the huntsman. "Tell me
what you enjoy the most, big man."

"I will leave you two to discuss the joys of food," Francesca
said, hurrying back to the main room of the inn, where she
heard Pippino ask Roza a naughty question.

"Tell me, pretty one, do you enjoy a good fuck?"

Before her former maidservant could answer, Francesca said,
"Pippino! Do you recall how Alonza insisted you treat me when
I first came to the inn? Well, that is how I am insisting that you
treat my Roza now. Keep your cock in your breeches, or you'll be
spending the winter in the snow. Do you understand me?"

"Cara, be fair," he complained. "We have spent the summer
in the forest with no human contact. Once the others get here
there will be quite a demand for this pretty girl's company. You
should really keep a whore or two at the inn. Old Alonza
wouldn't hear of it, but what is a man to do when he needs a
woman, I ask you?"

"The inn can offer you food, shelter, and the companionship of your mates. I, like Alonza, will have no slatterns toiling
for me, Pippino," Francesca told him sternly.

"Damn me," the huntsman said, "if you don't sound just
like the old woman."

Carlo and Matteo now entered the inn, and Pippino's attention turned to an old friend and the man by his side.

"Are they all like that one?" Roza asked her mistress.

"Some worse," Francesca told her. "You just have to be
firm, and come to me or Carlo if any of them frighten you or

attempt to force you when you have said no. Pippino is correct when he says old Alonza would not put up with any nonsense. She didn't, and neither will I."

That night as she and her husband lay together, he said, "So, it has begun, and it would appear that we have become inn-keepers. How many did Bernardo say would come this year?" He wrapped his arms about her.

"Fewer than before," Francesca told him. "We will manage, my love." She snuggled closer to him, pressing her breasts against him.

"Poor Pippino," Carlo said softly. He drew her nightgown up and off of her lush body, tossing it to the floor. His big hand smoothed down the length of her back, cupping and squeezing her buttocks in his palm. "Pippino must soothe his cock by himself while I get to soothe mine with you." He kissed her a slow, teasing kiss.

"Or perhaps I will soothe your cock myself," Francesca said, quickly reaching down and taking him in her hand. "What will the little huntsman do, my love? This, perhaps? Or mayhap this?" She taunted him first by squeezing his burgeoning cock and then rubbing it up and down slowly, slowly as it pulsed in her hand. Turning, she bent and took him into her mouth, her tongue teasing its way about the head of his cock, then suddenly sucking him eagerly while he groaned at the sensation of her warm mouth drawing on his throbbing cock. His hand tangled in her red-gold hair, encouraging her.

"Mmmm," Francesca purred as she eased her hold on him, licking the thick column up and down.

He retaliated, his other hand pushing between her soft thighs to find the tiny pleasure nub she possessed. A single fin-ger easily slid between her moist nether lips and successfully gained his goal. Now it was Francesca's turn to gasp with her pleasure as the skillful finger tortured her. She released his cock from between her lips, unable to concentrate on two sensations at once. Her body arched up to meet his hand, his finger.

"Oh, villain!" she whispered hotly.

He laughed softly. "You have a wicked yet heavenly mouth, my love," he told her. Then with a final flick of his finger he sent her over the edge even as he mounted her, pushing himself slowly into her warm body.

She felt him filling her and cried out softly. It felt so good to be filled by his thickness, his length. Wrapping her legs about his she demanded of him, "Deeper! Faster! Faster!" And he complied with her shameless wishes, feeding her heated desire until she was writhing and sobbing beneath him.

"Temptress!" he groaned into her ear. "You find your huntsman a better lover than your duke, don't you? You give yourself more shamelessly, more freely as the innkeeper than you did as my *duchessa*."

"The huntsman is more exciting," she gasped. "Oh, God, don't stop! I'll die if you do, my Carlo!"

He laughed wickedly. "Oh, you will die, my love, but it will be long before I stop," he promised her. Then he began to fuck her fiercely, until he had to cover her mouth with his hand to prevent her screams of pleasure from being heard by all in the inn. The duke had been a passionate man, but the huntsman was wilder and even more passionate. The *duchessa* had been a contented recipient of her husband's love, but the beautiful innkeeper was more reckless in her lust with her huntsman.

Francesca let him bring her to the edge twice before she finally begged for release. He gave it to her gladly, for he was not certain how much longer he could maintain himself. She flew among the stars as the greatest pleasure she had ever known swept over her. Her body shook with her own release and the sound of his voice crying her name as he unleashed his seed into her eager body. "My love! My love!" she whispered desperately as his arms closed tightly about her.

They did not speak after that. There were no words. But they slept more soundly than either of them had in months. The duke of Terreno Boscoso and his *duchessa* had somehow been overwhelmed by the passions of the huntsman and his innkeeper wife. They were not gone. Perhaps one day they would reappear. Perhaps not. And when the morning came they arose, smiling wordlessly at one another, and prepared for the day ahead.

"I'm surprised to see them up on time," Terza murmured to Roza. "Much went on in their room last night. I thought it would never cease."

"They seem happier today," Roza noted. "It is as if they found peace together at last." Then she asked, "Is there a trundle beneath your bed?"

"Are you not content with Balbina? It is warmer in her chamber near the hearth than in my chamber upstairs."

"I had to sleep in the pantry last night," Roza admitted. "Balbina could hardly wait to get that big fellow, Bernardo, in her bed, and he was more than willing."

"She had the reputation of being a woman with a fine lustful nature back at the castle," Terza said. "Of course I'll share my little chamber with you, but our mistress should know, lest she think I've invited that Pippino into my bed."

Roza giggled. "She would never think that of you, Terza. Not Pippino!"

"I'm sure there are some who appreciate his charms," Terza answered, chuckling.

During the next few days more and more of the huntsmen began returning to the winter inn, happy to find it still available to them despite the French occupation. After all, it was not very likely that the French knew of the duke's huntsmen or the winter inn deep in the forest. And they were all relieved by that knowledge. While they were facing the hard truth that change had come to Terreno Boscoso, at least the inn, despite the change in innkeepers, was very much the same.

Chapter 17

The inhabitants of the inn settled into their winter schedule. Seventeen men had arrived this season. Not quite as many as two years ago, but more than enough to take care of. Francesca thanked heaven she had her companions from the castle to help her.

November ended, and December began. It was toward the end of that month that the priest arrived. Francesca was surprised to see him, for she had not considered he would still come, but he reassured her that he had been careful. "The French will not find the inn."

"What news?" Carlo asked him. The cleric knew him only as the huntsman.

The priest sighed and then told them, "It is said that Duke Rafaello and the *duchessa* have disappeared, although the French prefer telling all who will listen that they were executed as traitors to King Louis. Of course, no one saw the deed done or viewed the bodies."

"I thought that castle was inviolate," Carlo said carefully. "Did not the duke barricade himself within with his family?"

"Someone noticed one day that there were no men-at-arms upon the castle heights," the priest began. "Comte du Barry ordered the castle's drawbridge taken down, and no one prevented the French as they hacked it to bits, enough to get what remained lowered. When they entered the castle they found it deserted. No one remained.

"The duke and his wife were gone. There were no servants or animals or men-at-arms. It was as if they had never existed. Some believe the French tale, but others do not."

"Then where is the duke?" Francesca asked the priest.

The cleric crossed himself. "I suspect, my daughter, that only God has the answer to that mystery. I do not believe the French, however. I think the duke and his wife may have sought refuge with her family in Florence. Many others do also. Where is Alonza?" he asked Francesca.

"She has died," Francesca told him, and they crossed themselves. "The duke appointed me to manage the inn if I would take Alonza's position. I was weary of hiding from the French, as were my friends. We gladly left the town. Carlo and I were wed before I returned. He and his friend, Matteo, maintain the outside for us."

"It is honest work," the priest said. "But what will you do when the spring comes, my daughter?"

"We will remain here at the inn, for we fear returning to the town while the French occupy it," she answered him.

He nodded in agreement. "Of course," he said. " 'Tis very wise."

The priest remained for several weeks, leaving in mid-January when there was a brief thaw. But before he departed he learned a secret that Francesca had been keeping close to her heart. He scolded her gently for it, saying, "You must tell him, my daughter."

"I will," Francesca promised the cleric. "I wanted to make certain myself."

"She is more than certain, as am I," Terza, who was with her mistress, said tartly to the priest. "She should have revealed her condition weeks ago, but she fears he will want her to sit by the fire for the next few months, and of course she will not. Nor should she."

"When is the blessed event to be, my daughter?" the priest asked.

"Terza says sometime in July," Francesca answered.

"I will be here then to see the infant baptized," the priest promised.

"*Now will you tell him?*" Terza demanded to know.

"Tonight," Francesca promised.

The priest departed the inn that same day. He would return to the town and give what comfort he could to those who remained. She was sorry to see him go, for she missed the comfort of her church here in the forest, as she had been her whole life used to having her faith as her companion. It was difficult when there was no priest.

That evening, the meal over and most of the inn's other inhabitants gone to their beds, Francesca and Carlo sat by the fire in the kitchen, which they found cozy.

"The priest told me before he left that I must share my secret with you, my love," Francesca began.

"You have a secret?" he asked her, amused. "What can it be?"

"You are teasing me," she replied.

"I love teasing you," he told her, leering naughtily at her.

Francesca laughed. "Perhaps I shall keep my secret, then," she said.

"You know I hate secrets!" Carlo reminded her. "I will apologize if you will tell me your secret."

"Hmm." She pretended to consider. "Well," Francesca began, "perhaps I will relent, since you are being so nice."

He leaned forward and, catching a hand, kissed the inside of her wrist. "You and I should never have secrets from each other," Carlo told her. "Tell me, my love."

"We are having a baby," Francesca said simply. "Terza says sometime in July."

His handsome face registered his surprise, but then he said, "You cannot have a baby here, Cara. There is no doctor, nor a midwife to take care of you!"

"Most women birth their children without a doctor or even a midwife," she said.

"And many die from the lack of care," he replied. "I will not have you dying because we have no proper support. You are not some peasant to spawn in a field! We must find a way to get you to Florence for your sake and my heir's."

"No." She said it quietly, but he heard the firm tone behind the word.

"Cara, be reasonable," he pleaded with her. "You cannot remain here in the forest when you are enceinte with my heir. You need to be where our child can be delivered safely, kept safely. An inn in the forest is not that place."

"And you think putting me in danger by exposing me to all sorts of risks while I attempt to reach Florence will keep us safer?" she demanded. "No, Carlo. I will remain here, where I now belong, and my women will help me deliver. Your heir will not be born in Florence. This child will be born in Terreno Boscoso. Perhaps not in the castle of the Cesares, where his sire was born and his ancestors were born, but he or she will come into the world in this duchy, not in some foreign place."

"I am not content with this foolish decision, madam." He was suddenly the duke he was born to be.

"Then be discontent if you will," she responded. "I will not, cannot, be forced from my home." Then, pulling her hand from his, Francesca rose and left him sitting before the kitchen fire.

He didn't know what to do. She was right. Attempting to force her to leave the inn for Florence could put her in more danger than simply letting her have her own way.

But he could not help being concerned. He would speak to Terza the next day and see whether she would agree with him, for Francesca, if she listened to anyone, listened to her longtime serving woman.

But Terza agreed with her mistress. "What if someone recognized her on the road?" she said to him. "There is no real disguise that can hide her great beauty. The Milanese might turn her over to the French to gain their favor. They would care for her until the child was born, and then murder them both. No, no, my lord! My lady is safer here and so is the child. Remember who you really are and that this child is your heir."

He accepted his defeat then, and with his wife's permission told the rest of the inn's inhabitants proudly that he would soon be a father. The huntsmen cheered him and then spent the winter's day getting drunk in his son's honor, for a man like Carlo would certainly sire a son. Among them only Bernardo remained sober. He had suspected that Francesca was with child, for he had noticed her suddenly growing plumper.

He had kept his suspicions to himself. He was also quite aware of who Carlo really was, for in the duke's youth when he had been simply his father's heir, Duke Titus had shared that information with his head huntsman so he might keep an eye on the boy. It was Bernardo who had actually taught the duke to hunt. He was therefore fully knowledgeable of who Francesca really was and how important the child she now carried was. He made it his mission to watch over her as he had once watched over her husband, for he admired her bravery and practical nature. She might have been born to wealth and privilege, but she was no overproud aristo.

The winter months passed peacefully. The snows were heavy, but then they began to melt with the coming spring. The days grew a little longer and slowly warmer. The huntsmen began to leave again for their forest haunts. Finally they were all gone but for Bernardo, who remained. "You need another man here," he said when asked why. "With Cara so heavy with child now it is important to have enough protection. If the French were to venture this deep into the forest, another man would be a deterrent." And he could not be moved, nor would he speak on the matter further.

The duke was not unhappy with his company. "He knows who we are," he said to Francesca. "He has known all along but kept silent, and is unlikely to acknowledge it."

"He is a good man," she replied. "I am honestly glad he remained. Have you noticed of late how oddly Matteo is behaving? I believe our months here in the forest have not agreed with him. I wish we might send him away, but perhaps I am being unfair. Still, I do not trust him as I once did."

"He is not used to the isolation," Carlo said. "He is, after all, a castle servant. I think it is easier for women to adjust to this lonely life. And having to treat you and me as equals, and calling us by our Christian names, is difficult for him."

"Husband, only Balbina is content, as she has Bernardo to fuck her when she wants him, and he is always glad to service her. But what of Terza and Roza? Perhaps my faithful Terza is content because she is with me and we have been together since I was a child. But poor little Roza is young. I suspect she harbored dreams of marrying one day. There is no opportunity here for her to wed. Yet she is loyal to me, bless her."

"Matteo is probably going through a mood," he told her. "It is spring, after all. I will take him out in another day or two so we may set some rabbit traps."

"Be watchful nonetheless, even if you think me foolish, my love," Francesca advised her husband.

He put a loving arm about her, resting his free hand on her great belly. "He will be a big lad," he noted, and then chuckled as the infant kicked at the hand.

"Terza says I am as big if not a bit bigger than my mother was when the twins were born," Francesca said softly.

He grinned down at her. "I like the idea of two heirs, as long as you are safe." Then he kissed the top of her head.

"It could be two heiresses," she warned him. "You may desire a son, my lord, but only God almighty knows what will be."

"Terreno Boscoso has had two ruling *duchessas* in its time," Rafaello told her. "Of course, they were then compelled to wed with distant Cesare cousins to maintain the purity of our family descent."

"You mean a daughter can rule if she is firstborn?" Francesca was surprised.

"If there are no sons, yes," he answered. "And in the case of the two *duchessas* who ruled, there were no brothers."

"So, you will be content if our child is a daughter," she said.

"I will be content as long as you are both safe from any harm," he declared.

"I will keep praying for a son," Francesca said. "A son first is always best."

"It is," Rafaello agreed. "And we will call him Carlo, after his father. Carlo Rafaello Titus."

"I am just sorry we cannot communicate with my parents in Florence to let them know we are alive and we have a child coming," Francesca said sadly.

"When the child or children are born and I can tell them you are all well, I will find a way," he promised her.

Space was cleared for a summer garden, and it was planted so they might have food into the autumn and even some to store. The days grew longer, and Francesca's belly seemed to grow larger. Terza was now certain her mistress carried twins, telling all who would listen that Francesca's mother had been every bit as large with her twins, Luca and Lucianna.

"Her labor was surely long and difficult," Balbina said. "God and his blessed Mother help our mistress."

"No," Terza told them. "Her labor was swift, to our amazement. Her previous labors had been hard, but with her twins Mistress Orianna popped those two out as quickly as a raindrop rolling down a window. Pray it will be so for our mistress. And then, when she birthed her last child, it was as it had been with all the others but the twins. I never understood it, nor did anyone else."

Francesca's time finally came. She began her labors in early evening, and the first of the twins was born just before midnight. "Tell me! Tell me!" she demanded of her women, who were all attending her.

"A son!" Terza said. "And listen to him howl with his impatience," she chuckled, handing the infant to Balbina, who saw the little one cleaned and then swaddled. The plump cook held the baby boy against her ample bosom, quieting him, a large smile upon her face. "Shall I take him to the duke?" she asked.

"Yes, take him to Carlo, his father," Francesca corrected her gently. Then she gasped. "The pains are beginning again!" she exclaimed. And two hours later she birthed the second of the twins.

"A daughter!" Terza told her, "just like your mama."

"Let me see her," Francesca said happily.

"Let Roza clean and swaddle her first," Terza advised. "You still have a bit of work left to do. You have delivered your babies every bit as easily and quickly as your mama did all those years ago. She would be very proud of you."

"Prouder if we still held the duchy," Francesca murmured.

"You are alive and the infants seem healthy," Terza told her. "Be grateful and thank Santa Anna, your patron, and the blessed Mother, who was her daughter," the serving woman advised.

"I will," Francesca promised. She quickly expelled the afterbirth, and Terza cleaned all evidence of the births away. It was then that Roza put the female twin into her mother's arms. The infant was awake but quiet. She stared briefly at her mother, and then, as if satisfied with what she saw, closed her eyes and slept. "Take her to her father and bring me my son," Francesca said. She had barely seen the boy before he had been removed so his father might view his heir.

But before that might be done Rafaello came into the bedchamber, holding little Carlo in his arms. "What a lad!" he explained, well pleased.

"And here is your daughter," she said, handing him the baby as he set their son in the crook of her arm. "I should like to call her Giovanna, after my father. Giovanna Maria Blanca. Maria for the blessed Mother, and Blanca for my sister Bianca."

"Will your mother object to Blanca?" he asked her gently.

"This is not my mother's daughter," Francesca said. "She is ours. It is not likely my mother will ever see this grandchild, even if we can manage somehow to bring them word of these births, my love."

He nodded. "Carlo and Giovanna. They are good names," he agreed. "The priest arrived this evening before dark. We must choose godparents for the twins and let them be baptized quickly, so he may be on his way again."

"Bernardo will serve both children as their godfather. Terza will be godmother to each twin," Francesca decided. "With your approval, of course."

"I will not argue such choices," he agreed with her. "They will be so proud of the honor," Rafaello chuckled, "and honestly I prefer it. Had you birthed these infants in the castle we should have had to choose some high-and-mighty lordling who would have sent a rich gift without seeing either Carlo or Giovanna. Bernardo and Terza will help raise them and protect them. Yes, you have chosen well, my love."

The twin infants were baptized in the dining hall the day following their birth. Francesca was carried there so she might observe the proceedings. This was where the priest always held his services when he visited the inn in the winter. Overwhelmed at first by the great honor bestowed upon them, Bernardo and Terza performed their duties perfectly, and each child howled, outraged to be awakened as cool water was poured over its small head. The priest was pleased by this, claiming any de-mons inhabiting the two innocents had now been driven away by the holy baptismal waters and would not return.

The priest then departed, promising to see them again sometime in December.

It was full summer now. Francesca quickly recovered her strength and nursed her infants happily, and took up some of her duties as the innkeeper once again. Rafaello doted on his two children, marveling at how quickly they grew. July came to an end, and then August. It was September, and the few apple trees in the inn's small orchard needed picking. Francesca realized they must begin in earnest to prepare for the arrival of their guests in late October and early November.

Though the twins' cradles were in their bedchamber Francesca and her husband had begun to make love again. The birth of their children had released them from their self-imposed abstinence, and they were more eager than ever to share their passion.

"Do you think we wake the twins when we cry out while lovemaking?" he wondered one night. "You pleasure me so, my love, I cannot help myself."

"If they are awakened they make no sound," Francesca said, caressing his smooth chest with teasing fingers. She bent to kiss his nipples. "And when they do, then they must go in with Terza and Roza." She nipped and licked where she had just kissed.

"Good," he responded, pushing her upon her back and licking each of her nipples in turn. "Jesu! You excite me! I suspect you will always be this alluring, my love, may God have mercy on me." Then he began to kiss her passionately, his lips devouring her, and his head spun with the simple pleasure she gave him.

She murmured her own pleasure, returning his kisses, her

body eagerly yielding to him, her heart beating wildly. Was a husband supposed to continue to excite his wife after the birth of their children? When he nudged her thighs she opened to him eagerly. She wanted his thick length filling her with pleasure, sending her spinning through a cosmos of delight. She cried out as he did. "Carlo! Carlo!" she whispered in his ear. "Ohh, how I love you, my sweet husband!"

"And I you, beloved wife," he answered her, groaning as the hot walls of her sheath closed tightly around him. "Jesu, Cara, you are so sweet. So sweet!" He began to move in her, his heart beating with a mixture of excitement and unbridled lust.

Her body rose to meet his every downward thrust. She whispered encouragement in his ear, repeating her vow of love over and over again until they were both dizzy. And then, unable to restrain himself any longer, he released his tribute into her eager womb, reveling in her cry as her body shuddered with her own pleasure. Afterwards he cradled her in his arms, nuzzling the top of her head with his lips, telling her softly of his great love for her. And they slept until Francesca arose to nurse the twins, content and happy with the life she now led. How odd that she should be happier here in the forest as an innkeeper than in their castle as the wife of a ruler.

The trees were now beginning to put on their autumn colors. One afternoon Rafaello and Matteo were up on the inn's roof, making certain the slates were all in good order. Terza and Francesca were in the dining hall of the inn, polishing the tables, when they heard the rain that had been threatening all day begin. And then there was a loud thump. Startled, the two women looked at each other. Then they heard Bernardo shout in his deep voice, "Villain! What have you done?"

Dropping her cleaning cloth, Francesca ran outside, followed by Terza. Seeing her husband lying motionless on the ground, there was no doubt in her mind that Rafaello was dead. She gave one shriek of heartbreak, and then, looking to the roof, saw Matteo cowering. "Get down!" she ordered the man. "Get down now, for if you do not, as God is my witness, I will come up and pull you down myself! *Get down!*" Her voice was icy.

"It was an accident," Matteo cried, but he remained where he was. "It was an accident, my lady. The wet slates caused him to lose his balance, I swear it."

"*Get down, liar!* Before I kill you with my own bare hands I would learn why you have done this thing. Why have you killed the duke? To what purpose? Was he not always generous and fair to you, Matteo? Tell me why."

While she was speaking, Bernardo had quickly climbed to the inn's roof. Swiftly he scrambled across the wet slates and reached out to capture Matteo before he might escape. "Speak, villain!" he demanded of the now-terrified serving man. "Tell her why, or will you go to your death with another sin on your black soul?"

"The French!" Matteo gasped, barely able to speak with his fright. "The French promised to pay me to do the deed even before we fled the castle. They gave me a gold coin and said there were nine more should I be successful. But there was no opportunity at the castle. I have had to wait this long."

"Gold? You slew my husband for gold? This was not a cruel, unfair, or unkind master, Matteo. This was a good man."

"I will get my gold now," Matteo said, unheeding of her words. "With ten pieces of gold I can buy a little farm, find a wife," he told her. "I have done the French a great service. Now there is no duke of Terreno Boscoso to trouble them."

"There is Duke Carlo," Francesca said quietly. She was torn

between anger and despair. She could barely look at Rafaello's body. If she did not see it perhaps she could convince herself this was all a nasty dream.

"That infant? No three-month-old child can rule," Matteo said.

"No, but I can, you fool! I can rule, along with the council, in my son's name," Francesca told him.

"You said we would never return to the castle as long as the French were there," he said. He was not quite so afraid now. If he was quick he could escape the roof and make a run for it. With patience he could reach the town. Tell the French what he had done, tell them where the *duchessa* and her infants were hiding.

Francesca saw the sly look in Matteo's eyes as they shifted about, looking for the right moment to jump. "Kill him!" she said to Bernardo.

The huntsman shook the surprised servant by the collar. "Slowly or quickly, my lady?"

"Just do it. I do not want to hear the sound of his voice again." She looked at Matteo. "You will burn in hell for what you have done this day, traitor, but God will protect me and my children."

Bernardo let the serving man live long enough to hear her curse. Then, without a moment's hesitation, he snapped the man's neck. It was that sound that finally forced Francesca to realize the true state of things. Her strength evaporated, and she fell to her knees beside her husband's broken body, weeping furiously. "My love, my love!" she whispered over and over again, until finally a sobbing Terza, with Roza's help, lifted her mistress and brought her again into the inn.

As she did, Bernardo sought a spade and began to dig a

grave next to the house. Matteo's body, which he had tossed from the roof before descending, he would take deeper into the forest and leave for the wild animals. The man did not deserve a Christian burial for his wicked crime. But as he finished digging, Terza came out to speak with him.

"She will not have him simply put into the ground. There must be a coffin. One day, she says, she will take him home to be buried in his family's crypt. Roza and I will wash him and dress him in clean garments."

"There is little to constructing a coffin," Bernardo said. "If it will give her some measure of peace I will gladly do it, and we will bury him on the morrow. Have you prepared a place for him, Terza?"

"Set him on one of the tables in the dining hall. Your fellow huntsmen are not here yet, and no one will ever know," she replied.

Bernardo agreed, thinking to himself he would certainly never eat at that particular table. Then, carrying the duke into the inn, he set him gently down on a table nearest the door. His neck had been broken in the fall. There was no blood in evidence. "Where is she?" he asked Terza as he prepared to return outside again.

"We took her to her bedchamber. Roza is with her. I could give her nothing to ease her anxiety, for she must feed the twins."

Bernardo set the duke's body neatly, straightening out his legs, crossing his arms over his chest. "Then I will leave you to your unhappy task," he said.

Roza shortly joined Terza. "She has fed the twins and now sleeps, but restlessly," she reported to her senior.

Terza nodded. Together the two women stripped the duke's

body and washed it. Then they dressed him in clean garments. It was not the elegant clothing of his high rank, for that had been left behind when they fled the castle, but the simple garments of an innkeeper and hunter. Terza found two footed candelabra in the inn's cellar, and bringing them up, set candles in the several holders and lit them.

Balbina came from her kitchen and seeing her master laid out so neatly, began to weep loudly. "What will happen to us now?" she wailed.

"Nothing, you foolish woman!" Terza snapped. "We will go on with the mistress guiding us, as she always has. The duke was the duke no matter what, but the *duchessa* is strong and she is brave. She is every bit her mother's daughter. On the morrow we will bury the duke. Then we will give the lady time to mourn while we continue to ready the inn for our visitors."

"But will the lady recover from this terrible loss?" Balbina wondered.

"She must, for there are her children to consider. I have told you that she is like her mother, and *Signora* Orianna put her children above all else. So will the lady now," Terza told the cook. "For now the inn is her home, but wherever she goes Roza and I will be with her."

"And I also," Bernardo told the three women. "I have known the duke since he was a lad coming into the forest to join us. We became friends, and now I will guard his wife and his children with my own life. As long as I live no harm will come to them."

Shortly afterwards Francesca came into the dining hall. She knelt at the foot of the table and prayed. Her thoughts were jumbled, and sometimes she lost track of what she was thinking. Rafaello was gone. He was dead. She could not believe her life had been altered so quickly, in such a brief time. This morning they had made love, and been happy.

Now he was dead, dead, dead. She felt the tears slipping down her cheeks, but she made no sound. The initial shock was over for her. She had the twins to consider. She rose to her feet and spoke to the two women and Bernardo. Balbina had already returned to her kitchen, weeping as she cast a final look at the duke.

"Roza, you will remain with the twins tonight. They have nursed very well, and with luck will not awaken now until dawn. Bernardo, the coffin?"

"Will be ready for you by the morning, my lady. It will be simple, for I have neither the time nor the materials with which to make the duke a coffin befitting his high station. I hope it will serve, however," he answered her.

Francesca nodded. "It will be fine," she told him, "and I thank you. It will allow me to take him home one day and inter him with his father and his mother."

"You plan to return, then?" Bernardo said.

"One day," Francesca said. "It is my son, the duke's, heritage. I will attempt to regain it for him eventually."

The *duchessa* of Terreno Boscoso sat by her husband's body all night long, praying. When the morning came Bernardo carried the dead man outside and set him gently in the simple wood coffin he had spent much of the night building. Francesca bent down and kissed Rafaello's cold lips a final time. Then she instructed Bernardo to nail the coffin shut. With all of their help the funereal container was set in the grave. Each of them stood silently, praying for the soul of the young duke, and then Bernardo began to fill it in with the moist earth. When he was finished the three women returned into the house. There was work to be done if they were to be ready for their guests.

It had been a mild autumn, but as November began the wind started to blow from the north once again, and the huntsmen began coming in from the forest. Each noticed almost immediately that Carlo was among the missing. Bernardo told them simply that the innkeeper had died. When they had all arrived he would tell them the full story, but he did not want to repeat himself over and over. They were excited by the twins and most became doting towards the children. They saw Francesca's sorrow and were respectful.

By the end of the month Bernardo reckoned that most of those who sheltered with them had arrived, although the number was even smaller than the previous year, having fallen to fifteen. They had finished their meal one evening and were seated by the fire in the inn's main room, dicing and talking, when the big huntsman sought their attention. "The time has come for you to learn the facts of Carlo's death," he began. Almost immediately the room grew quiet, and all eyes turned to him. "You have noticed the absence of Matteo as well, I am certain. It was Matteo who murdered Carlo," Bernardo spun his tale. "Matteo had sought to take liberties with little Roza. Because she is no light-skirts, she told Carlo, and Carlo warned Matteo to keep away from the girl.

"Sadly he did not listen, and sought to rape Roza in the henhouse when she went to gather eggs. Her screams brought Carlo to rescue her before any harm was done. Carlo had Matteo bound to the stable doors, and he whipped him for his attempted crime. Matteo then swore to respect Roza. Several days later Carlo and Matteo were up on the roof of the inn, seeking any damage. It began to rain, and Matteo threw Carlo off the roof to revenge himself. Sadly the innkeeper's neck was broken. I dispatched Matteo myself shortly afterwards, and put his body in the forest for the beasts. A vicious murderer does not deserve a grave. So, there is the sad tale of how our good friend Carlo died." Bernardo concluded the tale that he and Francesca had devised.

The room was silent as his last word died. Only the crackle of the fire in the hearth and the blowing wind could be heard. Then the men began to speak quietly among themselves, and Bernardo left them to find Francesca, who he knew was in the kitchen.

"You have told them?" she greeted him.

"I have. Some may ask me questions here and there, but the story was plausible and they are satisfied to have heard it."

"There is only the priest to tell now, if he arrives next month," Francesca said. "I will want him to bless the grave."

"If you want I will go and seek him out," Bernardo said.

"No," she replied. "He will come, and I feel the children and I are safer with you here watching over us."

"I will not return to the forest for hunting," he assured her. "I am yours to command now, my lady."

December came, and the priest arrived as usual, just before the Feast of the Nativity. At his back was a nasty snowstorm. He was told of Carlo's death and went immediately to the grave to bless it, the snow now falling about him. Bernardo held a lantern so they might both see in the dusk, which was obscured even more by the falling snow. The priest found himself both shocked and heartbroken.

He joined Francesca in the kitchen by the hearth when he and Bernardo returned from the outside. "I can think of nothing that would ease your sorrow," he told her. "Nonetheless I can pray with you, my daughter."

"Nothing will ever take my sorrow from me," she told him quietly.

The priest nodded, understanding. Then he said, "The French have departed Terreno Boscoso in the past month. It seems King Louis died on the last day of August. The new king is but a boy just turned thirteen. Before he died King Louis appointed his daughter, Anne of Beaujeu, to be the lad's regent and guardian. This choice, however, has much angered the Duke of Orleans, who quarrels with her over the responsibility of young King Charles, for if the boy dies it is Orleans who will be king."

Francesca attempted to control her excitement. "Why did the French withdraw? The Comte du Barry must be furious."

"They withdrew because they were called home by the regent who seeks whatever method she can to protect her position as her brother's guardian," the priest said.

"You are certain the French are gone?" Francesca said to him.

"Indeed, yes," he answered her. "The people are returning to the town and there is to be a celebration soon."

"But what of the duke and *duchessa*?" Bernardo asked.

"The council does not believe them dead, and seeks for them," the priest responded.

"We must be certain of this," Francesca said. "I cannot endanger the twins."

"I will go myself when this storm has abated," Bernardo said.

"And if all is well, and as our good priest says, then I

must go home," Francesca said. "My son cannot be denied his heritage."

The priest looked puzzled by their conversation, and seeing it, Francesca said to Terza and Bernardo, "We must tell him."

They nodded in agreement.

"Good Father, I am the *duchessa* of Terreno Boscoso," Francesca began. "My husband was not Carlo, a huntsman, but Rafaello Cesare, your duke." Then she went on to explain everything, beginning with her flight from Rafaello when he first proposed.

She concluded her lengthy recitation by saying, "If the French are truly gone, then I must bring my children home. It is my little Carlo who is now this duchy's duke."

The priest was astounded but he did not disbelieve her. "Who else knows this? The infant duke must be kept safe, my lady."

"The servants who came with me from the castle. Balbina was our cook. Terza and Roza, my personal serving women. And, of course, Bernardo."

"And that lovely tale that was told the others? All false?" the priest said.

"Matteo betrayed the duke to the French before we fled the castle," Francesca told him. "He believed now he might complete the betrayal, but we caught him before he was able to expose us."

The priest nodded. "A foolish man. But now that I know the truth I will help you."

Chapter 18

King Louis had brought an end to what was known as the Hundred Years' War. Under his reign France had become peaceful and was showing the beginnings of true prosperity. Agriculture and commerce were beginning to thrive, but France had no source of precious metals, which was why King Louis had been so interested in Terreno Boscoso's gold mine. He was to find himself very disappointed when Commander d'Aumont reported to him that the mine no longer produced gold and that he had been misled by the Comte du Barry. He was forced, however, in order to save face, to leave his troops in that unimportant little duchy, claiming it was an ally of Milan and therefore a danger to France. The Comte du Barry found himself banned from court.

Louis had not been well liked. He was stingy, with himself in particular, greedy, and cruel. Yet he had managed through the deaths of his surviving brother and other male relations to acquire much of what became France. He had been very generous to his wife, and she in return had given him children while turning a blind eye to her husband's mistresses. The queen did not live at court. Now, however, Louis was dead, and while he had legally created his daughter, Anne, a clever young woman, the little king's regent and guardian, there were those who sought to wrest this powerful position from Anne of Beaujeu's elegant hands.

Needing all the military aid she could get to protect her brother, King Charles VIII, Anne gave orders for the small contingent of troops in Terreno Boscoso to be withdrawn immediately. So it was that the few folk remaining in the town awoke one morning to discover all of the French marching away. Raoul du Barry refused to leave even as the town's citizens began returning to their homes again. The duke's council began to seek for their lord, but no one had seen them go when they fled. And no one had seen them since. The council began to fear their ruler was dead.

The priest was not able to leave the winter forest until the very end of January.

Francesca had instructed the cleric that if the French were truly gone to find a council member and tell him only that the family was hidden in the forest and would soon be returning to the town once the roads were more passable. "Do not tell them that my husband is dead," she advised the priest.

The *duchessa* had decided not to let Bernardo leave them. "I am fearful without you watching over us," she said, and he acquiesced. He had already told her he would go with them when they left the forest.

It had been decided that Francesca and her children would

go back to the castle as quickly as they could. Terza would be by her side, but Balbina and Roza must remain until the spring departure of the huntsmen. But the roads did not become passable until two months later, in late March. Francesca had considered telling the huntsmen at the inn who she was, but decided against it, for she was afraid for her son in particular. After Matteo's treacherous behavior she was not ready to trust anyone other than those close to her. The twins were now eight months old, and she worried about the trip they must make in the uncertain and whimsical early spring weather. But without her they would starve. She had no choice but to take them with her.

Using the excuse of an ill grandmother to assuage the curiosity of the inn's guests, they departed early one morning. Giovanna was placed in a warm basket that hung from Terza's saddle. Her brother was similarly housed with his mother. They would not return the way they had come, but rather seek the road that Alonza and Francesca had taken when they went from the forest to the town. It was a little bit longer, but it would be safer, as they might shelter in a farmhouse each night, which would be better for the twins. Exiting the forest on to the roadway by midday, they stopped so Francesca might nurse her children. In the afternoon, as the babies didn't seem to mind, the horses now cantered gently. Indeed they napped quite peaceably.

"We have our own food," Bernardo assured the farmer from whom they requested shelter that night. Francesca understood the food was still in short supply. The farmer made his barn available to them. "May we drink from your well?"

The farmer nodded and admired the twins. "Those are fine babies you have, mistress. You and your man should be proud." Then he left them to themselves.

"Fool," Bernardo muttered. "As if a lovely young thing like you would marry the likes of me, my lady."

Terza giggled. "Indeed," she agreed with him.

"It is better he believe what he thinks," Francesca said with a smile. "I take no offense, Bernardo."

They had not eaten since they departed the inn that morning. Now they devoured the cold roasted venison, the bread, and the cheese Balbina had packed for them. The water from the farmer's well was sweet. Francesca nursed her babies again before settling them down in an empty feeding trough Terza filled first with fresh hay before covering the hay with a soft woolen cloth. The twins slept immediately, with their mother and Terza on either side of the trough. Bernardo took himself a distance from the women to make his bed in the hay.

They slept soundly, awakening just before dawn. The twins were fed once again. The *duchessa* and her companions ate their bread and cheese before saddling their horses. The two babies were settled for the day in their baskets, and they left the barn as the sun was peeping over the skyline, and the farmer coming from his house. Bernardo thanked him for his hospitality.

"Are you going to the town?" he asked them. "Everyone who fled is hurrying to return now that the French have departed. Now we must find our duke and his wife."

"Perhaps they fled to her family in Florence," Bernardo suggested.

"Well, wherever they got to, the French couldn't find them, although that comte who seemed to be their leader tried to tell everyone that they were executed," the farmer said. "If that were true you can bet their bodies would have been displayed as proof, but they were not," the farmer remarked. "Well, Godspeed!" And he waved them off.

Their second day and night on the road mirrored the first. And then on the afternoon of the third day they reached the town. Francesca at that point pushed back the hood of her cape, revealing her red-gold hair and her face. Suddenly she heard a cry.

"It is the *duchessa*!"

And suddenly they were being surrounded by the townsfolk, who joyously escorted them to the castle. To her great surprise Captain Arnaldo and a group of men appeared to join them. Bernardo remained close to Francesca and her small son.

The captain came to ride on the other side of her. "Welcome home, my lady," he said. His gaze went to the babies, and he looked questioningly at her. Then he asked her, "Where is the duke, my lady?"

"This infant boy is your duke," she said softly. "He is called Carlo. My husband is dead. I have returned because this is our son's heritage and the French are now gone."

Captain Arnaldo nodded, taking in the baby with his auburn hair and blue-green eyes. He was a miniature of his father. "We will have to remove the Comte du Barry from the castle, my lady. He would not go and claims he will now rule Terreno Boscoso."

Francesca laughed a bitter laugh. "He will be dead before the sunset," she said.

"Can we get into the castle, Captain?"

"The drawbridge, or what remains of it, is passable," the captain replied.

"Who serves him?"

"Few, and most his own servants."

Francesca turned to Bernardo. "You know what to do," she said.

"I do, my lady, and it shall be done immediately," Bernardo told her.

"I would see him first so that he dies knowing that my son's duchy, like a phoenix, has risen from the ashes he and the French caused. That I am responsible for his death, and my son will grow up to rule Terreno Boscoso," Francesca said.

"I will bring him to you first, my lady. Do you wish him to suffer?"

"I should, for I am a Florentine, but no. Just strangle him."

Bernardo smiled a slow smile. "As you wish, my lady," he promised her.

"Captain Arnaldo, this is Bernardo, who guards me and my children. I shall tell you all this evening. Bernardo, this is the captain of the castle's men-at-arms, whom I thought surely would be in Switzerland."

The two men nodded warily at one another, each gauging the other.

"I wanted to be certain that all was entirely lost before I deserted our duchy," Captain Arnaldo explained. "When the French departed I somehow knew it was not."

They crossed the damaged drawbridge and entered into the castle's courtyard. Francesca left the children with Terza and two men-at-arms while she and the others entered the building. Bernardo grabbed a surprised servant by the nape of his neck.

"Where is your master?" he asked.

Looking up at the big huntsman, the servant could hardly speak, but he finally managed to get the words out. "In . . . the hall."

"Leave this place, and thank God your life is spared. Do not come back," Bernardo warned the shaking man, who when released fled from the courtyard.

They made their way to the hall where the Comte du Barry was sprawled in a chair at the high board. He was drunk, but not so much that his eyes didn't widen at the sight of the *duchessa* and the men by her side.

"Get out of the duke's seat," Francesca said. "How dare you defile it, Frenchman?"

To his credit the Comte du Barry rose and stared down at her. "Where did you come from, bitch?" he asked her.

Bernardo stepped up to the high board and slapped the comte across his face. "You will speak to the *duchessa* in a more civil manner, Frenchman," he growled. He towered over his opponent, glaring in a very fierce manner. "You are bold for a man who will shortly meet his maker. Are you ready to die, then?"

Raoul du Barry turned a pasty white. Suddenly sober, he now looked terrified. For a moment he could not speak.

"I believe my mistress told you to leave the high board," Bernardo growled.

Finally du Barry began to babble, "This duchy is no more. This is France, and I am the king's representative."

"That greedy old bugger you called King Louis is now dead. In his place a child sits. Your soldiers have been called home," Bernardo said. "Show me your authority. You have no authority. Terreno Boscoso does not belong to France. It belongs to its duke and to its people." Bernardo then reached out, his fingers grasping at the comte's doublet. He yanked the frightened man from behind the table and then flung him from the dais. Then Bernardo stepped down and picked up du Barry from the floor where he had landed. His big hands were now wrapped around the Frenchman's neck. "My lady?" he asked Francesca.

She nodded without a word.

Bernardo slowly choked the Comte du Barry, whose pale face first turned pink, then deep red, and finally purple.

His eyes bulged from his head, and Francesca wondered if they would pop from his face. Satisfied at last that the comte had suffered enough, she gave Bernardo another nod, and the big huntsman snapped his victim's neck, ending his life.

"Remind me never to offend you, my lady," Captain Arnaldo said wryly. He had, like so many others, always thought the *duchessa* a charming woman, an exquisite ornament. He was surprised to see how determined, how fierce, she was in her revenge.

He knew that strength of character would be applied to guiding her infant son to manhood. Terreno Boscoso was in good hands.

"See he is buried," Francesca told Bernardo. "Make his own men dig the grave in unhallowed ground. And no priest." Then she turned to Captain Arnaldo. "I want double the men-at-arms we used to have, and I want them as quickly as possible. Can you manage that for us?"

"I can," he answered.

"Is the council in the town? I will want an immediate meeting so Duke Carlo's rights can be confirmed quickly."

"You should tell the people of Duke Rafaello's death yourself," the captain suggested. Is she a woman to take my proposal? he wondered nervously.

"Yes, you are right," Francesca agreed. "But not until the council has first been informed. And my husband's body must be returned to the castle so it may be interred in the Cesare crypt below the castle." She sighed. "There is so much to do, but it will be done and done properly."

A majority of the council had returned to the town, and as news of the *duchessa*'s return had already spread, they were not surprised to be called to the castle two days later.

They came, and the *duchessa*, already in the council chamber, greeted them warmly. When they were finally all seated she spoke.

"I will not demur," she began. "Duke Rafaello is dead since November."

The chamber was suddenly eerily silent as all eyes were fastened on Francesca.

"But do not despair, for last summer God blessed us with twin infants, a son and a daughter. Here is your new duke." And reaching down to the basket beside her chair, Francesca lifted up her son for them to see. "This is Duke Carlo Cesare."

The baby, in a well-rested mood, smiled at them all. He waggled his fat little fingers at them, and the royal council of Terreno Boscoso was immediately enchanted.

But then one of them said, "He will need a guardian, a regent, my lady."

"I am his guardian and will be his regent," Francesca said firmly.

"But Terreno Boscoso has never been ruled by a woman," another council member said nervously.

"You are incorrect, Signore Augusto. You do not know your own history. Duke Rafaello told me that this duchy has had two ruling *duchessas*. The first was *Duchessa* Iniga, some five hundred years back, and just a hundred and fifty years ago, *Duchessa* Sancia. I will not govern poorly, I promise you. But it is I who will rule Terreno Boscoso until Duke Carlo reaches his eighteenth year. My son shall have the best teachers to educate him. Captain Arnaldo and my bodyguard, Bernardo, shall teach Carlo the arts of warfare. I shall teach him manners and how to rule properly." She put the little duke back in his basket and nodded to Bernardo to take him to his nursery. "Now, good sirs, it is time for our second order of business. We must build an army, for never again shall this duchy be threatened by others assuming we are weak, especially as our duke and the little duke of Milan and the new French king are all children. France and Milan quarrel over regents, and will be kept busy for several years to come with that argument. That will not happen here in Terreno Boscoso. Will it?"

"No! No!" the voices of the council murmured. But then one asked Francesca, "What if you choose to wed again, my lady?"

"I will not marry again," Francesca told them. "I had a good husband. I have children. My responsibilities to Terreno Boscoso are too great. I have no wish for another husband, good sirs."

The council chamber was silent with her words.

"And no lover will rule me or this duchy," she reassured them with a little laugh.

"My lady, we suggested no such thing," a council member spoke up quickly.

"No, you did not, but do not deny the thought bloomed in each of your heads, good sirs. 'Tis only natural you would be concerned by such a thing, but you need have no fears. The path I must take is clear. My son's interests must be protected before all else. Now, are there any other questions?"

"Who is to pay for this army you wish to raise?" one of the three noble council members asked sharply.

"We will levy a tax," Francesca said. "Or I can allow the duchy to go unprotected and put us all in jeopardy of conquest once again, if you choose."

"How much of a tax?" the noble persisted.

"That must be decided only after we have investigated what

a small army of about a thousand would cost us," she told him. "We cannot simply impose a tax. It could be too heavy, or not enough. But now, good sirs, I think we can adjourn this meeting. From now on we shall meet weekly, for I shall need your wisdom and I do value your thoughts." Francesca arose. "Good day to you all," she said, and left the council chamber.

"You have given them something to consider," Captain Arnaldo said once they had departed the council chamber, "as well as frightened them." He chuckled. "It was masterfully done, my lady, if you will permit me to say it."

"You are permitted," Francesca said with a grin. "It was necessary for them to understand from the beginning that I will brook no interference with my son or this duchy. I will listen to anyone's advice, but I will rule until Carlo is old enough to do so himself. And hopefully he will learn from me and from others. Poor child. He will never remember his father, nor have Rafaello to teach him. He will not have the many years of irresponsibility that my husband had to enjoy. The burden of this duchy is now upon his infant shoulders." A single tear slipped down her cheek. "My poor little son."

Captain Arnaldo pretended to ignore her sadness, for he knew she would not want him to acknowledge it. Instead he asked her, "Did you mean it when you told the council that you would never marry again?"

"Yes. I must put any happiness I might have with another aside. A second husband would want children, and who is to say he might not put the future of his son ahead of Rafaello's son. The Cesare line must continue without any interference or peril."

"I had not considered that, my lady. You are a wise woman." The captain nodded.

"I am the *duchessa* of Terreno Boscoso. My loyalty can only lie with my husband's heir and what is best for the duchy," Francesca told him quietly. "Obtain the men-at-arms we need, my captain. Then we will set about to build a small army. Will you see that the townsfolk are told to come to the main square tomorrow at noon?"

He nodded and bowed over her hand. Then Captain Arnaldo hurried off, and Francesca hurried to the nursery to see her babies.

"You look worn," Terza noted as her mistress joined her.

"I am," Francesca admitted. "Tomorrow I must tell our people of the new duke. Did the French steal any of my clothing? Will I have something impressive to wear?"

"Oddly your apartments were left untouched," Terza said. "They are exactly as I left them, my lady."

"We need nursemaids for the twins, and someone to cook until Balbina returns," Francesca said. "We have eaten all the rations she sent with us."

"A few of the servants returned today," Terza informed her mistress. "And they have said the others who fled the French to the countryside will be back too."

"Is there someone who can care for the twins? I need you to help me prepare for tomorrow," Francesca said.

"They are sleeping now. If you will remain with them I will find someone," Terza said, and with her mistress's approval, she hurried off. She returned quickly with two women following her. They appeared somewhere between older youth and middle years. They curtsied to the *duchessa*, who stood now to greet them. "Here are Cerelia and Donata," Terza said. "They have children of their own, and will watch over the little duke and his sister, if it pleases my lady."

Both women smiled at Francesca. They were clean and appeared capable.

"Duke Carlo must be your prime concern," Francesca told the two. "His sister is Lady Giovanna. I am still nursing them, so I will come here to the nursery several times daily, or I may request you bring my children to me. We will have a larger nursery staff as soon as possible, but the duke and his sister will be your charges."

"We are honored that you put your trust in us, my lady. I am Cerelia, and I will watch over little Duke Carlo."

"And I am Donata," the other woman said. "It is a privilege to care for the Lady Giovanna."

"Where were you when the French occupied the town?" the *duchessa* asked.

"We fled to the countryside," Cerelia said. "My husband is a shoemaker in the town, and Donata's is a leather worker. We returned some days ago to find our houses wrecked and in poor condition."

"Can your men spare you?" Francesca asked them.

"We have always served the Cesare family," Donata said simply.

"I am grateful, then, for your loyalty," the *duchessa* told them. "I leave my babies in your care. I shall return later to nurse them." Then Francesca, in the company of Terza, departed the nursery. Entering her apartments she was pleased to see that the French had indeed, as Terza said, left them intact. Her jewelry was hidden at the inn, of course, but her clothing was there for her. Francesca reached for a brightly colored gown.

"No," Terza said. "You are in mourning, my lady. We must choose something darker." She withdrew a forest green gown. "This is both respectful and flattering."

Francesca looked at the gown. It was one that her mother had ordered made for her. Oddly she had never worn it. "Yes," she said. "It will do nicely."

In the hall that evening Francesca noted that Piero, their majordomo, had returned. There were two other servants who served her a hot meal. "Who is cooking?" she asked, curious.

"It is Balbina's assistant," Piero said. "Welcome home, my lady." He bowed.

"Tell her Balbina will not be back for several months, but she will return sometime in the spring," Francesca told him. "And see that the drawbridge is restored."

Piero bowed, acknowledging her words.

Francesca wept softly to herself that night in the bed that she and Rafaello had once shared. She almost imagined she could smell him on the pillows. She did manage, however, after a brief while, to sleep. It was not a restful sleep, but she considered that after a while she would become used to sleeping alone again. In the morning she awoke, and after feeding her infants ate a small breakfast before dressing. Oddly the dark green gown with its elegant gold embroidery and the delicate fall of creamy lace that dripped from her sleeves was very impressive.

Terza dressed her mistress's hair in a severe style to try to make her appear older than her twenty years. She draped the only jewelry, a double length of pearls, about Francesca's graceful neck. She fixed simple gold and pearl ear bobs in her mistress's ears. Francesca refused a cape, explaining a cape could cover her gown and jewelry, and she would not look as impressive as she wanted to look.

"Very well, then," Terza said, handing her a pair of leather gloves. "Let us go."

"Where is the duke?" the *duchessa* asked.

"Cerelia will bring him to the hall, suitably garbed," Terza said. "She and Donata spent all last night fashioning a proper garment for the baby. He cannot be displayed as just an infant. He must look his part despite his youth."

"How devoted these servants are to the Cesare family," Francesca noted softly.

In the hall Captain Arnaldo and Bernardo were waiting for them. Cerelia stood next to the big huntsman, holding little Carlo. The baby was garbed in a little pale blue velvet robe that had been embroidered at its neck with gold thread. Seeing his mother, he cried out for her, smiling as if pleased with his new clothing.

"There is an honor guard waiting in the courtyard for you, my lady," Captain Arnaldo said.

"You must ride by my side," she answered him. "Bernardo, you will be on my other side with the duke in his basket."

They nodded silently and then hurried to the courtyard, with Terza and Cerelia following. Francesca mounted her horse as the men mounted theirs. Terza made certain her mistress's gown was spread gracefully over the horse's flanks. Cerelia tucked the little duke into his basket by Bernardo's side. A half dozen men-at-arms preceded them as they rode from the castle courtyard. Another six men-at-arms followed behind them.

They rode slowly and carefully across the damaged draw-bridge and down the hill into the town. Reaching the main square, they found it full. When word had been spread that the *duchessa* would be speaking this morning, many still outside the town had hurried back to hear what she would say. There were already rumors, but they had come to hear fact.

The mounted party rode to the center of the square. Francesca turned her horse to face the majority of the citizens gathered. It was silent and so she spoke loudly for all to hear. "Citizens of Terreno Boscoso, like you, I thank God almighty that the French have gone. Now I bring you news both tragic and yet hopeful." The people in the square seemed to press closer so as not to miss a word. "Duke Rafaello is dead."

A great cry of sorrow rose from those gathered.

Francesca held up her hand to quiet them, and when there was total silence once again she continued. "But four months before my husband's murder, God blessed us with twin infants, a son and a daughter. He is tiny, but he will grow, with our help, into the man his grandfather and his father were. Good people of Terreno Boscoso, I bring you Duke Carlo Cesare."

Then she nodded to Bernardo, who held up her little son for everyone in the square to see. After a moment of stunned silence the people began to cheer wildly. The baby, not at all frightened, seemed to raise his hand in greeting. "Look at that! Look at that!" they heard people saying. And then the cry went up, "Long live Duke Carlo! Long live Duke Carlo! Long live the *Duchessa* Francesca!"

They left the now-noisy square, and as they rode, Francesca said to Bernardo, "How did you get him to wave at his people? He is so tiny, and it will be spoken of for years to come."

"I used a single finger to raise his little arm. The velvet of his gown hid what I was doing," Bernardo explained with a broad grin. "It seemed a good way to get the people to quickly take the wee duke to their hearts."

Francesca laughed aloud, and for the first time since Rafaello's murder she laughed long and heartily. "It was masterfully done, my old friend," she told him. "You must not leave our side, Bernardo. I hope you will not miss the forest."

"When he's old enough I'll teach him to hunt," Bernardo said.

"You must teach his sister as well. I will not raise her to be a silly girl," Francesca said to him. "She must be a strong and fearless woman, for who knows what she will face in her lifetime."

"She will hopefully be like her mother," Captain Arnaldo said quietly.

"I am my mother's daughter, it would seem," Francesca told them. "I am not a wild romantic like my elder sister, Bianca. Though it be a radical idea, a woman must be strong in order to survive. I am just that and I am fortunate in having you both by my side and by my son's side. The next few years will not be easy, but, God willing, Carlo will live to reach his majority, to marry one day, and to give me grandchildren, one of whom will follow in his father's footsteps. It is enough," she said as they rode up the castle hill.

She missed Rafaello and regretted the years they would not have together. But they had done their duty and produced two children. A son who would one day rule, and a daughter for whom she would make the most advantageous marriage. A marriage that would be of value to this duchy. How odd, Francesca thought. She no longer thought of Florence as her country. Terreno Boscoso was her country, her home.

And while her bed was empty now, her heart was full and grateful for the time she and Rafaello had had together. Their children were the only things that counted now. Francesca smiled to herself. She had never considered it until recently, but she was indeed Orianna Pietro d'Angelo's daughter. She wondered if the world was big enough for both of them.

Epilogue

s she had promised the duchy, Francesca turned over the responsibilities of the duchy to her son, Duke Carlo, when he had reached the age of eighteen. A year later he married Carlotta, the youngest daughter of his father's old friend, Valiant Cordassci and his wife, Louisa di Genoa. Both families were pleased, especially when a son was born to the young couple within a year.

In the years during which her son had reached his majority his mother had built alliances with other countries and raised an army to protect the duchy. Never again would Terreno Boscoso be vulnerable to others. True to her word, Francesca had never remarried, although Orianna Pietro d'Angelo had tried her very best to convince her otherwise. Captain Arnaldo and Bernardo grew old in the ducal service.

FRANCESCA

The young duke had been educated by the finest tutors his mother could find, brought from Florence and Rome. He learned the art of warfare from the captain, and how to hunt and be a man from Bernardo, who began taking the boy into the forest when he was only five. His elegant manners were learned at his mother's side. He grew into a kind man and a wise, just ruler.

People said he reminded them of his late father, and when they did Carlo thanked them, for Rafaello Cesare had been well loved. But only in his features did he resemble his sire. Unlike the gentle and trusting man who had given him life, Carlo had learned to be practical, resourceful, and observant, like his clever mother was. He could not be taken unawares, as Rafaello had been.

Francesca had not neglected her daughter, Giovanna, although most of her attention had been focused on the duchy. Giovanna was educated as her brother had been, and taught, with the help of the faithful Terza and Roza, the female skills her mother was too busy to teach her. Her marriage at seventeen to a French duke was considered a coup for her family and a great triumph for Terreno Boscoso. Within ten months Giovanna fulfilled her duty as his wife by producing twin sons.

No longer needed now by either the duchy or her children, Francesca spent much of her time traveling to visit her now-elderly parents and her sisters. She was always accompanied by Captain Arnaldo and Bernardo, until they could no longer travel. She then settled into her own small home back in the duchy, finally dying at the age of eighty.

Those observing her body as it lay in state in the duchy's cathedral said she had a smile on her face. Duke Carlo had been with his mother at the end, and only he had heard her last word as that smile had touched her lips.

It had been *"Rafaello!"*

About the Author

Bertrice Small is the *New York Times* bestselling author of fifty-four novels and four novellas, as well as the recipient of numerous awards, including a Lifetime Achievement Award from *Romantic Times*. She lives on the North Fork of eastern Long Island in Southold, which was founded in 1640 and is the oldest English-speaking town in the state of New York. Now widowed, she is the mother of a son, Thomas, and grandmother to a tribe of wonderful grandchildren. Longtime readers will be happy to learn that her beloved felines, twelve-year-old Finnegan, the long-haired black kitty, and eight-year-old Sylvester, the black-and-white bed cat, are still her dearest companions. Readers can contact the author by going to her message board on her Web site, www.bertricesmall.com, or writing to her at P.O. Box 764, Southold, NY, or bertricesmall@hotmail.com.